P9-DEK-854

Praise for
THE ROMANOV PROPHECY
by Steve Berry

"Perfect for thriller fans and history buffs alike. Fabulous plot twists are matched by fascinating details about tsars, secret burials, Fabergé eggs, and Rasputin. Steve Berry is a writer on the rise."

—DAVID MORRELL,
bestselling author of *The Protector*

"The fate of Mother Russia ups the ante for Berry's formula: based on international intrigue, swashbuckling action, indestructible hero[es] from the American South. . . . Not to be missed."

—*Kirkus Reviews*

"Readers who enjoy [the] books of Dan Brown and Daniel Silva will enjoy *The Romanov Prophecy*. This is a wild roller-coaster ride, with explosive action and compelling suspense, delving into one of the great mysteries of our time."

—SHARON KAY PENMAN,
bestselling author of *Dragon's Lair*
and *Time and Chance*

"Berry has clearly done his research. Fact and fiction are woven deftly."

—*Atlanta* magazine

"Berry has woven a strong combination of historical facts and people . . . to create a clever novel . . . [and] proves he has the talent to be one of the new up-and-coming voices— the next John le Carré or Daniel Silva—in international intrigue fiction. . . . A slam dunk."

—*The Florida Times-Union*

BY STEVE BERRY

The Amber Room
The Romanov Prophecy
The Third Secret
The Templar Legacy
The Alexandria Link
The Venetian Betrayal
The Charlemagne Pursuit
The Paris Vendetta

THE
ROMANOV
PROPHECY

A Novel

STEVE
BERRY

BALLANTINE BOOKS • NEW YORK

The Romanov Prophecy is a work of fiction. Though some characters, incidents,
and dialogues are based on the historical record, the work as a whole is a prod-
uct of the author's imagination.

2005 Ballantine Books Premium Mass Market Edition

Published in the United States by Ballantine Books, an imprint of The Random
House Publishing Group, a division of Random House, Inc., New York.

BALLANTINE and colophon are registered trademarks of Random House, Inc.

Originally published in hardcover in the United States by Ballantine Books, an
imprint of The Random House Publishing Group, a division of Random House,
Inc., in 2004.

This book contains an excerpt from the forthcoming hardcover edition of *The
Venetian Betrayal*. This excerpt has been set for this edition only and may not
reflect the final content of the forthcoming novel.

ISBN 978-0-345-50439-5

Cover design: Beck Stvan
Cover photographs: © Adri Berger/Getty Images; Romanov emblem © Corbis/
Bettmann

Printed in the United States of America

www.ballantinebooks.com

OPM   9   8   7   6

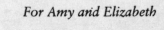
For Amy and Elizabeth

Russia—a country in which things that just don't happen happen.

—Peter the Great

A year shall come of Russia's blackest dread; Then will the crown fall from the royal head, The throne of tsars will perish in the mud, The food of many will be death and blood.

—Mikhail Lermontov (*1830*)

Russia: mysterious dark continent, "a riddle wrapped in a mystery inside an enigma" in Winston Churchill's phrase, remote, inaccessible to foreigners, inexplicable even to natives. That is the myth, encouraged by Russians themselves, who would prefer that no one discover who they really are and how they really live.

—Robert Kaiser, *Russia: The People and the Power* (*1984*)

For all its trials, for all its mistakes, the story of Russia at the end of the [twentieth] century must be counted as a kind of revival, a resurrection.

—David Remnick, *Resurrection: The Struggle for a New Russia* (*1997*)

ACKNOWLEDGMENTS

Again, some thanks. First, Pam Ahearn, my agent and friend. She's taught me much, including what was the right title for this book. Next, to all the folks at Random House: Gina Centrello, an extraordinary publisher who gave me a chance; Mark Tavani, whose wise editorial advice is everywhere in this manuscript; Kim Hovey, who runs a top-notch publicity team, which includes Cindy Murray; Beck Stvan, the artist responsible for the gorgeous cover image; Laura Jorstad, an eagle-eyed copy editor; Carole Lowenstein, who made the pages shine; and finally all those in Marketing, Promotions, and Sales—nothing could have been achieved without their dedicated efforts. Also, many thanks to Dan Brown, who offered nothing but kindness to a rookie writer and proved that success does not spoil generosity. As with *The Amber Room,* I cannot forget Fran Downing, Nancy Pridgen, and Daiva Woodworth. Every writer should be blessed with such a wonderful group of critics. And finally, above all, my wife, Amy, and daughter, Elizabeth. Together, they make life both interesting and wonderful.

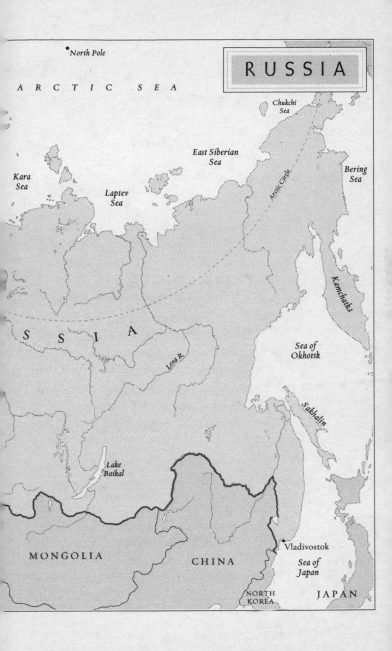

TIMELINE OF RELEVANT EVENTS
OF RUSSIAN HISTORY

FEBRUARY 21, 1613	Mikhail Feodorovich proclaimed tsar
OCTOBER 20, 1894	Nicholas II ascends the throne
APRIL 5, 1898	Nicholas II presents Lilies-of-the-Valley egg, created by Carl Fabergé, to his mother
DECEMBER 16, 1916	Rasputin murdered by Felix Youssoupov
MARCH 15, 1917	Nicholas II abdicates his throne; he and his family are arrested and held
OCTOBER 1917	Bolshevik Revolution; Lenin takes power
1918	Russian civil war begins; Whites fight Reds
JULY 17, 1918	Nicholas II, his wife, Alexandra, and their five children are murdered in Yekaterinburg
APRIL 1919	Felix Youssoupov flees Russia
1921	Russian civil war ends; Reds, led by Lenin, triumph
SEPTEMBER 27, 1967	Felix Youssoupov dies
MAY 1979	Grave site of Nicholas II and his family is located outside Yekaterinburg

DECEMBER 1991	Soviet Union dissolves
JULY 1991	The remains of Nicholas II and his family are exhumed; two of the imperial children are not found in the mass grave
1994	The remains are positively identified, but no evidence of the two missing children is ever found

INTRODUCTION

The idea for this novel came during a tour of the Kremlin. The guide kept mentioning "the third Rome." I was unfamiliar with the phrase, so she told me that Ivan the Great, who ruled Russia in the fifteenth century, once said, "two Romes have fallen [meaning Rome and Constantinople], a third now stands [Moscow], and a fourth there will never be." That intriguing thought instantly spurred my imagination, and over the next few days, a story developed that dealt with Nicholas II, his family, and their murder, coupled with the political struggles of modern-day Russia.

The original title was *The Fourth Rome*, for obvious reasons. But once the manuscript was bought, my editor felt a change was needed. If you're Stephen King, you can call your book whatever you want. But if you're Steve Berry, the title itself needs to attract readers. We knew it had to be *The Romanov Something*. So, after listing about a hundred or so nouns and agonizing over each one, my agent, Pam Ahearn, suggested *prophecy*.

It was perfect.

I'm often asked about the research for this book. Actually, locating primary and secondary sources on the Romanovs and Nicholas II was easy. The trouble came with their lack of consistency. I read many firsthand reports, and the conflicts between them were amazing. I began to wonder if they'd all been present at the same event. There's a Russian saying quoted in the book—"He lies like an eyewitness"—which is right on target.

Miles Lord, the hero of *The Romanov Prophecy,* remains one of my favorite characters. I don't want to lose him, as the world lost the Romanovs, so he might return someday for another Russian adventure. Many have asked if there's any of me in Miles. Of course we're both lawyers, and we both visited the same places while in Russia. But that's where the similarities end. I only wish I was more like him.

I learned a lot writing this story. What happened to Nicholas II and his family; the princess trees found through-out western North Carolina; the strange personality of Felix Yussoupov; Rasputin's predictions; Fabergé's eggs; and those amazing Borzois. And I was astonished by its success. Like my first novel, this one became a national bestseller in both hardback and paperback. Currently, it's published in eighteen countries. And every time I see it on a shelf I think about that day, walking through the Kremlin.

Hope you like it.

Steve Berry
August 2006

PROLOGUE

ALEXANDER PALACE
TSARSKOE SELO, RUSSIA
OCTOBER 28, 1916

ALEXANDRA, EMPRESS OF ALL RUSSIA, TURNED FROM HER bedside vigil as the door swung open, the first time in hours her gaze had been diverted from the pitiful child lying prone beneath the sheets.

Her Friend rushed into the bedroom, and she burst into tears. "Finally, Father Gregorii. Thanks to precious God. Alexei needs you terribly."

Rasputin swept close to the bed and made the sign of the cross. His blue silk blouse and velvet trousers reeked of alcohol, which tempered his usual stench, one her court ladies had said reminded them of a goat. But Alexandra had never cared about any odor. Not from Father Gregorii.

She'd sent the guards to look for him hours before, mindful of the stories of how he loved the Gypsies on the outskirts of the capital. Many times he would exhaust the night there with drink, in the company of prostitutes. One of the guardsmen even reported that the dear father had paraded across tabletops with his trousers down, proclaiming the delight his ample organ bestowed on the ladies of the Imperial Court. Alexandra refused to believe such talk about her Friend and promptly had the guard reassigned far from the capital.

"I have been searching for you since twilight," she said, trying to get his attention.

But Rasputin's focus was on the boy. He fell to his knees. Alexei was unconscious and had been for nearly an hour. Late in the afternoon, the boy had been playing in the garden when he fell. Within two hours the cycle of pain had started.

Alexandra watched as Rasputin peeled back the blanket and studied the right leg, blue and swollen to the point of grotesqueness. Blood was pulsating out of control beneath the skin, the hematoma now the size of a small melon, the leg drawn up against the chest. Her son's gaunt face was devoid of color, except for dark smears beneath both eyes.

She gently brushed the child's light brown hair.

Thank God the screaming had stopped. The spasms had been coming every quarter of an hour with morbid regularity. A high fever had already made him delirious, but he'd continued to sound a constant wail that ripped her heart.

Once he became lucid and pleaded, "Oh Lord, have mercy on me," and asked, "Mama, won't you help me?" Then he wanted to know if the pain would stop if he died. She could not bring herself to tell him the truth.

What had she done? This was all her fault. It was well known that women passed on the trait for hemophilia, but were never affected. Her uncle, brother, and nephews had all died from the disease. But she never considered herself a carrier. Four daughters had taught her nothing. Only when the blessed son finally arrived twelve years ago had she learned the painful reality. Beforehand, not one doctor had cautioned her of the possibility. But did she ever ask? No one seemed willing to volunteer anything. Even direct questions were many times avoided with nonsensical answers. That was why Father Gregorii was so special. The *starets* never held back.

Rasputin closed his eyes and nestled close to the stricken

boy. Flecks of dried food littered his wiry beard. The gold cross she'd given him hung around his neck. He grasped it tight. The room was lit only by candles. She could hear him muttering, but could not make out the words. And she dare not say anything. Though she was Empress of All Russia, the tsarina, she never challenged Father Gregorii.

Only he could stop the bleeding. Through him God protected her precious Alexei. The tsarevich. Sole heir to the throne. Next tsar of Russia.

But only if he lived.

The boy opened his eyes.

"Don't be afraid, Alexei, everything is all right," Rasputin whispered. The voice was calm and melodious, but firm in its conclusion. He stroked Alexei's sweaty body from head to toe. "I have driven away your horrid pains. Nothing will hurt you anymore. Tomorrow you will be well, and we will play our jolly games again."

Rasputin continued to caress the boy.

"Remember what I told you about Siberia. It is full of huge forests and endless steppes, so large no one has seen the end of it. And it all belongs to your mama and papa and, one day, when you are healthy, strong, and big, it will be yours." He clutched the boy's hand in his. "One day I will take you to Siberia and show it all to you. The people there are so different from here. The majesty of it all, Alexei. You must see it." The voice stayed calm.

The boy's eyes brightened. Life returned, as quick as it had left hours ago. He started to raise himself from the pillow.

Alexandra became concerned, afraid he would inflict a fresh injury. "Take care, Alexei. You must be careful."

"Leave me alone, Mama. I must listen." Her son turned to Rasputin. "Tell me another story, Father."

Rasputin smiled and told him about humpbacked horses, the legless soldier and eyeless rider, and an unfaithful tsarina who was turned into a white duck. He spoke of the wildflowers on the vast Siberian steppes, where plants have souls and speak to one another; how the animals, too, could speak and how he, as a child, had learned to understand what horses whispered in the stable.

"See, Mama. I've always told you horses could speak."

Tears welled in her eyes at the miracle before her. "You are so right. So right."

"And you will tell me everything you heard from the horses, won't you?" Alexei asked.

Rasputin smiled approvingly. "Tomorrow. I'll tell you more tomorrow. Now you must rest." He stroked the boy until the tsarevich dozed back to sleep.

Rasputin stood. "The Little One will survive."

"How can you be sure?"

"How can you not?"

His tone was indignant and she instantly regretted her doubting. She'd many times thought her own lack of faith was the cause of Alexei's pain. God was perhaps testing her through the curse of hemophilia to see the strength of her beliefs.

Rasputin stepped around the bed. He knelt before her chair and grasped her hand. "Mama, you must not forsake our Lord. Do not doubt His power."

Only the *starets* was allowed to address her with such informality. She was the *Matushka,* Little Mother; her husband, Nicholas II, the *Batiushka,* Little Father. It was how the peasantry viewed them—as stern parents. Everyone around her said Rasputin was a mere peasant himself. Perhaps so. But he alone could relieve Alexei's suffering. This peasant from Siberia with his tangled beard, stinking body, and long greasy hair was heaven's emissary.

"God has refused to listen to my prayers, Father. He has forsaken me."

Rasputin sprang to his feet. "Why do you speak this way?" He grasped her face and twisted her toward the bed. "Look at the Little One. He suffers horribly because you do not believe."

No one other than her husband would dare touch her without permission. But she did not resist. In fact, she welcomed it. He whipped her head back and bore a gaze deep into her eyes. The full expression of his personality seemed concentrated in those pale blue irises. They were unavoidable, like phosphorescent flames at once piercing and caressing, far off, yet intent. They could see directly into her soul, and she'd never been able to resist them.

"*Matushka,* you must not speak of our Lord this way. The Little One needs you to believe. He needs you to put your faith in God."

"My faith is in you."

He released her. "I am nothing. Merely the instrument through which God acts. I do nothing." He pointed skyward. "He does it all."

Tears sprang in her eyes and she slumped from the chair in shame. Her hair was unkempt, the once beautiful face sallow and wizened from years of worry. Her eyes ached from crying. She hoped no one entered the room. Only with the *starets* could she openly express herself as a woman and mother. She started to cry and wrapped her arms around his legs, her cheeks pressed tight to clothes that stank of horses and mud.

"You are the only one who can help him," she said.

Rasputin stood rigid. Like a tree trunk, she thought. Trees were able to withstand the harshest Russian winter, then bloom anew every spring. This holy man, whom God had certainly sent, was her tree.

"Mama, this solves nothing. God wants your devotion, not your tears. He is not impressed with emotion. He demands faith. The kind of faith that never doubts—"

She felt Rasputin tremble. She released her hold and stared up. His face had gone blank, his eyes rolled to the top of his head. A shiver quaked through him. His legs went limp and he crumpled to the floor.

"What is it?" she asked.

He did not reply.

She grabbed him by his shirt and shook him. "Speak to me, *starets*."

Slowly he opened his eyes. "I see heaps, masses of corpses, several grand dukes and hundreds of counts. The Neva will be all red with blood."

"What do you mean, Father?"

"A vision, Mama. It has come again. Do you realize before long I shall die in terrible agony?"

What was he saying?

He grabbed her arms and pulled her close. Fear filled his face, but he wasn't really looking at her. He was focused far off, beyond her.

"I shall leave this life before the new year. Remember, Mama, if I be killed by common assassins the tsar has nothing to fear. He will remain on his throne with nothing to fear for your children. They will reign for hundreds of years. But, Mama, if I am murdered by boyars, their hands will remain soiled by my blood for twenty-five years. They will leave Russia. Brother will rise against brother, and they will kill each other in hate. Then there will be no nobles in the country."

She was frightened. "Father, why are you speaking like this?"

His eyes came back from beyond and focused on her. "If one of the tsar's relatives carries out my murder, none of your family will live more than two years. They will all be killed by the Russian people. Be concerned for your salvation and tell your relatives I paid for them with my life."

"Father, this is nonsense."

"It is a vision, and I have had it more than once. The night is dark with the suffering that is before us. I shall not see it. My hour is near, but though it is bitter, I do not fear it."

He started to tremble again.

"Oh, Lord. The evil is so great that the Earth will tremble with famine and sickness. Mother Russia will be lost."

She shook him again. "Father, you must not talk like this. Alexei needs you."

A calm overtook him.

"Fear not, Mama. There is another vision. Salvation. This is the first time it has come to me. Oh, what a prophecy. I see it clearly."

PART
ONE

1

IN FIFTEEN SECONDS MILES LORD'S LIFE CHANGED FOREVER.

He first saw the sedan. A dark blue Volvo station wagon, the tint so deep that it appeared black in the bright midday sun. He next noticed the front tires cutting right, weaving a path around traffic on busy Nikolskaya Prospekt. Then the rear window, reflective as a mirror, descended, and a distorted reflection of the surrounding buildings was replaced by a dark rectangle pierced by the barrel of a gun.

Bullets exploded from the gun.

He dived flat. Screams arose around him as he slammed onto the oily pavement. The sidewalk was packed with afternoon shoppers, tourists, and workers, all now lunging for cover as lead raked a trail across the weathered stone of Stalinist-era buildings.

He rolled over and looked up at Artemy Bely, his lunch companion. He'd met the Russian two days back and taken him to be an amicable young lawyer with the Justice Ministry. Lawyer to lawyer they'd eaten dinner last night and breakfast this morning, talking of the new Russia and the great changes coming, both marveling at being part of history. His mouth opened to shout a warning, but before he could utter a sound Bely's chest erupted and blood and sinew splattered on the plate-glass window beyond.

The automatic fire came with a constant *rat-tat-tat* that reminded him of old gangster movies. The plate glass gave way and jagged shards crashed to the sidewalk. Bely's body crumpled on top of him. A coppery stench rose from the gaping wounds. He shoved the lifeless Russian off, worried about the red tide soaking into his suit and dripping from his hands. He hardly knew Bely. Was he HIV-positive?

The Volvo screeched to a stop.

He looked to his left.

Car doors popped open and two men sprang out, both armed with automatic weapons. They wore the blue-and-gray uniforms with red lapels of the *militsya*—the police. Neither, though, sported the regulation gray caps with red brim. The man from the front seat had the sloped forehead, bushy hair, and bulbous nose of a Cro-Magnon. The man who slid from the rear was stocky with a pockmarked face and dark, slicked-back hair. The man's right eye caught Lord's attention. The space between the pupil and eyebrow was wide, creating a noticeable droop—as if one eye was closed, the other open—and provided the only indication of emotion on an otherwise expressionless face.

Droopy said to Cro-Magnon in Russian, "The damn *chornye* survived."

Did he hear right?

Chornye.

The Russian equivalent for *nigger.*

His was the only black face he'd seen since arriving in Moscow eight weeks ago, so he knew he had a problem. He recalled something from a Russian travel book he'd read a few months back. *Anyone dark-skinned can expect to arouse a certain amount of curiosity.* What an understatement.

Cro-Magnon acknowledged the comment with a nod. The

two men stood thirty yards away, and Lord wasn't about to wait around to find out what they wanted. He sprang to his feet and raced in the opposite direction. With a quick glance over his shoulder he saw the two calmly crouch and ready themselves to shoot. An intersection loomed ahead, and he leaped the remaining distance just as gunfire blasted from behind.

Bullets strafed the stone, puffing cloud bursts into the chilly air.

More people dived for cover.

He sprang from the sidewalk and faced a *tolkuchki*—street market—lining the curb as far as he could see.

"Gunmen. Run," he screamed in Russian.

A *bobushka* peddling dolls understood instantly and shuffled to a nearby doorway, jerking tight a scarf around her weathered face. Half a dozen children hawking newspapers and Pepsis darted into a grocery. Vendors abandoned their kiosks and scattered like roaches. The appearance of the *mafiya* was not uncommon. He knew that a hundred or more gangs operated throughout Moscow. People being shot, knifed, or blown up had become as common as traffic jams, simply the risk of doing business on the streets.

He bolted ahead into the crowded *prospekt,* traffic merely inching along and starting to congeal in the mayhem. A horn blared and a braking taxi stopped just short of him. His bloodied hands came down hard on the hood. The driver continued to lean on the horn. He looked back and saw the two men with guns round the corner. The crowd parted, which provided a clear shot. He dived behind the taxi as bullets obliterated the driver's side.

The horn stopped blaring.

He raised himself up and stared into the driver's bloodied face, smushed against the passenger-side window, one eye cocked open, the pane stained crimson. The men were now fifty yards away, on the other side of the congested *prospekt*. He studied the storefronts on both sides of the street and registered a men's fashion salon, children's clothing boutique, and several antiques galleries. He searched for someplace in which to disappear and chose McDonald's. For some reason the golden arches harked of safety.

He raced down the sidewalk and shoved open its glass doors. Several hundred people packed the chest-high tables and booths. More stood in line. He recalled that this was at one point the busiest restaurant in the world.

He was gulping air fast and a scent of grilled burgers, fries, and cigarettes accompanied each breath. His hands and clothes were still bloody. Several women started to scream that he'd been shot. A panic overtook the young crowds and there was a mad push for the doors. He shouldered forward, deeper into the throng, and quickly realized this was a mistake. He pushed through the dining room toward stairs that led down to bathrooms. He slipped out of the panicked mob and skipped down the stairs three at a time, his bloodied right hand gliding across a slick iron rail.

"Back. Away. Back," deep voices ordered in Russian from above.

Gunfire erupted.

More screams and rushed footsteps.

He found the bottom of the stairs and faced three closed doors. One led to the ladies' room, the other to the men's. He opened the third. A large storage room spanned before him, its walls shiny white tile like the rest of the restaurant. In one corner three people huddled around a table smoking. He noticed their T-shirts—Lenin's face superimposed over McDonald's golden arches. Their gazes met his.

"Gunmen. Hide," he said in Russian.

Without a word, all three bolted from the table and shot toward the far end of the brightly lit room. The lead man flung open a door, and they disappeared outside. Lord stopped only an instant to slam shut the door from which he'd entered and lock it from the inside, then he followed.

He dashed out into the chilly afternoon and stood in an alley behind the multistory building that accommodated the restaurant. He half expected Gypsies or bemedaled war veterans to be in residence. Every nook and cranny of Moscow seemed to provide shelter to one or another dispossessed social group.

Dingy buildings surrounded him, the coarsely hewn stone blackened and scarred from decades of unregulated auto emissions. He'd often wondered what those same fumes did to lungs. He tried to get his bearings. He was about a hundred yards north of Red Square. Where was the nearest Metro station? That could be his best means of escape. There were always policemen in the stations. But policemen were chasing him. Or were they? He'd read how the *mafiya* many times donned police uniforms. Most times the streets were littered with police—too damn many—all sporting nightsticks and automatic weapons. Yet today he'd seen not one.

A thud came from inside the building.

His head whipped around.

The door at the far end of the storage room leading from the bathrooms was being forced. He started running in the direction of the main street, just as gunfire echoed from inside.

He found the sidewalk and turned right, running as fast as his suit would allow. He reached up, unbuttoned his collar, and yanked down his tie. Now at least he could breathe. It would only be a few moments before his pursuers rounded the corner from behind. He quickly swerved right and vaulted a waist-high, chain-link fence encircling one of the innumerable parking lots dotting Moscow's inner ring.

He slowed to a trot and let his eyes shoot left and right. The lot was full of Ladas, Chaikas, and Volgas. Some Fords.

A few German sedans. Most filthy with soot and dented from abuse. He looked back. The two men had cleared the corner a hundred yards back and were now racing in his direction.

He rushed forward down the center of the grassy lot. Bullets ricocheted off the cars to his right. He dived behind a dark Mitsubishi and peered around its rear bumper. The two men were positioned on the other side of the fence, Cro-Magnon standing, his gun aimed forward, Droopy still trotting toward the fence.

A car engine revved.

Smoke poured from the exhaust. Brake lights lit.

It was a cream-colored Lada that had been parked to the opposite side of the center lane. The car quickly backed out of its space. He saw fear on the driver's face. He'd most likely heard the bullets and decided to leave fast.

Droopy jumped the fence.

Lord rushed from his hiding place and vaulted onto the Lada's hood, his hands clasping the windshield wipers. Thank heaven the damn thing had wipers. He knew most drivers kept them locked in the glove compartment to thwart thieves. The Lada's driver gave him a startled look but kept rolling forward toward the busy boulevard. Through the rear window Lord saw Droopy, fifty yards behind, crouching to fire and Cro-Magnon scaling the fence. He thought of the taxi driver and decided it wasn't right to involve this man. As the Lada exited onto the six-lane boulevard, he rolled off the hood and onto the sidewalk.

Bullets arrived in the next second.

The Lada whipped left and sped away.

Lord continued to roll until he was in the street, hoping a slight depression below the curb would be enough to block Droopy's firing angle.

The earth and concrete churned as bullets dug in.

A crowd waiting for a bus scattered.

He glanced to his left. A bus was no more than fifty feet away and rolling toward him. Air brakes engaged. Tires squealed. The scent of sulfur exhaust was nearly suffocating. He twirled his body into the street as the bus screeched to a stop. The vehicle was now between him and the gunmen. Thank God no cars were using the boulevard's outermost lane.

He stood and darted across the six-lane road. Traffic all came one way, from the north. He crisscrossed the lanes and made a point of staying perpendicular with the bus. Halfway, he was forced to pause and wait for a line of cars to pass. There'd only be a few moments more until the gunmen rounded the bus. He took advantage of a break in traffic and ran across the final two lanes, onto the sidewalk, jumping the curb.

Ahead was a busy construction site. Bare girders rose four stories into a rapidly clouding afternoon sky. He'd still not seen one policeman other than the two on his tail. Over the whirl of traffic came the roar of cranes and cement mixers. Unlike back home in Atlanta, no fences of any kind delineated the unsafe zone.

He trotted onto the work site and glanced back to see the gunmen starting their own bisection of the crowded boulevard, dodging cars, horns protesting their progress. Workers milled about the construction site, paying him little attention. He wondered how many black men dressed in bloody suits ran onto the job site every day. But it was all part of the new Moscow. The safest course was surely to stay out of the way.

Behind, the two gunmen found the sidewalk. They were now less than fifty yards away.

Ahead, a cement mixer churned gray mortar into a steel trough as a helmeted worker monitored the progress. The trough rested on a large wooden platform chained to a cable that ran four stories up to a roof crane. The worker tending the mixture backed away and the entire assembly rose.

Lord decided up was as good a place as any and raced for the ascending platform, leaping forward, gripping the platform's bottom edge. Crusted concrete caked on the surface made it difficult to maintain a hold, but thoughts of Droopy and his pal kept his fingers secure.

The platform rose, and he swung himself upward.

The unbalanced movement caused a sway, chains groaning from the added weight, but he managed to climb up and flatten his body against the trough. The added weight and movement tipped everything his way, and mortar sloshed onto him.

He glanced over the side.

The two gunmen had seen what he did. He was fifty feet in the air and climbing. They stopped their advance and took aim. He felt the mortar-encrusted wood beneath him and stared at the steel trough.

No choice.

He quickly rolled into the trough, sending wet mortar oozing over the side. Cold mud enveloped him and sent a chill through his already shaking body.

Gunfire started.

Bullets ripped the wooden underside and pelted the trough. He shrank into the cement and heard the recoil of lead off steel.

Suddenly, sirens.

Coming closer.

The shooting stopped.

He peered out toward the boulevard and saw three police cars speeding south, his way. Apparently the gunmen had heard the sirens, too, and hastily retreated. He then saw the dark blue Volvo that had started everything appear from the north and speed down the boulevard. The two gunmen backed toward it, but seemed unable to resist a few parting shots.

He watched as they finally climbed into the Volvo and roared away.

Only then did he raise up on his knees and release a sigh of relief.

LORD CLIMBED OUT OF THE POLICE CAR. HE WAS BACK ON
Nikolskaya Prospekt, where the shooting had begun. At the
construction site he'd been lowered to the ground and hosed
down to cleanse away the mortar and blood. His suit jacket
was gone, as was his tie. His white dress shirt and dark
trousers were soaking wet and stained gray. In the chilly afternoon they felt like a cold compress. He was wrapped in a
musty wool blanket one of the workers had produced that
smelled of horses. He was calm. Amazing, considering.

The *prospekt* was filled with squad cars and ambulances,
light bars flashing, a multitude of uniformed officers everywhere. Traffic was at a standstill. Officers had secured the
street at both ends, all the way to the McDonald's.

Lord was led to a short, heavy-chested man with a bull
neck and close-cropped reddish whiskers sprouting from
fleshy cheeks. Deep lines streaked his brow. His nose was
askew, as if from a break that had never healed, and his complexion carried the sallow pale all too common with Russians. He wore a loose-fitting gray suit and a dark shirt under
a charcoal overcoat. His shoes were dog-eared and dirty.

"I am Inspector Orleg. *Militsya*." He offered a hand. Lord
noticed liver spots freckling the wrist and forearm. "You one
here when shots were fired?"

The inspector spoke in accented English, and Lord debated whether to answer in Russian. It would surely ease

their communication. Most Russians assumed Americans were too arrogant or too lazy to master their language—particularly black Americans, whom he'd found they viewed as something of a circus oddity. He'd visited Moscow nearly a dozen times over the past decade and had learned to keep his linguistic talent to himself—garnering in the process an opportunity to listen in on comments between lawyers and businessmen who thought they were protected by a language barrier. At the moment, he was highly suspicious of everyone. His previous dealings with the police had been confined to a few disputes over parking and one incident where he was forced to pay fifty rubles to avoid a bogus traffic violation. It wasn't unusual for the Moscow police to shake down foreigners. *What do you expect from somebody who earns a hundred rubles a month?* an officer had asked while pocketing his fifty dollars.

"The shooters were police," he said in English.

The Russian shook his head. "They dress like police. *Militsya* not gun people down."

"These did." He glanced beyond the inspector at the bloodied remains of Artemy Bely. The young Russian was sprawled faceup on the sidewalk, his eyes open, brown-red ribbons seeping from holes in his chest. "How many were hit?"

"Pyát."

"Five? How many dead?"

"Chetýre."

"You don't seem concerned. Four people shot dead in the middle of the day on a public street."

Orleg shrugged. "Little can be done. The roof is tough to control."

"The roof" was the common way to refer to the *mafiya* who populated Moscow and most of western Russia. He'd never learned how the term came into being. Maybe it was because that was how people paid—through the roof—or

STEVE BERRY / 22

perhaps it was a metaphor for the odd pinnacle of Russian life. The nicest cars, largest *dachas,* and best clothes were owned by gang members. No effort was made to conceal their wealth. On the contrary, the *mafiya* tended to flaunt their prosperity to both the government and the people. It was a separate social class, one that had emerged with startling speed. His contacts within the business community considered protection payments just another facet of company overhead, as necessary to survival as a good workforce and steady inventory. More than one Russian acquaintance had told him that when the gentlemen in the Armani suits paid a visit and pronounced, *Bog zaveshchaet delit'sia*— God instructs us to share—they were to be taken seriously.

"My interest," Orleg said, "is why those men chase you."

Lord motioned to Bely. "Why don't you cover him up?"

"He not mind."

"I do. I knew him."

"How?"

He found his wallet. The laminated security badge he'd been given weeks ago had survived the cement bath. He handed it to Orleg.

"You part of Tsar Commission?"

The implied question seemed to ask why an American would be involved with something so Russian. He was liking the inspector less and less. Mocking him seemed the best way to show how he felt.

"I part of Tsar Commission."

"Your duties?"

"That confidential."

"May be important to this."

His attempt at sarcasm was going unnoticed. "Take it up with the commission."

Orleg pointed to the body. "And this one?"

He told him that Artemy Bely was a lawyer in the Justice

Ministry, assigned to the commission, who'd been helpful in arranging access to the Soviet archives. On a personal level, he knew little more than that Bely was unmarried, lived in a communal apartment north of Moscow, and would have loved to visit Atlanta one day.

He stepped close and gazed down at the body.

It had been awhile since he last saw a mutilated corpse. But he'd seen worse during six months of reserve duty that turned into a year in Afghanistan. He was there as a lawyer, not a soldier, sent for his language skills—a political liaison attached to a State Department contingent—present to aid a governmental transition after the Taliban was driven out. His law firm thought it important to have someone involved. Good for the image. Good for his future. But he'd found himself wanting to do more than shuffle paper. So he helped bury the dead. The Afghans had suffered heavy losses. More than the press had ever noted. He could still feel the scorching sun and brutal wind, both of which had only sped decomposition and made the grim task more difficult. Death was simply not pleasant. No matter where.

"Explosive tips," Orleg said behind him. "Go in small, come out large. Take much with them along way." The inspector's voice carried no compassion.

Lord glanced back at the blank stare, the rheumy eyes. Orleg smelled faintly of alcohol and mint. He'd resented the flippant remark about covering the body. So he undraped the blanket from around him, bent down, and laid it across Bely.

"We cover our dead," he told Orleg.

"Too many here to bother."

He stared at the face of cynicism. This policeman had probably seen a lot. Watched how his government gradually lost control, himself working, like most Russians, on the mere promise of payment, or for barter, or for black-market U.S. dollars. Ninety-plus years of communism had left a mark. *Bespridel,* the Russians called it. Anarchy. Indelible as a tattoo. Scarring a nation to ruin.

"Justice Ministry is frequent target," Orleg said. "Involve themselves in things with little concern for safety. They have been warned." He motioned to the body. "Not first or last lawyer to die."

Lord said nothing.

"Maybe our new tsar will solve all?" Orleg asked.

He stood and faced the inspector, their toes parallel, bodies close. "Anything is better than this."

Orleg appraised him with a glare, and he wasn't sure if the policeman agreed with him or not. "You never answer me. Why men chase you?"

He heard again what Droopy said as he slid out of the Volvo. *The damn* chornye *survived.* Should he tell Orleg anything? Something about the inspector didn't seem right. But his paranoia could simply be the aftereffect of what had happened. What he needed was to get back to the hotel and discuss all this with Taylor Hayes.

"I have no idea—other than I got a good view of them. Look, you've seen my security clearance and know where to find me. I'm soaking wet, cold as hell, and what's left of my clothes has blood soaked into them. I'd like to change. Could one of your men drive me to the Volkhov?"

The inspector did not immediately reply. He just stared with a measured mien Lord thought intentional.

Orleg returned his security card.

"Of course, Mr. Commission Lawyer. As you say. I have car made available."

LORD WAS DRIVEN TO THE VOLKHOV'S MAIN ENTRANCE IN A police cruiser. The doorman let him inside without a word. Though his hotel identification was ruined, there was no need to show it. He was the only man of color staying there, instantly recognizable, though he was given a strange look at the tattered condition of his clothes.

The Volkhov was a pre-revolutionary hotel built in the early 1900s. It sat near the center of Moscow, northwest of the Kremlin and Red Square, the Bolshoi Theater diagonally across a busy square. During Soviet times the massive Lenin Museum and monument to Karl Marx had been in full view from the street-side rooms. Both were now gone. Thanks to a coalition of American and European investors, over the last decade the hotel had been restored to its former glory. The opulent lobby and lounges, with their murals and crystal chandeliers, conveyed a tsarist atmosphere of pomp and privilege. But the paintings on the walls—all from Russian artists—reflected capitalism because each was marked for sale. Likewise, the addition of a modern business center, health club, and indoor pool brought the old facility further into the new millennium.

He rushed straight to the main desk and inquired if Taylor Hayes was in his room. The clerk informed him that Hayes was in the business center. He debated whether or not he should change clothes first, but decided he could not wait.

He bounded across the lobby and spotted Hayes through a glass wall, sitting before a computer terminal.

Hayes was one of four senior managing partners at Pridgen & Woodworth. The firm employed nearly two hundred lawyers, making it one of the largest legal factories in the southeastern United States. Some of the world's biggest insurers, banks, and corporations paid the firm monthly retainers. Its offices in downtown Atlanta dominated two floors of an elegant blue-tinted skyscraper.

Hayes possessed both an MBA and a law degree, his reputation that of a proficient practitioner in global economics and international law. He was blessed with a lean athletic body, and his maturity was reflected in brown hair streaked with gray. He was a regular on CNN as an on-camera commentator and cast a strong television presence, his gray-blue eyes flashing a personality Lord often thought a combination of showman, bully, and academician.

Rarely did his mentor appear in court, and even less frequently did he participate in weekly meetings among the four dozen lawyers—Lord included—who manned the firm's International Division. Lord had worked directly with Hayes several times, accompanying him to Europe and Canada, handling research and drafting chores delegated his way. Only in the past few weeks had they spent any prolonged time together, their relationship along the way evolving from "Mr. Hayes" to "Taylor."

Hayes stayed on the road, traveling at least three weeks every month, catering to the firm's wide array of international clients who didn't mind paying $450 an hour for their lawyer to make house calls. Twelve years before, when Lord joined the firm, Hayes had taken an instant liking to him. He later learned Hayes had specifically asked that he be assigned to International. Certainly an honors graduation from the University of Virginia Law School, a master's in Eastern European history from Emory University, and his language proficiency qualified him. Hayes started assigning him all over Europe, especially in the Eastern bloc. Pridgen & Woodworth represented a wide portfolio of clients heavily invested in the Czech Republic, Poland, Hungary, the Baltic states, and Russia. Satisfied clients meant a steady rise within the firm to senior associate—and soon, he hoped, junior partner. One day, maybe, he was going to be the head of International.

Provided, of course, he lived to see that day.

He yanked open the glass door to the business center and entered. Hayes peered up from the computer terminal. "What the hell happened to you?"

"Not here."

A dozen men dotted the room. His boss seemed to instantly understand and, without another word, they moved toward one of several lounges dotting the hotel's ground floor, this one adorned with an impressive stained-glass ceiling and pink marble fountain. Over the past few weeks its tables had become their official meeting place.

They slid into a booth.

Lord grabbed a waiter's attention and tapped his throat, the sign he wanted vodka. Actually, he *needed* vodka.

"Talk to me, Miles," Hayes said.

He told him what had happened. Everything. Including the comment he heard one of the gunmen utter and Inspector Orleg's speculation that the killing was directed at Bely and the Justice Ministry. Then he said, "Taylor, I think those guys were after me."

Hayes shook his head. "You don't know that. It could be you got a good look at their faces, and they decided to eliminate a witness. You just happened to be the only black guy around."

"There were hundreds of people on that street. Why single me out?"

STEVE BERRY / 28

"Because you were with Bely. That police inspector's right. It could have been a hit on Bely. They could have been watching all day, waiting for the right time. From the sound of it, I think it was."

"We don't know that."

"Miles, you just met Bely a couple of days ago. You don't know beans about him. People die around here all the time, for a variety of unnatural reasons."

Lord glanced down at the dark splotches on his clothes and thought again about AIDS. The waiter arrived with his drink. Hayes tossed the man a few rubles. Lord sucked a breath and gulped a long swallow, letting the fiery alcohol calm his nerves. He'd always liked Russian vodka. It truly was the best in the world. "I only hope to God he's HIV-negative. I'm still wearing his blood." He tabled the glass. "You think I ought to get out of the country?"

"You want to?"

"Shit, no. History is about to be made here. I don't want to cut and run. This is something I can tell my grandkids about. I was there when the tsar of all Russia was restored to the throne."

"Then don't go."

Another swig of vodka. "I also want to be around to see my grandchildren."

"How did you get away?"

"Ran like hell. It was strange, but I thought of my grand-father and 'coon hunting to keep me going."

A curious look came to Hayes's face.

"The sport of local rednecks back in the nineteen forties. Take a nigger out in the woods, let the dogs get a good whiff, then give him a thirty-minute head start." Another swallow of vodka. "Assholes never caught my granddaddy."

"You want me to arrange protection?" Hayes asked. "A bodyguard?"

"I think that'd be a good idea."

"I'd like to keep you here in Moscow. This could get real sticky, and I need you."

And Lord wanted to stay. So he kept telling himself Droopy and Cro-Magnon went after him because he saw them kill Bely. A witness, nothing more. That had to be it. What else could it be? "I left all my stuff in the archives. I thought I'd only be gone for a quick lunch."

"I'll call and have it brought over."

"No. I think I'll take a shower and go get it myself. I have more work to do anyway."

"Onto something?"

"Not really. Just tying up loose ends. I'll let you know if anything pans out. Work will take my mind off this."

"What about tomorrow? Can you still do the briefing?"

The waiter returned with a fresh vodka glass.

"Damn right."

Hayes smiled. "Now that's the attitude. I knew you were a tough sonovabitch."

4

2:30 PM

HAYES SHOULDERED THROUGH THE THRONG OF COMMUTERS streaming out of the Metro train. Platforms that a moment ago were deserted now teemed with thousands of Muscovites, all shoving toward four escalators that reached six hundred feet up to street level. An impressive sight, but it was the silence that caught his attention. It always did. Nothing but soles to stone and the scrape of one coat against another. Occasionally a voice would carry, but, overall, the procession of eight million people that paraded in every morning and then out every evening on the busiest subway system in the world was somber.

The Metro was Stalin's showcase. A vain attempt in the 1930s to openly celebrate socialist achievement with the largest and longest tunneling ever completed by humankind. The stations dotting the city became works of art adorned with florid stucco, neoclassical marble piers, elaborate chandeliers, gold, and glass. Not one person ever questioned the initial cost or subsequent upkeep. Now the price for that foolishness was an indispensable transportation system that demanded billions of rubles each year for maintenance, but brought in only a few kopecks a ride.

Yeltsin and his successors had tried to raise the fare, but the public furor was so great they'd all backed down. That had been their problem, Hayes thought. Too much populism for a nation as fickle as Russia. Be right. Be wrong. But don't be indecisive. Hayes firmly believed Russians would have respected their leaders more if they'd raised the fares, then shot anybody who openly protested. That was a lesson many Russian tsars and communist premiers had failed to learn—Nicholas II and Mikhail Gorbachev particularly.

He stepped off the escalator and followed the crowd out narrow doors into a brisk afternoon. He was north of Moscow center, beyond the overloaded four-lane motorway that encircled the city and was curiously called the Garden Ring. This particular Metro station was a dilapidated tile-and-glass oval with a flat roof, not one of Stalin's finest. In fact, the entire part of town would not find its way into any travel brochures. The station entrance was lined with a procession of haggard men and women, their skin drawn, hair matted, clothes a stinking mess, hocking everything—from toiletries to bootleg cassettes to dried fish—trying to raise a few rubles or, even better, U.S. dollars. He often wondered if anyone actually bought the shriveled salty fish carcasses, which looked even worse than they smelled. The only source of fish nearby was the Moskva River and, based on what he knew of Soviet and Russian waste disposal, there would be no telling what extras came with the meal.

He buttoned his overcoat and pushed his way down a buckled sidewalk, trying to fit in. He'd changed out of his suit into a pair of olive corduroys, a dark twill shirt, and black sneakers. Any hints of Western fashion were nothing but requests for trouble.

He found the club to which he'd been directed. It sat in the middle of a run-down block among a bakery, a grocery, a record store, and an ice-cream parlor. No placard announced its presence, only a small sign that beckoned visitors with a promise written in Cyrillic of exciting entertainment.

The interior was a dimly lit rectangle. Some vain attempt at ambience radiated from cheap walnut paneling. A blue fog laced the warm air. The room's center was dominated by an enormous plywood maze. He'd seen this novelty before, downtown, in the swankier haunts of the new rich. Those were neon monstrosities, molded out of tile and marble. This was a poor man's version, fashioned of bare boards and illuminated by fluorescent fixtures that threw down harsh blue rays.

A crowd encircled the display. These were not the type of men who tended to congregate in the more elaborate places munching salmon, herring, and beetroot salad, while armed lieutenants guarded the front door and roulette and blackjack were played for thousands of dollars in an adjoining room. It could cost two hundred rubles just to walk through the door at those places. For the men here—surly blue-collar workers from nearby factories and foundries—two hundred dollars was six months' wages.

"About time," Feliks Orleg said in Russian.

Hayes had not noticed the police inspector's approach. His attention had been on the maze. He motioned to the crowd and asked in Russian, "What's the attraction?"

"You'll see."

He stepped close and noticed that what appeared as one unit was actually three separate mazes intertwined. From small doors at the far end, three rats sprang. The rodents seemed to understand what was expected of them and raced forward undaunted while men howled and screamed. One of the spectators reached out to bang the side and a burly man with prizefighter forearms appeared from nowhere and restrained him.

"Moscow's version of the Kentucky Derby," Orleg said.

"This go on all day?"

The rats scooted around the twists and turns.

"All fucking day. They piss away what little they earn."

One of the rats found the finish line and a portion of the crowd erupted in cheers. He wondered what it paid, but decided to get down to business. "I want to know what happened today."

"The *chornye* was like a rat. Very fast through the streets."

"He should never have had the chance to run."

Orleg downed a swallow of the clear drink in his hand. "Apparently, the shooters missed."

The crowd was starting to quiet down, preparing for the next race. Hayes led Orleg to an empty table in a far corner. "I'm not in the mood for smart-ass, Orleg. The idea was to kill him. How hard could that have been?"

Orleg savored another sip before swallowing. "Like I said, the fools missed. When they chased him, your Mr. Lord escaped. Quite inventive, I was told. It took a lot for me to clear that area of police patrols for those few minutes. They should have had an easy opportunity. Instead, they killed three Russian citizens."

"I thought these men were professionals."

Orleg laughed. "Mean bastards, yes. Professionals? I don't think so. They're gangsters. What did you expect?" Orleg emptied the glass. "You want another hit made on him?"

"Fuck, no. In fact, I don't want one hair on Lord's head touched."

Orleg said nothing, but his eyes made clear that he didn't like being ordered by a foreigner.

"Leave it alone. It was a bad idea to start with. Lord thinks it was a hit on Bely. Good. Let him think that. We can't afford any more attention."

"The shooters said your lawyer handled himself like a pro."

"He was an athlete in college. Football and track. But two Kalashnikovs should have compensated."

Orleg sat back in the chair. "Maybe you should handle things yourself."

"Maybe I will. But for now, you make sure those idiots back off. They had their chance. I don't want another hit. And if they don't follow this order, assure them they will not like the people their bosses send for a visit."

The inspector shook his head. "When I was a boy we hunted down rich people and tortured them. Now we are paid to protect them." He spat on the floor. "Whole thing makes me sick."

"Who said anything about rich?"

"You think I do not know what is happening here?"

Hayes leaned close. "You don't know shit, Orleg. Do yourself a favor and don't ask too many questions. Follow orders and it'll be far better for your health."

"Fucking American. The whole world is completely upside down. I remember a time when you people worried whether we would even let you leave this country. Now you own us."

"Get with the program. Times are changing. Either keep up or get out of the way. You wanted to be a player? Be one. That requires obedience."

"Don't you worry about me, lawyer. But what of your Lord problem?"

"You don't worry about that. I'll handle him."

5

3:35 PM

LORD WAS BACK IN THE RUSSIAN ARCHIVES, A GLOOMY GRAN-
ite building that once had served as the Institute of Marxism-
Leninism. Now it was the Center for the Preservation and
Study of Documents of Contemporary History—more evidence of the Russian penchant for superfluous titles.

He'd been surprised on his first visit to find images of
Marx, Engels, and Lenin still on the pediment outside the
main entrance, along with the call FORWARD TO THE VICTORY
OF COMMUNISM. Nearly all reminders of the Soviet era had
been stripped from every town, street, and building across
the country, replaced by the double-headed eagle the Romanov dynasty had displayed for three hundred years. He'd
been told that the red granite statue of Lenin was one of the
few left standing in Russia.

He'd calmed down after a hot shower and more vodka. He
was dressed in the only other suit he'd brought from Atlanta,
a charcoal gray with a faint chalk stripe. He was going to
have to visit one of the Moscow shops during the next couple of days and purchase another, since one suit would not
be enough for the busy weeks ahead.

Before the communist fall, the archives had been considered too heretical for the general public, inaccessible to all but
the most stalwart communists, and that distinction partially

remained. Why, Lord had yet to understand. The shelves were stocked mainly with nonsensical personal papers—books, letters, diaries, government records, and other unpublished material—innocuous writings that possessed no historical significance. To make matters more of a challenge there was no indexing system, just a random organization by year, person, or geographic region. Totally haphazard, certainly designed more to confuse than enlighten. As if no one wanted the past found, which was most likely the case.

And there was little help.

The staff archivists were leftovers from the Soviet regime, part of the party hierarchy who had once enjoyed benefits not available to ordinary Muscovites. Though the party was gone, a cadre of loyal elderly women remained, many of whom, Lord believed, firmly wished for a return to totalitarian order. The lack of help was why he'd requested Artemy Bely's assistance, and he'd accomplished more in the past few days than in the weeks before.

Only a few idlers milled among the metal shelves. Most of the records, particularly those on Lenin, had once been locked away behind steel doors in underground vaults. Yeltsin had ended that secrecy and ordered everything moved aboveground, opening the building to academicians and journalists.

But not entirely.

A large section remained closed—the so-called Protective Papers—similar to what a TOP SECRET stamp did to any Freedom of Information request back home. Lord's Tsarist Commission credentials, however, overrode any supposed former state secrets. His pass, arranged by Hayes, was authority from the government to look wherever he desired, including through the Protective Papers.

He sat down at his reserved table and forced his mind to concentrate on the pages spread before him. His job was to bolster Stefan Baklanov's claim to the Russian throne.

Baklanov, a Romanov by birth, was the leading contender for selection by the Tsarist Commission. He was also heavily entrenched with Western businesses, many of which were Pridgen & Woodworth clients, so Hayes had sent Lord into the archives to make sure there was nothing that might impugn Baklanov's claim to power. The last thing anyone needed was for there to have been a state investigation, or implications Baklanov's family had been German sympathizers during World War II—anything that might cause the people to doubt his commitment to them or to Russia.

Lord's assignment had led him to the last Romanov to occupy the Russian throne—Nicholas II—and what happened in Siberia on July 16, 1918. He'd read many published accounts and several unpublished ones during the past few weeks. All were, at best, contradictory. It took a detailed study of each report, culling out obvious falsehoods and combining facts, to glean any useful information. His growing notes now formed a cumulative narrative of that fateful night in Russian history.

Nicholas rustled from a sound sleep. A soldier stood over him. It wasn't often over the course of the past few months that he'd been able to actually sleep, and he resented the intrusion. But there was little he could do. He'd once been the Tsar of All Russia, Nicholas II, the embodiment of the Almighty on Earth. But a year ago last March he'd been forced to do the unthinkable for a divine monarch—abdicate in the face of violence. The provisional government that followed him was mainly liberals from the Duma and a coalition of radical socialists. It was to be a caretaker body until a constituent assembly could be elected, but the Germans had allowed Lenin to cross their territory and reenter Russia, hoping he'd wreak political havoc.

And he had.

Toppling the weak provisional government ten months back in what the guards proudly called the October Revolution.

Why was his cousin, the kaiser, doing this to him? Did he hate him that much? Was winning the World War important enough to sacrifice a ruling dynasty?

Apparently so.

Just two months after seizing power, to no one's surprise, Lenin signed a cease-fire with the Germans, and Russia abandoned the Great War, leaving the Allies without an eastern front to occupy the advancing Germans. Britain, France, and the United States could not be happy. He understood the dangerous game Lenin was playing. Promising the people peace to gain their confidence, but needing to delay its implementation in order to placate the Allies, while at the same time not offending his real ally, the kaiser. The Treaty of Brest-Litovsk, signed five months back, was nothing short of devastating. Germany gained a quarter of Russia's territory and nearly a third of its people. That action, he'd been told, had generated great resentment. The talk among the guards was that all of the Bolshevik enemies had finally coalesced under a unified White banner, chosen in startling contrast to the communist Red flag. A mass of recruits had already gravitated to the Whites. Peasants particularly were drawn, since land was still denied them.

A civil war now raged.

White versus Red.

And he was merely Citizen Romanov, prisoner of the Red Bolsheviks.

Ruler of no one.

He and his family had first been held in the Alexander Palace at Tsarskoe Selo, not far from Petrograd. Then they were moved east to Tobolsk, in central Russia, a river town full of whitewashed churches and log cabins. The people there had been openly loyal, showing great respect to their fallen tsar and his family. They'd daily gathered in large numbers outside the confinement house, removing their hats and crossing themselves. Hardly a day went by without a delivery of cakes, candles, and icons. The guards themselves, members of the honored Rifle Regiment, had been friendly and had taken the time to talk and play cards. They'd been allowed books and newspapers, even correspondence. The food had been excellent and every comfort was shown them.

All in all, not a bad prison.

Then, seventy-eight days ago, another move.

This time here, to Yekaterinburg, on the eastern slope of the Ural Mountains, deep in the heart of Mother Russia where Bolsheviks dominated. Ten thousand Red Army troops wandered the streets. The local population was bitterly opposed to anything tsarist. The house of a wealthy merchant, a man named Ipatiev, had been commandeered and converted into a makeshift prison. The House of Special Purpose, Nicholas had heard it called. A high wooden fence had been erected, the glass in all the windows smeared with lime and iron-barred, none to be opened on pain of being shot. All the doors had been removed from the bedrooms and lavatories. He'd been forced to listen while his family was jeered with insults, compelled to view without comment lewd pictures of his wife and Rasputin scrawled on the walls. Yesterday he'd almost come to blows with one of the impertinent bastards. The guard had written on his daughters' bedroom wall: OUR RUSSIAN TSAR CALLED NICK. PULLED OFF HIS THRONE BY HIS PRICK.

Enough of that, he thought.

"What time is it?" he finally asked the guard standing over him.

"Two AM.*"*

"What is wrong?"

"It is necessary that your family be moved. The White Army is approaching the city. An attack is imminent. It would be dangerous to be in the upper rooms, if there was shooting in the streets."

The words excited Nicholas. He'd heard the guards' whispers. The White Army had stormed across Siberia, taking town after town, regaining territory from the Reds. Over the past few days the rumble of artillery could be heard in the distance. That sound had given him hope. Perhaps his generals were finally coming and things would be put right again.

"Rise and dress," the guard said.

The man withdrew and Nicholas roused his wife. His son, Alexei, slept in a bed on the far side of the modest bedroom.

He and Alexei quietly dressed in their military field shirts, trousers, boots, and forage caps, while Alexandra withdrew to their daughters' room. Unfortunately, Alexei could not walk. Yet another hemophilic hemorrhage two days before had crippled him, so Nicholas gently carried the thin thirteen-year-old into the hall.

His four daughters appeared.

Each was dressed in a plain black skirt and white blouse, their mother following, limping with her cane. His precious Sunshine was barely able to walk anymore—sciatica from her childhood had progressively worsened. The almost constant worry she endured for Alexei had destroyed her health, graying her once chestnut hair and fading the loving glow in eyes that had captivated him since the first day they'd met as teenagers. Her breath seemed to come quick, many times in painful gasps, her lips occasionally turning blue. She complained about her heart and back, but he wondered if the afflictions were real or just side effects of the unutterable grief she experienced, wondering if today was the day death would snatch her son.

"What is this, Papa?" Olga asked.

She was twenty-two, his firstborn. Thoughtful and intelligent, she was in many ways like her mother, occasionally brooding and sulky.

"Perhaps our salvation," he mouthed.

A look of excitement crept across her pretty face. Her sister Tatiana, one year her junior, and Maria, two years younger, came close, carrying pillows. Tatiana was tall and stately, the leader of the girls—Governess, they all called her—and she was her mother's favorite. Maria was pretty and gentle—eyes like saucers—and flirtatious. Her desire was to marry a Russian soldier and have twenty children. His two middle daughters had heard what he said.

He motioned for silence.

Anastasia, seventeen, lingered with her mother, carrying King Charles, the cocker spaniel their jailers had allowed her to retain. She was short and plump with the reputation of a rebel—a monkey for jokes, *her sisters would say*—but her deep blue eyes were charming and he'd never been able to resist them.

The remaining four captives quickly joined them.

Dr. Botkin, Alexei's physician. Trupp, Nicholas's valet. Demidova, Alexandra's maid. And Kharitonov, the cook. Demidova likewise clutched a pillow, but Nicholas knew this one was special. Sewn deep within its feathers was a box containing jewels, and Demidova's task was never to allow the pillow from her sight. Alexandra and the girls likewise harbored treasure, their corsets concealing diamonds, emeralds, rubies, and ropes of pearl.

Alexandra limped close and asked him, *"Do you know what's happening?"*

"The Whites are nearby."

Her tired face showed wonderment. *"Could this be?"*

"This way, please," a familiar voice said from the stairway.

Nicholas turned and faced Yurovsky.

The man had arrived twelve days before with a squad from the Bolshevik Secret Police, replacing the previous commandant and his undisciplined factory-worker guards. At first the change seemed positive, but Nicholas quickly determined that these new men were professionals. Perhaps even Magyars, prisoners of war from the Austro-Hungarian army, hired by the Bolsheviks for jobs native Russians abhorred. Yurovsky was their leader. A dark man with black hair, black beard, and an unhurried way in his manner and speech. He gave orders calmly and expected them to be obeyed. Ox Command was the name with which they'd christened him, and Nicholas had quickly concluded that this demon enjoyed oppressing people.

"We must hurry," Yurovsky said. "Time is short."

Nicholas signaled for quiet and the entourage followed a wooden staircase down to the ground floor. Alexei slept soundly on his shoulder. Anastasia released the dog, which scurried away.

They were led outside, across a courtyard, to a semi-basement room with one arched window. Dingy striped wallpaper covered the plaster walls. There was no furniture.

"Wait here for the cars to arrive," Yurovsky said.

"Where are we going?" Nicholas asked.

"Away," was all their jailer said.

"No chairs?" Alexandra said. "May we not sit?"

Yurovsky shrugged and instructed one of his men. Two chairs appeared. Alexandra took one, Maria positioning the pillow she held behind her mother's back. Nicholas sat Alexei in the other. Tatiana placed her pillow behind her brother and made the boy comfortable. Demidova continued to clutch her pillow close with crossed arms.

More artillery rumbled in the distance. The sound brought Nicholas hope.

Yurovsky said, "It is necessary that we photograph you. There are people who believe you have already escaped. So I need you to stand here."

Yurovsky positioned everyone. When he finished, the daughters stood behind their seated mother, Nicholas stood beside Alexei, the four non–family members behind him. Over the course of sixteen months they'd been ordered to do many strange things. This one, being awakened in the middle of the night for a picture and then being whisked away, was no exception. When Yurovsky left the room and closed the door, no one said a word.

A moment later the door reopened.

But no photographer with a tripod camera entered. Instead, eleven armed men paraded in. Yurovsky came last. The Russian's right hand was stuffed into his trouser pocket. He was holding a sheet of paper in the other.

He started reading.

"In view of the fact that your relatives are continuing their attack on the Soviet Russia, the Ural Executive Committee has decided to execute you."

Nicholas was having trouble hearing. A vehicle engine was revving outside, loud and clamorous. Strange. He looked at his family, then faced Yurovsky and said, "What? What?"

The Russian's expression never broke. He simply repeated the declaration in the same monotone. Then his right hand came from his pocket.

Nicholas saw the gun.

A Colt pistol.

The barrel approached his head.

6

A WEAK FEELING ALWAYS CAME TO LORD'S STOMACH WHEN he read about that night. He tried to imagine what it must have been like when the shooting started. The terror they must have felt. Nowhere to go. Nothing to do but die horribly.

He'd been drawn back to the event because of what he'd found in the Protective Papers. He'd stumbled onto the note ten days back, scrawled on a plain brittle sheet in outdated Russian script, the black ink barely legible. It was inside a crimson leather bag that had been sewn shut. A label on the outside indicated: ACQUIRED JULY 10, 1925. NOT TO BE OPENED UNTIL JANUARY 1, 1950. It was impossible to determine if that instruction had been heeded.

He reached into his briefcase and found the copy he'd carefully translated. The date at the top read April 10, 1922:

```
The situation with Yurovsky is troubling. I
do not believe the reports filed from
Yekaterinburg were accurate and the
information concerning Felix Yussoupov
corroborates that. It is unfortunate the
White Guardsman you persuaded to talk was
not more forthcoming. Perhaps too much pain
can be counterproductive. The mention of
Kolya Maks is interesting. I have heard this
```

name before. The village of Starodug has
likewise been noted by two other similarly
persuaded White Guardsmen. There is something
occurring, of that I am certain, but I fear
my body will not endure for me to learn
what. I greatly worry about the future of
all our endeavors after I am gone. Stalin is
frightening. There is a rigidness about him
that insulates all emotion from his decision
making. If the leadership of our new nation
falls to him, I fear the dream may die.

I wonder if one or more of the imperials
may have escaped Yekaterinburg. It certainly
appears that way. Comrade Yussoupov apparently
believes so. Perhaps he thinks he can offer
the next generation a reprieve. Perhaps the
tsarina was not as foolish as we all believed.
Maybe the *starets*'s ramblings have more
meaning than we first thought. Over the past
few weeks, thinking of the Romanovs, I have
found myself recalling the words of an old
Russian poem: The knights are dust and their
good swords rust. Their souls are with the
saints we trust.

He and Artemy Bely both believed the document was
penned in Lenin's own hand. It wouldn't be unusual. The
communists had preserved thousands of Lenin's writings.
But this particular document had not been found where it
should have been. Instead, Lord had located it among papers
repatriated from the Nazis after World War II. Hitler's invading armies had stolen not only Russian art, but also
archival material by the tons. Document depositories in
Leningrad, Stalingrad, Kiev, and Moscow were stripped

clean. Only after the war, when Stalin sent his Extraordinary Commission to reclaim the country's heritage, had many of these caches found their way back to the Motherland.

There was, though, one other relevant paper within the crimson leather bag. A single sheet of parchment with a frilly border of flowers and leaves. The handwriting was in English, the script distinctly feminine:

October 28, 1916.

Dear beloved Soul of my Soul, my own Wee One, Sweet Angel, oh, me loves you so, always together, night and day, I feel what you are going through and your poor heart. God have mercy, give you strength and wisdom. He won't forsake you. He will help, recompense this mad suffering and end this separation at such a time when one needs being together.

Our Friend has just left. He saved Baby once again. Oh merciful Jesus thank the Lord we have him. The pain was immense, my heart torn apart from witnessing, but Baby now sleeps peacefully. I am assured that tomorrow he will be well.

Such sunny weather, no clouds. That means, trust and hope, yet all is pitch black around, but God is above all; we know not His way, nor how He will help, but He will hark unto all prayers. Our Friend is most insistent on that.

I must tell you that just before he left our Friend went into a strange convulsion. I was most frightened thinking he may be ill. What would Baby do without him. He fell to the floor and began muttering about leaving this world before the new year and seeing masses of corpses, several grand dukes and hundreds of counts. The Neva will be all red with blood, he said. His words terrified me.

Looking toward heaven, he told me that if he be

murdered by boyars their hands will remain soiled by blood for twenty-five years. They will leave Russia. Brother will rise against brother, they will kill each other in hate, and there will be no nobles in the country. Most disturbing, he said that if one of our relatives carries out his murder, none of our family will live more than two years. We will all be killed by the Russian people.

He made me rise and immediately write this down. Then he said not to despair. There would be salvation. The one with the most guilt will see the error of his way. He will assure that the blood of our body resurrects itself. His rantings bordered on nonsense and I wondered, for the first time, if the stench of alcohol upon him had affected his brain. He kept saying that only a raven and an eagle can succeed where all fail and that the innocence of beasts will guard and lead the way, being the final arbiter of success. He said God will provide a way to be sure of righteousness. Most troubling was his statement that twelve must die before the resurrection can be complete.

I tried to question him but he went silent, insisting that I write the prophecy down exactly and convey the vision to you. He talked as if something might happen to us, but I assured him that Papa has the country well in hand. He was not comforted and his words troubled me all night. Oh my precious one, I hold you tight in my arms and will never let anyone touch your shining soul. I kiss, kiss, kiss and bless you and you always understand. I hope you come to me soon.

Your Wify

Lord knew that the writer was Alexandra, the last tsarina of Russia. She had kept a diary for decades. So had her husband, Nicholas, and both journals subsequently provided an unprecedented look into the royal court. Nearly seven hundred of their letters were found in Yekaterinburg after the execution. He'd read other diary excerpts and most of the letters. Several recent books had published them verbatim. He knew the reference to "our Friend" was their way of describing Rasputin, since both Alexandra and Nicholas thought their letters were being scrutinized by others. Unfortunately, their unfettered confidence in Rasputin was not shared by anyone else.

"So deep in thought," a voice said in Russian.

He glanced up.

An older man stood on the opposite side of the table. He was fair-skinned with pale blue eyes, a thin chest, and freckled wrists. His head was half bald and graying fuzz dusted the sallow skin on his neck from ear to ear. He wore steel-rimmed glasses and a bow tie. Lord immediately recalled that he'd seen the man poring through the records, one of several individuals who seemed to be working as hard as he was.

"Actually, I was back in 1916 for an instant. Reading this stuff is like time travel," Lord said in Russian.

The older man smiled. Lord estimated his age to be nearing, if not more than, sixty.

"I quite agree. It is one of the reasons I like coming here. A reminder of something that once was."

He instantly warmed to the congenial manner and stood from the table. "I'm Miles Lord."

"I know who you are."

A wave of suspicion swept over him and his gaze unconsciously darted around the room.

His visitor seemed to sense the fear. "I assure you, Mr. Lord, I am no threat. Just a tired historian looking for a little conversation with someone of similar interests."

He relaxed. "How do you know me?"

The man smiled. "You are not a favorite of the women who staff this depository. They resent being ordered about by an American—"

"And a black?"

The man smiled. "Unfortunately, this country is not progressively minded on the issue of race. We are a fair-skinned nation. But your commission credentials cannot be ignored."

"And who are you?"

"Semyon Pashenko, professor of history, Moscow State University." The older man offered his hand and Lord accepted. "Where is the other gentleman who accompanied you in days past? A lawyer, I believe. We talked for a few moments among the stacks."

He debated whether to lie, but decided the truth would be better. "He was killed this morning on Nikolskaya Prospekt. In a shooting."

Shock filled the older man's face. "I saw something on the television about that earlier. So terrible." He shook his head. "This country will be the ruin of itself if something is not done soon."

Lord sat and offered a seat.

"Were you involved?" Pashenko asked, settling into a chair.

"I was there." He decided to keep the rest of what happened to himself.

Pashenko shook his head. "That sort of display says nothing for who or what we are. Westerners, like yourself, must think us barbarians."

"Not at all. Every nation goes through periods like this. We had our own during the western expansion and in the nineteen twenties and thirties."

"But I believe our situation is more than merely growing pains."

"The past few years have been difficult for Russia. It was hard enough when there was a government. Yeltsin and

Putin tried to keep order. But now, with little semblance of authority, it's nothing short of anarchy."

Pashenko nodded. "Unfortunately, this is nothing new for our nation."

"Are you an academician?"

"A historian. I have devoted my life to the study of our beloved Mother Rus."

He grinned at the ancient term. "I would imagine there hasn't been much use for your specialty in some time."

"Regretfully. The communists had their own version of history."

He recalled something he'd read once. *Russia is a country with an unpredictable past.* "Did you teach, then?"

"For thirty years. I saw them all. Stalin, Khrushchev, Brezhnev. Each one inflicted his own peculiar damage. It is sinful what happened. But even now, we find it hard to let go. People still line up each day to walk past Lenin's body." Pashenko lowered his voice. "A butcher, revered as a saint. Did you notice the flowers around his statue out front." He shook his head. "Disgusting."

Lord decided to be careful with his words. Though this was the postcommunist era, soon to be the new tsarist era, he was still an American working under credentials granted by a shaky Russian government. "Something tells me that if tanks rolled through Red Square tomorrow, everyone who works in this archive would be there to cheer them on."

"They are no better than street beggars," Pashenko said. "They enjoyed privilege, kept the leaders' secrets, and in return received a choice apartment, some extra bread, a few more days off in summer. You must work and earn what you get, is that not what America stands for?"

Lord didn't answer. Instead, he asked, "What do you think of the Tsarist Commission?"

"I voted yes. How could a tsar do any worse?"

He'd found that attitude quite prevalent.

"It is unusual to find an American able to speak our language so well."

He shrugged. "You have a fascinating country."

"Have you always had an interest?"

"Since childhood. I started reading about Peter the Great and Ivan the Terrible."

"And now you are a part of our Tsarist Commission. About to make history." Pashenko motioned to the sheets on the table. "Those are quite old. Do they come from the Protective Papers?"

"I found both a couple of weeks ago."

"I recognize the script. Alexandra herself penned that one. She wrote all her letters and diaries in English. The Russians hated her because she was born a German princess. I always thought that an unfair criticism. Alexandra was a most misunderstood woman."

He offered the sheet, deciding that this Russian's brain might be worth picking. Pashenko read the letter, then said when he finished, "She was colorful in her prose, but this is mild. She and Nicholas wrote many romantic letters."

"It's sad handling them. I feel like an intruder. I was reading earlier about the execution. Yurovsky must have been one devil of a man."

"Yurovsky's son said that his father always regretted his involvement. But who knows? For twenty years after he gave lectures to Bolshevik groups about the murders, proud of what he did."

He handed Pashenko the note penned by Lenin. "Take a look at this."

The Russian read the page slowly, then said, "Definitely Lenin. I am familiar with his writing style, too. Curious."

"My thought exactly."

Pashenko's eyes lit up. "Surely you do not believe those

stories that two of the royal family survived the execution at Yekaterinburg?"

He shrugged. "To this day the bodies of Alexei and Anastasia have never been found. Now this."

Pashenko grinned. "Americans really are conspiratorialists. A plot into everything."

"It's my job at the moment."

"You must support Stefan Baklanov's claim, correct?"

He was a little surprised and wondered about his transparency.

Pashenko motioned to the surroundings. "The women, again, Mr. Lord. They know all. Your document inquiries are recorded and, believe me, they pay attention. Have you met our so-called Heir Apparent?"

He shook his head. "But the man I work for has."

"Baklanov is no better fit to rule than Mikhail Romanov was four hundred years ago. Too weak. Unlike poor Mikhail, who had his father to make decisions for him, Baklanov will be on his own, and many would revel in his failure."

This Russian academician had a point. From all he'd read about Baklanov, the man seemed more concerned with a return of tsarist prestige than with actually governing the nation.

"May I make a suggestion, Mr. Lord?"

"Certainly."

"Have you been to the archives in St. Petersburg?"

He shook his head.

"A look there might be productive. They house many of Lenin's writings. Most of the tsar and tsarina's diaries and letters are stored there, too." He pointed to the sheets. "It might help discover the meaning of what you have found."

The suggestion seemed a good one. "Thank you, I just might do that." He glanced at his watch. "If you'll excuse me, I have more to read before this place closes. But I enjoyed talking. I'll be around for a few more days. Maybe we can chat again."

"I, too, will be in and out. If you don't mind, I think I might just sit here a little while. May I read those two sheets again?"

"Of course."

Ten minutes later when he returned, the writings by Alexandra and Lenin lay on the table, but Semyon Pashenko was gone.

7

A DARK BMW PICKED HAYES UP IN FRONT OF THE VOLKHOV. After a fifteen-minute trek through surprisingly light traffic, the driver wheeled into a gated courtyard. The house beyond was late classical, built in the early part of the nineteenth century, then and now one of Moscow's showpieces. During the communist tenure it had been the Center for State Literature and Arts, but after the fall, like most things, the building went on the auction block and was eventually snapped up by one of the country's new rich.

Hayes stepped from the car and told the driver to wait.

As usual, two men armed with Kalashnikovs patrolled the courtyard. The house's blue stucco facade appeared gray in the dimming afternoon light. He sucked in a breath, bitter with carbon fumes, and stepped resolutely down a brick walk through a lovely autumn garden. He entered the house through an unlocked pine door.

The interior was characteristic for a dwelling built nearly two hundred years ago. The floor plan was an irregular hodgepodge, the formal reception areas knotted toward the front facing the street, various private living quarters in the rear. The decor was period and he assumed original, though he'd never asked the owner. He wound his way through a maze of tight corridors and found the paneled salon where the meeting always occurred.

Four men waited, each sipping drinks and smoking cigars.

He'd met them a year ago, and all of their subsequent communication had been through code names. Hayes was known as Lincoln, the other four by their chosen labels—Stalin, Lenin, Khrushchev, and Brezhnev. The idea had come from a popular print Moscow gift shops peddled. It depicted various Russian tsars, empresses, and Soviet premiers gathered around a table, drinking and smoking, with Mother Russia the single topic of discussion. Of course, no such meeting had ever occurred, but the artist graphically fantasized how each individual personality might have reacted given such an event. The four men had chosen their designated label carefully, reveling in the prospect that their meetings were not unlike the painting—and that the fate of the Motherland now rested in their hands.

The four extended a welcome and Lenin poured Hayes a vodka from a carafe chilling in a sterling ice bucket. A plate of smoked salmon and marinated mushrooms was offered. He declined. "I'm afraid I have bad news," he said in Russian, then told them about Miles Lord surviving.

"There is another matter," Brezhnev said. "We did not know until today this lawyer was an African."

Hayes thought the observation curious. "He's not. He's American. But if you mean his color, what does it matter?"

Stalin leaned forward. Unlike his namesake, he seemed always to be the voice of reason. "Americans have such a hard time understanding the Russian sensitivity to fate."

"And where exactly does fate tie in here?"

"Tell us about Mr. Lord," Brezhnev asked.

The entire subject bothered Hayes. He'd thought it strange they'd so nonchalantly ordered Lord's murder without knowing anything at all about him. At their last meeting Lenin had given him Inspector Orleg's telephone number and told him to arrange the murder through him. The instruction had bothered him at first—such a valuable assistant would be difficult to replace—but too much was at stake to be concerned about one lawyer. So he'd done as they asked. Now more questions. Ones that made little sense.

"Came to my firm right out of law school. Phi Beta Kappa at the University of Virginia. Always been interested in Russia, took a master's degree in Eastern European studies. Good with languages. Damn hard to find a lawyer who can speak Russian. I thought he'd be an asset, and I was right. Many of our clients rely on him exclusively."

"Personal information?" Khrushchev asked.

"Born and raised in South Carolina, somewhat affluent. His father was a preacher. One of those tent revivalists who traveled from town to town healing people. From what Lord tells me, he and his father didn't get along. Miles is thirty-eight or thirty-nine, never been married. Lives a fairly basic life, from all I see. Works hard. One of our top producers. Has never given me any trouble."

Lenin leaned back in the chair. "Why the interest in Russia?"

"Beats the shit out of me. From conversations he seems genuinely fascinated. Always has been. He's a history buff, his office is full of books and treatises. He's even done some lecturing at a couple of our local universities and at a few state bar meetings. Now let *me* ask something. Why is all this important?"

Stalin sat back. "That is immaterial, given what happened today. The problem of Mr. Lord will have to wait. What should concern us now is what happens tomorrow."

Hayes wasn't ready to change subjects. "For the record,

I wasn't in favor of killing Lord. I told you I could handle him, whatever your apprehensions may have been."

"As you will," Brezhnev said. "We have decided that Mr. Lord is to be your concern."

"I'm glad we agree. He won't be a problem. But no one has yet to explain how he *was* a problem."

Khrushchev said, "Your assistant has been intent in the archives."

"That's what I sent him there to do. On your instructions, I might add."

The assigned task was simple. Find anything that could affect Stefan Baklanov's claim to the throne. And Lord had searched nearly ten hours a day for the past six weeks and reported everything he'd found. Hayes suspected something he'd passed on to the group had piqued these men's interest.

"It is not necessary," Stalin said, "that you know everything. Nor do I believe you really want to. Suffice it to say that we deemed the elimination of Mr. Lord the most economical way to handle the matter. That effort failed, so we are willing to take your advice. For now."

A grin accompanied the statement. Hayes didn't particularly like the condescending way these four treated him. He wasn't some errand boy. He was the fifth member of what he'd privately dubbed the Secret Chancellory. But he decided to keep his irritation to himself and changed the subject. "I assume the decision has been made that the new monarch will be absolute?"

"The question of the tsar's power is still a matter of debate," Lenin said.

He understood that some aspects of what they were doing were uniquely Russian, to be decided solely by Russians. And as long as those decisions did nothing to jeopardize the enormous financial contribution his clients were making and the sizable return he stood to enjoy, he didn't care. "What is the status of our influence with the commission?"

"We have nine who will vote as we say, no matter what," Lenin said. "The other eight are being approached."

"The rules will require unanimity," Brezhnev said.

Lenin sighed. "I wonder how we ever let that pass."

Unanimity had been an integral part of the resolution that created the Tsarist Commission. The people had approved both the idea of a tsar and a commission, with the check and balance that all seventeen commissioners must vote yes. One vote was enough to derail any attempt at stacking the deck.

"The other eight will be secure by the time a vote is taken," Stalin made clear.

"Are your people working on the matter?" Hayes asked.

"As we speak." Stalin sipped from his drink. "But we will need more funds, Mr. Hayes. These men are proving expensive to purchase."

Western currency was financing nearly everything the Secret Chancellory was doing, and that bothered Hayes. He paid all the bills, but possessed only a limited voice.

"How much?" he asked.

"Twenty million dollars."

He held his emotions in check. That was on top of another ten million provided thirty days ago. He wondered how much of the money was actually making its way to commission members and how much was staying with the men around him, but he dared not ask.

Stalin handed him two laminated badges. "Here are your commission credentials. They will allow you, and your Mr. Lord, access to the Kremlin. They also authorize entrance into the Facets Palace. You have the same privileges as commission staff members."

He was impressed. He'd not expected to be actually present at the sessions.

Khrushchev smiled. "We thought it better that you be there in person. There will be a lot of American press. You should be able to blend into the surroundings and keep us informed. None of the commission members know you or the extent of your connections. Your observations should be helpful in our coming discussions."

"We have also decided that we wish your role to expand," Stalin said.

"In what way?" he asked.

"It is important the commission encounter no distractions during its deliberations. We will ensure that its session is brief, but there is a danger from outside influences."

He'd sensed during their last meeting that something was bothering these four men. Something Stalin had said earlier when he questioned him about Lord. *Americans have such a hard time understanding Russian sensitivity to fate.*

"What would you have me do?"

"Whatever becomes necessary. Granted, any one of us could get the people we represent to handle a problem, but we need a certain element of deniability. Unfortunately, unlike the old Soviet Union, the new Russia does not hold its secrets closely. Our records are open, our press aggressive, foreign influence great. You, on the other hand, have international credibility. And, besides, who would suspect you of any nefarious activity?" Stalin curled his thin lips into a wiry smile.

"And how would I handle any situation that might arise?"

Stalin reached into his jacket pocket and withdrew a card. On it was written a telephone number. "There are men waiting at that number. If you were to instruct that they plunge themselves into the Moskva River and never surface, they would. We suggest you use that loyalty wisely."

8

WEDNESDAY, OCTOBER 13

LORD STARED THROUGH THE MERCEDES'S TINTED WINDOW AT the Kremlin's crimson walls. Bells in the clock tower high above pealed loud for eight AM. He and Taylor Hayes were being driven across Red Square. The driver was a bushy-headed Russian whom Lord might otherwise have found frightening, had Hayes not arranged the transportation himself.

Red Square was devoid of people. Out of respect to the communists, a few of whom still lingered in the Duma, the cobbled expanse remained cordoned off until one PM each day, when Lenin's tomb closed to visitors. He thought the gesture ridiculous, but it seemed enough to satisfy the egos of those who once dominated this nation of 150 million.

A uniformed guard reacted to a bright orange sticker on the car's windshield and waved the vehicle through Savior's Gate. He felt excitement at entering the Kremlin through this portal. The Spasskaya Tower above him had been erected in 1491 by Ivan III, part of his massive reconstruction of the Kremlin, and the gate had admitted every new tsar and tsa-rina to the ancestral seat of power. Today it was designated the official entrance for the Tsarist Commission and its staff.

He was still shaky. Thoughts of his chase yesterday not far from this site kept racing through his mind. Hayes had assured him over breakfast that no chances would be taken, his safety would be guaranteed, and he was relying on his boss to make good on that assurance. He trusted Hayes. Respected him. He desperately wanted to be a part of what was happening, but he wondered if perhaps he was being foolish.

What would his father say if he could see him now?

The Reverend Grover Lord didn't much care for lawyers. He liked to describe them as *locusts on the landscape of society.* His father once visited the White House, part of a contingent of southern ministers invited for a photo op when the president signed off on a vain attempt at restoring prayer to the public schools. Less than a year later the Supreme Court struck down the law as unconstitutional. *Godless locusts,* his father had raved from the pulpit.

Grover Lord didn't approve of his son becoming a lawyer and demonstrated his disgust by not providing one dime for law school, though he could have easily paid the entire bill. That had forced Lord to finance his own way with student loans and night jobs. He'd earned good grades and graduated with honors. He'd secured an excellent job and risen through the ranks. Now he was about to witness history.

So screw Grover Lord, he thought.

The car motored into the Kremlin yard.

He admired what was once the Presidium of the Supreme Soviet, a compact neoclassical rectangle. The red banner of the Bolsheviks no longer flew overhead. Instead, an imperial double-headed eagle flapped in the morning breeze. He also noticed the absence of Lenin's monument that had once sat off to the right, and remembered the uproar that had accompanied its removal. For once Yeltsin had ignored popular dissent and ordered the iron image melted for scrap.

He marveled at the construction that surrounded him. The Kremlin epitomized the Russian penchant for big things.

They'd always been impressed with city squares that could accommodate missile launchers, bells so large they could never be hoisted into their towers, and rockets so powerful as to be uncontrollable. Bigger was not only better, it was glorious.

The car slowed and veered right.

The Cathedrals of the Archangel Michael and Annunciation rose to the left, those of the Dormition and Twelve Apostles to the right. More unnecessarily obese buildings. Ivan III had commissioned them all, an extravagance that earned him the label "Great." Lord knew that many chapters in Russian history had opened and closed within those ancient edifices, each topped with gilded onion domes and elaborate Byzantine crosses. He'd visited them, but never dreamed that he'd be chauffeured into Cathedral Square in an official limousine, part of a national effort to restore the Russian monarchy. Not bad for a South Carolina preacher's son.

"Some shit," Hayes said.

Lord smiled. "You got that right."

The car rolled to a stop.

They stepped out into a frosty morning, the sky bright blue and cloud-free, unusual for a Russian autumn. Perhaps an omen of good things, Lord hoped.

He'd never been inside the Palace of Facets. Tourists weren't allowed. It was one of the few structures within the Kremlin that endured in its original form. Ivan the Great had erected it in 1491, naming his masterpiece for the diamond-patterned limestone blocks that covered its exterior.

He buttoned his overcoat and followed Hayes up the ceremonial Red Staircase. The original stairs had been destroyed by Stalin, this reincarnation fashioned a few years back from ancient paintings. From here, tsars had once made their way to the adjacent Cathedral of the Dormition to be crowned.

And it was from this exact spot Napoléon had watched the fires that destroyed Moscow in 1812.

They headed for the Great Hall.

He'd only seen pictures of that ancient room and, as he followed Hayes inside, he quickly concluded none of those images did the space justice. He knew its size was fifty-four hundred square feet, the largest room in fifteenth-century Moscow, designed solely to impress foreign dignitaries. Today iron chandeliers burned bright and cast the massive center pillar and rich murals in sparkling gold, the scenes illustrating biblical subjects and the wisdom of the tsars.

Lord imagined the scene before him as it would have been in 1613.

The House of Ruirik, which for seven hundred years had ruled—Ivan the Great and Ivan the Terrible its most notable rulers—had died out. Subsequently, three men had tried to be tsar, but none succeeded. The Time of Troubles then ensued, twelve years of anguish while many sought to establish a new dynasty. Finally, the boyars, tired of chaos, came to Moscow—within the walls that surrounded him now—and selected a new ruling family. The Romanovs. But Mikhail, the first Romanov tsar, found a nation in utter turmoil. Brigands and thieves roamed the forests. Widespread hunger and disease wreaked havoc. Trade and commerce had nearly ceased. Taxes remained uncollected, the treasury nearly empty.

Not all that dissimilar to now, Lord concluded.

Seventy years of communism leaving the same stain as twelve years with no tsar.

For a moment he visualized himself as a boyar who'd participated in that selection, clad in fine garments of velvet and brocade, wearing a sable hat, perched at one of the oak benches that lined the gilded walls.

What a moment that must have been.

"Amazing," Hayes whispered. "Through the centuries these fools couldn't get a wheat field to harvest more than one season, but they could build this."

He agreed.

A U-shaped row of tables draped in red velvet dominated one end of the room. He counted seventeen high-backed chairs and watched as each was filled with a male delegate. No women had made the top seventeen. There'd been no regional elections. Just a thirty-day qualifying period, then one nationwide vote, the seventeen people garnering a plurality becoming the commissioners. In essence, a gigantic popularity contest, but perhaps the simplest means to ensure that no one faction dominated the voting.

He followed Hayes to a row of chairs and sat with the rest of the staff and reporters. Television cameras had been installed to broadcast the sessions live.

The meeting was called to order by a delegate selected yesterday to act as chair. The man cleared his throat and started reading from a prepared statement.

"On July 16, 1918, our most noble tsar, Nicholas II, and all the heirs of his body were taken from this life. Our mandate is to rectify the ensuing years and restore to this nation its tsar. The people have selected this commission to choose the person who will rule this country. That decision is not without precedent. Another group of men met here, in this same room, in 1613 and chose the first Romanov ruler, Mikhail. His issue ruled this nation until the second decade of the twentieth century. We have gathered here to right the wrong that was done at that time.

"Last evening we took prayer with Adrian, Patriarch of All Russia. He called upon God to guide us in this endeavor. I state to all listening that this commission will be conducted in a fair, open, and courteous manner. Debate will be encouraged, as only with discussion can truth be determined. Now let all who may have business before us draw near and be heard."

Lord patiently watched the entire morning session. The time was consumed with introductory remarks, parliamentary matters, and agenda setting. The delegates agreed that an initial list of candidates would be presented the next day, with a representative personally offering a candidate for consideration. A period of three days was approved for further nominations and debate. On the fourth day a vote would be taken to narrow the list down to three. Another round of intense debate would occur, and then a final selection would be made two days later. Unanimity would only be required on the last vote, as the national referendum mandated. All other votes would be by simple majority. If no candidate was selected after this six-day process, then the whole procedure would start again. But there seemed a general consensus that, for the sake of national confidence, every effort would be made to select an acceptable person on the first attempt.

Shortly before the noon break, Lord and Hayes retreated from the Great Hall into the Sacred Vestibule. Hayes led him into one of the far portals, where the bushy-headed driver from that morning waited.

"Miles, this is Ilya Zivon. He'll be your bodyguard when you leave the Kremlin."

He studied the sphinxlike Russian, an icy glint radiating back from a vacant face. The man's neck was as broad as his jaw, and Lord was comforted by an apparent hard, athletic physique.

"Ilya will look after you. He comes highly recommended. He's ex-military and knows his way around this town."

"I appreciate this, Taylor. I really do."

Hayes smiled and glanced at his watch. "It's nearly twelve and you need to get to the briefing. I'll handle things here. But I'll be at the hotel before you start." Hayes turned to Zivon. "You keep an eye on this fellow, just like we discussed."

9

12:30 PM

LORD ENTERED THE VOLKHOV'S CONFERENCE ROOM. THE
windowless rectangle was filled with three dozen men and
women, all dressed in conservative attire. Waiters were just
finishing serving drinks. The warm air, like the rest of the
hotel, carried the scent of an ashtray. Ilya Zivon waited outside, just beyond the double doors leading to the hotel lobby.
Lord felt better knowing the burly Russian was nearby.

The faces before him were etched with concern. He knew
their predicament. They'd been encouraged to invest in the
reemerging Russia by an anxious Washington, and the lure
of fresh markets had been too tempting to resist. But nearly
constant political instability, a daily threat from the *mafiya,*
and protection payments that were sapping away profits had
turned a rosy investment opportunity into a nightmare. The
ones here were the major American players in the new Russia: transportation, construction, soft drinks, mining, oil,
communications, computers, fast food, heavy equipment,
and banking. Pridgen & Woodworth had been hired to look
after their collective interests, each relying on Taylor Hayes's
reputation as a hard-nosed negotiator with the right contacts
within the emerging Russia. This was Lord's first meeting
with the group as a whole, though he knew many on an individual basis.

Hayes followed him inside and lightly patted him on the shoulder. "Okay, Miles, do your thing."

He stepped to the front of the brightly lit room. "Good afternoon. I'm Miles Lord." A quiet came over the gathering. "Some of you I've already met. To those I haven't, nice to have you here. Taylor Hayes thought a briefing might help answer your questions. Things are going to start happening fast and we might not have time to talk during the days ahead—"

"You're goddamn right we have questions," a stout blond woman yelled with a New England twang. Lord knew her to be the head of Pepsico's Eastern European operations. "I want to know what's going on. My board is nervous as shit about all this."

As they should be, Lord thought. But he kept his face tight. "You don't give me a chance to even get started, do you?"

"We don't need speeches. We need information."

"I can give you the raw data. Current national industrial output is down forty percent. The inflation rate is approaching one hundred fifty percent. Unemployment is low, about two percent, but *under*employment is the real problem—"

"We've heard all that," another CEO said. Lord didn't know the man. "Chemists are baking bread, engineers manning assembly lines. The Moscow newspapers are full of that crap."

"But things aren't so bad that they can't get worse," Lord said. "There's a popular joke. Yeltsin and the governments that followed him managed in two decades to do what the Soviets failed to accomplish in seventy-five years: make the people long for communism." A few snickers came. "The communists still have a solid grassroots organization. Revolution Day every November is marked by impressive demonstrations. They preach nostalgia. No crime, minimal poverty, social guarantees. That message has a certain appeal to a nation deep in despair." He paused. "But the emergence of a fascist fanatical leader—neither a communist nor a democrat, but a demagogue—is the most dangerous scenario. That's particularly true given Russia's considerable nuclear capability."

A few heads nodded. At least they were listening.

"How did all this happen?" a wiry little man asked. Lord vaguely recalled that he was in computers. "I've never been able to understand how we got to this point."

Lord stepped back toward the front wall. "Russians have always been big on the concept of a national idea. The Russian national character has never been based on individuality or market activity. It's much more spiritual, much deeper."

"Be a whole lot easier if we could Westernize the whole place," one of the men said.

He always bristled at the notion of Westernizing Russia. The nation would never be fully associated with the West, nor exclusively with the East. Instead it was, and always had been, a unique mixture. He believed the smart investor would be the one who understood Russian pride. He explained what he thought, then returned to answering the question.

"The Russian government finally realized it needed something that stood above politics. Something that could be a rallying point for the people. Maybe even a concept they could use to govern. Eighteen months ago, when the Duma put out a call for a national idea along that line, it was surprised with what the Institute of Public Opinion and Market Research brought back. *God, Tsar, and Country.* In other words, bring back the monarchy. Radical? Certainly. But when the issue was put to a national vote, the people overwhelmingly said yes."

"Why do you think?" one of the men asked.

"I can only give you my opinion. First, there's a real fear of a resurgence of communism. We saw it years ago when Zyuganov challenged Yeltsin and nearly won. But a majority of Russians do not want a return to totalitarianism, and every poll says that. Still, that wouldn't stop a populist from preying on difficult times and sweeping into office with false promises.

"The second reason is more deeply set. The people simply believe the current form of government is incapable of solving the country's problems. And quite frankly, I think they're right. Look at crime. Each one of you, I'm sure, pays protection money to one or more *mafiya*. You have no choice. Either that or end up going home in a body bag."

He thought again of what happened yesterday, but he said nothing. Hayes had advised him to keep that to himself. The people in this room, he'd warned, were nervous enough without wondering whether their lawyers were now a target.

"There is a pervasive belief that if you're not stealing, you're cheating yourself. Less than twenty percent of the population even bothers to pay taxes. There's almost a total internal breakdown. It's easy to see why people would believe anything is better than the current situation. But there's also a certain nostalgia with regard to the tsar."

"It's nuts," one of the men voiced. "A damn king."

He understood how Americans viewed autocracy. But the combination of Tatar and Slav that melded into a modern Russian seemed to yearn for autocratic leadership, and it was that battle for supremacy that had kept Russian society sharp through the centuries.

"The nostalgia is easy to understand," he said. "Only in the past decade has the real story about Nicholas II and his family been told. All across Russia there's a sentiment that what happened in July 1918 was wrong. Russians feel cheated by Soviet ideology, which passed the tsar off as the embodiment of evil."

"Okay, the tsar's coming back—," one of the men started.

"Not exactly," Lord said. "That's a misconception the

press doesn't fully understand. That's why Taylor thought this session would be beneficial." He could see he had their full attention. "The *concept* of the tsar is coming back, but there are two questions that need to be answered. Who is to be tsar? And what is the extent of his power?"

"Or her," one of the women said.

He shook his head. "No. Only he. Of that we're sure. Since 1797 Russian law has decreed lineage would pass only through the male line. We assume that law will be maintained."

"Okay," said another man, "answer the two questions."

"The first one is easy. The tsar will be whomever the seventeen representatives of the commission choose. Russians are keen on commissions. Most in the past have been nothing more than rubber stamps for the Soviet Central Committee, but this one will work entirely outside of the government, which isn't all that hard at the moment since there's barely any government left.

"Candidates will be presented and their claims evaluated. The strongest contender at the moment is our candidate, Stefan Baklanov. He has a distinct Western philosophy, but his Romanov bloodline is direct. You're paying us to make sure his claim is the one the commission eventually recognizes. Taylor is lobbying hard to make that happen. I've spent the past weeks in the Russian archives making sure there's nothing that could affect that claim."

"Amazing they let you near anything," a voice said.

"Not really," Lord said. "We're not actually involved with the Tsarist Commission, though we have credentials that imply that. We're here to look after *your* interests and to make sure Stefan Baklanov is selected. Just like back home, lobbying is an art form here, too."

A man in the back row stood. "Mr. Lord, we all have careers on the line. You understand the gravity of this? We're talking about a possible reversion from a semi-democracy to an autocracy. That has got to have a spillover effect on our investments."

He was ready with an answer. "We have no idea at this point how much authority the new tsar will have. As yet, we don't know whether the tsar will be a figurehead or the ruler of all Russia."

"Get real, Lord," one of the men said. "These idiots aren't going to turn complete political power over to a single man."

"The consensus is that's exactly what they will do."

"This can't be happening," another said.

"It may not be all that bad," Lord quickly said. "Russia is broke. It needs foreign investment. You might find an autocrat easier to deal with than the *mafiya*."

A few muttered their assent, but one man asked, "And that problem is going to go away?"

"We can only hope."

"What do you think, Taylor?" another man asked.

Hayes stood from his place at a back table and stepped to the front of the room. "I think what Miles told you is absolutely correct. We are about to witness the restoration of the Tsar of All Russia. The re-creation of an absolute monarchy. Pretty amazing, if you ask me."

"Pretty damn scary," one of the men said.

Hayes smiled. "Don't worry. You're paying us big bucks to look after your interests. The commission has opened for business. We'll be there doing what you hired us to do. All you have to do is trust us."

10

2:30 PM

HAYES ENTERED THE TINY CONFERENCE ROOM ON THE SEV-enth floor. The office building rose in central Moscow, a strikingly modern rectangle with a gray-tinted glass facade. He always appreciated the choice of meeting locations. His benefactors seemed to revel in luxury.

Stalin sat at the coffin-shaped conference table.

Dmitry Yakovlev was the *mafiya*'s representative in the Secret Chancellory. In his midforties, with a shock of corn-colored hair spilling over a tanned brow, the man radiated charm and control. For once, the three hundred or so gangs that occupied western Russia had all agreed on a single en-voy to represent their mutual interests. Too much was at stake to argue over protocol. The criminal element appar-ently understood survival, and well knew what an absolute monarch with the full support of the people could do for them. Or *to* them.

In many ways, Hayes realized, Stalin was the center of everything. Gang influence reached deep into the govern-ment, business, and the military. Russians even had a name for it: *Vori v Zakone*—Thieves in Law—a description Hayes liked. But their threat of violence was real since a contract killing was a far cheaper and faster way to settle a dispute than the courts.

"How was the opening session?" Stalin asked in perfect English.

"The commissioners organized themselves, as expected. They'll get down to business tomorrow. The timetable is six days to a first vote."

The Russian seemed impressed. "Less than a week was what you predicted."

"I told you I know what I'm doing. Was the transfer made?"

There was a hesitation that signaled irritation. "I am unaccustomed to such directness."

What was not said, but nonetheless clear, was that he was unaccustomed to such directness *from a foreigner.* Hayes decided to employ tact, though he, too, was irritated. "No disrespect intended. It's only that the payments have not been made, as agreed, and I'm accustomed to arrangements being honored."

On the table was a sheet of paper. Stalin slid it across to him. "That's the new Swiss account in Zurich you requested. Same bank as before. Five million, U.S., went in this morning. That's all the payments due to date."

Hayes was pleased. For a decade he'd represented the *mafiya* in their American diversifications. Millions of dollars had been laundered through North American financial institutions, most funneled into legitimate businesses seeking capital, more used to purchase stocks, securities, gold, and art. Pridgen & Woodworth had earned millions in legal fees through his representation, all made thanks to a combination of friendly American laws and even friendlier bureaucrats. No one knew the money source and, to date, the activity had not attracted any official attention. Hayes had used his representation to expand his influence in the firm and attract a huge array of foreign clients that turned to him simply because he understood how business was done in the new Russia—how to use fear and anxiety—how uncertainty could be a friend if one knew precisely how to alleviate it. Which he did.

Stalin smirked. "This is becoming quite profitable for you, Taylor."

"I told you I wasn't going to take the risks for my health."

"Apparently not."

"What was all that about yesterday? What you said about expanding my role in this whole affair."

"Just as I said. We may need certain matters handled and you come with a measure of deniability."

"I want to know what you're not telling me."

"It is truly not important at the moment. There is no need for concern; we are simply being cautious."

Hayes reached into his trouser pocket and withdrew the card Stalin had given him the day before. "Will I need to make the call?"

Stalin chuckled. "Does the notion of such loyalty—that on your order men would submerge themselves in the river— appeal to you?"

"I want to know why I might need them."

"Let us hope you won't. Now tell me about the power concentration. What was mentioned today at the session?"

He decided to let the matter drop. "Power will be concentrated in the tsar. But there will still be a council of ministers and a Duma that will have to be dealt with."

Stalin pondered the information. "It seems our nature to be volatile. Monarchy, republic, democracy, communism . . . none of it really works here." He paused, then added with a smile, "Thank goodness."

Hayes asked what he really wanted to know, "What of Stefan Baklanov? Will he cooperate?"

Stalin glanced at his watch. "I assume you will have the answer to that question shortly."

11

GREEN GLADE ESTATE
4:30 PM

HAYES ADMIRED THE SHOTGUN, A FOX SIDE-BY-SIDE WITH A Turkish walnut stock, hand-rubbed to an oil finish. The pistol grip was lean and straight with a beavertail fore-end and hard rubber butt plate. He tested the action, boxlike, with automatic ejectors. He knew the price ranged from seven thousand dollars for a basic model to twenty-five thousand for an exhibition-grade. Truly, an impressive weapon.

"Your shot," Lenin said.

Hayes shouldered the gun and took aim into a cloudy afternoon sky. He steadied the barrel with a feather-light touch.

"Pull," he yelled.

A clay pigeon shot from the thrower. He followed the black dot in the sight, moved ahead, and fired.

The target disintegrated in a shower of debris.

"You're a good shot," Khrushchev said.

"Hunting is my passion."

He spent at least nine weeks a year traveling the world on expeditions. Canadian caribou and geese. Asian pheasant and wild sheep. European red stag and fox. African Cape buffalo and antelope. Not to mention the duck, deer, grouse, and wild turkey he routinely sought in the woods of northern Georgia and the mountains of western North Carolina. His office in Atlanta was littered with trophies. The past couple of months had been so intense that he'd not had a chance to shoot, so he was grateful for this outing.

He'd left Moscow right after his meeting with Stalin, a car and driver delivering him to an estate thirty miles south of town. The manor house was a lovely red brick veined with ivy. It was owned by another member of the Secret Chancellory—Georgy Ostanovich, better known to Hayes as Lenin.

Ostanovich came from the military. He was a thin, cadaverous man with steel-gray eyes encircled by thick-lensed glasses. He was a general, though he never wore a uniform, a line officer who'd led troops in the assault of Grozny at the outset of the Chechen war. That conflict had deprived him of one lung, which was why he now labored with each breath. After the war he'd become an outspoken critic of Yeltsin and his weak military policies, and only Yeltsin's fall from power had prevented him from losing his rank and commission. Top officers were worried about their future under a tsar, so the army's presence in any conspiracy was deemed critical, and Ostanovich had been chosen its collective representative.

Lenin stood up to the mark and prepared to shoot.

"Pull," the Russian yelled.

A second later, he scored a direct hit.

"Excellent," Hayes said. "With the sun going down, the shots are getting difficult."

Stefan Baklanov, the Heir Apparent, stood off to one side, his single-action shotgun open. Baklanov was a short man, balding and barrel-chested, with light green eyes and a thick Hemingway beard. He was nearing fifty, his face seemingly devoid of emotion and that worried Hayes. In the realm of politics, whether a candidate could actually govern was often immaterial. The question was whether or not it *appeared* he could lead. Though Hayes had no doubt that all seventeen members of the Tsarist Commission would eventually be bribed, their votes assured, a suitable candidate must still be presented for their perusal and, even more important, the damn fool had to be able to lead afterward—or at least effectively implement orders from the men who'd put him there.

Baklanov stepped up to the mark. Lenin and Khrushchev moved back.

"I am curious," Baklanov said in his baritone voice. "Will the monarchy be absolute?"

"No other way will work," Lenin said.

Hayes broke his gun and extracted the spent cartridge. Only the four men stood on the elevated brick terrace. The fir and beech groves beyond were dotted with autumn's copper. Past a pavilion, in the far distance, a herd of bison mingled on an open plain.

"Will I be given full command of the military?" Baklanov asked.

"Within reason," Lenin said. "This is not Nicholas's time. We have . . . modern considerations."

"And will I control the army?"

"What would be your policies concerning the military?" Lenin asked.

"I was unaware I would be allowed my own policies."

The sarcasm was clear and Hayes saw Lenin did not appreciate it. Baklanov seemed to notice. "I realize, General, you believe the military is vastly underfunded and our defensive capabilities have been hampered by political instability. But I do not believe our destiny lies in a strong military. The Soviets bankrupted this nation by building bombs while our roads crumbled and people went hungry. Our destiny is to fulfill those basic needs."

Hayes knew this wasn't what Lenin wanted to hear. Russian line officers earned less each month than street merchants.

Military housing had become no more than slum tenements. Hardware had not been maintained in years, the most sophisticated equipment outmoded to the point of obsolescence.

"Of course, General, certain funding allowances will have to be made to correct past deficiencies. We do need a strong military . . . for defense capability." It was a clear signal that Baklanov was willing to compromise. "But I am wondering, will the royal property be restored?"

Hayes almost smiled. The Heir Apparent seemed to enjoy his hosts' predicament. The word *tsar* was an ancient Russian corruption of the Latin *caesar,* and he thought the analogy quite appropriate. This man might just make an excellent Caesar. He possessed an unbridled arrogance that bordered on foolishness. Perhaps Baklanov had forgotten that the patience of Caesar's colleagues in ancient Rome eventually ran out.

"What did you have in mind?" Khrushchev asked.

Khrushchev—Maxim Zubarev—came from the government. He had a brash, swaggering way about him. Perhaps, Hayes often thought, it was compensation for a horse face and crinkly brown eyes, neither of which was flattering. He represented a sizable bloc of officials in the Moscow central bureaucracy concerned about their influence under a restored monarchy. Zubarev realized, and had expressed many times, that national order existed only because the people were tolerating governmental authority until the Tsarist Commission finished its work. Ministers wanting to survive that metamorphosis would have to adapt, and fast. Hence their need for a voice in a surreptitious manipulation of the system.

Baklanov faced Khrushchev. "I would require that ownership of the palaces possessed by my family at the time of the revolution be restored. They were Romanov property, stolen by thieves."

Lenin sighed. "How do you plan to maintain them?"

"I don't. The state will, of course. But perhaps we could enter into some sort of arrangement similar to the English monarchy. Most will remain accessible to the public, entrance fees used for maintenance. But all Crown property and images will belong to the Crown, to be licensed to the world for a fee. The English royals raise millions each year that way."

Lenin shrugged. "I see no problem. The people certainly can't afford those monstrosities."

"Of course," Baklanov said, "I would reconvert the Catherine Palace at Tsarskoe Selo into a summer residence again. In Moscow, I would want exclusive control of the Kremlin Palaces, the Facets being the center of my court there."

"Do you realize the cost of such extravagance?" Lenin said.

Baklanov stared at the man. "The people will not want their tsar living in a cottage. Cost is your problem, gentlemen. Pomp and circumstance is essential for the ability to rule."

Hayes admired the man's daring. It made him think of Jimmy Walker bucking the bosses of Tammany Hall in the New York of the 1920s. But such a course came with risks. Walker ended up resigning, the public thinking him a crook, the Hall abandoning him for not taking orders.

Baklanov rested the gun butt on his shiny right boot. Hayes took a moment and admired the wool suit—Savile Row if he wasn't mistaken—Charvet cotton shirt, Canali tie, and felt hat with a chamois tuft. If nothing else, the Russian knew how to present himself.

"The Soviets spent decades indoctrinating us on the evils of the Romanovs. Lies, every last word," Baklanov said. "The people want a monarchy with all the trappings. Something the rest of the world will take notice of. That can only be done with great spectacle and circumstance. We shall start with an elaborate coronation, then a gesture of allegiance from the people to their new ruler—say, a million souls in Red Square. After that, palaces will be expected."

"And what of your court?" Lenin asked. "Will St. Petersburg be your capital?"

"Without a doubt. The communists chose Moscow. A move back will symbolize change."

"And will you have an assortment of grand dukes and duchesses?" Lenin inquired, the general's disgust undisguised.

"Of course. Succession must be preserved."

"But you despise your family," Lenin said.

"My sons will receive their birthright. Beyond that, I will create a new ruling class. What better way to reward the patriots who made all this possible?"

Khrushchev spoke up. "There are those among us who want a boyar class created from the ranks of the new rich and gangs. The people expect the tsar to put a stop to the *mafiya,* not reward it."

Hayes wondered if Khrushchev would be as bold if Stalin were here. Stalin and Brezhnev had been left out of the meeting intentionally. The division had been Hayes's idea, a variation on the good cop–bad cop scenario.

"I agree," Baklanov said. "A slow evolution will be beneficial to all concerned. I am more interested that the heirs of my body inherit and the Romanov dynasty continue."

Baklanov's three children, all sons, ranged in age from twenty-five to thirty-three. To a man, they hated their father, but the prospect of the oldest becoming tsarevich and the other two grand dukes had enticed a family truce. Baklanov's wife was a hopeless alcoholic, but she was Orthodox by birth, Russian, with some royal blood. She'd spent the last thirty days in an Austrian spa drying out and had repeatedly assured everyone she would gladly forgo the bottle in return for becoming the next Tsarina of All Russia.

"The continuation of the dynasty is something we are all interested in," Lenin said. "Your firstborn seems a reasonable man. He promises that your policies will be continued."

"And what will be my policies?"

Hayes had been waiting for an opening. "To do exactly as we say." He was tired of tiptoeing around this bastard.

Baklanov openly bristled at the bluntness. Good, Hayes thought. He needs to get used to it.

"I was unaware an American would be playing a role in this transition."

Hayes zeroed in a tight gaze. "This American is the one funding your lifestyle."

Baklanov looked at Lenin. "Is that true?"

"We have no desire to spend our rubles on you. The foreigners offered. We accepted. They have much to lose, or gain, from the years ahead."

Hayes went on, "We'll ensure that you will be the next tsar. You'll also get absolute power. There will be a Duma, but it will be as impotent as a castrated bull. All proposals for law would have to be approved by you and the state council."

Baklanov nodded in approval. "Stolypin's philosophy. Make the Duma an appendage of the state to endorse government policy, not to check or administer it. Sovereignty to the monarch."

Petr Stolypin had been one of Nicholas II's last prime ministers. So much a bloody defender of tsarist order that the hangman's noose, used to quell peasant revolts, was tagged the Stolypin Necktie, and railway cars to Siberia for political exiles named Stolypin Carriages. But he'd been assassinated, shot at the Kiev opera by a revolutionary while Nicholas II watched.

"Perhaps there is a lesson to be learned from Stolypin's fate?" Hayes said.

Baklanov did not reply, but his bearded face conveyed that he understood the threat. "How will the state council be chosen?"

Lenin said, "Half elected, half selected by you."

"An attempt," Hayes said, "to interject an element of democracy into the process for public relations. But we'll make sure the council is controllable. In matters of policy you will listen to us exclusively. It's taken an enormous amount of work to bring everyone together on this project. You are the centerpiece. We understand that. Discretion is to everyone's advantage, so you won't get any public flak from us. But your obedience cannot, and will not, be in question."

"And if I refuse, once the mantle of power is mine?"

"Then your fate," Lenin said, "will be the same as your ancestors'. Let's see. Ivan VI spent his life in solitary confinement. Peter II was beaten to death. Paul I strangled. Alexander II bombed. Nicholas II shot. You Romanovs have not fared well when it comes to assassination. A death suitable to your station can be easily arranged. Then we'll see if the next Romanov will be more cooperative."

Baklanov said nothing. He merely turned back toward the graying woods and slammed the breech on his gun shut. He motioned to the target attendant.

A disk launched into the air.

He fired and missed.

"Oh, dear," Khrushchev said. "I see we're going to have to work on your aim."

12

LORD WAS DISTURBED THAT HAYES HAD SUDDENLY LEFT THE city. He felt better with his boss nearby. He was still nervous from the day before, and Ilya Zivon had gone home for the night, promising to be waiting in the Volkhov's lobby at seven AM tomorrow. Lord had pledged to stay in his room, but he was restless and decided to descend to the ground floor for a drink.

As usual, an older woman was perched behind a simulated wood desk at the end of the hotel's third-floor corridor—no way to get to or from the elevators without passing her. She was a *dezhurnaya*. Another holdover from the Soviet time when every floor of every hotel was staffed with one, all on the KGB payroll, providing a method for monitoring foreign guests. Now they were nothing more than elaborate stewards.

"Going out, Mr. Lord?"

"Just down to the bar."

"Were you at the commission proceedings today?"

He'd made no secret of his commission activities, arriving and leaving each day with his credentials clipped to his suit.

He nodded.

"Will they find us a new tsar?"

"Do you want them to?"

"Very much. This country needs a return to its roots. That is our problem."

He was curious.

"We are a huge place that forgets its past easily. The tsar, a Romanov, will give us back our roots." She sounded proud.

"What if the chosen one is not a Romanov?"

"Then it will not work," she declared. "Tell them not to even consider such. The people want a Romanov. The closest there is to Nicholas II."

They chatted a little longer, and before he headed for the elevator he promised to pass the woman's thoughts along.

Downstairs, he walked toward the same lounge he and Hayes had taken refuge in yesterday after the shooting. He was passing one of the restaurants when a familiar face emerged. It was the older man from the archives, with three others.

"Good evening, Professor Pashenko," Lord said in Russian, getting the man's attention.

"Mr. Lord. What a coincidence. You here for dinner?"

"This is my hotel."

"I am with friends. We often dine here. The restaurant is quite good." Pashenko introduced his companions.

After some small talk, Lord excused himself. "It was good to see you again, Professor." He motioned ahead. "I was on my way for a quick drink before bed."

"Might I join you?" Pashenko asked. "I so enjoyed our talk."

He hesitated a moment, then said, "If you like. Some company would be welcome."

Pashenko bid his friends good night and followed him into the lounge. A light piano medley floated across the darkened room. Only about half the tables were occupied. They sat and Lord asked a waiter to bring a carafe of vodka. "You disappeared quickly yesterday," he said.

"I could see that you were busy. And I had taken up enough of your time."

The waiter arrived with drinks, and his guest graciously paid before he had a chance to get out his money. He thought about what the woman upstairs had said. "Professor, might I ask you something?"

"Of course."

"If the commission chose someone other than a Romanov, what would be the effect?"

Pashenko poured a drink for them both. "It would be a mistake. The throne belonged to the Romanov family at the time of the revolution."

"Some would argue that Nicholas gave up the throne when he abdicated in March 1917."

Pashenko chuckled. "With a gun to his head. I hardly think anyone would seriously say he freely abandoned his throne and his son's birthright."

"Who do you believe has the best claim?"

The Russian lifted one eyebrow. "A difficult question. Are you familiar with the Russian law of succession?"

He nodded. "The Emperor Paul established the act in 1797. Five criteria were set. Any pretender must be male, as long as there is an eligible male. He must be Orthodox. His mother and wife must have been Orthodox. Any marriage must be to a woman of equal rank from a ruling house. And he can only marry with permission of the ruling tsar. Lose any one of the five and you're out of the running."

Pashenko grinned. "You do know our history. And divorce?"

"The Russians never cared about that. Divorced women married routinely into the royal family. I always found that interesting. An almost fanatical devotion to Orthodox doctrine, yet a practical bending in the name of politics."

"You understand there is no guarantee the Tsarist Commission will adhere to the Succession Act."

"I believe they'll have to. That law has never been repealed, except by communist manifesto, which no one recognizes as valid."

Pashenko cocked his head to one side. "But would not the five criteria literally rule out all pretenders?"

It was a point he and Hayes had discussed. The man was right—the succession law was a problem. And the few Romanovs who survived the revolution weren't making things any easier. They'd divided themselves into five distinct clans, only two of which—the Mikhailovichi and the Vladimirovichi—possessed strong enough genetic ties to vie for the throne.

"It is a dilemma," the professor said. "But we have an unusual situation here. An entire ruling family was eliminated. It is easy to see why there would be confusion over succession. The commission will have to unravel this puzzle and select a suitable tsar the people will accept."

"I'm concerned about the process. Baklanov claims that several of the Vladimirovichi are traitors. I've been told he plans to produce evidence to support his allegations, if any of their names are placed in nomination."

"And you worry about him?"

"Very much."

"Have you found anything that could jeopardize his claim?"

Lord shook his head. "Nothing that relates to him. He's Mikhailovichi, the closest by blood to Nicholas II. His grandmother was Xenia, Nicholas's sister. They fled Russia to Denmark in 1917, after the Bolsheviks came to power. Their seven children grew up in the West and subsequently scattered. Baklanov's parents lived in Germany and France. He went to the best schools, but he'd not been in direct line until the premature deaths of his cousins. Now he's the eldest male. I haven't found anything, as yet, that could hurt him."

Except, he thought, the possibility that a direct descendant of Nicholas and Alexandra may be walking around somewhere. But that was too fanciful an idea to merit consideration.

Or, at least, until yesterday it seemed that way.

Pashenko held his vodka glass close to his aged face. "I am familiar with Baklanov. His only problem may be his wife. She's Orthodox with a touch of royal blood. But, of course, not a member of any ruling house. Yet how could she be? There are so few left. Surely the Vladimirovichi will claim this a disqualification, but in my opinion the commission will be forced to ignore that requirement. I fear no one can meet it. And certainly none of the surviving descendants can claim permission of the tsar to marry, since there has been no tsar for decades."

Lord had already come to that conclusion himself.

"I don't think the Russian people will care about marriage," Pashenko went on. "It's what the new tsar and tsarina do after that will count far more. These surviving Romanovs can be petty. They have a history of infighting. That cannot be tolerated, especially publicly at the commission."

Recalling again Lenin's note and Alexandra's message, he decided to see what Pashenko knew. "Have you given any more thought to what I showed you yesterday in the archives?"

The older man grinned. "I understand your worry. What if there is a direct descendant from Nicholas II still alive? That would negate every claim from every Romanov, save that one. Surely, Mr. Lord, you cannot believe anyone survived the massacre at Yekaterinburg?"

"I don't know what to believe. But, no, if the accounts of the massacre are accurate, no one survived. Still, Lenin seemed to doubt the reports. I mean, there's no way Yurovsky was going to tell Moscow he was two bodies short."

"I agree. Though there is now indisputable evidence that

was precisely the case. The bones of Alexei and Anastasia are gone."

Lord recalled 1979, when a retired geologist, Alexander Audonin, and a Russian filmmaker, Geli Ryabov, found where Yurovsky and his henchmen had buried the murdered Imperial family. They spent months talking with relatives of guards and members of the Ural Soviet, and scouring suppressed papers and books, one of which was a handwritten account by Yurovsky himself, given to them by the chief executioner's eldest son, which filled in many gaps and detailed precisely where the bodies had been hidden. But the Soviet political climate had made all those who'd possessed the account fearful of revealing its existence, let alone searching for the bodies. It was not until 1991, after the communist fall, that Audonin and Ryabov followed the clues and exhumed the bones, which were positively identified through DNA analysis. Pashenko was correct. Only nine skeletons came from the ground. And though there had been a thorough search of the grave site, the remains of Nicholas II's two youngest children were never found.

"They could simply be buried at another spot," Pashenko noted.

"But what did Lenin mean when he said that the reports on what happened in Yekaterinburg weren't entirely accurate?"

"Hard to say. Lenin was a complex man. There's no doubt he alone ordered the entire family shot. Records clearly demonstrate the orders came from Moscow and were personally approved by Lenin. The last thing he wanted was the White Army to liberate the tsar. The Whites weren't royalists, but the act could have been a rallying point that would have spelled the end of the revolution."

"What do you think he meant when he wrote, *The information concerning Felix Yussoupov corroborates the apparently false reports from Yekaterinburg?*"

"Now *that* is interesting. I've thought about that, along with Alexandra's account of what Rasputin told her. That is new information, Mr. Lord. I consider myself quite schooled in tsarist history, but I have never read anything connecting Yussoupov and the royal family *after* 1918."

He refilled his vodka glass. "Yussoupov murdered Rasputin. Many say that act hastened the monarchy's downfall. Both Nicholas and Alexandra hated Yussoupov for what he did."

"Which adds to the mystery. Why would the royal family have anything to do with him?"

"If I recall, most of the grand dukes and duchesses applauded the decision to kill the *starets*."

"Quite true. And that was, perhaps, Rasputin's greatest damage. He divided the Romanov family. It was Nicholas and Alexandra versus everyone else."

"Rasputin was such an enigma," Lord said. "A Siberian peasant who could directly influence the Tsar of All Russia. A charlatan with imperial power."

"Many would debate that he was a charlatan. A large number of his prophecies came true. He said the tsarevich would not die of hemophilia, and he didn't. He foretold that the Empress Alexandra would see his birthplace in Siberia, and she did—on the way to Tobolsk as a prisoner. He also said that if a member of the royal family killed him, the tsar's family would not survive two years. Yussoupov married a royal niece, murdered the *starets* in December 1916, and the Romanov family was slaughtered nineteen months later. Not bad for a charlatan."

Lord was not impressed by holy men with a supposed conduit to God. His father had claimed to be one. Thousands had flocked to revivals to hear him shout the word and heal the sick. Of course, all that was forgotten hours later when one of the choir women arrived at his room. He'd read a lot about Rasputin and how he had seduced women the same way.

He flushed the thoughts of his father away and said, "It's never been proven that any of Rasputin's predictions were memorialized while he was alive. Most came later from his daughter, who seemed to believe it was her life's destiny to vindicate her father's image. I've read her book."

"That may be true, until today."

"What do you mean?"

"Alexandra's note talks about the royal family dying within two years. The sheet was dated in her own hand, October 28, 1916. That was two months *before* Rasputin was murdered. Apparently, he told her something. A prophecy, she said. And she memorialized it. So you have a historically important document in your possession, Mr. Lord."

He'd not considered the full implications of his discovery, but the professor was right.

"Do you intend to go to St. Petersburg?" Pashenko asked.

"I didn't before. But I think I will now."

"A good decision. Your credentials can gain you access to parts of the archives none of us have been able to see. Maybe there will be more to find, especially since now you know what to look for."

"That's the whole problem, Professor. I really don't know what I'm looking for."

The academician seemed unconcerned. "Not to worry. I have a feeling you will do just fine."

ST. PETERSBURG
THURSDAY, OCTOBER 14
12:30 PM

LORD SETTLED INTO THE ARCHIVE, LOCATED ON THE FOURTH floor of a post-revolutionary building that faced busy Nevsky Prospekt. He'd managed to book two seats on a nine AM Aeroflot shuttle from Moscow. The flight, though smooth, was nerve-racking, budget cuts and a lack of trained personnel taking their toll on the Russian national airline. But he was in a hurry and didn't have time to drive or take the train for the eight-hundred-mile round trip.

Ilya Zivon had been waiting in the Volkhov's lobby at seven AM as promised, ready for another day of escorting. The Russian had been surprised when Lord told him to drive to the airport and had wanted to call Taylor Hayes for instructions. But Lord informed him that Hayes was out of town and had left no telephone number. Unfortunately, the return flight for the afternoon was full, so he'd reserved two tickets on the overnight train from St. Petersburg back to Moscow.

Whereas Moscow projected an air of reality, with dirty streets and unimaginative structures, St. Petersburg was a fairy-tale city of baroque palaces, cathedrals, and canals. While the rest of the nation slept under a dull gray sameness, here pink granite and yellow and green stucco facades thrilled the eyes. He recalled how the Russian novelist Nikolai Gogol had described the city: *Everything in it breathed falsehood.* Then and now the city seemed busy with itself, its great architects all Italian, the layout reflecting a distinctive European air. It had served as the capital until the communists took over in 1917, and there was serious discussion of moving the center of power back once the new tsar was coronated.

The traffic from the airport south of town had been light for a weekday morning in a city of five million. His commission credentials had at first been questioned, but a call to Moscow had verified his identity, and he was given access to the archive's entire collection, including the Protective Papers.

The St. Petersburg depository, though small, contained a wealth of firsthand writings from Nicholas, Alexandra, and Lenin. And just as Semyon Pashenko had said, the tsar and tsarina's diaries and letters were all there, taken from Tsarskoe Selo and Yekaterinburg after the royal family was murdered.

What sprang from the pages was a portrait of two people clearly in love. Alexandra wrote with the flair of a romantic poet, her writings strewn with expressions of physical passion. Lord spent two hours thumbing through boxes of her correspondence, more to get a feel as to how this complex and intense woman composed her thoughts than to find anything.

It was midafternoon when he came across a set of diaries from 1916. The bound volumes were stuffed into a musty cardboard container labeled N & A. He was always amazed at how Russians stored records. So meticulous about their creation, yet so careless in their preservation. The diaries were stacked in chronological order, inscriptions in the front of each clothbound book revealing most to be gifts from

Alexandra's daughters. A few had swastikas embroidered on the cover. A little strange to see the image, but he knew that before Hitler adopted the design it was an ancient mark of well-being that Alexandra used liberally.

He thumbed through several volumes and found nothing beyond the usual rants of two love-torn mates. Then he came upon two stacks of correspondence. From his briefcase he obtained the photocopy of Alexandra's letter to Nicholas dated October 28, 1916. Comparing the copy to the originals, he discovered that the handwriting, along with the frilly border of flowers and leaves, was identical.

Why had this one letter been secreted away in Moscow?

Perhaps more of the Soviet purge of tsarist history, he assumed. Or simple paranoia. But what made this single letter so important that it was sealed in a pouch with instructions not to open for twenty-five years? One thing was certain. Semyon Pashenko was right. He clearly possessed a historically important document.

He spent the remainder of the afternoon reviewing what he could find on Lenin. It was nearly four o'clock when he first noticed the man. He was short and thin, his anxious eyes watery. He was dressed in a baggy beige suit and, for some reason, Lord more than once thought the stranger's gaze lingered longer than it should. But Zivon sat nearby, on guard, and he chalked his suspicions up to paranoia and told himself to calm down.

Near five o'clock he finally found something, again in Lenin's own hand. Ordinarily it would mean nothing, but Yussoupov's name drew his attention, his mind cross-referencing with the Moscow note.

Felix Yussoupov lives on the rue Gutenburg near Bois de Boulogne. He associates with the large population of Russian aristocracy that has invaded Paris. The fools

think the Revolution will die and that they will shortly
return to their position and wealth. I am told that one
former dowager keeps a suitcase packed and ready,
thinking she will be leaving soon for home. My agents
report reading correspondence between Yussoupov and
Kolya Maks. At least three letters. This is a concern. I
realize now the mistake we made relying on the Ural
Soviet to handle the executions. The developing reports
are becoming troublesome. We already have one woman
under arrest who claims to be Anastasia. She came to our
attention because of her constant letters to King George
V, pleading for his help in escaping. The Ural Committee
reports that two of the tsar's daughters are being hidden
in a remote village. They have identified them as Maria
and Anastasia. I have dispatched agents to check.
Another woman has appeared in Berlin and conclusively
asserts that she is Anastasia. Informants report that she
bears a striking resemblance to the daughter.

This is all troubling. If not for the fear I harbor about
what happened at Yekaterinburg, I would dismiss these
reports as nonsense. But I am afraid there is more to it.
We should have killed Yussoupov with the rest of the
bourgeoisie. That arrogant ass is at the center of
something. He openly hates our government. His wife
has Romanov blood and some have talked of a restoration
with him as tsar. That is foolish dreaming by foolish
men. The Motherland is gone to them, this much they
should clearly understand.

He finished the rest of the page but there was no further
reference to Felix Yussoupov. Certainly Lenin was concerned that Yurovsky, the man in charge of the Romanovs'
execution at Yekaterinburg, had filed a false report about
what had happened.

Were eleven people murdered in that cellar, or only nine? Or perhaps eight?

Who knew?

Lord thought about the royal pretenders who'd surfaced by 1920. Lenin referred to a woman from Berlin. She came to be known as Anna Anderson and was the most celebrated of all the subsequent pretenders. Movies and books detailed her story, and for decades she basked in a celebrity limelight, steadfastly maintaining, until her death in 1984, that she was the tsar's youngest daughter. But DNA testing on tissue that survived her death conclusively proved that she was not related to the Romanovs in any way.

There was also a persuasive account circulated through Europe in the 1920s that Alexandra and her daughters were actually not murdered at Yekaterinburg, but instead had been spirited away before Nicholas and Alexei were shot. The women were supposedly held in Perm, a provincial town not far from Yekaterinburg. Lord remembered a book, *The File on the Tsar,* which went into great detail trying to prove that assertion. But later documents that the authors had no access to—not to mention the subsequent location of the royal bones—demonstrated conclusively that Alexandra and at least three of her daughters had died at Yekaterinburg.

It was all so confusing, hard to ever know what was real and what had been concocted. He agreed with Churchill. *Russia is a riddle, wrapped in a mystery, inside an enigma.*

From his briefcase he retrieved another copy he'd made in the Moscow archive. It was attached to a note written in longhand by Lenin. He'd not shown this to either Hayes or Semyon Pashenko because it really wasn't material. Until now.

It was a typed excerpt from an affidavit given by one of the Yekaterinburg guards, dated October 1918, three months after the Romanov murders.

The tsar was no longer young, his beard going gray. He daily wore a soldier's shirt with an officer's belt fastened by a buckle around his waist. His eyes were kind, and I got the impression that he was a simple, frank, talkative person. Sometimes I felt he was going to speak to me. He looked as if he would like to talk. The tsarina was not a bit like him. She was severe looking and had the appearance and manners of a haughty woman. Sometimes the guards discussed things and we decided that she looked exactly like a tsarina should. She seemed older than the tsar. Gray hair was plainly visible at her temples, her face not the face of a young woman. All my evil thoughts about the tsar disappeared after I had stayed a certain time among the guards. After I had seen them several times I began to feel entirely different toward them. I began to pity them. I pitied them as human beings. I longed for their suffering to end. But I realized what was coming. The talk of their fate was clear. Yurovsky made sure we all understood the task at hand. After a while, I started saying to myself that something should be done to let them escape.

What had he stumbled upon? And why had no one found any of this before? But he kept reminding himself that only in the past few years had access to the archives been opened. The Protective Papers were still closed to the vast majority of researchers, and the sheer chaos of Russian record keeping made finding anything a matter of luck.

He needed to get back to Moscow and report to Taylor Hayes. It was possible that Stefan Baklanov's claim could be brought into question. There might be a pretender out there, someone with a bloodline closer to Nicholas II than Baklanov's. Sensationalist journalism and popular fiction had long proclaimed a pretender's existence. One movie studio had even released to millions of children a full-length animated feature on Anastasia that postulated her survival. But just as with Elvis and Jimmy Hoffa, the record was heavy on speculation and devoid of conclusive evidence.

Or was it?

HAYES HUNG UP THE PHONE AND TRIED TO CONTROL HIS TEM-per. He'd traveled from Moscow to Green Glade for both business and relaxation. He'd left word for Lord at the hotel that he'd been called out of town and that he should continue in the archives, promising to get in touch with Lord by mid-afternoon. Intentionally, he did not include any means of location. But Ilya Zivon had been ordered to keep a close eye on Lord and to report everything.

"That was Zivon," he said. "Lord spent the day in St. Petersburg going through the archives."

"You were unaware of this?" Lenin asked.

"Totally. I thought he was working in Moscow. Zivon said that Lord told him to drive to the airport this morning. They're taking the Red Arrow back to Moscow tonight."

Khrushchev was openly agitated. Rare for him, Hayes thought. Of the five, the government representative stayed the coolest, rarely raising his voice. He was also careful with his vodka, perhaps thinking sobriety gave him an edge.

Stefan Baklanov was gone from Green Glade, driven the

previous day to another property not far away where he could be kept secluded until his first appearance before the commission in two days. It was a little past seven PM and Hayes should have been headed back to Moscow. He was just about to leave when the call came from St. Petersburg.

"Zivon slipped away at dinner and called his employers. They directed him here," Hayes said. "He also said that Lord talked to a man at the archives yesterday in Moscow. Semyon Pashenko was the name. The hotel concierge told Zivon this morning that Lord had drinks with a man of the same description last evening."

"And the description?" Khrushchev asked.

"Late fifties, early sixties. Thin. Light blue eyes. Bald. Start of a beard on his face and neck."

Hayes observed the look exchanged between Lenin and Khrushchev. He'd sensed all week they were keeping something from him, and he was liking the situation less and less. "Who is he? Since you obviously know."

Lenin sighed. "A problem."

"That much I gather. How about details?"

Khrushchev said, "Have you ever heard of the Holy Band?"

He shook his head.

"In the nineteenth century, Tsar Alexander II's brother started a group that came to be known by that name. The fear of assassination was tremendous at the time. Alexander had freed the serfs and wasn't popular. This Holy Band was something of a joke. Nothing but aristocrats who pledged themselves to defend the tsar's life. In reality they could hardly defend themselves and, in the end, Alexander died from an assassin's bomb. Pashenko heads a contemporary group made up of anything but amateurs. His Holy Band was formed sometime in the nineteen twenties, as best we can determine, and has survived to this day."

"That's after Nicholas II and his family were murdered," Hayes said. "There was no tsar to protect."

"But that is the problem," Lenin said. "Rumors have persisted for decades that descendants of Nicholas survived the massacre."

"Bullshit," Hayes said. "I've read about all the pretenders. They're nuts. Every one of them."

"Perhaps. But the Holy Band survives."

"Has this got something to do with what Lord found in the archives?"

"It has everything to do with it," Lenin said. "And now that Pashenko has made repeated contact, Lord must be dealt with immediately."

"Another hit?"

"Definitely. And tonight."

He decided not to argue the merits. "How am I supposed to get men to St. Petersburg before midnight?"

"Air transportation can be arranged."

"Care to tell me why this is so urgent?"

"Frankly," Khrushchev said, "details are not important. Suffice it to say, the problem could jeopardize everything we are working to achieve. This Lord is apparently a free spirit. One you cannot control. No more chances can be taken. Use the phone number we provided and have men dispatched. That *chornye* cannot be allowed to return to Moscow alive."

1 4

LORD AND HIS BODYGUARD ARRIVED AT THE TRAIN STATION. The concrete platforms were clogged with people trudging past in heavy coats, some adorned with curly astrakhan wool collars, most clutching bulky suitcases or shopping bags. No one seemed to pay him any attention. And other than the man in the archives, whom he'd thought might be watching, he'd sensed no danger all day.

He and Zivon had enjoyed a leisurely dinner at the Grand Hotel Europe, then spent the rest of the evening in one of the lounges listening to a string quartet. He'd wanted to stroll Nevsky Prospekt, but Zivon had been hesitant about parading the streets at night. So they'd stayed inside and taken a taxi directly to the station, allowing just enough time to climb aboard.

The evening was cold and Uprising Square bustled with traffic. He imagined the bloody exchanges between tsarist police and demonstrators that had started the revolution in 1917, the battle for control of the square raging for two days. The train station itself was another Stalinist creation, the grandiose green-and-white facade more fitting for a palace than a rail terminal. Next door, construction continued on a new high-speed rail terminal for a line being built to Moscow. The multibillion-dollar project was designed by an Illinois architectural firm, working through a British engineering concern, and the head architect had been present at the Volkhov briefing yesterday, understandably jittery about his future.

Lord had booked a first-class sleeping compartment with two berths. He'd ridden the Red Arrow express several times and recalled the days when sheets and mattresses were filthy, the compartments less than clean. But things had noticeably changed, the ride now regarded as one of the more luxurious in Europe.

The train left on time at 11:55 PM, which would put them in Moscow at 7:55 tomorrow morning. Four hundred and five miles in eight hours.

"I'm not all that sleepy," he told Zivon. "I think I'll go to the saloon car for a drink. You can wait here, if you like."

Zivon nodded and said he would catch a quick nap. Lord left the compartment and moved forward through two more sleeping cars, down a narrow, one-person-wide corridor. A trace of coal smoke from a samovar at the far end of each car burned his eyes.

The saloon car was equipped with comfortable leather seats and oak adornments. He took a window table and, in the gloomy light, watched the countryside whiz past.

He ordered a Pepsi, his stomach not in the mood for vodka, and opened his briefcase, reviewing the notes made earlier on the documents he'd found. He was convinced that he'd stumbled onto something, and he wondered what effect any of it would have on Stefan Baklanov's claim.

There was a lot at stake—to Russia, as well as to the corporations Pridgen & Woodworth represented. He didn't want to do anything to jeopardize either's future, or his own with the firm.

But there was no denying his lingering doubts.

He rubbed his eyes. Damn, he was tired. Late hours were nothing unusual, but the strain from the past few weeks was beginning to wear on him.

He settled back in the plush leather seat and sipped his drink. There certainly had been no class in law school on any of this. And twelve years of clawing his way up the firm had not prepared him, either. Lawyers like him were supposed to work in offices, courthouses, and libraries, the only intrigue being how to bill enough to make the effort worthwhile, and how to garner recognition from senior partners like Taylor Hayes—people who would ultimately make the decision on his future.

People he wanted to impress.

Like his father.

He could still see Grover Lord lying in the open casket, the mouth that had hollered the word of God closed in death, the lips and face ashen. They'd dressed him in one of his best suits and tied the tie with a dimple the reverend had always liked. The gold cufflinks were there, along with his watch. Lord remembered thinking how those three pieces of jewelry could have paid for a good slice of his education. Nearly a thousand of the faithful had turned out for the service. There'd been fainting and crying and singing. His mother had wanted him to speak. But what would he say? He couldn't proclaim the man a charlatan, a hypocrite, a lousy father. So he'd refused to say anything, and his mother never forgave him. Even now, their relationship remained chilly. She was Mrs. Grover Lord, and proud of the fact.

He rubbed his eyes again as sleep started to take hold.

His gaze drifted down the long car to the faces of others up for a late refreshment. One man caught his attention. Young, blond, stocky. He sat alone sipping a clear drink, and the man's presence sent a chill down Lord's spine. Was he a threat? But the inquiry was answered when a young woman with a small child appeared. Both sat with the man and all three of them started chatting.

He told himself to get a grip.

But then he noticed at the far end of the car a middle-aged man nursing a beer, the face gaunt, lips thin, the same anxious watery eyes he'd seen that afternoon.

The man from the archives, still dressed in the same baggy beige suit.

Lord came alert.

Too much of a coincidence.

He needed to get back to Zivon, but didn't want to make his concern obvious. So he tipped back the rest of his Pepsi, then slowly snapped his briefcase shut. He stood and tossed a few rubles on the table. He hoped his actions signaled calm, but on the way out, in the glass door, he saw the man's reflection stand and head toward him.

He yanked open the sliding door and darted from the saloon, slamming the door shut. As he turned into the next car, he saw the man hustling his way.

Shit.

He made his way forward and entered the car with his compartment. A quick glance back through the glass and he saw the man enter the car behind, still coming his way.

He slid open his compartment door.

Zivon was gone.

He slammed the door shut. Perhaps his bodyguard was in the lavatory. He rushed down the narrow aisle and rounded a slight angle in the corridor that led to the far exit. The lavatory door was closed, its OCCUPIED notice not engaged.

He slid open the door.

Empty.

Where the hell was Zivon?

He stepped inside the lavatory. But before he did, he cracked open the exit door to give the appearance that someone had passed through to the next car. He slid the lavatory door shut, but did not engage the lock so the OCCUPIED wouldn't show from the outside.

He stood motionless, pressed tight against the stainless steel door, breathing hard. His heart pounded. Footsteps approached and he braced himself, ready to use his briefcase as a weapon. From the door's other side, the exit for the sleeper car slid open with a dull scrape.

A second later it closed.

He waited a full minute.

Hearing nothing, he inched open the lavatory door. No one was in the hall. He slammed the door shut and engaged the lock. It was the second time in two days he'd successfully run for his life. He laid his briefcase on the toilet and took a moment to rinse sweat from his face in the washbasin. A can of disinfectant rested on the sink. He used the spray to cleanse the bar of soap, then washed his hands and face, careful not to swallow the water, a laminated sign warning in Cyrillic that nothing was potable. He used his handkerchief to dry his face. No paper towels had been provided.

He stared at himself in the mirror.

His brown eyes were weary, the angular features of his face drawn, and his hair needed a cut. What was going on? And where was Zivon? Some bodyguard. He splashed more water on his face and rinsed out his mouth, careful again not to swallow. A strange irony, he thought. Goddamn superpower with the ability to blow up the world a thousand times over, but can't manage clean water on a train.

He tried to regain his composure. Through an oval window the night raced past. Another train whizzed by in the opposite direction, the rush of cars lasting what seemed minutes.

He took a deep breath, grabbed his briefcase, and slid open the door.

The way was blocked by a tall, stocky man with a pockmarked face, his shiny black hair pulled back in a ponytail. Lord stared into the eyes and instantly noticed the wide space between the right pupil and brow.

Droopy.

A fist slammed into Lord's stomach.

He doubled over, air strangling in his throat, a wave of nausea gripping him. The force of the blow drove him into the outer wall, his head popping hard against the window, winking the scene before him in and out.

He settled onto the toilet.

Droopy stepped into the lavatory and shut the door. "Now, Mr. Lord, we finish."

He'd managed to retain a grip on his briefcase and momentarily thought of swinging it upward, but in the tight confines the blow would be meaningless. Air started to grab in his lungs. The initial shock was replaced by fear. A cold, shivering terror.

A knife snapped open in Droopy's hand.

There'd only be a moment.

His gaze cut to the disinfectant. He lunged forward, grabbed the can, pointed, and sprayed his assailant's face. The caustic mist soaked into the eyes and the man shrieked. Lord brought his right knee up into the groin. Droopy doubled over, the knife clattering to the tile floor. With both hands Lord crashed the briefcase down and Droopy crumpled forward.

Lord pounded again. Then again.

He leapt over the body and slid the metal door open, bolting into the corridor. Waiting for him was Cro-Magnon, the same sloped forehead, bushy hair, and bulbous nose from two days ago.

"In a hurry, Mr. Lord?"

He kicked the Russian's left knee with the toe of his loafer, knocking the man down. To his right, a silver samovar steamed with hot water, a glass decanter ready for patrons looking for coffee. He slung the scalding liquid at Cro-Magnon.

The man cried out in pain.

Lord spun in the opposite direction and shot for the exit adjacent to the lavatory. He could hear Droopy getting to his feet, calling out to Cro-Magnon.

He raced out of the sleeper into the next car and hustled down the narrow hall as fast as the confined space would allow. He was hoping a steward would appear. Anyone. He maintained a grasp on his briefcase and found the exit into the next car. Behind, he heard the door at the far end open and caught a glimpse of his two assailants starting after him.

He kept moving, then decided this was pointless. Eventually he was going to run out of train.

He shot a glance back.

The angle of the car gave him a moment of privacy. The hall before him was lined with more sleeping compartments. He figured he was still in the first-class section. He needed to duck into one, if only for a moment, enough time to let the pursuers pass. Maybe then he could backtrack and find Zivon.

He tried the next paneled door.

Locked.

The one after was locked, too.

There'd only be another second.

He grasped a latch handle and looked back. Shadows of approaching figures dimmed the hall in the forward car. As the shoulder of one man came into view, he yanked on the panel.

It opened.

He slipped in and slammed the door shut.

"Who are you?" a female voice asked in Russian.

He spun around.

Perched on the bed, not three feet away, was a woman. She was thin as a figure skater, with shoulder-length blond hair. He took in her oval face, her milky white skin, the blunt tip of her upturned nose. She was a curious mixture of tomboyishness and femininity. And her blue eyes carried not a hint of concern.

"Don't be afraid," he said in Russian. "My name is Miles Lord. I have a big problem."

"That still does not explain why you barged into my compartment."

"Two men are after me."

She stood and stepped close. She was short, rising only to his shoulders, and wore a pair of dark jeans that seemed made only for her. A curvy jacket with padded shoulders covered a blue turtleneck sweater. A faint smell of sweet perfume blossomed from her.

"Are you *mafiya*?" she asked.

He shook his head. "But the men after me may be. They killed a man two days ago and tried to kill me."

"Step back," she said.

He brushed past toward the compartment's solitary window. She slid open the door, glanced out casually, then shut it.

"There are three men at the far end."

"Three?"

"Yes. One has a black ponytail. The other is craggy with a wide nose, like a Tatar."

Droopy and Cro-Magnon.

"The third is muscular. No neck. Blond hair."

It sounded like Zivon. His mind raced at the possibilities. "Are the three talking?"

She nodded. "They are also knocking on compartment doors, headed this way."

The concern that immediately filled his eyes was apparently evident. She pointed to the bin above the door. "Climb up there and stay quiet."

The recess was large enough for two good-sized pieces of luggage, more than enough room to accommodate him in the fetal position. He sprang onto one of the berths and hauled himself up. She handed him his briefcase. He'd just settled in when a knock came on the compartment door.

She answered the call.

"We are looking for a black man, dressed in a suit, carrying a briefcase." The voice was Zivon's.

"I have seen no such man," she said.

"Do not lie to us," Cro-Magnon said. "We are not to be misled. Have you seen him?" The tone was harsh.

"I have seen no such man. I want no trouble from you."

"Your face is familiar," Droopy said.

"I am Akilina Petrovna of the Moscow Circus."

A moment passed.

"That is it. I have seen you perform."

"How wonderful. Perhaps you should continue your search elsewhere. I need some sleep. I have a performance in the evening."

She slammed the compartment door shut.

He heard the lock engage.

And for the third time in two days, he heaved a deep sigh of relief.

He waited a full minute before climbing down. A cold sweat drenched his chest. His hostess sat on the opposite berth.

"Why do these men want to kill you?" The tone of her voice was soft. Still not a hint of concern.

"I have no idea. I'm a lawyer from America, here working with the Tsarist Commission. Until two days ago, I didn't think anybody even knew I was alive, other than my boss."

He sat on the opposite bed. The adrenaline was receding, replaced by a throbbing in every muscle of his body. Fatigue was setting in. But he still had a major problem. "One of those men, the first who spoke to you, was supposed to be my bodyguard. Apparently there's a lot more to him than I thought."

The features on her compact face wrinkled. "I would not recommend turning to him for help. The three appeared to be working together."

He asked, "Is this an everyday thing in Russia? Strange men slipping into your compartment? Mobsters at your door. You seem to have no fear."

"Should I?"

"I'm not saying you should. God knows, I'm harmless. But in America this could be construed as a dangerous situation."

She shrugged. "You don't appear dangerous. Actually, when I saw you, I thought of my grandmother."

He waited for her to explain.

"She grew up in the time of Khrushchev and Brezhnev. The Americans used to send spies to test the soil for radioactivity, trying to find the missile silos. Everyone was warned about them, told they were dangerous, told to be on the lookout. Once, my grandmother was out in the woods and met a strange man gathering mushrooms. He was dressed as a peasant and carried a wicker basket like people do in the woods. She was completely unafraid and walked straight up to him and said, 'Hello, spy.' He stared at her, shocked, but didn't deny the allegation. Instead, he said, 'I was trained so well. I learned everything about Russia I could. How did you know I was a spy?' 'That's easy,' my grandmother said. 'I've lived here all my life and you're the first black man I've ever seen in these woods.' The same is true for you, Miles Lord. You're the first black man I've ever seen on this train."

He smiled. "Your grandmother sounds like a practical woman."

"She was. Until the communists took her one night. Somehow, a seventy-year-old woman threatened an empire."

He'd read about how Stalin slaughtered twenty million in the name of the Motherland, and how the party secretaries and Soviet presidents who came after him weren't any better.

What had Lenin said? *Better to arrest a hundred innocent people than run the risk of one enemy of the regime remaining free.*

"I'm sorry," he said.

"Why should you be?"

"I don't know. It's the appropriate thing to say. What do you want me to say? Too bad your grandmother was butchered by a bunch of fanatics?"

"That's what they were."

"That why you covered for me?"

She shrugged. "I hate the government and the *mafiya*. One and the same."

"Do you think those men were *mafiya*?"

"No doubt."

"I need to find a steward and talk to the conductor."

She smiled. "That would be foolish. Everyone is for sale in this land. If those men seek you, they will buy influence on this train."

She was right. The police weren't much better than the *mafiya*. He thought of Inspector Orleg. He had disliked the burly Russian from the moment they'd met. "What do you suggest?"

"I have no suggestions. You are the lawyer for the Tsarist Commission. You think of what to do."

He noticed her overnight bag on the bed, a MOSCOW CIRCUS emblem embroidered on its side. "You told them you performed in the circus. That true?"

"Of course."

"What's your talent?"

"You tell me. What do you believe I could do?"

"Your petite size would make you an ideal tumbler." He stared at her dark tennis shoes. "Your feet are tight and compact. I'd wager long toes. Your arms are short, but muscular. I'd say an acrobat, maybe the balance beam."

She smiled. "You're quite good. Have you ever seen me perform?"

"I haven't been to the circus in many years."

He wondered about her age. She appeared to be in her late twenties or early thirties.

"How did you come to speak our language so well?" she asked.

"I've studied it for years." His mind turned to the more immediate problem. "I need to get out of here and leave you be. You've done more than anyone could ask."

"Where would you go?"

"I'll find an empty compartment somewhere. Then try to get off this train tomorrow without anyone seeing me."

"Don't be foolish. Those men will search this train all night. The only safe place is here."

She tossed her travel bag to the floor between them and stretched out on her bunk. Then she reached up and switched off the light above the pillow. "Go to sleep, Miles Lord. You're safe here. They will not come back."

He was too tired to argue. And there was no sense arguing since she was right. So he loosened his tie and slipped off his suit jacket, then lay on his bunk and did what she said.

Lord opened his eyes.

Wheels still clanged on steel rails beneath him. He glanced at the luminous dial on his watch. Five twenty AM. He'd been asleep five hours.

He'd dreamed of his father. The Misunderstood Son sermon he'd heard so many times. Grover Lord loved to mix politics and religion, communists and atheists his main targets, his eldest son the example he liked to parade before the faithful. The concept played well to southern congregations, and the reverend was great at screaming fear, passing the plate, then pocketing his 80 percent before moving on to the next town.

His mother defended the bastard till the end, refusing to believe what she must have known. It had fallen to him, as the oldest, to retrieve his father's body from an Alabama motel. The woman with whom he'd spent the night had been whisked away, hysterical, after awakening to find herself naked with the corpse of the Reverend Grover Lord. Only then had he discovered what he'd long suspected—two half brothers the good reverend had supported out of the collection plate for years. Why the five children back home weren't enough, he assumed only God and Grover Lord knew. Apparently the Adultery and Evils of the Flesh sermon had gone unheeded.

He glanced across the darkened compartment. Akilina Petrovna rested quietly under a white quilt. He could barely discern her rhythmic breathing over the monotonous rattle of the tracks. He'd gotten himself into something bad, and no matter how much history was about to be made, he nccdcd to gct thc hcll out of Russia. Thank goodness he'd brought his passport with him. Tomorrow he'd leave for Atlanta on the first flight he could book. But right now, the sway of the compartment and the click of wheels, along with the darkness that surrounded him, allowed sleep to once again take hold.

15

"Miles Lord."

He opened his eyes to find Akilina Petrovna staring down at him.

"We are approaching Moscow."

"What time is it?"

"A little past seven."

He shoved away the blanket and sat up. Akilina sat back on the edge of her berth a couple of feet away. His mouth felt like it'd been rinsed with Elmer's glue. He needed a shower and a shave, but there was no time. He also needed to contact Taylor Hayes, but there was a problem. A big problem. And his hostess seemed to know.

"Those men will be waiting at the station."

He licked the film off his teeth. "Don't I know."

"There is a way off."

"How?"

"We will cross the Garden Ring in a few minutes and the train will slow. There is a speed limit beyond. When I was small we would hop on and off the Petersburg express. It was an easy way to and from downtown."

He didn't particularly relish the idea of jumping from a moving train, but he couldn't risk a reunion with Droopy and Cro-Magnon.

The train started to slow.

"See," she said.

"You know where we are?"

She glanced out the window. "About twenty kilometers from the station. I would suggest you leave quickly."

He reached for his briefcase and snapped open the locks. There wasn't much there—just the few copies of what he'd found in the Moscow and St. Petersburg archives and some other unimportant papers. He folded all of them and stuffed them into his jacket. He felt for his passport and wallet. Both were still in his pockets. "This briefcase would just be in the way."

She took the leather case from him. "I will hold on to it for you. If you want it back, come to the circus."

He smiled. "Thanks. I might just do that." But on another trip at another time, he thought.

He stood and slipped on his jacket.

She moved toward the door. "I will check the hall to see if all is clear."

He lightly grasped her arm. "Thanks. For everything."

"You are welcome, Miles Lord. You brought interest to an otherwise boring ride."

They were close and he savored the same flowery scent from last night. Akilina Petrovna was attractive, though her face bore hints of life's harsh effects. Soviet propaganda once proclaimed communist women the most liberated in the world. No factory could run without them. Service industries would literally collapse if not for their contribution. But time was never kind to them. He'd long admired the beauty of young Russian women, but pitied the inevitable effects society would wreak. And he wondered what this lovely woman would look like in twenty years.

He stepped back, out of the doorway, as she slid open the panel and left.

A minute later it reopened.

"Come," she said.

The corridor in both directions was empty. They were about three-quarters of the way back in the long car. To the left, beyond another steaming samovar, was an exit door. Through its glass the stark reality of urban Moscow whizzed past. Unlike American or European trains, the portal was not alarmed or locked.

Akilina wrenched the handle down and pulled the steel door inward. The clatter of wheel to rail increased.

"Good luck, Miles Lord," she said as he passed.

He took one last look into her blue eyes, then leapt out to the hard earth. He pounded the cold ground and rolled away.

The last car passed and the morning lapsed into an eerie quiet as the train roared southward.

He'd landed in a weedy lot between blocks of dingy apartment buildings. He was glad he'd jumped when he had. Any farther and there may not have been anything but concrete to greet him. Sounds of morning traffic filled the air from beyond the buildings, a pungent scent of carbon exhaust filling his nostrils.

He stood and brushed off his clothes. Another suit destroyed. But what the hell. He was leaving Russia today, anyway.

He needed a telephone, so he made his way to a boulevard lined with shops and businesses opening for the day. Buses deposited passengers, then steamed away with a belch of black exhaust. He spied two *militsya* across the street in their blue-and-gray uniforms. Unlike Droopy and Cro-Magnon, these wore regulation gray caps with red brims. He decided to avoid them.

He spotted a grocery a few yards down the sidewalk and ducked inside. The man tending the shelves was thin and old. "You have a telephone I might use?" he asked in Russian.

The man tossed him a grave look and did not reply. Lord reached into his pocket and brought out ten rubles. The man accepted the money and pointed to the counter. He stepped over, dialed the Volkhov, and told the hotel operator to connect him with Taylor Hayes's room. The phone rang a dozen times. When the hotel operator came back on, he told her to try the restaurant. Two minutes later Hayes was on the line.

"Miles, where the hell are you?"

"Taylor, we have a big problem."

He told Hayes what had happened. A few times he let his gaze drift to the man tending his shelves, wondering if he could understand English, but the traffic noise spilling in from outside helped mask the conversation.

"They're after *me,* Taylor. Not Bely or anybody else. Me."

"All right. Calm down."

"Calm down? That bodyguard you gave me is in with them."

"What do you mean?"

"I mean he joined up with the other two looking for me."

"I understand—"

"No, you don't, Taylor. Until you've been chased by Russian mobsters, you can't understand."

"Miles, listen to me. Panic is not going to get you out of this. Go to the nearest police."

"Shit, no. I don't trust anybody in this rat hole. The whole goddamn country is on the take. You got to help me, Taylor. You're the only one I trust."

"What did you go to St. Petersburg for? I told you to stay low."

He explained about Semyon Pashenko and what the older man had told him. "And he was right, Taylor. There was stuff there."

"Does it affect Baklanov's claim to the throne?"

"It might."

"You're telling me Lenin thought some of the tsar's family survived the massacre at Yekaterinburg?"

"He was sure interested in the subject. There are enough written references to make you wonder."

"Jesus. Just what we need."

"Look, it's probably nothing at all. Come on, it's been almost a hundred years since Nicholas II was murdered. Surely somebody would have surfaced by now." At the mention of the tsar's name, the store clerk perked up. He lowered his voice. "But that's not my real worry at the moment. Getting out of here alive is."

"Where are the papers?"

"On me."

"Okay. Find the subway and take a train to Red Square. Lenin's tomb—"

"Why not the hotel?"

"Could be watched. Let's stay public. The tomb will be opening shortly. There are army guards all over the place. You'll be safe there. They can't all be on the take."

Paranoia was taking over. But Hayes was right. Listen to him.

"Wait outside the tomb. I'll be there with the cavalry shortly. Understand?"

"Just hurry."

16

8:30 AM

LORD'S ENTRANCE TO THE METRO WAS A STATION IN THE northern part of town. The subway train was packed in a suffocating closeness with stinking commuters. He clung to a steel pole and felt the clatter of wheels to rail. At least no one seemed threatening. All of them appeared wary. Like himself.

He left the Metro at the Historical Museum and crossed a busy street, passing through Resurrection Gate. Red Square opened beyond. He marveled at the recently rebuilt gate, the original seventeenth-century white towers and redbrick archways having fallen victim to Stalin.

The compactness of Red Square had always struck him as odd. Communist television spectaculars had made the cobbled space look endless. In reality, it was only a third longer than a football field and less than half as wide. The imposing redbrick walls of the Kremlin stood to the southwest side. On the northeast rose the GUM department store, the massive baroque building resembling more a nineteenth-century train station than a bastion of capitalism. The north end was dominated by the Historical Museum and its white-tiled roof. A double-headed Romanov eagle now decorated the top of the building, the Red Star gone the way of the communists. At the south end stood St. Basil's Cathedral, an explosion of pinnacles, onion domes, and spade-shaped gables. Its collage of colors, flooded in arc light and splashed onto the blackness of a Moscow night, was the city's most recognizable symbol.

Steel barricades at either end prevented pedestrians from entering the square. Lord knew the area remained cordoned off every day until one PM, when Lenin's tomb closed.

And he saw that Hayes was right.

There were at least two dozen uniformed *militsya* in and around the boxlike tomb. A small queue of visitors had already formed in front of the granite mausoleum. The building sat on the highest point of the square, nestled close to the Kremlin wall, a row of towering silver firs standing guard on either side, flanking the walls beyond.

He rounded the barricade and followed a tour group toward the tomb. He buttoned his jacket against the chill and wished he'd brought his wool coat, but it was back in the compartment of the Red Arrow he and Ilya Zivon had briefly shared. Bells chimed in the clock tower above the walls. Tourists wearing oversized down jackets and cameras milled about. Garish colors clearly tagged them. Most Russians seemed to favor black, gray, brown, and navy blue. Gloves were a giveaway, too. True Russians shunned them, even in the dead of winter.

He followed the tour group to the front of the mausoleum. One of the *militsya* ambled toward him, a young, pale-faced man dressed in an olive-green greatcoat and blue fur *shlapa*. He noticed the lack of a weapon, the guard's function purely ceremonial. Too bad.

"Are you here to tour the shrine?" the guard asked in Russian.

Though he understood him perfectly, he decided to feign ignorance. He shook his head. "No Russian. English?"

The guard's face stayed frozen. "Passport," the man said in English.

The last thing Lord wanted was to attract attention. He quickly glanced around, searching for Taylor Hayes or anybody coming his way.

"Passport," the guard said again.

Another guard moved in his direction.

He reached into his back pocket and found his passport. The blue cover would immediately identify him as American. He handed it to the guard, but nerves caused his grip to slip and the booklet dropped to the cobbles. He bent down to retrieve it and felt a *swoosh* as something whipped past his right ear and sank into the guard's chest. He looked up to see a ribbon of red pouring from a hole in the man's green coat. The guard gasped for breath, his eyes rolled skyward, then his body folded to the pavement.

Lord spun around and spied a gunman a hundred yards away atop the GUM department store.

The gunman leveled his rifle and re-aimed.

Pocketing the passport, Lord rushed past the crowd and leapt up the granite steps, shoving people to the ground and screaming in English and Russian, "Gunman. Run."

Tourists scattered.

He dived forward just as another bullet ricocheted off the glazed stone beside him. He landed hard on the black labradorite of the tomb's foyer and rolled inside just as another bullet obliterated more red granite at the doorway.

Two more guards rushed up from inside the tomb.

"There's a gunman outside," he screamed in Russian. "On top of GUM."

Neither guard was armed, but one darted into a small cubicle and dialed a phone. Lord inched toward the doorway. People were racing in every direction. But none was in danger. He was the target. The gunman was still on the roof, wedged between a row of arc lights. Suddenly a dark Volvo station wagon zoomed out of a side street south of GUM, directly in front of St. Basil's. The car screeched to a stop and two doors popped open.

Droopy and Cro-Magnon stepped out, then sprinted toward the tomb.

He had only one way to go, so he bolted down the staircase into the bowels of the mausoleum. People were crowded at the base of the stairs, fear in their eyes. He shouldered past them, turned twice, and entered the main vault. He raced around the walkway that encircled Lenin's glass coffin, giving the waxy corpse only a momentary glance. Two more guards were on the other side. Neither voiced a word. He bounded up a slick marble staircase and popped out a side exit. Instead of turning right, back toward Red Square, he darted left.

A quick glance confirmed that the rifleman had spotted him. But the angle wasn't right. The shooter needed to move, and Lord saw the man do just that.

He was now in the green space behind the mausoleum's receding tiers. A stairway, chained shut, rose to his left. He knew it led up to the rooftop reviewing platform. No point going there. He needed to stay low.

He ran forward toward the Kremlin wall. When he glanced back he saw the gunman take up a new position toward the end of the arc lights. Lord was now in the area behind the tomb. Stone busts commemorated the graves of such men as Sverdlov, Brezhnev, Kalinin, and Stalin.

Two shots rang out.

He dived to the concrete path, using the trunk of one of the silver firs for cover. A bullet raked the tree's boughs, careering off the Kremlin wall behind him, while another ricocheted off one of the stone monuments. He couldn't go right, toward the Historical Museum. Too open. Left allowed the mausoleum to work as a shield. But then the gunman wasn't as immediate a problem as the men he'd seen climb out of the Volvo.

He turned left and ran straight ahead, down a narrow path among the graves of party leaders. He stayed in a crouch and moved as fast as he could, using the tree trunks for protection.

Emerging on the other side of the tomb, shots started again from the GUM roof. Bullets chipped away at the Kremlin wall. The gunman couldn't be that bad a shot, so Lord reasoned that he was being herded in a predetermined direction, one where Droopy and Cro-Magnon would surely be waiting.

He glanced left beyond the granite reviewing stands toward Red Square. Droopy and Cro-Magnon spotted him and raced his way.

Three police cars roared into the square from the south, their lights flashing, sirens blaring. Their appearance halted Droopy and Cro-Magnon's rapid approach. He stopped, too, huddling close to a stone monolith for protection.

Droopy and Cro-Magnon looked back toward GUM's roof. The gunman high above signaled, then disappeared. They apparently took his cue and beat a retreat to the Volvo.

Police cars roared into the square, one obliterating a free-standing barricade. Uniformed *militsya* poured out, weapons in hand. Lord looked left, back from where he had come. More *militsya* were running toward him down the narrow path parallel to the wall, their greatcoats unbuttoned, breath condensing in the cool, dry air.

And they were armed.

There was nowhere for him to go.

He raised his hands above his head and stood.

The first policeman to approach slammed him to the ground and burrowed the barrel of a gun into the nape of his neck.

17

11:OO AM

LORD WAS HANDCUFFED AND TRANSPORTED FROM RED Square in a police cruiser. The *militsya* were anything but courteous, and he reminded himself that he wasn't in the United States. So he kept silent and spoke English when acknowledging his name and American citizenship. There was no sign of Taylor Hayes anywhere.

From the little bit of conversation he overheard, the guard had been shot dead. Two other guards were wounded, one seriously. The gunman had fled the rooftop. No trace of him had been found. Apparently, none of the guards or *militsya* noticed the dark Volvo station wagon and its two occupants. He decided to offer nothing until he was able to talk face-to-face with Hayes. There seemed little doubt now that the phones at the Volkhov were being monitored. How else would anyone have known where he was? That would imply, perhaps, some faction of the government was involved with whatever was occurring.

Yet Droopy and Cro-Magnon had fled at the approach of the police.

He needed to get to Hayes. His employer would know what to do. Perhaps some element of the police could help? But he doubted it. He had little trust left for any Russian.

He was whisked through the streets in a wailing squad car

directly to central headquarters. The modern, multistory building faced the Moskva River, the former Russian White House on the opposite bank. He was taken to the third floor and led down a dismal corridor lined with rows of empty chairs to an office where Inspector Feliks Orleg greeted him. The pudgy Russian was dressed in the same dark suit from three days before, when they had first met on Nikolskaya Prospekt before the bleeding body of Artemy Bely.

"Mr. Lord. Come in. Sit," Orleg said in English.

The office was a claustrophobic cubicle with grimy plaster walls. There was a black metal desk, file cabinet, and two chairs. The floor was a gritty tile, the ceiling nicotine-stained, and Lord could see why—Orleg puffed hard on a black Turkish cigarette. The blue fog was intense, but at least it tempered the body odor blossoming from the inspector.

Orleg ordered the handcuffs removed. The door was closed and they were left alone.

"No need for restraints. Correct, Mr. Lord?"

"Why am I being treated like a criminal?"

Orleg sat behind the desk in a rickety oak chair that squealed. The inspector's tie hung loose, a yellowed collar unbuttoned. "Twice you were where somebody died. This time, policeman."

"I didn't shoot anyone."

"But violence follows you. Why?"

He liked the obstinate inspector less today than at their first meeting. The Russian had liquid eyes that screwed up when he spoke. Disdain filled his face, and Lord wondered what was actually moving through the bastard's mind while the face maintained an icy facade. He didn't like the odd flutter in his chest. Was that fear? Or apprehension?

"I want to make a phone call," he said.

Orleg puffed on his cigarette. "To?"

"That's not your concern."

STEVE BERRY / 126

A thin smile accompanied a vacuous stare. "We are not America, Mr. Lord. No rights for people in custody."

"I want to call the American embassy."

"You diplomat?"

"I work for the Tsarist Commission. You know that."

Another irritating smile. "That confer privilege?"

"I didn't say that it did. But I am here in this country on a pass from the government."

Orleg laughed. "Government, Mr. Lord? No government. We wait for tsar to return." No effort was made to conceal the sarcasm.

"I assume you voted no?"

Orleg's face turned serious. "Assume nothing. Much safer that way."

He didn't like the implications. But before he could respond, the phone on the desk rang. The shrill startled him. Orleg lifted the handset while still fingering the cigarette with his other hand. He answered in Russian and instructed the person on the other end to put the call through.

"What may I do for you?" Orleg said into the mouthpiece, still in Russian.

There was a pause while Orleg listened.

"I have the *chornye* here," the inspector said.

Lord's interest perked, but he did nothing that revealed he understood what Orleg was saying. The policeman apparently felt safe behind the language barrier.

"A guard is dead. The men you sent were not successful. No contact was made. I told you the situation could have been handled better. I agree. Yes. He does have great luck."

The caller was apparently the source of all his problems. And he'd been right about Orleg. The sonovabitch was not to be trusted.

"I will keep him here until your people arrive. This time it will be done correctly. No more gangsters. I will kill him myself."

Chilly fingers danced down Lord's spine.

"Do not worry. I have him under personal watch. He is here, sitting right before me." A smile formed on the Russian's face. "He doesn't understand a word I'm saying."

There was a pause, then Orleg bolted upright in the chair. The inspector's gaze met Lord's.

"What?" Orleg said. "He speaks—"

Lord brought both legs up and slammed the heavy desk across the tile floor into Orleg. The inspector's chair rolled back and kissed the wall, pinning him tight. Lord then yanked the phone cord from the wall and leapt from the room. He slammed the door, then followed the empty hall, bounding down the staircase three steps at a time, retracing his route to the ground floor and the street.

Once out in the chilly midmorning air, he plunged into the sidewalk crowd.

18

HAYES EXITED THE CAB AT SPARROW HILLS AND PAID THE driver. The midday sky was a burnished platinum, the sun straining hard, as if through frosted glass, to compensate for a frigid breeze. The Moskva River looped sharply below him, forming a peninsula that supported the Luzhniki sports stadium. In the distance, toward the northeast, the bulbous gold and silver cupolas of the Kremlin cathedrals peaked through a cold haze like tombstones in a fog. It was from the hills around him that both Napoléon and Hitler had been thwarted. In 1917 revolutionary groups had held clandestine meetings among its trees, safe from the secret police, plotting an eventual downfall of the tsar. Now a new generation seemed intent on reversing their efforts.

To his right, Moscow State University rose above the trees in an overpowering array of capricious spires, ornate wings, and elaborate curlicues. It was another of Stalin's grandiose wedding-cake skyscrapers erected to impress the world. This one was the largest, built by German prisoners of war. He recalled a story about one prisoner who supposedly fashioned a pair of wings from scrap lumber and tried to fly home from the top. Like his nation and *führer,* he failed.

Feliks Orleg waited on a bench under a canopy of beech trees. Hayes was still fuming from what had happened two hours before, but cautioned himself to watch his words. This wasn't Atlanta. Or even America. He was just one part of an extensive team. Unfortunately, at the moment, the point man.

He sat on the bench and asked in Russian, "Have you found Lord?"

"Not yet. Has he called?"

"Would you? Obviously he doesn't trust me anymore, either. I tell him I'll be there to help and two killers show up. Now, thanks to you, he's not going to trust anybody. The idea was to eliminate the problem. Now the problem is wandering around Moscow."

"What is so important about killing this one man? We are wasting energy."

"That's not for you or me to question, Orleg. The only saving grace is he eluded *their* killers, not yours or mine."

A breeze moved past and leaves trickled from the trees. Hayes had worn his heavy wool coat and gloves, but a chill still crept through him.

"Did you report what happened?" Orleg asked.

He caught the edge in the inspector's voice. "Not yet. I'll do what I can. But they will not be pleased. That was stupid talking to me on the phone in front of him."

"How would I know he speaks Russian?"

Hayes was trying hard to keep control, but this arrogant policeman had placed him in a difficult situation. He faced Orleg. "Listen to me. Find him. Do you understand? Find him and kill him. And do it fast. No mistakes. No excuses. Just do it."

Orleg's face was tight. "I've taken enough orders from you."

He stood. "You can take that up with the people we both work for. I'll be glad to send a representative so you can lodge a complaint."

The Russian got the message. Though an American was his immediate supervisor, Russians were running the operation.

Dangerous Russians. Men who murdered businessmen, government ministers, military officers, foreigners. Anybody who became a problem.

Like incompetent police inspectors.

Orleg stood. "I'll find the damn *chornye* and I'll kill him. Then I might just kill you."

Hayes wasn't impressed with the Russian's bravado. "Take a number, Orleg. There are plenty in line ahead of you."

LORD TOOK REFUGE IN A CAFÉ. AFTER FLEEING POLICE HEAD-quarters he'd descended into the first Metro station he passed and boarded a train, changing routes several times. Then he left the Metro and dissolved into the evening crowds high above. He'd walked for an hour before concluding that no one was following.

The café was busy, filled with young people dressed in faded denim and dark leather jackets. A strong scent of espresso mellowed a thick nicotine cloud. He sat at a wall table and tried to eat something, having skipped breakfast and lunch, but a plate of stroganoff did nothing but sour his already churning stomach.

He'd been right about Inspector Orleg. It made sense the authorities were somehow involved. The telephone lines at the Volkhov were surely being monitored. But who had Orleg been talking with on the phone? And was all of this related to the Tsarist Commission? It had to be. But how? Perhaps the backing of Stefan Baklanov by the consortium of Western investors he and Hayes represented was viewed as a threat. But wasn't their effort supposed to be secret? And didn't a sizable bloc of Russians recognize Baklanov as the closest surviving Romanov? A recent poll gave him better than 50 percent of the popular support. That could be seen as a threat. Certainly the *mafiya* was involved. Droopy and Cro-Magnon were without a doubt members. What had Orleg said? *No more gangsters. I will kill him myself.*

The mob possessed deep ties within the government. Russian politics was as jagged as the exterior of the Facets Palace. Alliances changed by the hour. The only true allegiance was to the ruble. Or, more accurately, the dollar. This was all too much. He needed to get out of the country.

But how?

Thankfully, he still carried his passport, credit cards, and some cash. He also still possessed the information he'd been able to locate in the archives. But that wasn't of major concern any longer. Staying alive was his priority—and getting help.

But what to do?

He couldn't go to the police.

Maybe the American embassy? But that would be the first place they would stake out. Damn right. So far the bastards had appeared on a train from St. Petersburg and in Red Square, both places where he should have been the only person who knew he'd be there.

Except for Hayes.

What about him? His boss surely must be worried after hearing what had happened. Maybe Hayes could get to him? He had lots of contacts in the Russian government, but he would not realize the phones in the Volkhov were under scrutiny. Or maybe by now he did.

He sipped hot tea, which calmed his gut, and wondered what the reverend would do in the same situation. Strange that he thought of his father, but Grover Lord was a master of the tight spot. His blazing tongue had constantly bred trouble, but he'd laced every other word with *God* and *Jesus,* and never backed down. No. Fast talk wasn't going to be much help here.

But what *would* be?

He glanced at the table beside him. A young couple was huddled close reading one of the day's newspapers. He noticed the front-page article about the Tsarist Commission and read what he could.

During the third day of the initial session, five names had emerged as possible contenders. Baklanov was mentioned as the leading candidate, but relatives from two other branches of the Romanov family were vigorously arguing a closer blood connection with Nicholas II. The formal nominating process would not start for two more days, and anticipation was building over the debate that would ensue among the various men and their defenders.

Over the past couple of hours he'd overheard conversations from the tables around him about the pending selection. There seemed a genuine appreciation of the unfolding events—and surprisingly, the young Russians supported the creation of a modern-day monarchy. Perhaps they'd heard their grandparents speak of the tsar. The typical Russian seemed to want the nation to have grand goals. But he wondered whether an autocracy could effectively function in the twenty-first century. The only solace, he concluded, was that Russia was perhaps one of the last places left on Earth where a monarchy might actually have a chance at working.

But his problem was more immediate.

He couldn't check into a hotel. Registrations were still reported nightly by every licensed establishment. He couldn't catch a plane or train—the debarkation points would surely be watched. Nor could he rent a car without a Russian driver's license. He also couldn't just walk into the Volkhov. He was essentially trapped, the whole country his prison. He needed to get to the American embassy. There he could find people who'd listen. But he couldn't pick up a phone and dial. Surely, whoever was monitoring the Volkhov's phones would keep a close ear to the lines into the embassy. He needed somebody else to make contact and somewhere to lay low until that contact was made.

He glanced again at the newspaper and noticed an advertisement. It was for the circus and announced shows nightly at six, the ad beckoning visitors with promises of lively family entertainment.

He glanced at his watch. Five fifteen PM.

He thought of Akilina Petrovna. Her tousled blond hair and pixie face. She'd impressed him with her courage and patience. He actually owed her his life. She still had his briefcase and had told him to come get it whenever.

So why not?

He stood from the table and started to leave. But a sobering thought suddenly occurred to him. He was heading for a woman to help ease him out of a tight spot.

Just like his father.

19

TRINITY MONASTERY OF ST. SERGIUS
SERGYEV POSAD
5:00 PM

HAYES WAS FIFTY MILES NORTHEAST OF MOSCOW, APPROACH-ing Russia's most sacred religious site. He knew its history. The irregularly shaped fortress had first risen above the surrounding forest in the fourteenth century. Tatars had quickly besieged and finally ransacked the citadel a hundred years later. In the seventeenth century Poles had tried and failed to breach the monastery walls. Peter the Great had sought refuge here during a revolt early in his reign. And now it was a place of pilgrimage for millions of Russian Orthodox, as sacred as the Vatican to Catholics, where St. Sergius lay in a silver sarcophagus, the faithful traveling from across the nation just to kiss his tomb.

He arrived as the site was closing for the day. He stepped from the car and quickly tied the belt of his overcoat, then slipped on a pair of black leather gloves. The sun was already below the horizon, an autumn night closing in, the sparkling blue-and-gold-starred onion domes dull in the fading light. A blistering wind howled with a rumble that reminded him of artillery fire.

Lenin had come with him. The other three members of the Secret Chancellory had unanimously decided that Hayes and

Lenin should be the ones to make the initial approach. The patriarch might appreciate the risks more if he saw and heard firsthand that a Russian military line officer was willing to stake his reputation on the coming venture.

He watched the cadaverous Lenin smooth his gray wool coat and deftly wrap a maroon scarf around his neck. They'd hardly spoken on the ride up. But each knew what had to be done.

A black-robed priest with a mosslike beard waited at the main gate while a steady procession of pilgrims streamed out on either side of him. The priest led them inside thick stone walls directly to the Cathedral of the Dormition. The church's interior was candlelit, shadows flickered across a gilded iconostasis towering behind the main altar, and acolytes busily closed the sanctuary for the day.

They followed the priest down into a subterranean room. They'd been told the meeting would occur in the crypt of All Saints Hallowed, the place where patriarchs of the Russian Orthodox Church lay buried. The vault below was tight, its walls and floor lined with light gray marble. An iron chandelier splashed dim rays across a vaulted ceiling. Elaborate tombs were decorated with gilded crosses, iron candelabra, and painted icons.

The man kneeling before the farthest tomb was at least seventy, tufts of bushy gray hair sprouting from a narrow head. His ruddy face was covered with a matted beard and a mustache thick as fleece. A hearing aid protruded from one ear and age spots dotted hands intertwined in prayer. Hayes had studied photographs of the man, but this was the first time he'd seen His Holiness, Patriarch Adrian, apostolic head of the thousand-year-old Russian Orthodox Church, in the flesh.

Their escort left them alone, footsteps retreating back up into the cathedral.

A door closed above.

The patriarch crossed himself and stood. "Gentlemen, good of you to come." The voice was deep and gravelly.

Lenin introduced himself and Hayes.

"I am familiar with you, General Ostanovich. My sources tell me I am to listen to what you propose and decide the merits."

"We appreciate the audience," Lenin said.

"I thought here in the crypt the safest place for our talk. It is private beyond reproach. Mother Earth will shield us from any inquisitive ears. And perhaps the souls of the great men buried here, my predecessors, might inspire me to the proper course."

Hayes wasn't fooled by the explanation. The proposal they were about to extend was not something a man in Adrian's position could afford to have become public. It was one thing to consequently benefit, quite another to openly participate in a treasonous conspiracy—particularly for a man who was supposed to be above politics.

"I wonder, gentlemen, why should I even consider what you propose? Since the end of the Great Interruption, my church has enjoyed an unparalleled resurgence. With the Soviets gone, there is no more persecution or restrictions. We have baptized new members by the tens of thousands, and churches are opening every day. Soon we will be back to where we were before the communists arrived."

"But there could be so much more," Lenin said.

The old man's eyes flashed bright like coals in a dying fire. "And it is that possibility that intrigues me. Please explain."

"An alliance with us will secure your place with the new tsar."

"But any tsar will have no choice but to work with the church. The people would demand no less."

"We live in a new age, Patriarch. A public relations campaign can cause more damage than any repressive police force ever could. Think about it. The people are starving, yet the church continues to erect gilded monuments. You parade about in embroidered robes, but lament when the faithful don't support their parishes with adequate contributions. All the support you now enjoy could be eroded by a few well-publicized scandals. Some of the men in our association control the largest media outlets—newspapers, radio, television—and much can be done with that power."

"I am shocked that a man of your stature would utter such threats, General." The words were strong, though voiced calmly.

Lenin appeared unfazed by the rebuke. "This is a difficult time, Patriarch. Much is at stake. Military officers are not paid enough to feed themselves, much less their families. There are invalids and disabled veterans receiving nothing in the way of a pension. Just last year, five hundred line officers killed themselves. An army that once shook the world is now decimated to the point of nothing. Our government has crippled the military complex. I doubt, Holiness, that any of our missiles could even leave their silos. This nation is defenseless. Our only saving grace is that no one, as yet, knows this."

The patriarch considered the diatribe. "How could my church be of aid to the coming change?"

"The tsar will need the full support of the church," Lenin said.

"He would have that anyway."

"By *full support* I mean whatever may be necessary to assure that popular opinion is controlled. The press must be free, at least in principle, the people allowed to voice dissent, within reason. The whole idea of a tsarist return is a break with the oppressive past. The church could be of valuable assistance to ensure a stable, long-lasting government."

"What you really mean is that others in league with you don't want to risk the church opposing them. I am not ignorant, General. I know the *mafiya* is part of your group. Not to mention the leeches from the government ministry who are every bit as bad. You, General, are one thing. They are quite another."

Hayes knew the old man was right. Government ministers were nearly universally on the take from either the *mafiya* or the new rich. Bribes were a standard way to conduct the public's business. So he asked, "Would you rather have communists?"

The patriarch turned to him. "What would an American know of this?"

"It has been my business for three decades to understand this country. I represent a huge conglomerate of American investors. Companies with billions at stake. Companies that could also make sizable contributions to *your* various parishes."

A mirthful grin came to the old man's bearded face. "Americans think money buys everything."

"Doesn't it?"

Adrian stepped close to one of the elaborate tombs, his hands clenched together, his back to his two guests. "A fourth Rome."

"Excuse me?" Lenin asked.

"A fourth Rome. That's what you propose. In the time of Ivan the Great, Rome, where the first pope sat, had already fallen. Then Constantinople, where the Eastern pope sat, succumbed. After that, Ivan proclaimed Moscow the third Rome. The only place left on Earth where the church and state merged into a single political entity—headed by him, of course. He predicted there would never be a fourth."

The patriarch turned and faced them.

"Ivan the Great married the last Byzantine princess and

visibly invested *his* Russia with *her* Byzantine heritage. After the fall of Constantinople to the Turks in 1453, he proclaimed Moscow the secular center of the Christian world. Clever, actually. It allowed him to decree himself head of the eternal union between church and state, imposing upon himself the sacred majesty of a universal priest-king, wielding authority in God's name. From Ivan on, every tsar was considered divinely appointed and Christians were required to obey. A theocratic autocracy, one that combined church and dynasty into an imperial heritage. It worked well for more than four hundred and fifty years until Nicholas II—when the communists murdered the tsar and dissolved the union of church and state. Now, perhaps, a reemergence?"

Lenin smiled. "But this time, Holiness, the union will be far-reaching. We propose a merger of all factions, including the church. A united effort to ensure a collective survival. As you say, a fourth Rome."

"Including the *mafiya*?"

Lenin nodded. "We have no choice. Their reach is too long. Perhaps in time they can be acclimated into mainstream society."

"That is too much to wish. They are draining the people. Their greed is largely to blame for our dire situation."

"I understand that, Holiness. But we have no choice. Thankfully, the *mafiya* factions, at least for the moment, are cooperating."

Hayes decided to seize the opportunity. "We can also help with your public relations problem."

The patriarch's eyebrows arched. "I was unaware my church had such a problem."

"Let's be frank, Holiness. If you did not have a problem, we would not be here, beneath Orthodox Russia's holiest cathedral, plotting the manipulation of a restored monarchy."

"Go on, Mr. Hayes."

He was beginning to like Patriarch Adrian. He seemed an entirely practical man. "Church attendance is down. Few Russians want to see their children become clerics, and even fewer are donating to parishes. Your cash flow has got to be at critical levels. You also have a possible civil war on your hands. From what I've been told, a good number of priests and bishops favor making Orthodoxy the national religion, to the exclusion of all others. Yeltsin refused to do that, vetoing the bill that tried, then passing a watered-down version. But he had no choice. The United States would have cut off funds if religious persecution began, and Russia needs foreign aid. Without some governmental sanction, your church may well founder."

"I will not deny that a schism is brewing between ultratraditionalists and modernists."

Hayes kept his momentum. "Foreign missionaries are eroding your base. You've got ministers flocking from all over America looking for Russian converts. That variety in theology creates problems, doesn't it? Hard to keep the flock faithful when others start preaching alternatives."

"Unfortunately, we Russians do not handle choices well."

"What was the first people's democratic election?" Lenin said. "God created Adam and Eve, then said to Adam, 'Now, choose a wife.'"

The patriarch smiled.

Hayes continued, "What you want, Holiness, is state protection without state repression. You want Orthodoxy, but don't want to surrender control. We offer you that luxury."

"Specifics, please."

Lenin said, "You, as patriarch, will remain head of the church. The new tsar will assert himself as head, but there will be no interference with church administration. In fact, the tsar will openly encourage people to Orthodoxy. The Romanovs were always dedicated that way, Nicholas II particularly. This dedication is also consistent with a Russian nationalist philosophy the new tsar will expound. In return, you will assure the church promulgates a pro-tsarist position and supports the new government in whatever it does. Your priests should be our allies. In this way the church and state will be joined, but the masses need never know. A fourth Rome, modified to a new reality."

The old man went silent, clearly considering the proposal.

"All right, gentlemen. You may consider the church at your disposal."

"That was fast," Hayes said.

"Not at all. I have been thinking about this since you first made contact. I merely wanted to talk face-to-face and gauge the men I will be in league with. I am pleased."

Both acknowledged the compliment.

"But I ask that you deal only with me on this matter."

Lenin understood. "Would you like a representative to attend our meetings? That courtesy would be extended."

Adrian nodded. "I will appoint a priest. He and I will be the only two privy to this arrangement. I will be in touch with the name."

20

MOSCOW, 5:40 PM

THE RAIN STOPPED JUST AS LORD EXITED THE METRO STATION. Tsventnoy Boulevard was damp from a good dousing, the air noticeably colder, a chilling fog draping the city. He still wore no coat other than his suit jacket and looked out of place among the dense crowd wrapped in wool and fur. He was glad night had fallen. That and the fog should help conceal him.

He followed a crush of people toward the theater across the street. He knew the Moscow Circus was a popular tourist stop, one of the premier shows in the world. He'd gone himself once years ago to marvel at the dancing bears and trained dogs.

He had twenty minutes until the performance started. Perhaps during intermission he could get a message backstage to Akilina Petrovna. If not, he'd find her after. Maybe she could get in touch with the American embassy. Perhaps she could get in and out of the Volkhov and talk with Taylor Hayes. Surely she had an apartment where he could wait in safety.

The theater was fifty yards down the street on the opposite side. He was just about to cross and head for a ticket booth when a voice from behind yelled, *"Stoi."* Stop.

He kept shouldering ahead.

The voice said again, *"Stoi."*

He glanced back over his left shoulder and saw a policeman. The man was shoving through the crowd, arm raised, eyes locked straight ahead. Lord increased his pace and quickly crossed the congested street, dissolving into the bustling crowd on the far side. A tour bus was off-loading its passengers, and he joined a steady procession of Japanese as they made their way into the brightly lit theater. Another glance back and he did not see the policeman.

Maybe he'd simply imagined the officer was after him.

He kept his head low and followed the noisy crowd. At the ticket booth he paid the ten-ruble admission and darted inside, hoping Akilina Petrovna was there.

AKILINA DONNED HER COSTUME. THE COMMUNAL DRESSING room buzzed with its usual bustle, performers rushing in and out. No one was afforded the luxury of private dressing quarters. That was something she'd seen only in American movies, which depicted circus life romantically.

She was tired, having gotten little sleep last night. The trip from St. Petersburg to Moscow had been interesting, to say the least, and throughout the day she'd thought about Miles Lord. She'd told him the truth. He was the first black man she'd ever seen on that train. And no, she'd never been frightened of him. Maybe *his* fear had disarmed her.

Lord projected none of the stereotypical descriptions she recalled from childhood, when teachers in the state-run schools deplored the hideous evil of the Negroid race. She remembered comments about their inferior brains, weak immune systems, and total inability to govern themselves. Americans once enslaved them, a point the propagandists hammered home to emphasize the failure of capitalism. She'd even seen photographs of lynchings where white men

gathered in ghostly white robes and pointed hoods and
gawked at the spectacle.

Miles Lord, though, seemed nothing like any of that. His
skin was the color of the rusty Voina River she remembered
from visits to her grandmother's village. His brown hair was
short and neat. His body was compact and sinewy. He carried an air that was formal but friendly, his throaty voice
memorable. He'd seemed genuinely surprised by her invi-
tation to spend the night in her compartment, perhaps unaccustomed to such openness in women. She hoped his
sophistication ran deeper, since he seemed interesting.

Exiting the train, she'd seen the three men chasing Lord
leave the station and climb into a dark blue Volvo waiting on
the street. She'd stuffed Lord's attaché case into her
overnight bag and kept it, just as she'd promised, hoping he
might want it back.

All day she'd wondered if Lord was all right. Men had not
played much of a role in her life the past few years. The circus performed almost every night, twice nightly in the summer. When not in Moscow, the troupe traveled extensively.
She'd visited nearly all of Russia and most of Europe, and
even New York City for a performance at Madison Square
Garden. There was little time for male companionship beyond an occasional dinner or a conversation during a long
plane or train ride.

She was a year shy of thirty and wondered if marriage
would ever come. Her father had always hoped she'd settle
down, give up performing, and start a family. But she'd
watched what had happened to her friends who'd married.
Laboring all day at a factory or store, only to come home and
tend to the household, the process repeated interminably day
after day. There had been no equality between men and
women, though the Soviets had proudly proclaimed communist women the most liberated in the world. And little comfort

came in marriage. Husbands and wives usually worked separately, at different times, even vacationing separately since rarely were both simultaneously excused from their jobs. She understood why one in three marriages ended in divorce. Why most couples birthed only one child. There was no time or money to cope with anything more. Such a life had never appealed to her. As her grandmother used to say, *To know a person, you have to eat salt together.*

She took her place before the mirror and squirted water into her hair, tightening the damp braids into a bun. She wore little makeup on stage, just enough to abate the harsh, blue-white floods. She was pale-skinned, having inherited an almost total lack of pigment, blond hair, and stark blue eyes from her Slavic mother. Her talent came from her father. He'd worked as an aerialist with the circus for decades. Luckily, his abilities had translated into a larger apartment, more food rations, and a better clothing allowance. Thank goodness the arts had always been an important element of communist propaganda. The circus, along with the ballet and opera, had been exported for decades—an attempt to show the world that Hollywood did not hold a monopoly on fun.

Now the entire troupe was a moneymaking proposition. The circus was owned by a Moscow conglomerate that continued to parade the spectacle across the globe, the difference being that profit was the goal instead of propaganda. She actually earned a decent salary for somebody living in post-Soviet Russia. But the minute she could no longer dazzle an audience from the balance beam she would most likely find herself among the millions of unemployed. Which was why she kept her body in excellent shape, watched her diet carefully, and regulated her sleep habits precisely. Last night had been the first night in quite a while she hadn't slept a full eight hours.

She thought again of Miles Lord.

Earlier, at her apartment, she'd opened the briefcase. She recalled him removing some papers, but was hoping there might be something that might shed insight into a man she found fascinating. There'd been nothing beyond a blank pad, three ballpoint pens, a few cards from the hotel Volkhov, and an Aeroflot ticket for yesterday from Moscow to St. Petersburg.

Miles Lord. American lawyer with the Tsarist Commission.

Maybe she'd see him again.

LORD SAT PATIENTLY THROUGH THE ENTIRE FIRST HALF OF THE show. No *militsya* had followed him inside—at least no uniformed policemen—and he hoped no plainclothed men were around. The arena was impressive, an indoor amphitheater rising in a half circle around a colorful stage. Padded red benches accommodated what he estimated to be a couple of thousand people, mainly tourists and children, all sitting close, sharing in the emotion radiating from the performers' faces. The surroundings bordered on the surreal, and the trampolinists, trained dogs, trapeze artists, clowns, and jugglers had, at least for a while, taken his mind off the situation.

Intermission came and he decided to stay in his seat. The less moving around, the better. He was only a few rows from the main floor, in a direct line of sight with the ring, and he hoped that when Akilina Petrovna appeared she would see him.

A bell dinged and an announcer noted that the second half would start in five minutes. His gaze circled the expansive arena one more time.

A face registered.

The man was perched on the far side, dressed in a dark

leather jacket and jeans. It was the man in the baggy beige suit from the St. Petersburg archives yesterday and the train last night. He was nestled amid a group of tourists who were busily grabbing a few last photos before the start of the show.

Lord's heart raced. His gut went hollow.

Then he saw Droopy.

The demon entered from the left, between Lord and his other problem. The dark hair shone with oily dressing, pulled tight in a ponytail. He wore a tan sweater over dark trousers.

As the lights came down and music blared for the second act, Lord stood to leave. But at the top of the aisle, no more than fifty feet away, stood Cro-Magnon, a smile on his pock-marked face.

Lord sat. Nowhere to go.

The first act was Akilina Petrovna, who bounded onto the stage barefoot, wearing a sequined blue leotard. She skipped to the lively beat of the music and quickly mounted the beam, starting her act to applause.

A wave of panic swelled inside him. He glanced back and saw that Cro-Magnon was still at the top of the aisle, but then he spotted the deeply lined gray slab face of Droopy, the demon now sitting about halfway down. Coal-black eyes—Gypsy eyes, he concluded—focused with a look that signaled the end of a hunt. The man's right hand nestled inside his jacket, which he peeled back enough to exhibit the hilt of a gun.

He turned back toward the stage.

Akilina Petrovna was strutting across the beam in an amazing display of poise. The music softened and she kept step to the gentle beat with agile movements. He focused hard, willing her to glance his way.

And she did.

For an instant their eyes met and he caught a glint of recognition. Then he registered something else. Fear? Did she likewise recognize the men behind him? Or did she read the terror in his own gaze? If she realized any of that, she did not let it affect her concentration. She continued to impress the crowd with a slow, athletic dance while perched atop a four-inch oak beam.

She performed a one-handed pirouette, then leapt from the beam. The crowd applauded as clowns burst onto the stage riding tiny bicycles. As stagehands carted away the heavy balance beam, Lord decided he had no choice. He bolted from his seat and sprang onto the stage, just as one of the clowns rode by, honking a horn. The crowd roared with laughter, thinking him part of the show. He glanced left and saw both Droopy and the man from St. Petersburg rise. He slipped behind the curtain and ran straight into Akilina Petrovna.

"I've got to get out of here," he told her in Russian.

She grabbed his hand and yanked him deeper backstage, past two animal cages holding white poodles.

"I saw the men. You seem to stay in trouble, Miles Lord."

"Tell me about it."

They passed more performers busily going about their preparations. No one seemed to pay them any attention. "I need to duck in somewhere," he said. "We can't keep running."

She led him down a hallway crowded with old posters tacked to a dirty wall. A sour whiff of urine and wet fur tempered the air. Doors lined the narrow corridor on both sides.

She twisted one of the knobs. "In here."

It was a closet that contained mops and brooms, but there was enough room for him to squeeze inside.

"Stay here until I come back," she said.

The door closed.

In the blackness, he tried to catch his breath. Footsteps passed outside in both directions. He couldn't believe this was happening. The policeman outside must have alerted Feliks Orleg. Droopy, Cro-Magnon, and Orleg were all connected. No doubt about it. What was he going to do? Half the job of any good lawyer was telling his client what a damn fool he or she was being. He should take his own advice. He needed to get the hell out of Russia.

The door swung open.

In the hall light, he registered three male faces.

The first he did not recognize, but the man held a long silver blade tight against Droopy's neck. The other face belonged to the man from yesterday in St. Petersburg. He was clutching a revolver, its barrel aimed straight at him.

Then Lord saw Akilina Petrovna.

She stood calmly beside the man with the gun.

PART
TWO

21

"WHO ARE YOU?" LORD ASKED.

The man standing beside Akilina said, "There is no time to explain, Mr. Lord. We need to leave here quickly."

He was not persuaded.

"We do not know how many more are here. We are not your enemy, Mr. Lord. He is." The man motioned toward Droopy.

"A bit hard to believe with a gun pointed at me."

The man lowered the revolver. "Quite right. Now, we must go. My associate will deal with this man while we take our leave."

He stared at Akilina and asked, "You with him?"

She shook her head.

"We must go, Mr. Lord," the man said.

His expression telegraphed to her, *Should we?*

"I think so," she said.

He decided to trust her instincts. His hadn't been so good lately. "All right."

The man turned to his associate and spat out something in a dialect Lord did not recognize. Droopy was forcibly led down the hall toward a door at the far end.

"This way," the man said.

"Why does she have to come?" he asked, motioning to Akilina. "She has no involvement."

"I was instructed to bring her."

"By whom?"

"We can talk about this on the way. Right now we have to leave."

He decided not to argue any further.

They followed the man outside into the cold night, stopping only to allow Akilina to retrieve a pair of shoes and a coat. The exit opened into an alley behind the theater. Droopy was being stuffed into the backseat of a black Ford near the alley's end. Their host walked to a light-colored Mercedes, opened the rear door, and invited them inside. Then he climbed into the front seat. Another man was already behind the wheel, the engine idling. A light rain started to fall as they left the theater.

"Who are you?" Lord asked again.

The man did not reply. Instead he handed him a business card.

SEMYON PASHENKO

Professor of History
Moscow State University

He was beginning to understand. "So my meeting him was not coincidental?"

"Hardly. Professor Pashenko realized the great danger both of you were in and directed us to keep watch. That was what I was doing in St. Petersburg. Apparently, I did not do a good job."

"I thought you were with the others."

The man nodded. "I can see that, but the professor instructed me only to make contact when forced. What was about to happen back in the theater, I think, would qualify."

The car wove through heavy evening traffic, its windshield wipers clunking back and forth, not doing much good. They were headed south, past the Kremlin, toward Gorky

Park and the river. Lord noticed the driver's interest in cars around him and surmised that the many turns were designed to avoid any tails that might be lurking.

"You think we're safe?" Akilina whispered.

"I hope so."

"You know this Pashenko?"

He nodded. "But that means nothing. Hard to know anybody around here." Then he added with a weak smile, "Present company excepted, of course."

Their route had taken them away from the blocks of anonymous high-rises and neoclassical oddities, the hundreds of apartment buildings little more than *trushchaba*—slums—and life there, he knew, was a tense daily grind, noisy and crowded. But not everyone lived that way, and he noticed they'd turned onto one of the unobtrusive, tree-lined streets that radiated from the busy boulevard. This one ran north toward the Kremlin, linking two of the ring roads.

The Mercedes veered right into a lighted asphalt lot. A guard watched the entrance from a glass booth. The three-story apartment building beyond was unusual, fashioned not of concrete but of honey-colored bricks laid straight and true, a rarity for Russian masons. The few cars in the lined spaces were foreign and expensive. The man in the passenger's seat pointed a controller and commanded a garage door to rise. The driver steered the Mercedes inside, and the paneled door rolled shut.

They were led into a spacious lobby lit by a crystal chandelier. The smell was pine, not the horrid scent of mud and urine most apartment lobbies wafted—*The smell of cats,* one Moscow journalist had called it. A carpeted stairway led up to a third-floor apartment.

Semyon Pashenko answered a light knock on a white paneled door and invited them inside.

Lord quickly took in the parquet floor, Oriental rugs, brick fireplace, and Scandinavian furniture. Luxuries in both the Soviet Union and new Russia. The walls were a soothing beige, broken periodically by elegantly framed prints depicting Siberian wildlife. The air smelled of boiled cabbage and potatoes. "You live well, Professor."

"A gift from my father. To my dismay, he was a devoted communist and afforded the privilege of rank. I inherited the amenity and was allowed to purchase it when the government started divesting. Thankfully, I had the rubles."

Lord turned in the center of the room and faced his host. "I guess we should thank you."

Pashenko raised his hands. "No need. In fact, it is us who owe you thanks."

Lord was puzzled, but said nothing.

Pashenko motioned to upholstered chairs. "Why don't we sit. I have dinner warming in the kitchen. Some wine, perhaps?"

He glanced at Akilina, who shook her head. "No, thank you."

Pashenko noticed Akilina's costume and told one of the men to fetch her a bathrobe. They sat before a fire and Lord removed his jacket.

"I chop the wood at my *dacha* north of Moscow," Pashenko said. "I so like a fire, though this apartment is centrally heated."

Another Russian rarity, he thought. He also noticed the driver of the Mercedes take up a position at one of the windows, periodically peeking out through the closed curtains. The man peeled off his coat, exposing a handgun nestled in a shoulder harness.

"Who are you, Professor?" Lord asked.

"I am a Russian who is glad for the future."

"Could we dispense with the riddles? I'm tired, and it's been a long three days."

Pashenko bowed his head in an apparent apology. "From all reports, I agree. The incident in Red Square made the news. Curious there was no mention of you in the official reports, but Vitaly"—Pashenko motioned to the man from yesterday in St. Petersburg—"saw it all. The police arrived just in time."

"Your man was there?"

"He went to St. Petersburg to make sure your train ride was uneventful. But the same two gentlemen with whom you are, by now, intimately familiar interfered."

"How did he find me?"

"He saw you and Miss Petrovna together and watched while you jumped from the train. Another man with him followed your actions farther down the tracks and found you at the grocery using the telephone."

"What about my bodyguard?"

"We thought he might work for the *mafiya*. Now we are sure."

"Could I ask why I am involved?" Akilina said.

Pashenko leveled a gaze at her. "You involved yourself, my dear."

"I involved nothing. Mr. Lord happened into my compartment on the train last night. That's all."

Pashenko straightened in the chair. "I, too, was curious of your involvement. So I took the liberty of checking on you today. We have extensive contacts in the government."

Akilina's face tightened. "I don't appreciate you invading my privacy."

Pashenko gave a short laugh. "That is a concept we Russians know little of, my dear. Let's see. You were born here in Moscow. Your parents divorced when you were twelve. Since neither one of them could receive Soviet permission for another apartment, they were forced to live together afterward. Granted, their accommodations were a bit better than most, given your father's usefulness to the state as a performer, but it was nonetheless a stressful situation. By the way, I saw your father perform several times. He was a marvelous acrobat."

She acknowledged the compliment with a nod.

"Your father became involved with a Romanian national who was associated with the circus. She became pregnant, but returned home with the child. Your father tried to obtain an exit visa, but the authorities denied his requests. The communists were not in the habit of allowing their performers to leave. When he tried to leave without permission, he was detained and sent to a camp.

"Your mother remarried, but that marriage ended quickly in divorce. When she couldn't find a place to live after the second divorce—apartments were quite scarce, I remember well—she was forced to once again live with your father. By then, the authorities had decided to release him from the camp. So there, in that tiny apartment, the two of them languished in separate rooms until both died an early death. Quite a statement for our 'people's republic,' wouldn't you say?"

Akilina said nothing, but Lord could feel the pain radiating from her eyes.

"I lived with my grandmother in the country," she said to Pashenko, "so I didn't have to see my parents' torment. I didn't even talk with them the last three years. They died bitter, angry, and alone."

"Were you there when the Soviets took your grandmother away?" Pashenko asked.

She shook her head. "By then I had been placed in the special performers' school. I was told she died of old age. I only learned the truth later."

"You of all people should be a catalyst for change. Anything has to be better than what we had."

Lord felt for the woman sitting beside him. He wanted to assure her that things like that would never happen again. But that wouldn't be true. Instead, he asked, "Professor, do you know what's going on?"

A crease of concern laced the older man's face. "Yes, I do."

He waited for an explanation.

"Have you ever heard of the All-Russian Monarchist Assembly?" Semyon Pashenko asked.

Lord shook his head.

"I have," Akilina said. "They want to restore the tsar to power. After the Soviet fall, they used to hold big parties. I read about them in a magazine article."

He nodded. "They held big parties. Monstrous affairs with people dressed as nobles, Cossacks in tall hats, middle-aged men in White Army uniforms. All designed to garner publicity, to keep the tsarist issue alive in the hearts and minds of the people. They were once thought fanatics. Now, not so."

"I doubt that group could be credited with the national referendum on restoration," Akilina said.

"I would not be so sure. There was far more to the assembly than met the eye."

"Could you get to the point, Professor?" Lord asked.

Pashenko sat in an almost unnatural pose that communicated no emotion. "Mr. Lord, do you recall the Holy Band?"

"A group of noblemen who pledged their lives for the tsar's safety. Inept and cowardly. Not one of them was around when a bomb killed Alexander II in 1881."

"A later group took that same name," Pashenko said. "But I assure you, it was not inept. Instead, it survived Lenin, Stalin, and the Second World War. In fact, it still exists today. The public division is the All-Russian Monarchist Assembly. But there is also a private portion, which I head."

Lord's gaze tightened on Pashenko. "And the purpose of this Holy Band?"

"The safety of the tsar."

"But there hasn't been a tsar since 1918."

"But there has."

"What are you talking about?"

Pashenko's fingers templed at his lips. "In Alexandra's letter and Lenin's note, you found what we have been missing. I must confess that until the other day, when I read those words, I harbored my own doubts. But now I am sure. An heir survived Yekaterinburg."

Lord shook his head. "You can't be serious, Professor."

"I am. My group was formed shortly after July 1918. My uncle and great uncle were both members of that Holy Band. I was recruited decades ago and have now risen to its leadership. Our purpose is to guard the secret and implement its terms at the appropriate time. But thanks to the communist purges, many of our members died. To ensure security, the Originator made sure no one knew all of the secret's terms. So a large part of the message vanished, including the starting point. You have now rediscovered that beginning."

"What do you mean?"

"Do you still have the copies?"

He grabbed his jacket and handed Pashenko the folded sheets.

Pashenko motioned. "Here, in Lenin's note. 'The situation with Yurovsky is troubling. I do not believe the reports filed from Yekaterinburg were entirely accurate, and the information concerning Felix Yussoupov corroborates that. The mention of Kolya Maks is interesting. I have heard this name before. The village of Starodug has likewise been noted by two other similarly persuaded White Guardsmen.' The information we lost was the name—Kolya Maks—and the village—Starodug. It is the starting point of the quest."

"What quest?" he asked.

"To find Alexei and Anastasia."

Lord sat back in the chair. He was tired, but what this man was saying sent his mind reeling.

Pashenko went on, "When the royal Romanov bodies were finally exhumed in 1991 and later identified, we positively learned that two may have survived the massacre. The remains of Anastasia and Alexei have never been found to this day."

"Yurovsky claimed to have burned them separately," he said.

"What would you have claimed if you had been ordered to kill the imperial family and were two bodies short? You would lie because, otherwise, you would be shot for incompetence. Yurovsky told Moscow what they wanted to hear. But there are enough reports that have surfaced since the Soviet fall to cast great doubt on Yurovsky's declaration."

Pashenko was right. Affidavits gathered from Red Guardsmen and other participants attested that not everyone may have died that July night. Accounts varied from the bayoneting of moaning grand duchesses to the stabbing and rifle-butting of hysterical victims. There were many contradictions. But he also recalled the snippet of testimony he found, apparently from one of the Yekaterinburg guards, dated three months after the murders.

But I realized what was coming. The talk of their fate was clear. Yurovsky made sure we all understood the task at hand. After a while, I started saying to myself that something should be done to let them escape.

He pointed to the papers. "There's another sheet there, Professor. From one of the guards. I didn't show you. You may want to read it."

Pashenko shuffled through and read.

"This is consistent with other testimony," Pashenko said when he finished. "Great sympathy developed for the imperial family. Many of the guards hated them, stole what they could, but others felt differently. The Originator made use of that sympathy."

"Who is the Originator?" Akilina asked.

"Felix Yussoupov."

Lord was shocked. "The man who killed Rasputin?"

"The same." Pashenko shifted in the chair. "My father and uncle told me a story once. Something that happened at the Alexander Palace, in Tsarskoe Selo. It was passed down through the Holy Band, from the Originator himself. The date of the event is October 28, 1916."

Lord motioned to the letter Pashenko held. "That's the same date of that letter from Alexandra to Nicholas."

"Precisely. Alexei had suffered another hemophilic bout. The empress sent for Rasputin, and he came and eased the boy's suffering. Afterward, Alexandra broke down, and the *starets* berated her for not believing in both God and him. It was then that Rasputin prophesied that the one with the most guilt would see the error of his ways and assure that the blood of the imperial family resurrected itself. He also said only a raven and an eagle could succeed where all fail—"

"—and that the innocence of beasts will guard and lead the way, being the final arbiter of success," Lord said.

"The letter confirms the story I was told years ago. A letter you found hidden away in the state archives."

"So what does all this have to do with us?" he asked.

"Mr. Lord, you are the raven."

"Because I'm black?"

"In part. You are a rarity in this nation. But there is something more." Pashenko motioned to Akilina. "This beautiful lady. Your name, my dear, means 'eagle' in old Russian."

There was surprise on her face.

"Now you see why we are so curious. Only a raven and an eagle can succeed where all fail. The raven connects himself with the eagle. I am afraid, Miss Petrovna, you are a part of this whether you realize or not. That is why I had the circus watched. I was sure the two of you would reconnect. Your doing that is further confirmation of Rasputin's prophecy."

Lord almost laughed. "Rasputin was an opportunist. A corrupt peasant who manipulated the grief of a guilt-ridden tsarina. If not for the tsarevich's hemophilia, the *starets* could have never wormed his way into the imperial household."

"The fact remains Alexei was severely stricken and Rasputin could quell the attacks."

"We *know* now that a lowering of emotional stress can affect bleeding. Hypnosis has been used for some time on hemophiliacs. Stress affects blood flow and vascular wall strength. From everything I've read, Rasputin would simply calm the boy. He'd speak to him, tell him tales about Siberia, tell him everything was going to be fine. Alexei would usually drift off to sleep, which also helped."

"I, too, have read those explanations. But the fact remains Rasputin could affect the tsarevich. And he apparently foretold his own death weeks in advance, along with what would happen if royalty killed him. He also prophesied a resurrection. The one Felix Yussoupov implemented. Something the two of you are now part of completing."

Lord glanced over at Akilina. Her name and its linkage to him could be pure coincidence. Yet that coincidence was apparently decades in the making. *Only a raven and an eagle can succeed where all fail.* What was going on?

"Stefan Baklanov is unfit to rule this nation," Pashenko said. "He is a pompous fool with no ability to govern. It is only by a fluke of death that he is eligible. He will be easily manipulated, and I fear the Tsarist Commission will vest him with sweeping power—a gift the Duma will have no choice but to confirm. The people want a tsar, not a figurehead." Pashenko leveled his gaze. "Mr. Lord, I realize it is your task to support Baklanov's claim. But I believe there is a direct blood heir of Nicholas II out there. Precisely where, I have no idea. Only you and Miss Petrovna can learn that."

He sighed. "This is too much, Professor. Way too much."

A slight smile came onto the older man's face. "Understandable. But before I tell either of you any more, I am going into the kitchen to see about dinner. Why don't you talk in private. You have a decision to make."

"About what?" Akilina asked.

Pashenko rose from the chair. "Your future. And Russia's."

22

8:40 PM

HAYES LAY BACK AND GRIPPED THE IRON BAR ABOVE HIS head. He shoved the weights up from their cradle and sweated through ten presses, his biceps and shoulders aching from the stress. He was glad the Volkhov was equipped with a health club. Though pushing sixty, he was determined to surrender nothing to time. There was no reason he couldn't live another forty years. And he needed that time. There was so much to do, and only now was he in a position to succeed. After Stefan Baklanov's coronation, he'd be able to work at will and do what he wanted. He was already eyeing a lovely chalet in the Austrian Alps, a place where he could enjoy the outdoors, hunt, fish, and be the lord of his own manor. The thought was intoxicating. More than enough motivation to keep him moving forward, no matter what the task.

He finished another set of presses, grabbed a towel and patted moisture from his brow. He then left the exercise room and headed for the elevators.

Where was Lord? Why hadn't he called in? He'd told Orleg earlier that Lord may now doubt him. But he was not convinced. It could be that Lord assumed the hotel phones were being monitored. Lord knew enough about Russian paranoia to know how easy it would be for either the government or a private group to accomplish that task. That might explain why he hadn't heard from Lord since his abrupt departure from Feliks Orleg's office. But he could have called the firm in Atlanta and arranged for contact. Yet a check there not an hour before had revealed no calls had come through.

What a mess.

Miles Lord was becoming a real problem.

He stepped off the elevator into a wood-paneled lobby on the sixth floor. Every floor had one, a sitting area with magazines and newspapers. Filling two leather chairs were Brezhnev and Stalin. He was scheduled to meet with them and the rest of the Secret Chancellory in two hours at a villa south of town, so he wondered about their presence here and now.

"Gentlemen. To what do I owe this honor?"

Stalin stood. "There is a problem that requires action. We must talk, and you could not be located by telephone."

"As you can see, I was working up a sweat."

"Might we go to your room?" Brezhnev asked.

He led the way past the *dezhurnaya,* who did not look up from her magazine. When they were inside his room with the door locked, Stalin said, "Mr. Lord was located earlier at the circus. Our men tried to intercept him. One was disabled by Lord, the other by men who were apparently likewise searching. Our man had to kill his captor to escape."

"Who interfered?" Hayes asked.

"That is the problem. It is time you learn some things." Brezhnev sat forward in the chair. "There has long been speculation that some of the imperial family may have survived the death sentence the Soviets imposed in 1918. Your Mr. Lord came across some interesting material in the Protective Papers, information that we had not been privy to. We thought the matter at first serious, but containable. Now, such is not the case. The man Mr. Lord made contact with in Moscow is Semyon Pashenko. He is a professor of history at the university. But he also heads a group dedicated to tsarist restoration."

"How could that threaten what we have in motion?" Hayes asked.

Brezhnev sat back and Hayes took him in.

Vladimir Kulikov represented a large coalition of the country's new rich, the lucky few who'd managed to turn a tremendous profit since the fall of the Soviet Union. A short and serious man, his face was weather-beaten—like a peasant's, Hayes had often thought—his nose beaklike, the hair short, sparse, and gray. He gave off an air of superiority that often infuriated the other three in the Secret Chancellory.

The new rich were not particularly liked by the military or the government. Most were ex–party officials blessed with a web of connections—clever men who manipulated a chaotic system to their personal advantage. None of them worked hard. And many of the American businessmen Hayes represented financed them.

"Until his death," Brezhnev said, "Lenin was quite interested in what happened at Yekaterinburg. Stalin likewise was consumed, so much so that he sealed every piece of paper dealing with the Romanovs in the state archives. He then killed or banished to the camps anyone with knowledge. His fanaticism is one reason that learning anything firsthand is now so difficult. Stalin worried about a Romanov survivor, but twenty million deaths can stir up a lot of chaos, and no opposition to him ever collated. Pashenko's group is somehow connected with the possibility of one or more Romanov survivors. How, we're not sure. But there have been rumors for decades that a Romanov was hidden until the time was right to reveal his or her whereabouts."

Stalin said, "We now know that only two of the children could have survived, Alexei and Anastasia, since their bodies were never found. Of course, even if either or both survived the massacre they would have died long ago, the boy espe-cially because of his hemophilia. So we're talking about their children or grandchildren, if there were any. And they would be direct Romanov. Stefan Baklanov's claim would be mean-ingless."

Hayes saw concern on Stalin's face, but he couldn't be-lieve what he was hearing. "There's no way any of those people survived. They were shot at close range, then bayo-neted."

Stalin ran a hand along the armchair, tracing the wood carvings. "I told you at our last meeting, Americans have a hard time understanding the Russian sensitivity to fate. Here is an example. There are Soviet documents I have seen where the KGB conducted interrogations. Rasputin pre-dicted that Romanov blood would be resurrected. He sup-posedly said that an eagle and a raven would accomplish the resurrection. Your Mr. Lord found a writing that confirms this prediction." He leaned forward. "Would not Mr. Lord qualify as that raven?"

"Because he's black?"

Stalin shrugged. "As good a reason as any."

He couldn't believe a man with Stalin's reputation was trying to convince him that a scoundrel peasant from the early part of the twentieth century had somehow predicted the reemergence of the Romanov dynasty. And, even more, an African American from South Carolina was somehow a part of all that. "I may not understand your sensitivity to fate, but I fully understand common sense. This is crap."

"Semyon Pashenko doesn't think so," Brezhnev was quick to say. "He stationed men at the circus for a reason, and he was right. Lord showed up. Our men reported that a circus performer was on the train last night. A woman. Ak-ilina Petrovna. They even talked with her and thought noth-ing of it at the time, but she was led from the theater with

Lord and driven off by Pashenko's men. Why, if there is nothing to this but fiction?"

A good question, Hayes silently admitted.

Stalin's face was severe. "*Akilina* means 'eagle' in old Russian. You speak our language. Did you know that?"

He shook his head.

"This is serious," Stalin said. "There are things at work we really do not fully understand. Until a few months ago, when the referendum passed, no one seriously thought a tsarist return possible, much less one that could be used for political advantage. But now both are possible. We must stop whatever is happening immediately, before it can gestate into something more. Use the telephone number we provided, assemble the men, and find your Mr. Lord."

"It's already being done."

"Do more."

"Why not do it yourself?"

"Because you have freedom of movement none of us enjoys. This task is yours to handle. It might even move beyond our borders."

"Orleg is looking for Lord right now."

"Perhaps a police bulletin regarding the Red Square shooting could multiply the number of eyes," Brezhnev said. "A policeman was killed. The *militsya* would be anxious to find the gunman. They might even solve our problem with a well-placed shot."

23

Lord said, "I'm sorry about what happened to your parents."

Akilina had been sitting still, eyes down, since Pashenko had left the room.

"My father wanted to be with his son. He intended on marrying the mother, but to emigrate you must secure permission of your parents—an absurd Soviet rule that stopped anyone from leaving. My grandmother, of course, gave her consent, but my grandfather had been missing since World War Two."

"Yet your father still had to have his okay?"

She nodded. "He was never declared dead. None of the missing ever were. No father, no permission, no visa. The repercussions came fast. My father was dropped from the circus and not allowed to perform anywhere. It was all he knew how to do."

"Why didn't you see them the last few years?"

"Neither could be tolerated. All my mother could see was another woman who'd birthed her ex-husband's baby. All he could see was somebody who'd left him for another man. Their duty was to endure the situation for the collective good." The resentment was clear now. "They sent me to my grandmother. I hated them at first for doing it, but as I got older I simply could not stand to be around either of them, so I stayed away. They died within a few months of each other. Simple flu that became pneumonia. I often won-der if my fate will be the same. When I can no longer please the crowds, where will I end up?"

He didn't know what to say.

"It is hard for Americans to understand how things were. How they still are, to some extent. You could not live where you wanted, do what you wanted. Our choices were made for us early in life."

He knew what she was referring to, the *raspredeleniye*. Distribution. A decision made at age sixteen as to what a person was to do with the rest of his or her life. Those with clout possessed a choice. Those without took what was available. Those in disfavor did what they were told.

"Party members' children were always looked after," she said. "They got the best assignments in Moscow. That was where everyone wanted to be."

"Except you?"

"I hated it. There was nothing but misery here for me. But I was compelled to return. My talents were needed by the state."

"You didn't want to perform?"

"Did you know what you wanted to do for the rest of your life at age sixteen?"

He silently conceded her point.

"Several of my friends chose suicide. Far preferable to spending the rest of your life at the Arctic Circle or in some remote Siberian village doing something you de-spise. I had a friend from school who wanted to be a doc-tor. She was an excellent student, but lacked the requisite party affiliation to be selected for university. Others of far less ability were allowed to attend over her. She ended up working in a toy factory." She stared at him hard. "You are lucky, Miles Lord. When you get old or disabled, there are government benefits to help. We have no such thing. The communists spoke of the tsar and his extravagance. They were no better."

He was beginning to understand even more the Russian preference for the distant past.

"I told you on the train about my grandmother. It was all true. She was taken off one night and never seen again. She worked in a state store and watched while managers pilfered the shelves, blaming the thefts on others. She finally wrote a letter to Moscow, complaining. She was fired, her pension canceled, her work papers stamped with the badge of an informant. No one would hire her. So she took up verse. Her crime was poetry."

He tilted his head to one side. "What do you mean?"

"She liked to write about the Russian winter, hunger, and the cries of children. How the government was indifferent to common people. The local party Soviet considered that a threat to national order. She became noticed—an individual rising above the community. That was her crime. She might become a rallying point for opposition. Someone who could galvanize support. So she was made to disappear. We are perhaps the only country in the world that executed its poets."

"Akilina, I can understand the hatred all of you have for the communists. But there needs to be an element of reality here. Before 1917 the tsar was a fairly inept leader who didn't necessarily care if his police killed civilians. Hundreds died on Bloody Sunday in 1905 merely for protesting his policies. It was a brutal regime that used force to survive, just like the communists."

"The tsar represents a link with our heritage. One that stretches back hundreds of years. He is the embodiment of Russia."

He sat back in the chair and took a few deep breaths. He studied the fire in the hearth and listened as the wood crackled into flames. "Akilina, he wants us to go after this supposed heir, who may or may not be alive. And all because some faith-healing idiot, nearly a century ago, predicted we would."

"I want to go."

He stared at her. "Why?"

"Since we met, I have felt strange. As if it was meant that you and I would connect. There was no fear when you entered my compartment, and I never once questioned my decision to let you spend the night. Something inside told me to do it. I also knew I would see you again."

He wasn't as mystical as this attractive Russian seemed to be. "My father was a preacher. He traveled from town to town lying to people. He loved to scream the word of God, but all he did was take advantage of people's poverty and play off their fears. He was the most unholy man I ever knew. Cheated on his wife, his kids, and his God."

"But he fathered you."

"He was there when my mother conceived, but he didn't father me. I raised myself."

She motioned to her chest. "He is still inside. Whether you want to admit it or not."

No, he didn't want to admit that. At one point, years ago, he'd seriously considered changing his last name. Only his mother's pleas had stopped him. "You realize, Akilina, this could all be made up."

"For what purpose? You have wondered for days why men are trying to kill you. This professor has provided an answer."

"Let them go find this Romanov survivor themselves. They have my information."

"Rasputin said only you and I could succeed."

He shook his head. "You don't really believe that?"

"I don't know what to believe. My grandmother told me, when I was a child, that she saw good things for me in life. Maybe she was right."

Not necessarily the answer he wanted, but there was something inside nudging him forward, too. If nothing else, this so-called quest would get him out of Moscow, away from Droopy and Cro-Magnon. And he couldn't deny being fascinated by the whole thing. Pashenko was right. There were an awful lot of coincidences that had come together over the past few days. He didn't for one minute believe Gregorii Rasputin had been able to predict the future, but he was intrigued by Felix Yussoupov's involvement. *The Originator,* Pashenko had called him, almost with reverence.

He recalled the man's history. Yussoupov was a bisexual transvestite who had murdered Rasputin out of a false belief that the fate of a nation rested on what he did. He took an almost perverse pride in his accomplishment and basked in the limelight of that foolish act for fifty years thereafter. He was another hypocritical showboat, a dangerous and malevolent fraud, like Rasputin and like Lord's own father. Yet Yussoupov was apparently involved in something that bespoke unselfishness.

"All right, Akilina. We'll do it. Why not? What else have I to do?" He glanced over at the kitchen door as Semyon Pashenko stepped back into the den.

"I just received some disturbing news," the older man said. "One of our associates, the one who carted away the man at the circus, did not show up at the assigned location with his prisoner. He's been found dead."

Droopy had escaped. Not a comforting prospect.

"I'm sorry," Akilina said. "He saved our lives."

Pashenko looked listless. "He knew the risks when he joined our Holy Band. He is not the first to die for this cause."

The older man sat down in a chair, a tired look in his eyes. "And will probably not be the last."

"We've decided," Lord said, "to do it."

"I thought you might. But do not forget what Rasputin said. *Twelve must die before the search is complete.*"

Lord wasn't necessarily concerned about any hundred-year-old prophecy. Mystics had been wrong before. Droopy and Cro-Magnon, though, were real, their threat immediate.

"You realize, Mr. Lord," Pashenko said, "that you were the object of the killing on Nikolskaya Prospekt four days ago, not Artemy Bely. Men are after you. Men whom I suspect already know some of what we know. These men will want to stop you."

"I assume," Lord said, "no one will know where we're going except you?"

"That's right. And it will stay that way. Only you, I, and Miss Petrovna know the details of the starting point."

"That's not entirely true. The man I work for knows of Alexandra's writing. But I don't see how he would connect any of this. And if he did, he would tell no one."

"Do you have any reason not to trust your employer?"

"I showed him that stuff two weeks ago and he never said a word about it. I don't think he even gave it much thought." He shifted in his seat. "Okay, since we've agreed to do it, how about explaining the *more* you alluded to earlier."

Pashenko sat up, emotion returning to his face. "The Originator set the search up in steps, each independent of the other. If the right person, with the right words, appeared at each step, information for the next would be provided. Only Yussoupov knew the entire plan and, if he is to be believed, he told no one.

"We now know that somewhere in the village of Starodug is the first leg. I checked after our talk a few days ago. Kolya Maks was one of Nicholas's palace guards who turned, after the revolution, to the Bolsheviks. By the time of the Romanov murders he was a member of the Ural Soviet. In the revolution's infancy, before Moscow asserted dominant control, local soviets ruled their respective geographic areas. So the Ural Soviet controlled the tsar's fate far more than the Kremlin. The Ural region was staunchly anti-tsarist. They wanted Nicholas dead from the first day he set foot in Yekaterinburg."

"I recall all that," Lord said, thinking about the peace treaty Lenin had signed in March 1918 that removed Russia from World War I. "Lenin thought he was rid of the Germans. Hell, he practically begged for peace. The terms were so humiliating one of the Russian generals shot himself after the signing ceremony. Then the German ambassador was assassinated in Moscow on July 6, 1918. Lenin now faced the possibility of another German invasion. So he planned to use the Romanovs as a bargaining chip, thinking the kaiser cared enough to actually want them, especially Alexandra, who was a German-born princess."

"But the Germans did not want any Romanovs," Pashenko said. "That's when the family became a liability. So the Ural Soviet was ordered to kill them. Kolya Maks may have been part of that. He may even have been present at the execution."

"Professor, that man is surely dead," Akilina said. "Too many years have passed."

"But it was his duty to make sure the information survived. We must assume Maks stayed faithful to his oath."

Lord was perplexed. "Why don't you just go yourself and find Maks? I understand you didn't have the name until now, but why do we have to do it?"

"The Originator made sure that only the raven and the eagle could be given the information. Even if I went, or sent someone else, the information would not be passed on. We must respect Rasputin's prophecy. The *starets* said only you could succeed where all others fail. I, too, must stay faithful to my oath, and respect what the Originator designed."

Lord searched his mind for more details about Felix Yussoupov. The family was one of the wealthiest in Russia, and Felix had only inherited the family reins when his older brother was killed in a duel. He'd been a disappointment from birth. His mother had wanted a girl and to console herself she kept him in long hair and dresses until he was five.

"Wasn't Yussoupov fascinated by Rasputin?" he asked.

Pashenko nodded. "Some biographers even suggest a homosexual link, one Rasputin may have rejected, which might have led to Yussoupov's resentment. His wife was Nicholas II's favorite niece, regarded as perhaps the most eligible young woman in Russia. He possessed a deep loyalty to Nicholas, and thought it his duty to rid the tsar of the threatening influence of Rasputin. It was a misguided belief, encouraged by other nobles who resented the *starets*'s position at court."

"I never regarded Yussoupov as particularly intelligent. Much more a follower than a leader."

"That may have been intentional. In fact, it is our belief that is precisely the case." Pashenko paused. "Now that you have agreed, I can tell you more of the information passed down to me. My great-uncle and uncle both harbored their portion of the secret until death. It is the words that must be uttered to the next person in the chain, which I now believe is Kolya Maks, or his successor. *He that endureth to the end shall be saved.*"

Lord thought immediately of his father. "From the gospel of Matthew."

Pashenko nodded. "Those words should gain access to the second part of the journey."

"You realize that this all could be a wild goose chase," Lord declared.

"I no longer think so. Both Alexandra and Lenin mentioned the same information. Alexandra penned her letter in 1916, describing the incident with Rasputin that the Originator independently passed to us. Lenin, six years later, wrote what was learned from a tortured White Guardsman. He specifically noted Maks's name. No. There is something in Starodug. Something Lenin could not discover. After his stroke in 1922, Lenin more or less retired and lost his zeal. By 1924 he was dead. Four years later Stalin sealed everything, and it stayed sealed until 1991. *The Romanov business,* Stalin called it. He forbade anyone to even speak of the imperial family. So no one ever followed Yussoupov's trail, if anyone even realized there was a trail to follow."

"As I recall," Lord said, "Lenin didn't necessarily consider the tsar a rallying point for opposition. By 1918 the Romanovs were discredited. 'Nicholas the Bloody' and all that. The disinformation campaign the communists waged against the imperials was quite successful."

Pashenko nodded. "Some of the tsar and tsarina's writings were first published then. All Lenin's idea. That way the people could read firsthand how indifferent their royal family had become. Of course, the published material was selective and heavily edited. It was also designed to send a message abroad. Lenin hoped the kaiser might want Alexandra back. He thought perhaps dangling her fate might ensure German compliance with the peace treaty, or perhaps a way to bargain a return of Russian prisoners of war. But the Germans possessed an extensive spy network throughout Russia, particularly in the Ural region, so I imagine they knew that the entire imperial family was murdered in July 1918. Lenin was, in essence, bargaining with corpses."

"What of all the stories about the tsarina and her daughters surviving?"

"More disinformation put out by the Soviets. Lenin was unsure how the world would view the murdering of women and children. Moscow tried hard to paint what happened as a valid execution carried out in heroic fashion. So the communists invented a story that the female Romanovs were taken off and died later in a White Army battle. Lenin thought disinformation would keep the Germans guessing. Once he saw that no one cared for any Romanov, regardless of sex or age, the pretense was dropped."

"Yet the disinformation remained."

Pashenko grinned. "Some of that our Holy Band must take credit for. My predecessors did an excellent job of misdirection. Part of the Originator's plan was to keep the Soviets guessing and the world wondering. Though I am not certain, I believe the entire Anna Anderson affair was a Yussoupov creation. He sent her to perpetuate a hoax, which the world readily accepted."

"Until DNA testing came along and proved her a fraud."

"But that was only recently. My guess is, Yussoupov taught her all the details she would need. The rest was her own magnificent performance."

"That was all part of this?"

"And much more, Mr. Lord. Yussoupov lived until 1967 and personally assured that his plan worked. The disinformation was not only to keep the Soviets off guard, but also to keep the surviving Romanovs in line. They could never be sure if a direct heir survived, so no one faction ever had complete control over the family. Anna Anderson played her role so well that even a lot of the Romanovs swore under oath she was Anastasia. Yussoupov was brilliant in what he conceived. After a while, pretenders emerged everywhere. There were books, movies, court fights. The deception took on a life of its own."

"All to guard the real secret."

"Correct. Since Yussoupov's death the responsibility has fallen to others, myself included, but because of Soviet travel restrictions it was difficult to ensure success. Maybe God shines upon us with your appearance." Pashenko stared hard. "I am glad you decided to do this, Mr. Lord. This nation needs your service."

"I'm not sure how much service I'll be."

The older man looked at Akilina. "And you, too, my dear." Pashenko sat back in the chair. "Now, a few more details. Rasputin's prophecy foretells that beasts will be involved—how, I could not begin to say. And that God will provide a way to ensure the righteousness of the claim. This could be a reference to DNA testing. It can surely be used here to verify the authenticity of any person you locate. This is not Lenin's or Yussoupov's day. Science can help."

The apartment's serenity had calmed his nerves, and Lord was becoming too tired to think. Also, the aroma of cabbage and potatoes was inviting. "Professor, I'm starved."

"Of course. The men who brought you are preparing everything." Pashenko turned toward Akilina. "While we eat, I will send them to your apartment to retrieve what you might need. I would recommend securing your passport, because there is no indication where this quest might lead. Also, we have contacts within the organization that owns the circus. I will arrange a leave that will not jeopardize your career. If this turns out to be nothing, at least your job will be waiting."

"Thank you."

"What about your things, Mr. Lord?"

"I'll give the men my hotel key. They can bring my suitcase. I also need to get a message to my boss, Taylor Hayes."

"I would not recommend that. The prophecy speaks of secrecy and I believe we should respect that."

"But Taylor might be able to help."

"You require no help."

He was too tired to argue. Besides, Pashenko was probably right. The fewer who knew his destination, the better. He could always call Hayes later.

"You can sleep here tonight in safety," Pashenko said, "and start your quest tomorrow."

24

LORD DROVE THE BATTERED LADA DOWN A STRETCH OF TWO-lane highway. Pashenko had provided the vehicle along with a full tank of gas and five thousand U.S. dollars. Lord had asked for American currency rather than rubles since Pashenko had been right last night—there was no telling where this journey would lead. He still thought the entire venture a waste of time, but he felt 1,000 percent better now that he was five hours south of Moscow, motoring through the wooded terrain of southwestern Russia.

He was dressed in jeans and a sweater, Pashenko's men having retrieved his suitcase from the Volkhov without a problem. He was rested, and a hot shower and shave had done wonders. Akilina looked refreshed as well. Pashenko's men had obtained her clothes along with her passport and exit visa. To facilitate their extensive travel schedule, all of the circus performers were issued visas with no expiration date.

She'd sat quiet for most of the trip. She wore an olive mock turtleneck shirt, jeans, and suede pea coat—an outfit, she explained, bought in Munich the year before. Dark colors and a conservative tone fit her well. High lapels accented her thin shoulders and threw off an Annie Hall look that Lord liked.

Through the windshield he saw fields and forests. The soil was black, nothing like the red clay of northern Georgia. Potatoes were the region's claim to fame. He recalled with amusement the tale of Peter the Great, who'd decreed that the strange plant be grown by peasants of the area. *Apples of the earth,* Peter had called them. But potatoes were foreign to Russia and the tsar failed to say which part of the plant needed to be harvested. When, in desperation, they tried to eat every part except the root, the peasants became ill. Angry and disappointed, they burned the entire crop. It was only when someone tasted the charred inside of the root that the plant acquired a home.

Their route took them through several dismal unhealthy meccas for metal smelting and tractor production. The air was a bitter smog of carbon and acid, everything filthy with soot. The whole area had once been a battleground. Pagans resisting Christians, princes vying for power, Tatars seeking conquest. A place where, as one writer had said, *Russian earth drank Russian blood.*

Starodug was a slender strip of a town oozing an imperial feel from colonnaded shops and wood and brick buildings. White-barked birch trees lined the streets, its center dominated by a three-spired church topped with midnight-blue onion domes and gold stars that glistened in the last rays of a setting sun. A sickening feeling of decay permeated the place—clear from structures teetering in disrepair, pavement crumbling, and green space in need of attention.

"Any suggestions on finding Kolya Maks?" he asked Akilina as they idled down one of the streets.

She motioned ahead. "I don't think that will be a problem."

He stared out the dirty windshield and saw a sign for the Kafe Snezhinki—cakes, meat pies, and ice cream noted as specialties on the storefront sign. The establishment consumed the ground floor of a three-story brick building with gaily carved window frames. Also on the sign he saw—IOSIF MAKS, OWNER.

"That's unusual," he said.

Russians didn't generally advertise ownership. He glanced around and noticed few other store signs, none with names. He recalled Nevsky Prospekt in St. Petersburg and the Arabat section of Moscow. Both trendy spots where hundreds of high-priced boutiques lined the street for miles in a commercial can-can. Only a few of those shops displayed prices, much less ownership.

"An omen of the times, perhaps," Akilina said. "Capitalism creeping upon us. Even here, in rural Russia." A smile noted that she was kidding.

He parked the Lada and they climbed out into fading darkness. He led the way back to the Kafe Snezhinki. The sidewalk was empty except for a dog chasing a fleeing magpie. Few retail shops were lit. Outside of metropolitan regions Russian stores were only rarely open on the weekend. More remnants, he knew, of a Bolshevik past.

The café was sparsely decorated. Four rows of tables dotted the center. Glass cases held the day's food assortment. An aroma of bitter coffee filled the air. Three people sat at one table, a solo at another. No one seemed to pay them any attention, though he wondered how many black men appeared here on a given day.

The man behind the glass cases was short and stout with bushy copper hair and a shaggy mustache and beard to match. He wore an apron smeared with an assortment of stains and, as he approached, a smell of feta cheese came with him. He was wringing his hands dry with a dirty towel.

"You Iosif Maks?" Lord asked in Russian.

A strange look came back.

"Where are you from?" the man said in Russian.

He decided the less information the better. "Why does that matter?"

"Because you're in my store asking questions. Talking like a Russian."

"Then I assume you're Iosif Maks?"

"State your business."

The tone was gruff and unfriendly, and he wondered if the reason was prejudice or ignorance. "Look, Mr. Maks, we're not here to cause trouble. We're looking for a man named Kolya Maks. He's probably long dead, but would you know if any of his relatives still live here?"

The man's gaze was tight. "Who are you?"

"My name is Miles Lord. This is Akilina Petrovna. We've come from Moscow looking for Kolya Maks."

The big man tossed the towel aside and clasped his arms around his chest. "There are a lot of Makses living around here. I know of no Kolya."

"He would have lived here in Stalin's day, but his children or grandchildren might still be around."

"I am a Maks by my mother and have never been close with any of them."

"Then why is your last name Maks?" he quickly asked.

A flustered look crept onto the Russian's face. "I have no time for this. I have customers."

Akilina moved close to the glass counter. "Mr. Maks, this is important. We are in need of Kolya Maks's relatives. Could you not tell us if they live here?"

"What makes you think they live here?"

Lord heard footsteps behind him and turned as a tall policeman entered the café, dressed in the rural uniform of the *militsya,* his head covered with a blue fur *shlapa*. He unbuttoned and removed his greatcoat, then sat at one of the tables, waving at Iosif Maks. The proprietor understood and busily went about preparing a coffee. Lord moved close to the counter. The policeman made him nervous. He kept his voice low as he spoke to Maks's back.

"He that endureth to the end shall be saved."

Maks's head swiveled around. "What does that mean?"

"You tell me."

The Russian shook his head. "Crazy American. Are you all nuts?"

"Who said I'm American?"

Maks looked at Akilina. "Why are you with this *chornye*?"

He did not react to the derogatory remark. They needed to leave the café with minimal disruption. Yet there was something in Maks's eyes that contradicted his words. He wasn't sure, but the man might be sending him a message that now was not the time or the place. He decided to take a chance. "We're leaving, Mr. Maks. Any suggestions where to stay for the night?"

The proprietor finished preparing the coffee and headed around the far end for the policeman's table. He deposited the drink, then returned.

"Try the Okatyabrsky Hotel. Turn left at the corner, then three blocks toward the center of town."

"Thanks," he said.

But Maks did not return the pleasantry and retreated back behind the glass cases without saying another word. Lord and Akilina started for the exit but were forced to walk right by the policeman, who sat sipping his steaming coffee. He noticed the man's gaze linger far longer than it should have. Turning back toward the glass counter at the other side of the room, Lord saw that Iosif Maks noticed, too.

They found the Okatyabrsky. The hotel filled a four-story building, the street-side rooms all with rickety balconies. The lobby's floor was dusted with black dirt, the air heavy with the sulfur scent of bad plumbing. The clerk behind the desk was cantankerous, promptly declaring that the hotel did not accept foreigners. Akilina took charge of the situation and angrily informed him that Lord was her husband and she expected him to be treated with respect. After some haggling, one room was let at a higher-than-usual rate, and they trudged upstairs to the third floor.

The rooms were spacious but timeworn, the decor something out of a 1940s movie. The one concession to modern times was a small refrigerator that churned intermittently in one corner. The attached bath wasn't much better—no toilet seat or paper, and when Lord went to rinse his face, he learned that the hot and cold water ran, but not at the same time.

"I imagine not many tourists come this far south," he said, stepping out of the bath toweling his face dry.

Akilina was sitting on the edge of the bed. "This area was forbidden during communist times. Only recently have foreigners been allowed."

"I appreciate what you did down there with the clerk."

"I am sorry also for what Maks said to you. He had no right."

"I'm not so sure he meant it." He then explained what he'd gleaned from the Russian's eyes. "I think he was as nervous about that policeman as we were."

"Why? He said he knew nothing of Kolya Maks."

"I think he lied."

She smiled. "You are an optimistic raven."

"I don't know about optimistic. I'm assuming there's at least a grain of truth to this whole thing."

"I hope there is."

He was curious.

"What you said last night is true. Russians want to remember only the good in the tsarist government. But you were right. It was an autocracy, repressive and cruel. Still . . . this time it could be different." A smile creased her lips. "What we are doing may be a way to cheat the Soviets one last time. They thought themselves so clever. But the Romanovs may have survived. Would that not be fitting?"

Yes, it would, he thought.

"Are you hungry?" Akilina asked.

He was. "I think we ought to stay out of sight. I'll go downstairs and buy some food from the kiosk in the lobby. Her bread and cheese looked good. We can have a quiet dinner here."

She smiled. "That would be good."

Downstairs, Lord approached the old woman operating a small kiosk and selected a loaf of black bread, some cheese, a couple of sausages, and two beers. He paid with a five-dollar bill, which she eagerly accepted. He was heading back toward the staircase when he heard cars approach outside. Blue and red lights swirled in the darkness and strobed the lobby through street-side windows. He glanced out and saw three police cars wheel to a stop, car doors pop open.

He knew where they were headed.

He bounded up the stairs and into the room. "Get your stuff. Police are downstairs."

Akilina moved fast. She yanked up her shoulder bag and slipped on her coat.

He grabbed his bag and coat. "It won't take them long to learn this room number."

"Where are we going?"

He knew there was only one way to go—up to the fourth floor. "Come on." He headed out the door, which he gently closed.

They climbed the dimly lit oak steps as feet pounded up from below. They turned on the landing and tiptoed to the top floor. Footsteps thumped down the third-floor hall. Lord studied the seven rooms by the light of an exposed incandescent bulb. Three rooms faced the street, three were at the rear of the building, one was at the end of the hall. The doors to all of them were open, signifying that they were unoccupied.

The rapping of fists on wood echoed from below.

He signaled for quiet and pointed to the last room, the one that faced the rear of the building.

Akilina headed for it.

Along the way, Lord gently closed the doors on either side of the hall. Then he followed her inside and quietly locked the door.

More pounding came from below.

The room was dark and he dared not switch on the bedside lamp. He moved to the window and stared out. Thirty or so feet down was an alley filled with parked cars. He yanked up the glass and stuck his head out into the cold. No policemen were in sight. Perhaps they thought a surprise visit enough to ensure success. To the right of the window a gutter pipe snaked a path from the roof to the cobbles below.

He straightened. "We're trapped."

Akilina brushed past and crouched out the window. He heard heavy steps on the staircase coming their way. The policemen surely had learned that the third-floor room was empty. The closed doors should slow them down, but not for long.

Akilina unshouldered her bag and tossed it out the window. "Give me yours."

He did, but asked, "What are you doing?"

She tossed the bag out. "Watch what I do and follow."

She swung herself out the window and clung to the sill. He stared as she grabbed hold of the drainpipe and angled her weight, legs planted on the brick facade, hands wrapped around the moist iron. Deftly, she maneuvered down, using her legs for leverage, alternately grabbing and releasing as gravity worked her to the ground. In a few seconds, she hopped off the wall to the street.

He heard doors opening out in the hall. He didn't really think he could do what Akilina had just done, but there was little choice. In a few more seconds the room would be full of police.

He swung out the window and grabbed hold of the pipe. The metal chilled his hands and the dampness caused his grip to slip, but he clenched tight. He planted his feet against the brick and started down.

He heard pounding on the room door.

He dropped himself faster and passed the second-floor windows. Wood splintered from above as the locked door was apparently forced. He continued down but lost his grip as one of the wall braces appeared. He started to fall just as a head popped out the open window above. He braced himself for impact as he scraped the rough brick on the way down and his body pounded to the concrete.

He rolled once and slammed into the tire of one of the parked cars.

Glancing up, he saw a gun appear in the policeman's hand. He ignored the pain in his thigh and sprang to his feet, grabbing Akilina and shoving her to the other side of the car.

Two shots cracked in the night.

One bullet ricocheted off the hood. The other shattered the windshield.

"Come on, and stay down," he said.

They clung to their bags and crawled forward down the alley, using the parked cars for protection. A trail of bullets followed them, but the fourth-floor window did not afford the best firing angle. Glass shattered and metal screamed as bullets raked past. The end of the alley was just ahead and he wondered if more policemen would be waiting.

They left the alley.

Lord whirled his head in both directions. Shops on both sides were dark. No street lamps. He quickly shouldered his bag, grabbed Akilina's hand, and raced with her to the other side of the street.

A car slid around the corner to their right. Headlights blinded him. The vehicle raced straight toward them.

They froze in the middle of the street.

Brakes screeched as tires grabbed damp pavement.

The car skidded to a stop.

He noticed the vehicle was not official. No lights or markings. The face through the windshield, though, was recognizable.

Iosif Maks.

The Russian stuck his head out the driver's-side window and said, "Get in."

They climbed inside and Maks slammed the accelerator to the floor.

"Good timing," Lord said, glancing through the rear window.

The big Russian kept his eyes on the road but said, "Kolya Maks is dead. But his son will see you tomorrow."

25

MOSCOW
SUNDAY, OCTOBER 17
7:00 AM

HAYES SAT DOWN TO BREAKFAST IN THE VOLKHOV'S MAIN DIN-
ing room. The hotel offered an exquisite morning buffet. He
especially loved the sweet *blinys* the chef prepared with
powdered sugar and a fresh fruit topping. The day's *Izvestia*
was delivered by the waiter and he settled back to read the
morning news.

A front-page article recapped the Tsarist Commission's activities of the past week. After the opening session Wednesday, nominations had started on Thursday. Stefan Baklanov's
had been the first name placed forward, his candidacy prof-
fered, as arranged, by the popular mayor of Moscow. The Secret Chancellory thought using someone the people respected
would give further credibility to Baklanov, and the ploy had
apparently worked as the *Izvestia* reporter editorialized about
the support growing for Baklanov's selection.

Two rival clans of surviving Romanovs quickly nomi-
nated their senior members, asserting a closer blood and mar-
ital tie to Nicholas II. Three more names had been offered,
but the reporter gave none a serious chance, the three all distant Romanovs. A boxed story off to the right noted that there
actually might be a lot of Russians with Romanov blood.

Laboratories in St. Petersburg, Novosibirsk, and Moscow were offering, for fifty rubles, to test a person's blood and compare genetic markers to those of the imperial family. Apparently, a lot of people had paid the fee and taken the test.

The initial debate among commission members on the nominees had been intense, but Hayes knew it was just for show since, at last report, fourteen of seventeen members were bought. Debate had been his idea. Better to let the members appear in disagreement and be slowly swayed than for a quick decision to be made.

The story ended with a note that the nomination process would conclude the next day, an initial vote on narrowing the field to three candidates was scheduled for Tuesday, and then two more days of debate would be held before a final vote on Thursday.

By the coming Friday it should all be over.

Stefan Baklanov would become Stefan I, Tsar of All Russia. Hayes's clients would be happy, the Secret Chancellory would be satisfied, and he'd be several million dollars richer.

He finished the article, marveling at the Russian penchant for public shows. They even had coined a name for such spectacles: *pokazukha*. The best example he could recall was when Gerald Ford visited in the 1970s, his route from the airport made more picturesque by the fir trees that had been cut from a nearby forest and stuck upright in the snow.

The waiter brought his steaming *blinys* and coffee. He thumbed through the rest of the paper, glancing at stories here and there. One in particular caught his eye. ANASTASIA ALIVE AND LIVING WITH HER BROTHER THE TSAR. Shock slid down his spine until he read further and noted the article was a review of a play that had recently opened in Moscow:

Inspired by a cheesy conspiracy book found in a secondhand store, English playwright Lorna Gant became intrigued by stories surrounding the alleged incomplete execution of the royal family. "I was fascinated with the Anastasia/Anna Anderson thing," Gant said, referring to the most famous Anastasia wannabe.

The play suggests that Anastasia and her brother Alexei managed to escape death at Yekaterinburg in 1918. Their bodies have never been found and speculation has abounded for decades over what really happened. All fertile grist for the playwright's imagination.

"It has an Elvis-is-alive-and-living-in-Alaska-with-Marilyn ring to it," Gant says. "There's a dark humor and irony to the message."

He read on and saw that the play seemed more a farce of the idea than a serious rendition on possible Romanov survivors, the reviewer comparing it to "Chekhov meets Carol Burnett." In the end the reviewer recommended no one bother with the performance.

A chair sliding from the table interrupted his reading.

He glanced up from the paper as Feliks Orleg sat down.

"Your breakfast looks good," the inspector said.

"I'd order you some, but this is a bit too public a place for you." He made no attempt to hide his contempt.

Orleg slid the plate close and reached for the fork. Hayes decided to leave the bastard alone. Orleg draped syrup over the thin pancakes and eagerly devoured them.

He folded and tabled the newspaper. "Some coffee?" he asked, his sarcasm clear.

"Juice would be fine," the Russian muttered through a full mouth.

He hesitated, then signaled the waiter and told him to bring a tumbler of orange juice. Orleg finished the *blinys* and wiped his mouth with a cloth napkin. "I've heard this hotel prepares a fine breakfast, but I can hardly afford an appetizer."

"Luckily you might soon come into some wealth."

A smile creased the inspector's chapped lips. "I'm not doing this for the pleasure of the company, I assure you."

"And the purpose of this lovely Sunday-morning visit?"

"The police bulletin on Lord worked. He has been located."

His interest was piqued.

"In Starodug. About five hours south."

He instantly recalled the town from the materials Lord had found in the archives. Lenin mentioned it along with a name: Kolya Maks. What had the Soviet leader said? *The village of Starodug has likewise been noted by two other similarly persuaded White Guardsmen. There is something occurring, of that I am now certain.*

Now, so was he. Too many coincidences.

Lord had obviously gotten himself into something.

Sometime during Friday night, Lord's room had been mysteriously emptied. Members of the Secret Chancellory were clearly upset, and if they were worried, he was worried. They'd told him to handle the situation, and he intended to do just that.

"What happened?" he asked.

"Lord and a woman were found at a hotel."

He waited for more. Orleg was apparently enjoying the moment.

"What the local *militsya* lack in knowledge, they make up for in stupidity. They raided the hotel, but neglected to cover the rear. Lord and the woman escaped through a window. They tried to shoot him, but he managed to get away."

"Did they learn why he was there?"

"He was asking questions in a local eatery about a Kolya Maks."

Confirmation. "What orders did you give the locals?"

"I told them to do nothing until they hear from me."

"We need to leave immediately."

"I thought as much. That's why I'm here. And I've even had my breakfast now."

The waiter brought the orange juice.

Hayes stood from the table. "Drink up. I have to make a call before we go."

26

AKILINA WATCHED AS LORD SLOWED THE CAR. A COLD RAIN smacked the windshield. Last night, Iosif Maks had stashed them in a house west of Starodug. It was owned by another Maks family member who'd provided two pallets before an open hearth.

Maks had returned a couple of hours ago and explained that the police had come to his house late last night inquiring about a black man and Russian woman who'd visited his eatery earlier. He'd told them exactly what had happened, most of which was witnessed by the *militsya* officer. They apparently believed what he said, since they had not returned. Thankfully, no one witnessed the escape from the Okatyabrsky.

Maks also left them a vehicle, a banged-up, cream-colored Mercedes coupe caked in black mud, its leather seats brittle from exposure. And he provided directions to where the son of Kolya Maks lived.

The farmhouse was single-story and built of double planks caulked with a thick layer of oakum, the roof's bark shingles darkened by mildew. A stone chimney puffed a thick column of gray vapor into the cold air. An open field spread in the distance, plows and harrows stored under a lean-to.

The entire scene reminded Akilina of the cabin her grandmother had once occupied, a similar grove of white birch rising to one side. She'd always thought autumn such a sad time of year. The season arrived without warning, then evaporated overnight into winter. Its presence meant the end of green forests and grassy meadows—more reminders of her childhood, the village near the Urals where she was raised, and the school where they all wore matching dresses with pinafores and red ribbons. Between lessons they'd been drilled about the oppression workers suffered during tsarist times, how Lenin had changed all that, why capitalism was evil, and what the *kollektiv* expected from each of its members. Lenin's portrait had hung in every classroom, in every home. Any challenge to him was wrong. Comfort was derived in knowing that ideas were shared by everyone.

The individual did not exist.

But her father had been an individual.

All he'd wanted was to live with his new wife and child in Romania. But the *kollektiv* would not allow such a simple thing. Good parents were expected to be party members. They had to be. Those who did not possess "revolutionary ideals" should be reported. One famous story was of a son who informed on his father for selling documents to rebellious farmers. The son testified against the father and was later murdered by the farmers. Songs and poems were subsequently written about him, and all children were taught to idealize such dedication to the Motherland.

But why?

What was admirable about being a traitor to your own family?

"I've only been into rural Russia twice," Lord said, interrupting her thoughts. "Both under controlled circumstances. But this is quite different. It's another world."

"In tsarist times they called the village *mir*. Peace. A good description since few ever left their village. It was their world. A place for peace."

Outside, the factory smog of Starodug was gone, replaced with verdant trees, green hills, and hay fields that she imagined in summer were alive with meadowlarks.

Lord parked the car in front of the cabin.

The man who answered the door was short and sturdy with reddish brown hair and a face round and flush like a beet. He was, Akilina estimated, close to seventy, but moved with surprising agility. He studied them with scrutinizing eyes that she thought akin to those of a border guard, then invited them inside.

The cabin was spacious with a single bedroom, kitchen, and a cozy den. The furniture was a mismatched decor of necessity and practicality. The floors were wide planks, sanded smooth, their varnish nearly gone. There were no electric lights. All the rooms were lit by smoky oil lamps and a fireplace.

"I am Vassily Maks. Kolya was my father."

They were seated at a kitchen table. A wood-burning stove was warming a pot of *lapsha*—the homemade noodles Akilina had always loved. The scent of roasted meat was strong, lamb if she wasn't mistaken, tempered by the musty smell of cheap tobacco. One corner of the room was devoted to an icon surrounded by candles. Her grandmother had maintained a holy corner until the day she disappeared.

"I prepared lunch," Maks said. "I hope you're hungry."

"A meal would be welcome," Lord said. "It smells good."

"Cooking is one of the few pleasures I have left to enjoy." Maks stood and moved toward the stove. He stirred the simmering pot of noodles, his back to them. "My nephew said you had something to say."

Lord seemed to understand. "He that endureth to the end shall be saved."

The old man tabled the spoon, then sat back down. "I never believed I would hear those words. I thought them a figment of my father's imagination. And to be spoken by a man of color." Maks turned to Akilina. "Your name means 'eagle,' child."

"So I'm told."

"You are a lovely creature."

She smiled.

"I hope this quest does not endanger that beauty."

"How would it?" she asked.

The old man rubbed his bulbous nose. "When my father informed me of the duty expected, he warned that perhaps it might cost my life one day. I never took him seriously . . . until this moment."

"What is it you know?" Lord asked.

The old man let out a breath. "I think about what happened often. My father told me I would, but I didn't believe him. I can almost see them being awakened in the middle of the night and hustled downstairs. They think the White Army is about to overrun the town and free them. Yurovsky, the mad Jew, tells them an evacuation is necessary, but first a photo needs to be taken for Moscow, to prove them alive and well. He tells everyone where to stand. But there is to be no photo. Instead, men with guns come into the room and the tsar is told that he and his family are to be executed. Then, Yurovsky points his gun."

The old man paused and shook his head.

"Let me prepare our lunch. Then I will tell you all about what happened in Yekaterinburg that July night."

Yurovsky fired the Colt pistol and the head of Nicholas II, Tsar of All Russia, exploded in a shower of blood. The tsar fell back toward his son. Alexandra had just started to make the sign of the cross when the other gunmen opened fire.

Bullets raked the tsarina and toppled her from the chair. Yurovsky had specifically assigned a victim for each gunman and instructed that the shots be to the heart to minimize bleeding. But Nicholas's body erupted in a fury of impacts as the other eleven executioners decided to take aim at their once divine ruler.

The shooters were arrayed in rows of three. The second and third rows were firing over the shoulders of the first, so close that many on the first row were being burned by hot exhaust. Kolya Maks stood in the first row, his neck singed twice. He'd been instructed to shoot Olga, the oldest daughter, but could not bring himself to do it. He'd been sent to Yekaterinburg to orchestrate the family's escape, arriving three days earlier, but events had accelerated at lightning pace.

The guards had been called into Yurovsky's office earlier. The commandant had told them, "Today, we are going to be killing the entire family and the doctor and servants living with them. Warn the detachment not to be alarmed if they hear shots." Eleven men, including Maks, were selected. It had been a stroke of luck that Maks was chosen, but he'd come highly recommended from the Ural Soviet—a man who could be trusted to follow orders—and apparently Yurovsky was in need of loyalty.

Two Latvians immediately spoke up and said they would not shoot women. Maks had been impressed that such brutal men possessed a conscience. Yurovsky did not object to their refusal and replaced them with two more who eagerly stepped forward and expressed no reservations. The final regiment included six Latvians and five Russians, plus Yurovsky. Hardened men with the names of Nikulin, Ermakov, two Medvedevs, and Pavel. Names Kolya Maks would forever recall.

A truck was parked outside, its engine revved to cover the gunfire, which came in a fusillade. The smoke from the barrels

*clothed the scene in a thick, eerie fog. It was becoming diffi-
cult to see, to tell who was shooting whom. Maks reasoned
that several hours of hard drinking had dulled senses to the
point that no one other than himself, and perhaps Yurovsky,
was sober. Few would remember the details, only that they
fired at anything that moved. He'd been careful with his alcohol consumption, knowing his head had to stay clear.*

*Maks watched Olga's body crumple after a bullet to the
head. The shooters were aiming at each victim's heart, but
something strange was happening. The bullets simply ricocheted off the women's chests and darted around the room
like hail. One of the Latvians muttered that God was protect-
ing them. Another wondered aloud if all this was wise.*

*Maks watched as Grand Duchesses Tatiana and Marie
tried to cower in one corner, their arms raised for protection. Bullets raked their young bodies, some bouncing off,
others penetrating. Two men broke formation and moved
close, shooting both girls in the head.*

*The valet, the cook, and the doctor were all shot where
they stood, their bodies dropping like targets at an arcade.
The maid was the crazy one. She flailed wildly around the
room, screaming, shielding herself with a pillow. Several of
the shooters adjusted and fired into the pillow. The bullets
careered away. It was frightening. What protection did these
people possess? The maid's head finally succumbed to a
clean shot and her screams halted.*

"Stop firing," Yurovsky yelled.

The room went silent.

*"The shots will be heard from the street. Finish them off
with bayonets."*

*The shooters tossed their revolvers aside and grabbed
their American Winchester rifles, moving into the room.*

*Somehow, the maid had survived the shot to the head. She
bolted upright and started picking her way over the bleeding*

corpses, softly wailing. Two Latvians moved toward her and thrust their daggers into the pillow she still clutched. The blades were dull and did not penetrate. She grabbed one of the bayonets and started shrieking. The men moved toward her. One crashed his rifle butt down on her head. The pitiful moan that came reminded Maks of a wounded animal. More rifle butts went down and her moans stopped. Men jabbed their bayonets into the body as if exorcizing a demon, too many thrusts for Maks to count.

Maks moved toward the tsar. Thick rivulets of blood rushed over the field shirt and trousers. The others were concentrating their bayonets on the maid and one of the grand duchesses. Acrid smoke filled the air and stifled his breath. Yurovsky was examining the tsarina.

Maks bent down and rolled Nicholas to one side. The tsarevich was underneath, dressed in the same military field shirt, trousers, boots, and forage cap he'd seen the boy wear many times. Just like his father. He knew they enjoyed dressing alike.

The boy opened his eyes. The look was one of terror. Maks immediately clamped a hand over the boy's mouth. He then brought a finger to his lips.

"Stay still. Be dead," he mouthed.

The boy's eyes closed.

Maks stood and aimed his pistol down at the floor just beside the boy's head and fired. The bullet ripped into the planking and Alexei jarred. Maks fired again on the other side and hoped no one noticed the body jerk, but everyone seemed consumed with the surrounding carnage. Eleven victims, twelve executioners, the space tight, time short.

"Was the tsarevich still alive?" Yurovsky asked through the smoke.

"Not anymore," Maks said.

The answer seemed to satisfy the commandant.

Maks rolled the bloodied body of Nicholas II back on top of the boy. He looked up as one of the Latvians moved toward the youngest daughter, Anastasia. She'd fallen in the initial volley and lay prostrate on the floor amid a thickening sea of blood. The girl was moaning, and Maks wondered if some of the bullets had found their mark. The Latvian was raising his rifle butt to finish the job when Maks stopped him.

"Let me," he mouthed. "I have not had the pleasure."

A smile curled on the other man's face and he backed away. Maks stared down at the girl. Her chest heaved from labored breath, blood streamed off her dress, but it was hard to tell if it was hers or from her sister's body nearby.

May God forgive him.

He brought the rifle butt down onto the girl's head. He angled it for a glance, enough to pound her into unconsciousness, but hopefully not enough to kill her.

"I'll finish her," Maks said, reversing the rifle to prepare the bayonet.

Luckily, the Latvian moved to another corpse without an argument.

"Stop," Yurovsky yelled.

The room went eerily quiet. No more flesh being serrated with blades. No more gunshots. No more moans. Just twelve men standing in thick smoke, the overhead electric lamp like the sun in a storm.

"Open the doors and let the smoke disperse," Yurovsky said. "We can't see a damn thing. Then check for pulses and report."

Maks moved straight to Anastasia. There was a pulse, faint and light. "Grand Duchess Anastasia. Dead," he called out.

Other guards reported more deaths. Maks moved to the tsarevich and rolled Nicholas over. He felt the boy's pulse.

Beating strong. He wondered if he'd even been hit. "Tsarevich. Dead."

"Good fucking riddance," one of the Latvians said.

"We must remove these corpses quickly," Yurovsky said. "This room has to be cleaned before morning." The commandant faced one of the Russians. "Go get some sheets from upstairs." He turned back. "Start laying the bodies out straight."

Maks watched as a Latvian grabbed one of the grand duchesses. Exactly which was hard to tell.

"Look," the man cried.

Everyone's attention went to the bloodied young woman. Maks moved close with the others. Yurovsky came over. A glistening diamond shone through the ripped corset. The commandant bent down and fingered the stone. He then grabbed one of the bayonets and opened an incision in the corset, sliding the garment free from the dead torso. More jewels tinkered down, splattering the blood on the floor.

"The stones shielded them," Yurovsky said. "Bloody bastards sewed them into their clothes."

Some of the other men realized the fortune that lay around them and started for the women.

"No," Yurovsky shouted. "Later. But anything found is to be turned over to me. It belongs to the state. Anyone keeping even a button will be shot. Clear?"

No one said a word.

The man arrived with sheets. Maks knew that Yurovsky was in a hurry to get the bodies away from the house. He'd made that clear earlier. Dawn was only a few hours away and the White Army was just outside town, approaching fast.

The tsar's body was wrapped first and carried out to the waiting truck.

One of the grand duchesses was tossed on a stretcher. Suddenly, the girl bolted upright and started to scream.

Horror gripped everyone. It almost seemed like heaven was working against them. The doors and windows of the house were now open, so there could be no more gunshots. Yurovsky palmed one of the rifles and thrust the blade into the girl's chest. The blade barely penetrated. He quickly reversed the rifle and slammed the butt into her head. Maks heard the skull crack. Yurovsky then jammed the blade deep into the girl's neck and twisted. There was gurgling and wrenching, blood spouted, then all movement stopped.

"Get these witches out of here," Yurovsky muttered. "They are possessed."

Maks moved to Anastasia and wrapped her in one of the sheets. A commotion came from the hall. Another of the grand duchesses had come back to life, and Maks glanced out to see men descend upon her with rifle butts and knives. He used the distraction to move to the tsarevich, still lying in the blood of his parents.

He bent close. "Little One."

The boy opened his eyes.

"Make no sound. I must carry you to the truck. Understand?"

A slight nod.

"Any sound or movement and they will skewer you."

He rolled the boy in the sheet and shoulder-carried both Alexei and Anastasia outside. He hoped the grand duchess did not awaken from her sleep. He also hoped no one checked for a pulse. Outside he discovered the men were far more interested in what they were finding on the bodies. Watches, rings, bracelets, cigarette cases, and jewels.

"I repeat," Yurovsky said. "All to be returned or you will be shot. There was a watch downstairs that is now gone. I am going back for the last body. When I return, it should be here."

No one doubted what would happen if it wasn't, and one

of the Latvians removed the watch from his pocket and tossed it into the pile with the other booty.

Yurovsky returned with the last body. It was slung onto the back of the truck. The commandant carried a forage cap in his hands.

"The tsar's," he said, stuffing it onto one of the killer's head. "It fits."

The others laughed.

"They died hard," one of the Latvians said.

Yurovsky stared into the truck bed. "It is not easy to kill people."

A tarpaulin was spread over the bodies in the truck bed, sheets stretched underneath to soak up the blood. Yurovsky selected four men to accompany the truck, then stepped to the cab and climbed inside. The rest of the execution squad started to disperse to their assigned posts. Maks was not one of those selected to go and he approached the open passenger's-side window.

"Comrade Yurovsky. Might I come along? I would like to help finish."

Yurovsky angled his short neck. He was so dark in the night. Black beard. Black hair. Black leather jacket. All Maks could discern were the whites of his eyes through a chilling stare.

"Why not? Climb in with the others."

The truck motored out of the Ipatiev house through open gates. One of the other men noted the time out loud: three AM. They would have to hurry. Two bottles of vodka were produced and passed around among the men in the bed with the bodies. Maks took only shallow swigs.

He'd been sent to Yekaterinburg to lay the groundwork for an escape. There were generals in the tsar's former command who took their oath to the Crown seriously. There'd been rumors for months that the fate of the imperial family was sealed. But only in the last day had Maks learned what that meant.

His gaze drifted to the body pile under the tarp. He'd laid the boy and his sister on top, just under their mother. He wondered if the tsarevich recognized his fate. Perhaps that was what had kept him quiet.

The truck passed the racetrack on the outskirts of town. It rolled past swamps, pits, and abandoned mines. Beyond the Upper Isetsk factory and across the railroad tracks the route entered dense forest. A couple more miles and another set of railroad tracks interfered. The only structures anywhere were the booths manned by railway watchmen, who were all asleep at this hour.

Maks could feel the roadway turn to mud. The truck slid as tires grabbed slippery earth. The rear wheels bogged in a quagmire, spinning freely, and the driver tried in vain to free the transport. Steam started billowing from the hood. The driver shut down the overheating engine and Yurovsky climbed from the cab, pointed to the darkened railway booth they'd just passed, and told the driver, "Go wake the attendant and get some water." He turned toward the truck bed. "Find some lumber to help the tires get out of this shit. I am going to walk ahead and look for Ermakov and his crew."

Two of the men had already passed out drunk. Two more jumped from the bed and disappeared into the darkness. Maks feigned drunkenness and remained still in the bed. He watched as the driver trudged back to the railway booth and banged on the door. A lamp flickered inside and the door opened. Maks could hear the driver telling the watchman they needed water. There was more arguing and Maks heard the guardsmen, who'd moved off into the night, call out that they had located lumber.

It would have to be now.

He crawled toward the tarp and slowly peeled it back. A coppery stench turned his stomach. He rolled the tsarina's sheeted body over and grasped the bundle with the tsarevich.

"It is I, Little One. Be still and quiet."

The boy murmured something Maks could not understand.

He carried the bundle from the bed and deposited it in the woods a few meters off the road.

"Do not move," he whispered.

He quickly scampered back and cupped the bundle holding Anastasia. He gently laid her on the ground and replaced the tarp. He cradled her in his arms and deposited her in the woods beside her brother. He loosened the wrap around each child and checked the girl's pulse. Faint, but there.

Alexei looked at him.

"I know this is horrible. But you must stay here. Watch over your sister. Do not move. I will come back. When, I don't know. Understand?"

The boy nodded.

"You remember me, don't you?"

Alexei nodded again.

"Then trust me, Little One."

The boy hugged him with a desperate grasp that tugged at his heart.

"Sleep, for now. I will return."

Maks hustled back to the truck and climbed into the bed, taking up his prone position beside the other two men still passed out. He heard footsteps approaching through the darkness. He moaned and started to sit up.

"Get up, Kolya. We need your help," one of the men said as they approached. "We found lumber at the watch station."

He jumped down and helped the other two as they started

laying boards across the muddy road. The driver returned with a pail of water for the engine.

Yurovsky appeared a few minutes later. "Ermakov's people are just ahead."

The truck recranked with some effort and the boards provided the traction needed. Less than half a mile later they encountered a group of men waiting with torches. From their shouts it was obvious most were drunk. Maks recognized Peter Ermakov standing in the headlight beam. Yurovsky had only been ordered to carry out the sentence. The body disposal was Comrade Ermakov's responsibility. He was a worker at the Upper Isetsk plant who loved to kill so much that everyone called him Comrade Mauser.

Somebody yelled, "Why didn't you bring them to us alive?"

Maks knew what Ermakov had probably promised the men. Be good Soviets and do as you are told and I will let you have your way with the women while Papa Tsar watches. *The possibility of carnal lust on four virgins was surely enough of an incentive to get them to make the necessary preparations.*

A crowd gathered at the rear of the truck facing the tarpaulin, torches crackling in the night. One of them yanked the cover away.

"Shit, that stinks," somebody hollered.

"The stench of royalty," another said.

"Move the bodies off into the carts," Yurovsky ordered.

Somebody grumbled about not wanting to touch the filthy things, and Ermakov hopped onto the bed. "Get these damn corpses off the truck. We have only a couple of hours until dawn and there is much to do."

Maks realized that Ermakov was not a man to challenge. The men started hauling bloodied bundles and dropping them into droshkies. There were only four of the wooden carts and he hoped no one counted corpses. Only Yurovsky would know the exact number, but his commander moved off with Ermakov ahead of the truck. The rest of the men who'd come from the Ipatiev house were too drunk or too tired to care about whether there were nine or eleven bodies.

The sheets were removed as each corpse was tossed into a droshkie. Maks watched as some of the men started going through the pockets in the bloodied clothing. One of the men from the execution squad told the crowd about the finds made earlier.

Yurovsky appeared and a shot rang out. "There'll be none of that. We will strip them at the burial site. But anything found is to be handed over or you will be shot on the spot."

No one argued.

With only four carts, the decision was made that the truck should drive as far as it could with the remaining bodies, with the carts following. Maks sat on the edge of the truck bed and watched the carts roll behind as the vehicle inched forward. He knew they would have to stop at some point, leave the road, and hike into the woods. He'd heard earlier that a burial site in one of the abandoned mine shafts had been chosen. The Four Brothers, somebody called the location.

Twenty minutes passed as the truck rocked forward. Then the tires slid to a stop and Yurovsky leaped out of the cab. He walked back to where Ermakov was leading a cart. The commandant grabbed Ermakov and jammed a pistol into the man's neck.

"This is fucking shit," Yurovsky said. "The man in the truck says he can't locate the trail back to the mine. You were all just here yesterday. Now, no memory? You're hoping I'll tire and leave you with the bodies so they can be

*robbed. That will not happen. Either find the trail or I'll kill
you. The Ural Committee will support me, I assure you."*

*Two from the execution squad sprang to their feet and the
bolts of their rifles cocked in the night. Maks followed suit.*

*"All right, Comrade," Ermakov calmly said. "There is no
need for violence. I will personally lead the way."*

27

LORD SAW TEARS IN VASSILY MAKS'S EYES. HE WONDERED how many times the events had played out in the old man's mind.

"My father served in Nicholas's guard. He was assigned to Tsarskoe Selo, the Alexander Palace where the imperial family lived. The children knew his face. Especially Alexei."

"How did he come to be in Yekaterinburg?" Akilina asked.

"He was approached by Felix Yussoupov. Men were needed to infiltrate Yekaterinburg. Palace guards were favored by the Bolsheviks. They were showpieces the propagandists used to legitimatize the revolution—how Nicholas's most trusted men turned on him. Many did turn, weak souls scared for their hides, but a few were recruited as spies, like my father. He knew many of the revolution leaders, and they were glad to have him as part of the movement. It was simply luck he arrived at Yekaterinburg in time. Even more luck that Yurovsky selected him as part of the execution squad."

They were sitting at the kitchen table, having finished their lunch.

"Your father sounds like a brave man," Lord said.

"Enormously so. He took an oath to the tsar and lived that oath until the end."

Lord wanted to know about Alexei and Anastasia. "Did they survive?" he asked. "What happened?"

The old man's lips curled into a thin smile. "Something wonderful. But first, something awful."

The convoy moved on into the forest. The road was little more than a rough trail cut through mud, the going slow. When the truck became stuck between two trees, Yurovsky decided to abandon the vehicle and proceed on to the mine using the droshkies. The remaining bodies from the truck were loaded onto stretchers fashioned from the tarpaulin. The Four Brothers mine was no more than a hundred paces away and Maks helped carry the stretcher containing the corpse of the tsar.

"Lay them out on the ground," Yurovsky ordered when they arrived at the clearing.

"I thought I was in charge," Ermakov said.

"You were," the commandant made clear.

A fire was started. Each corpse was undressed, the clothing burned. With thirty or so drunken men, the scene was chaotic. But Maks was grateful for the confusion since it helped mask the loss of two victims.

"Diamonds," one of the men screamed.

The word drew the others.

"Kolya. Come with me," Yurovsky said, shouldering his way through the crowd.

The men were packed around a female corpse. One of Ermakov's men had discovered another corset filled with jewels. Yurovsky grabbed the diamond out of the man's hand, a Colt pistol gripped in his other.

"There'll be no looting. First man who does dies. Kill me and the committee guarantees retribution. Now do as I say and undress the bodies. Leave anything you find with me."

"For you to keep?" a voice asked.

"It is not mine nor yours, but the state's. I intend to turn all this over to the Ural Committee. Those are my orders."

"Fuck you, Jew," a voice said.

In the flickering light, Maks saw anger flash in Yurovsky's eyes. He knew enough about this sullen man to know that he didn't like being reminded of his heritage. His father was a glazier, his mother a seamstress, ten children between them. He'd grown up poor and hard, becoming a loyal party man after the failed 1905 revolution. He'd been banished to Yekaterinburg for revolutionary activity, but after the February revolt of the previous year, he'd been elected to the Ural Committee, and every day since he'd worked diligently for the party. He was no longer a Jew. He was a loyal communist. A man who took orders and could be depended upon to execute them precisely.

Dawn was breaking over the surrounding poplars.

"You are all dismissed," Yurovsky loudly said. "Except the men who came with me."

"You can't do that," Ermakov yelled.

"Either leave, or I will have you shot."

Rifles clicked to one side as guns were shouldered. The four from the execution squad had once again heeded the call of their commandant. The remaining group of men seemed to know that resisting would be foolish. Perhaps they might overpower these few, but the Ural Committee would not allow their transgression to go unpunished. Maks was not surprised when the drunken crowd disappeared down the trail.

When they were gone, Yurovsky stuffed his pistol under his belt. "Finish undressing the bodies."

Maks and two others accomplished the task while two men stood guard. It was hard to tell identities any longer, except for the tsarina, whose size and age helped distinguish her even in death. Maks felt a sickening in his stomach for these people he'd once served.

Two more corsets were found full of jewels. From the

tsarina came the most surprising find, an entire pearl belt sewn into the lining of her underwear.

"There are only nine bodies," Yurovsky suddenly said. "Where is the tsarevich and another of the women?"

No one said a word.

"Bastards. Those filthy stinking bastards," the commandant said. "They must have hidden them away on the way in, surely thinking something of value could be found. They're probably searching them right now."

Maks silently heaved a sigh of relief.

"What do we do?" one of the guards asked.

Yurovsky did not hesitate. "Not a damn thing. We report that nine went down into the shaft, two were burned. We'll try to find them when we're through. Is that clear to everyone?"

Maks realized none of the men present, especially Yurovsky, wanted to report that two bodies were unaccounted for. No explanation would spare them the committee's wrath. A collective silence confirmed that they were all in agreement.

More bloodied clothing was tossed into the fire, then nine naked corpses were laid prone beside a dark square in the earth. Maks noticed how the corset laces had left a line of running knots in the dead flesh. The grand duchesses also wore amulets around their necks with a picture of Rasputin and a prayer sewn in. These were yanked off and tossed into the cache pile. He recalled the beauty each of these women had projected in life and was saddened by how none remained in death.

One of the men reached down and fondled Alexandra's breasts.

A couple of the other men followed suit.

"I can rest in peace now that I have squeezed the empress' tits," one of them proclaimed, and the others joined his laughter.

Maks turned away and watched the fire crackle as cloth turned to ash.

"Toss the bodies down," Yurovsky said.

Each man dragged a corpse to the mine and dropped it over the edge. Several seconds of silence passed before a splash of water could be heard far below.

In less than a minute, all nine were gone.

VASSILY MAKS PAUSED, SUCKED IN A FEW LONG BREATHS, then sipped from a vodka glass. "Yurovsky then sat on a tree stump and ate a breakfast of boiled eggs. Nuns from the monastery had delivered them the day before for the tsarevich, and Yurovsky had instructed them that they should pack the eggs well. He knew exactly what was coming. After he stuffed his belly, he tossed grenades down the shaft to collapse the mine."

"You said something wonderful happened, too," Lord said.

The old man savored another sip of vodka. "That I did."

Maks left the burial site with the other men around ten AM. A guard was posted to keep an eye on the site and Yurovsky headed off to report to the Ural Committee on the night's activity. Luckily, the commandant had not ordered a search for the other two bodies, informing them that he would report they were burned separately.

Their instructions were to walk back to town and not attract attention. Maks thought the order strange considering how many men had been involved the previous night. There was no way the burial site would stay secret, particularly given the bitter feelings and a lure of wealth. Yurovsky specifically said they were not to speak to anyone about what happened and were to report for duty that afternoon at the Ipatiev house.

Maks allowed the other four to go ahead. He told them he

was going to take a different way back to town to clear his head. Cannon fire rumbled in the distance. His comrades warned that the White Army was within miles of Yekaterinburg, but he assured them no White would want to meet up with him.

Maks left his companions and lingered a good half an hour before trotting down the trail the truck had used the night before. In daylight Maks noted the thick forest, heavy with underbrush. He found the railway watch station, but did not approach. Instead, he got his bearings and located the spot in the road where the boards had been laid over the mud.

He glanced around. No one was in sight.

He pushed his way into the woods.

"Little One. Are you here?" He kept his voice to a low whisper. "It is me, Little One. Kolya. I have returned."

Nothing.

He moved deeper, shoving the prickly brush aside. "Alexei. I have come back. Reveal yourself. Time is short."

Only the birds replied.

He stopped in a clearing. The surrounding pines were old growth, their trunks wide with decades of life. One had succumbed to the ages and lay dead on its side, its exposed roots like the image of disjointed arms and legs he knew would never leave his mind. What a disgrace. Who were these demons who claim to be the people's representatives? Is what they propose for Russia any better than the supposed evil they rebelled against? How could it possibly be, considering this monstrous beginning.

Bolsheviks usually executed their prisoners with a bullet to the base of the neck. Why such barbarism here? Perhaps the indiscriminate slaughter of innocents was a pronouncement of what was to follow. And why all the secrecy? If Nicholas II was an enemy of the state, why not publicize his execution? The answer to that was easy—no one would sanction butchering women and children.

It was hideous.

Something snapped behind him.

His hand went to the pistol stuffed into his belt. He wrapped his fingers around the stock and whirled.

Down the barrel he spied the soft, almost angelic, face of Alexei Romanov.

His mother called him Wee One and Sunbeam. He was the focus of the entire family's attention. A bright, affectionate lad with a stubborn streak. Maks had heard the palace talk of his inattentiveness, his dislike of studies, his love of Russian peasant dress. He was spoiled and capricious, once ordering a band of the palace guards to march into the sea, and his father had many times joked about whether Russia would survive Alexei the Terrible.

But he was now tsar. Alexei II. The anointed, divine successor Maks was sworn to protect.

Beside Alexei stood his sister, who was in many ways like her brother. Her headstrong ways were legendary, her arrogance beyond the point of tolerance. Her forehead was bloodied, her dress shredded. Through rips in the clothing, he spied a corset. Both children were painted in blood, faces filthy, and they stank of death.

But they were alive.

Lord could not believe what he was hearing, but the old man spoke with such conviction that he could not doubt him. Two Romanovs survived the bloody massacre at Yekaterinburg and all because of one man's bravery. Many had postulated such an occurrence, relying on scant evidence and wild speculation.

But here was the truth.

"My father took them away from Yekaterinburg by nightfall. There were others waiting on the outskirts to help and they moved the children east. The farther from Moscow, the better."

"Why not go to the White Army?" he asked.

"For what? The Whites were not tsarists. They hated Romanovs as much as Reds. Nicholas falsely believed they were his salvation, but they would have probably killed the family. No one cared for Romanovs in 1918, except a precious few."

"The ones your father worked for?"

Maks nodded.

"Who were they?"

"I have no idea. That information was never passed to me."

Akilina asked, "What happened to the children?"

"My father took them away from the civil war that raged for two more years. Past the Urals, deep into Siberia. It was an easy matter to blend them in. No one beyond courtesans in St. Petersburg knew their faces, and most of those people were dead. Old clothes and filthy faces made a good disguise." Maks paused and sipped his drink. "They lived in Siberia with people who were part of the plan, and finally made it to Vladivostok on the Pacific. There, they were smuggled out. To where? I have no idea. That is another leg of your journey, to which I am not privy."

"What was their condition when your father found them?" Lord asked.

"Alexei was not hit by any bullet. The tsar's body had shielded him. Anastasia had wounds that healed. Both wore jeweled corsets. The family had sewn the stones into the fabric to be safe from thieves. Currency to be used later, they believed. But the move saved the children's lives."

"Along with what your father did."

Maks nodded. "He was a good man."

"What happened to him?" Akilina asked.

"He returned here and lived to old age. The purges spared him. He died thirty years ago."

Lord thought about Yakov Yurovsky. There'd not been so peaceful a fate for the head executioner. He recalled that Yurovsky had died twenty years after Yekaterinburg, also in July, of a bleeding ulcer. But not before Stalin ordered his daughter to a labor camp. The old party warrior tried to help her, but couldn't. Nobody cared that he'd been the one to kill the tsar. On his deathbed Yurovsky lamented at how fate had turned on him. But Lord understood how that could have happened. The Bible again. Romans 12:19. *Vengeance is mine, I will repay.*

"What do we do now?" he asked.

Maks shrugged. "That information will have to come from my father."

"How is that possible?"

"It is sealed in a metal box. I was never allowed to read or see what was inside. Only to convey this message to whoever came and spoke the words."

Lord was confused. "Where is this box?"

"On the day he died, I dressed him in his imperial uniform and buried the box with him. It has lain for thirty years on his chest."

He didn't like the implications.

"Yes, Raven. My father awaits you in the grave."

28

HAYES WATCHED FELIKS ORLEG FORCE THE WOODEN DOOR, the burly Russian's breath clouding in the cold dry air. A sign affixed to the brick above read: KAFE SNEZHINKI—IOSIF MAKS, OWNER.

The jam splintered as the door slammed inward. Orleg disappeared inside.

The street was empty, all of the surrounding shops closed. Stalin followed Hayes in. Darkness had enveloped them an hour ago, the drive from Moscow to Starodug taking nearly five hours. The Secret Chancellory had thought Stalin's presence important since the *mafiya* was seen as the most efficient unit to handle the matter, its representative now charged with full responsibility to do whatever was necessary.

They'd gone first to Iosif Maks's house on the outskirts of town. The local police had discreetly been monitoring the situation since morning and thought him at home, but Maks's wife informed them he'd gone into town to work for a while. A light in the rear of Maks's café breathed hope, and Stalin had sprung into action.

Droopy and Cro-Magnon had been dispatched to the rear of the building. Hayes recalled the names Lord had given his two assailants and thought the descriptions apt. He'd been told about Droopy's abduction at gunpoint from the Moscow

Circus and the death of his captor, the man as yet unidentified and unlinked to any Holy Band Semyon Pashenko may or may not head. This whole thing was turning strange, but the seriousness with which the Russians viewed everything was causing him concern. It wasn't often men like these became riled.

Orleg appeared out of a doorway that led to the rear of the building and rounded a set of glass cases, another man with bushy red hair and mustache in his grasp. Droopy and Cro-Magnon followed.

"He was on his way out the back door," Orleg said.

Stalin pointed to an oak chair. "Sit him there."

Hayes noticed a discreet signal Stalin gave Droopy and Cro-Magnon, both of whom seemed to instantly understand. The splintered front door was closed and positions were taken up at the windows, guns drawn. The local police had been warned off an hour ago by Orleg, an order from a Moscow inspector not something local *militsya* tended to ignore. Khrushchev had earlier used his government connections to advise the Starodug authorities that a police operation would be occurring in town, the effort linked to a Red Square killing, and there should be no interference.

"Mr. Maks," Stalin said. "This is a serious matter. I want you to understand that."

Hayes watched as Maks considered what was said. Not a shred of fear appeared in the man's face.

Stalin stepped close to the chair. "Yesterday, a man and a woman came here. You recall?"

"I have many visitors." The voice carried contempt.

"I'm sure you do. But I would imagine few *chornyes* frequent your eatery."

The stout Russian jutted his chin forward. "Fuck off."

There was confidence in the tone, but Stalin did not react to the rebuke. He simply motioned and Droopy and

Cro-Magnon moved in unison, pinning Maks facedown to the plank floor.

"Find something we can amuse ourselves with," Stalin said.

Droopy disappeared into the back room while Cro-Magnon maintained a grip. Orleg had been dispatched to the rear door as guard. The inspector thought it important he not be an active participant. Hayes considered this the wisest course as well. They might need *militsya* contacts in the weeks ahead, and Orleg was the best source they possessed inside the Moscow unit.

Droopy returned with a roll of duct tape. He wrapped Maks's wrists together tightly. Cro-Magnon yanked the Russian up and plopped him into the rickety oak chair. More tape was wrapped around the chest and legs, securing Maks firmly. A final strip was slapped across his mouth.

Stalin said, "Now, Mr. Maks, let me tell you what we know. An American by the name of Miles Lord and a Russian woman named Akilina Petrovna came here yesterday. They were asking about Kolya Maks, a person you claimed to have no knowledge about. I want to know who Kolya Maks is and why Lord and the woman are seeking him. You know the answer to my first inquiry, and I am certain you also have the answer to the second."

Maks shook his head.

"A foolish decision, Mr. Maks."

Droopy ripped off a short strip of the gray tape and handed it to Stalin. The two seemed to have done this before. Stalin brushed the hair from his tanned brow and bent down. He loosely pressed the wad of tape over Maks's nose. "When I squeeze that tape tight, your nostrils will be sealed. There will be a bit of air remaining in your lungs, but only a few moments' worth. You will suffocate in a matter of seconds. How about a demonstration?" Stalin squeezed the tape tight to the skin.

Hayes watched Maks's chest heave. But he knew the thick tape was used on ventilation ducts because it was airtight. The Russian's eyes started to bulge as blood cells searched for oxygen, the skin metamorphosing through a variety of colors, finally settling on ash white. The helpless man rocked in the chair, trying to breathe, but Cro-Magnon held him steady from behind.

Stalin casually reached up and peeled the tape back from the mouth. Gulps of air were instantly sucked in.

Color returned to Maks's face.

"Please answer my two questions," Stalin said.

All Maks did was breathe.

"You are obviously a brave man, Mr. Maks. For what, I am not sure. But your courage is to be admired." Stalin paused, seemingly allowing Maks to recover. "I want you to know, while we were at your residence your lovely wife invited us inside. Such a charming woman. We visited and she informed us where you were."

A wild look came onto Maks's face. Finally. Fear.

"Not to worry," Stalin said. "She is fine. She believes we work with the government, here to perform an official inquiry. Nothing more. But I assure you this procedure works equally well with women."

"Goddamn *mafiya*."

"This has nothing to do with *mafiya*. This is much bigger, and I believe you understand that."

"You will kill me no matter what I say."

"But I give you my word your wife will not be involved, if you simply tell me what I want to know."

The redheaded Russian seemed to consider the proposal.

"You believe what I am telling you?" Stalin calmly asked.

Maks said nothing.

"If you continue to remain silent, there should be no doubt in your mind that I will direct these men to retrieve your wife. I will bind her to a chair beside you, and you will watch her suffocate. Then, I will probably let you live, so the memory can haunt you the rest of your life."

Stalin spoke with a calm reserve, as if negotiating a business deal. Hayes was impressed with the ease in which this handsome man, crouched over in his Armani jeans and cashmere sweater, dished out misery.

"Kolya Maks is dead," Maks finally said. "His son, Vassily, lives about ten kilometers south of town on the main highway. As to why Lord sought him, I do not know. Vassily is my great-uncle. Members of the family have always operated businesses here in town with a sign out front. That was what Vassily asked of us, and I did as he asked."

"I believe you are lying, Mr. Maks. Are you of the Holy Band?"

Maks said nothing. Apparently, there was a limit to his cooperation.

"No. You would not admit that, would you? Part of your oath to the tsar."

Maks stared hard. "Ask Vassily."

"I shall," Stalin said, as he motioned.

Droopy slapped more tape over Maks's mouth.

The Russian rocked in the chair, trying to breathe. His attempt to break free sent the chair careering to the floor.

His struggle ended a minute later.

"A good man who will protect his wife," Stalin said, staring down at the corpse. "One to be admired."

"Will you honor your word?" Hayes asked.

Stalin stared at him with a look of genuine hurt. "Of course. What kind of person do you take me for?"

29

6:40 PM

LORD PARKED IN THE WOODS JUST OFF A MUDDY ROAD. A chilly dusk had evolved into a cold, moonless night. He wasn't wild about the prospect of digging up a thirty-year-old coffin, but little choice remained. He was now convinced two Romanovs had walked away from Yekaterinburg. Whether they eventually made it to safety and ultimately survived to parent offspring was another matter, but there seemed only one way to find out.

Vassily Maks had provided them with two shovels and a flashlight with weak batteries. He'd warned that the cemetery was deep into the forest, a good thirty kilometers from Starodug, nothing around but thick poplars and an old stone church used occasionally for funerals.

"The cemetery should be just ahead, down that trail," he said, as they climbed out of the car.

They were still using the vehicle Iosif Maks had provided that morning. Maks had said he would return by evening with their car. When he'd not arrived by six PM Vassily had told them to go on, he would explain to Iosif and they would both be waiting when they returned. The old man seemed as anxious as they were to learn what secret his father had harbored. He also noted that there was one other piece of information he needed to pass on, but only after they were privy to what his father knew. It was another safety device, one that he intended to pass to his nephew, Iosif, the man he was grooming to assume the duty of keeper once he was gone.

Lord wore a jacket and a pair of leather gloves brought from Atlanta, along with thick woolen socks. His jeans were the only pair of casual wear he'd packed before leaving for Russia. The sweater was bought in Moscow a couple of weeks back. His world should have been one of suits and ties, casual clothes simply for a Sunday afternoon, but events had taken a dramatic shift in the past few days.

Maks had also provided a little protection, an old bolt-action rifle that could easily be characterized as antique. But the weapon appeared well oiled, and Maks demonstrated how to load and fire. He warned them about bears that roamed at night, especially this time of year as they prepared for a winter's hibernation. Lord knew little about guns, having fired one only a couple of times while in Afghanistan. He wasn't necessarily comfortable with the idea of being armed, but he was even more uncomfortable with the prospect of encountering a hungry bear. It was Akilina who surprised him. She readily shouldered the rifle and popped off three shots into a tree fifty yards away. Another of her grandmother's lessons, she said. And he was glad. At least one of them knew what they were doing.

He grabbed the shovels and flashlight from the backseat. Their clothes bags were there, too. As soon as they were through, after a quick trip back to Vassily Maks, they intended to leave. Where they would go was unclear, but he'd already decided that if this journey proved a dead end, he was going to drive southwest to Kiev and catch a flight to the United States. He'd call Taylor Hayes from the safety of his Atlanta apartment.

"Let's go," he said. "Might as well get this over with."

Black columns of trees rose all around, their boughs rustled by a frigid breeze that chapped his skin. He used the flash-light sparingly, conserving the batteries for the dig.

The muted image of tombstones appeared in a clearing ahead. They were high in the Old World style, and even through the darkness it was obvious the plots had not been maintained. A layer of frost iced everything. The blackness of the sky above hinted that more rain might be on the way. No fence of any kind delineated boundaries and no gate sig-nified an entrance, the trail leading from the road simply dis-solving into the first line of markers. He could imagine a cortege of mourners led by a solemn, black-robed priest making their way down the path, a simple wooden coffin part of the procession, a rectangle in the black earth waiting.

A scan with the flashlight revealed that all the graves were overgrown with underbrush. A few cairns were scat-tered throughout, and most of the heaps of memorial stones sprouted bushy weeds and thorny vines. He shone the light on the markers. Some of the dates reached back two hun-dred years.

"Maks said the grave was farthest from the road in," he said, leading Akilina deeper into the cemetery.

The burial ground was spongy from rain that hadn't let up until midafternoon. Which should help with digging, he thought.

They found the grave.

He read the words chiseled beneath KOLYA MAKS.

HE THAT ENDURETH TO THE END SHALL BE SAVED.

Akilina slid the rifle off her shoulder. "Seems this may be the right path."

He handed her one of the shovels. "Let's find out."

The ground peeled up soft and clumpy and carried a sharp scent of peat. Vassily had said the oak coffin should be shal-low. Russians tended to bury their dead that way, and he hoped the old man was right.

Akilina worked near the stone marker while he burrowed at the other end. He decided to dig straight down to see how far they needed to go. About three feet in he struck something hard. He cleared away the wet dirt, revealing wood, rotting and splintered.

"That coffin is probably not going to come out," he said.

"Which doesn't speak well of the body."

They continued digging, clearing away layers of mud and, after twenty minutes, a dark rectangle was opened.

He shone the flashlight down.

Through gashes in the wood he saw the body. He used the shovel, pried off the remaining splinters, and exposed Kolya Maks.

The Russian wore the uniform of a palace guard. Occasional bursts of color flashed in the weak beam. Muted reds, dark blue, and what was once surely white, now charcoal from the black earth. Brass buttons and a gold belt buckle had survived, but little remained of the trousers and jacket beyond shreds, leather straps, and a belt.

Time had not been kind to the body, either. The flesh was gone from the face and hands. No features were left except the eye and nose sockets, an exposed jaw, and teeth clenched tight in death. Just as the son had said, the father cradled a metal box on what was left of his chest, rib bones protruding at odd angles, limp remnants of arms still crossed.

Lord had expected a smell, but none drifted up other than the musty odor of wet dirt and lichens. He used the shovel to peel back what was left of the arms. The little bit of coat sleeve crumbled away. A couple of sod worms scampered across the box lid. Akilina lifted the box out and set it gently on the ground. The exterior was dirty, but still intact. Bronze perhaps, he thought, to survive the moisture. He noticed a padlock on the front.

"It's heavy," she said.

He knelt down and tried the weight. She was right. He shook it back and forth. Something with mass slid inside. He laid the box back on the ground and grabbed the shovel.

"Stand back."

He pounded the point of the blade into the lock. It took three jabs to crack the hasp free. He was about to reach down and open the lid when a swirl of light streaked across the tree line. His head whirled around and he saw four dots in the distance—the headlights of two cars approaching fast down the lane where they'd parked. The car lights extinguished at about the point where they'd parked.

"Kill the light," he said. "And come on."

He left the shovels and grabbed the box. Akilina cradled the rifle.

He plunged into the trees and maneuvered through the underbrush to a point beyond the open grave, but far enough into the woods for cover. His clothes quickly dampened from wet foliage, and he was careful not to jostle the box, not sure of how fragile the contents might be. He slowly moved in the direction of their car, weaving a path around the cemetery back to where they'd parked. The wind freshened, now beating a loud rhythm with the branches.

Two flashlights clicked on in the distance.

Crouching down, he moved toward the burial clearing, stopping short, still in the trees. Four dark forms emerged from the end of the trail and entered the cemetery. Three stood tall and strode firm. One was hunched forward and moved slower. In the beams of one of the flashlights he spotted the face of Droopy. The other beam revealed the pudgy features of Inspector Feliks Orleg. As they came closer he could tell from the silhouette that the other man was Cro-Magnon, and the final form was Vassily Maks.

"Mr. Lord," Orleg called out in Russian. "We know you are here. Make this easy, would you please?"

"Who is he?" Akilina whispered in his ear.

"A problem," he mouthed.

"That man with the light was on the train," she whispered.

"Both of them were." He looked back at the rifle she held. "At least we're armed."

He watched through the undergrowth, around the dark streaks of trees, as the four forms moved toward the open grave, two flashlight beams leading the way.

"This where your father is buried?" he heard Orleg ask.

Vassily Maks moved toward the stone marker revealed by one of the lights. The wind momentarily masked the voices and he could not hear if the old man said anything. But he did hear when Orleg yelled in Russian, "Lord, either come out or I'll kill this old man. Your choice."

He wanted to reach back, take the rifle from Akilina, and rush forward, but all three of the other men were surely armed and certainly knew how to handle themselves. He, on the other hand, was scared to death and was betting his life on the prophecy of a charlatan murdered a hundred years ago. But before he could make any decision, Vassily Maks made it for him.

"Do not worry about me, Raven. I am prepared."

Maks started to run from his father's grave, back toward the cars. The other three forms stood still, but Lord could see Droopy's arm raise, the outline of a gun in his hand.

"If you can hear, Raven," Maks screamed. "Russian Hill."

One shot cracked in the night and the old man dropped to the ground.

The breath left Lord and he felt Akilina stiffen. They watched while Cro-Magnon calmly walked over and dragged the body back toward the grave, tossing it into the hole.

"We have to go," he whispered to her.

She didn't argue.

They crept from tree to tree, made their way through the

woods back toward the car, and stepped to where the three vehicles were parked.

Running footsteps were approaching from the direction of the cemetery.

Only one set.

He and Akilina crouched low in the foliage just beyond the muddy roadbed.

Droopy appeared with a flashlight in hand. Keys jingled in the dark, and the trunk to one of the two cars opened. Lord rushed from the woods. Droopy seemed to hear the steps and rose up from the trunk. Lord crashed the metal box onto the man's skull.

Droopy collapsed to the ground.

Lord looked down, satisfied that the man was out, then glanced into the trunk. A tiny light illuminated a dead stare from Iosif Maks.

What had Rasputin said? *Twelve must die before the resurrection can be complete.* Mother of God. Two more just had.

Akilina rushed forward and saw the body.

"Oh no," she muttered. "Both of them?"

"We don't have time for this. Get in our car." He gave her the keys. "But be quiet with the door. Don't crank the engine until I tell you." He handed her the box and took the rifle.

The cemetery was a good fifty yards up the road, the route soft and muddy. Not the easiest terrain to negotiate, especially in the dark. Cro-Magnon and Orleg were probably searching the woods, Droopy sent back to retrieve the other body, an open grave the perfect place to dump it. Lord had even left two shovels for them. It wouldn't be long, though, before they began to miss their associate.

He chambered a round, aimed at the right rear tire of one of the cars, and fired. He quickly chambered another and blew out the front tire of the other car. He then raced to his car and leaped in.

"Go. Now."

Akilina turned the key and slammed the gear into first. Tires spun as she maneuvered the front end left and straightened back out on the narrow road.

She floored the accelerator and they shot off into the dark.

They found the main highway and drove south. An hour passed with both of them quiet, the excitement of the moment ebbing with the realization that two men had just died.

It started to rain. Even the sky seemed to share their sorrow.

"I can't believe this is happening," Lord said, more to himself than to Akilina.

"What Professor Pashenko said must be true."

Not what he wanted to hear. "Pull over. Up there."

There was nothing around but dark fields and dense woods. He hadn't seen a house for miles. No cars had appeared behind them, and they'd passed only three going the opposite direction.

Akilina whipped the wheel left. "What are we doing?"

He reached for the metal box lying in the backseat. "Finding out if this was worth it."

He cradled the muddy box in his lap. The lock had shattered from the shovel blows and the bottom was dented from the blow to Droopy. He wrenched the hasp free, slowly opened the lid, and shone the flashlight inside.

The first thing he saw was the shimmer of gold.

He lifted out the ingot, about the size of a Hershey's chocolate bar. Thirty years underground had not diminished its glimmer. Stamped into the top was a number and the letters NR, a double-headed eagle between them. The mark of Nicholas II. He'd seen photographs of the symbol many times. The ingot was heavy, perhaps five pounds. Worth right now about thirty thousand dollars, if he correctly recalled the current price of an ounce of gold.

"It's from the royal treasury," he said.

"How do you know?"

"I know."

A small cloth bag that had deteriorated lay beneath. He fingered the outside and determined that it had once been velvet. In the weak beam of the flashlight it appeared a dark blue or maybe purple. He pressed down on the exterior. There was something hard inside, and something smaller. He handed the flashlight to Akilina and used both hands to peel back the rotting cloth.

A gold sheet covered in etched words appeared, as did a brass key. On the key was inscribed c.m.b. 716. The words on the sheet were written in Cyrillic. He read the inscription out loud:

```
The gold is for your use. Funds may be
necessary and your tsar understood his duty.
This sheet should also be melted and converted
to currency. Use the key to access the next
portal. Its location should already be clear.
If not, then your path ends here, as it
should. Only Hell's Bell can point the way
beyond. To the Raven and Eagle, good luck
and Godspeed. To any intruder, may the devil
be your eternal companion.
```

"But we don't know where the next portal is," Akilina said.

"Maybe we do."

She stared at him.

He could still hear the words Vassily Maks had screamed before dying.

Russian Hill.

His mind quickly reviewed what he'd read through the years. During the Russian civil war that raged from 1918 to

1920, White Army forces were heavily financed by American, British, and Japanese interests. The Red Bolsheviks were deemed a great danger, so gold, munitions, and other supplies were funneled to the Russian mainland through the frontier town of Vladivostok on the Pacific coast. Maks had told them earlier that the two Romanov children were herded east, away from the Red Army. The easternmost point was Vladivostok. Thousands of Russian refugees had taken the same route, some fleeing the Soviets, some seeking a fresh start, others just on the run. The American West Coast became a magnet not only for refugees, but also for the funding of the beleaguered White Army, which eventually was defeated by Lenin and the Reds.

He heard Vassily Maks scream once more.

North Beach lay to the east, Nob Hill to the south. Beautiful old houses, cafés, and offbeat retail stores dotted the summit and slope. It was a trendy part of a trendy city. But in the early 1800s it was where a group of Russian fur traders had been buried. Then, the rocky shore and steep terrain were populated only by Miwok and Ohlone tribes. It would be decades before white men dominated. The legend of the graves gave the spot its name.

Russian Hill.

San Francisco, California.

America.

That was where the two Romanovs had been taken.

He told Akilina what he thought. "It makes perfect sense. The United States is a big place. Easy to lose two teenagers there, and no one would have any idea who they were. Americans knew little about the Russian imperial family. Nobody really gave a damn. If Yussoupov is as smart as he's beginning to appear, that would be the percentage play." He held up the key and stared at the initials etched into it. C.M.B. 716. "My guess? This is the key to a safe deposit box in a San Francisco bank. We'll just have to find out which one when we get there, and hope it still exists."

"Could it?"

Lord shrugged. "San Francisco has an old financial district. There's a good chance. Even if the bank's gone, the boxes may have been left with a successor institution. It's a common practice." He paused. "Vassily told us that he had one other piece of information to give us after we got back from the cemetery. I'm betting that San Francisco was the next leg of the journey."

"He said he didn't know where the children were taken."

"We can't assume that was the truth. Just more deception until we retrieved the box. Our job now is to find Hell's Bell, whatever that is." He lifted the gold ingot. "Unfortunately, this is useless. We'd never get it out through customs. Not too many people nowadays would have imperial gold in their possession. I think you're right, Akilina. What Professor Pashenko said must be true. No Russian peasant would keep something like this and not melt it down a long time ago, unless it was more precious to him in its original form. Kolya Maks apparently took this seriously. As did Vassily and Iosif. They both died for it."

He stared out the darkened windshield. A wave of resolution shot through him. "You know where we are?"

She nodded. "Near the Ukraine border, almost out of Russia. This highway goes to Kiev."

"How far?"

"Four hundred kilometers. Maybe less."

He recalled reading State Department briefings before leaving for Moscow that noted the lack of border checks between Russia and Ukraine. It had proven simply too expensive to staff all the checkpoints, and with so many Russians living in Ukraine it was deemed an unnecessary bother.

He glanced through the rear windshield. An hour behind were Droopy, Cro-Magnon, and Feliks Orleg. Ahead was open.

"Let's go. We can catch a plane out of Kiev."

30

HAYES STUDIED THE FIVE FACES GATHERED IN THE PANELED room. It was the same room they'd used for the past seven weeks. Stalin, Lenin, Brezhnev, and Khrushchev were there, along with the priest whom Patriarch Adrian had assigned as his personal envoy. He was a short man with a frizzled beard the texture of steel wool and rheumy green eyes. The envoy had exercised enough foresight to dress in a simple suit and tie, showing no outward signs of association with the church. The man had been unceremoniously dubbed by the others Rasputin, a name the priest did not like.

All of the men had been summoned from a sound sleep and told to be present within the hour. Too much was at stake to wait until morning. Hayes was glad food and drink had been prepared. There were platters of sliced fish and salami, globs of red and black caviar heaped onto boiled eggs, cognac, vodka, and coffee.

He'd taken the past few minutes to explain what had happened the day before in Starodug. Two dead Makses, but no information. Both had stubbornly refused to say anything. Iosif Maks had merely pointed the way to Vassily, the old man leading them to the grave. Yet he'd said nothing, save for a shout to the raven.

"The grave was Kolya Maks's. Vassily Maks was his son," Stalin said. "Kolya was a member of the palace guard in Nicholas's time. He traded sides at the revolution and was in Yekaterinburg at the time of the imperial executions. He is not listed as having been on the death squad, but that means nothing, considering the accuracy of that era's record keeping. No statement was ever taken from him. He was buried in some sort of uniform that was not Soviet. I assume it was imperial."

Brezhnev shifted in the chair and turned to Hayes. "Your Mr. Lord obviously needed something from that grave. Something he now has."

Hayes and Stalin had personally gone to the grave late last night, after the men had returned with news of what happened. There was nothing to find, and the two Makses were left with their ancestor.

"Vassily Maks took us there so he could get that message to Lord," Hayes said. "It is the only reason he agreed to go."

"Why do you say that?" Lenin asked.

"He is a man who apparently took his duty to heart. He would not have revealed the grave's location, save for the fact he needed Lord to know something. He knew he was going to die. He just needed to complete his duty before that happened." His patience with his Russian associates was running thin. "Could you please tell me what this is all about? You have me parading across this country killing people, yet I have no idea why. What are Lord and the woman after? Are there Romanovs who survived Yekaterinburg?"

"I agree," Rasputin said. "I want to know what is happening. I was told the situation with succession was under control. There were no problems. Yet there is this sense of urgency."

Brezhnev banged his vodka glass onto a small table beside him. "For decades there have been rumors that some of the imperial family were not murdered. Grand duchesses and tsareviches have appeared all over the world. After our civil war ended in 1920, Lenin became convinced that a Romanov survivor existed. He learned that Felix Yussoupov had perhaps spirited away at least one Romanov. But he could never verify the fact, and his health failed before he could determine more."

Hayes was still skeptical. "Yussoupov murdered Rasputin. Nicholas and Alexandra hated him for that. Why in the world would he be involved with the imperial family?"

Khrushchev answered him. "Yussoupov was a unique individual. He suffered from the malady of sudden ideas. He murdered the *starets* on an impulse, thinking he was freeing the imperial family from a devil's grasp. Interestingly, his punishment was merely banishment to one of his estates in central Russia. That move saved his life, since he was not around when the February and October Revolutions occurred. A lot of Romanovs and nobles died then."

Hayes was something of a student of Russian history, the fate of the imperial family having served as fascinating reading on a long plane ride. He recalled that Grand Duke Michael, Nicholas's younger brother, was shot six days *before* Yekaterinburg. Alexandra's sister, Nicholas's cousin Serge, and four other grand dukes were all murdered the day *after,* thrown down a mine shaft in the Urals. More grand dukes and duchesses died in the months that followed. By 1919 the Romanov family was devastated. Only a precious few escaped to the West.

Khrushchev said, "Rasputin predicted that if he was murdered by boyars, their hands would remain soiled by blood. He also said that if an imperial relative carried out his murder none of the family would live more than two years, and they would be killed by the Russian people. Rasputin was murdered in December 1916 by the husband of a royal niece. The imperial family was wiped from the face of the Earth by August 1918."

Hayes was not impressed. "We have no proof that this prediction actually occurred."

Brezhnev leveled a tight gaze at him. "We do now. The writing your Mr. Lord found, in Alexandra's own hand, confirms that Rasputin told the tsarina his prediction in October 1916, two months before he died. This country's great founder"—Brezhnev's sarcasm was clear—"our beloved Lenin, evidently thought the matter quite serious. And Stalin was petrified enough to seal everything and kill anyone with knowledge."

Hayes had not realized the significance of what Lord had found until this moment.

Lenin said, "The provisional government offered Yussoupov the throne in March 1917, after both Nicholas and his brother, Michael, abdicated. The Romanov family was finished. So the government thought the Yussoupov family could take over. Felix was widely respected for killing Rasputin. The people thought him a savior. But he refused the offer. After the Soviets took full control, Yussoupov finally fled the nation."

"If Yussoupov was anything, he was a patriot," Khrushchev said. "Hitler offered him the governorship of Russia, once Germany had conquered, and he absolutely refused. The communists offered him a job as curator of several museums, and he said no. He loved Mother Russia and apparently never realized, until it was far too late, that murdering Rasputin was a mistake. He could never have intended for the imperial family to be killed. He apparently harbored enormous guilt over the tsar's death. So he formulated a plan."

"How do you know this?" Hayes asked.

Stalin smiled. "The archives have yielded their secrets since the communist fall. It's like a *matryoshky* doll—each layer peeled away to reveal the next. No one wanted this to happen, but we all believed now would be the time of revelation."

"You suspected all along a Romanov survived?"

"We suspected nothing," Brezhnev said. "We simply feared that whatever was put into place decades ago might come to fruition with the reemergence of imperial rule. It seems we were right. The involvement of your Mr. Lord was not expected, but perhaps it is fortunate the situation has developed as it has."

Stalin said, "Our state archives are full of reports from people who participated in the executions at Yekaterinburg. But Yussoupov was clever. He involved the fewest individuals possible with his plan. Lenin and Stalin's secret police learned only minor details. Nothing was ever confirmed."

Hayes sipped his coffee, then asked, "From what I recall, Yussoupov lived a modest life after fleeing Russia."

"He followed the tsar's lead and repatriated most of his foreign investments when World War One broke out," Brezhnev said. "Which meant his cash and stocks were here. The Bolsheviks seized all his Russian property, which included the art and jewels the Yussoupov family had amassed. But Felix was smarter than he appeared. He'd invested in Europe, especially Switzerland and France. He projected a modest lifestyle, but he always had money. Documents indicate that he traded in American railway stock in the nineteen twenties and converted his investment into gold before your Depression. The Soviets searched for the vault where that gold was deposited, but found nothing."

Lenin shifted in his chair. "He may also have managed tsarist investments that escaped Bolshevik reach. Many believed Nicholas II secreted millions of rubles away in foreign banks, and Yussoupov made many trips to the United States until his death in the late nineteen sixties."

Hayes was tired, but there was adrenaline flowing through his veins. "So what do we do now?"

"We must find Miles Lord and the woman," Khrushchev said. "I passed an alert to all border stations, but I am afraid it is too late. We don't maintain checks at the Ukrainian border any longer, and that was the nearest exit point. Mr. Hayes, you have the capacity to travel wherever and whenever it is necessary. We need you to be ready. Lord will most likely make contact. There is no reason for him to mistrust you. When he does, act quickly. I think you now understand the gravity of the situation."

"Oh, yes," he said. "I see the picture real clear."

31

ATLANTA, GEORGIA
7:15 AM

AKILINA WATCHED AS LORD SLID THE KEY INTO THE LOCK AND opened the door to his apartment. She followed him inside.

They'd slept in the Kiev airport Saturday night, catching an Aeroflot shuttle Sunday morning to Frankfurt, Germany. All of the afternoon and early-evening flights were booked, so they'd waited in the terminal for a late-night Delta nonstop to Atlanta, two seats available in coach, which Lord bought with half the money Semyon Pashenko had provided.

They'd stashed the gold bar in an airport locker in Kiev, worried the whole time how secure it would be, but Akilina agreed with Lord's conclusion—there was no way to bring the ingot out with them.

They'd both slept on the plane, but the time difference was taking its toll and they weren't through chasing the sun. In the Atlanta terminal Lord booked two seats on a flight to San Francisco, leaving at noon. They needed a shower and a change of clothes, so a twenty-minute taxi ride brought them to where Lord lived.

She was impressed with the apartment, which was far better than what Semyon Pashenko possessed, but probably common for an American, she concluded. The carpets were soft and clean, the furniture, to her way of thinking, elegant and expensive. It was a little chilly inside until Lord adjusted a wall thermostat and central heat warmed the rooms. A far cry from the radiators in her Moscow apartment, which tended to run either wide open or not at all. She noticed the overall neatness and decided that wasn't surprising. Miles Lord had appeared from the start as a person in control of himself.

"There are towels in the hall bathroom. Help yourself," he told her in Russian. "You can use that bedroom there to clean up."

Her English was okay, but limited. She'd had trouble understanding conversations at the airport, particularly what the customs officer had asked. Luckily, her performer's visa provided access into the country, no questions asked.

"I have a bath in my bedroom. I'll see you in a bit."

Lord left her to a shower and she took her time, letting the warm water caress her tired muscles. It was still the middle of the night to her body. In the bedroom she found a terry-cloth robe waiting on the bed and wrapped it around herself. Lord explained that they had an hour until they needed to head back to the airport for the flight west. She toweled her hair dry and let the tangled curls fall loose to her shoulders. Water running from the back bedroom confirmed that Lord was still in the shower.

She strolled into the den and took a moment to admire photographs framed on the wall and angled on two wood tables. Miles Lord had obviously come from a large family. There were several shots of him with an assortment of younger men and women at various stages in life. He was apparently the oldest, one picture of the entire family showed him in his late teens, four brothers and sisters not far behind.

A couple of shots revealed him in athletic gear, his face obstructed by a helmet and face guard, his shoulders padded beneath a numbered jersey. There was one image of his father, framed solo, standing off to the side. It showed a man of about forty with earnest, deep brown eyes and hair a close-cropped black that matched his skin. His brow glistened from sweat, and he stood before a pulpit, mouth open, ivory teeth glittering, right index finger pointed skyward. He wore a suit that seemed to fit well, and she noticed a glint of gold from cufflinks exposed on his outstretched arm. In the bottom right corner was some writing in black marker. She lifted the frame and tried to read the words, but her ability with Western alphabet was strained.

"It says, 'Son, come join me,'" Lord said in Russian.

She turned.

Lord stood in the open doorway, a maroon robe encasing his dark frame, bare feet protruding from the bottom. In the V formed by the collar she noticed a muscular chest dusted with a light brush of curly gray-brown hair.

"He gave me that picture trying to get me to become a part of his ministry."

"Why didn't you?"

He stepped close, smelling of soap and shampoo. She noticed he'd shaved, a two-day stubble on his neck and jaw gone, his cocoa complexion unmarred by the ridges of time and tragedy all so common in her homeland.

"My father cheated on my mother and left us penniless. I had no desire to follow in those footsteps."

She recalled his bitterness from Friday night in Semyon Pashenko's apartment. "And your mother?"

"She loved him. Still does. Never will she hear a foul word about him. His followers were the same. Grover Lord was a saint to all of them."

"No one knew?"

"No one would believe. He would have simply screamed discrimination and roared from the pulpit how hard it was for a successful black man to survive."

"We were taught in school about prejudice in this country. How blacks have no chance in a white society. Is that true?"

"It was, and some say it still is. But I don't think so. I'm not saying this country is perfect; it's far from that. But it is a land of opportunity, if you take advantage of the chances."

"Did you, Miles Lord?"

He smiled. "Why do you do that?"

A curious look came to her face.

"Use my whole name," he explained.

"A habit. I meant no offense."

"Call me Miles. And to answer your question, I'd like to think I took advantage of every opportunity. I studied hard, earned everything I ever achieved."

"Your interest in my land. Did that come early in life?"

He motioned to a row of bookcases across the sunlit room. "I was always fascinated by Russia. Your history makes for great reading. A country of extremes in size, politics, weather. Attitudes."

She watched him carefully as he spoke, listening to the emotion in his voice and watching his eyes.

"What happened in 1917 was so sad. The country was on the verge of a social renaissance. Poets, writers, painters, playwrights were at their peak. The press was free. Then it all died. Overnight."

"You want to be a part of our revival, don't you?"

He smiled. "Who would have ever thought a kid from South Carolina would be in this position?"

"Are you close with your brothers and sisters?"

He shrugged. "We're all scattered across the country. Too busy to take the time for a visit."

"Are they successful?"

"One's a doctor, two are schoolteachers, another's an accountant."

"Sounds like your father did not do so bad."

"He did nothing. My mother pushed us all."

Though she knew little about Grover Lord, she thought she understood. "Maybe his life was the example each of you needed."

He scoffed. "An example I could live without."

"Is he why you never married?"

He moved to one of the windows and glanced out at the sunny morning. "Not really. Just too busy to take the time."

The rumble of traffic could be heard in the distance. "I never married, either. I wanted to perform. Marriage in Russia can be difficult. We are not the land of opportunity."

"No one special in your life?"

For a moment she debated telling him about Tusya, but decided against it, saying only, "No one of importance."

"Do you really believe that restoring a tsar is the answer to all your country's troubles?"

She was glad he didn't press the point. Maybe he'd sensed her hesitancy. "Russians have always been led by somebody. If not a tsar, then a premier. What does it matter who leads, as long as the leadership is wise?"

"Apparently somebody wants to stop whatever it is we've become involved with. Perhaps they see a restored monarchy as a way to seize control?"

"They are thousands of miles away now."

"Thank God for that."

She said, "I keep thinking about the Makses. That old man and his nephew died for what they believed. Can it be that important?"

He stepped to the bookshelves and slid down one of the volumes. She noticed the photograph of Rasputin on the cover, a menacing shot of a bearded face and piercing eyes. "This opportunist may well hold the key to the future of your nation. I always thought him a fraud who had the good fortune to be in the right place at the right time. That shelf is lined with books about him. I've read about him for years, never believing him anything more than what my own father was."

"And now?"

He heaved a deep breath. "I don't know what to think. This whole thing is incredible. Felix Yussoupov somehow secreted away two Romanov children to America." He motioned to another shelf. "I have several biographies of Yussoupov. The portrait they paint is not one of a clever manipulator. More an idealistic bungler who couldn't even murder a man right."

She stepped close and took the book from his hands, staring deep into Rasputin's eyes on the cover. "They haunt, even now."

"My father used to say that divine mystery is impossible to decipher. I used to think that was simply a clever way to keep the faithful loyal—keep them coming back to hear more. Now I'm hoping he was wrong."

Her gaze caught his. "It's not good to hate your father."

"I never said I hated him."

"You didn't have to."

"I resent what he did. The mess he left behind. The hypocrisy."

"But maybe, like Rasputin, your father's legacy is more than you realize. Perhaps you are that legacy. The raven."

"You really believe all this, don't you?"

In the quiet of the warm apartment she was beginning to relax. "I only know that from the moment you entered my compartment on the train I have felt different. It's hard to explain. I am a woman from a simple family. My grandmother was murdered, my parents' lives destroyed. I have watched suffering all my life and wondered what could I do about it? Now maybe I can help change it all."

Lord reached into his pocket and withdrew the brass key

that had come from the metal box in the grave. The initials C.M.B. 716 were clear. "That's provided we find Hell's Bell and figure out what this key opens."

"I have confidence we will do both."

He shook his head. "I'm glad one of us does."

32

HAYES STUDIED STEFAN BAKLANOV. THE HEIR APPARENT was perched at a silk-draped table facing the seventeen members of the Tsarist Commission. The Grand Hall in the Palace of Facets was full of spectators and press, the still air laced by a blue fog from commissioners who seemed to continually enjoy tobacco in one form or another.

Baklanov was dressed in a dark suit and appeared unfazed by either the length or breadth of the commission's questions. This was his last appearance before a vote on the three finalists was taken in the morning. Nine names had been placed in nomination. Three were given no chance. Two were questionable. Four were serious contenders based on blood affiliation and compliance with the Succession Act of 1797. The initial round of debate had centered on marriages since 1918 and the dilution of bloodlines that may have once been strong. Each of the nine candidates had been given time before the commission to plead his respective case and answer questions. Hayes had arranged for Baklanov to go last.

"I keep thinking of my ancestor," Baklanov said into the microphone, his voice low, but strong. "In this chamber of the Facets Palace, boyars convened in January 1613 to choose a new tsar. The country was in turmoil from a dozen years of having no one on the throne. That group set precise conditions, just as you have done. After much debate, and many rejections, they unanimously chose a gentle sixteen-year-old—Michael Romanov. Interesting that he was found in the Ipatiev Monastery, the place where Romanov rule began and that—three hundred years later—another Ipatiev house, the House of Special Purpose, was where Romanov rule ended." Baklanov paused. "At least for a time."

"But was not Michael selected," one of the commissioners asked, "because he agreed to consult with the boyars before any decisions would be made? In essence making the boyar Duma a national assembly? Is that your plan?"

Baklanov shifted in his chair, but his face remained open and friendly. "That is not the only reason my ancestor was selected. Before voting, the assembly took a crude poll and found that there was widespread popular support for Michael Romanov's selection. The same is true here, Commissioner. All of the national polls indicate the people support my restoration. But to answer your question directly, Michael Romanov lived in different times.

"Russia has tried democracy and we can see each day the results. We are not a nation accustomed to distrusting its government. Democracy breeds constant challenge, and our history has not prepared us for that. Here, the people expect government to involve itself in their lives. Western society preaches the opposite.

"This country has seen no greatness since 1917. Our empire was once the largest on Earth, but now our existence is conditioned on the generosity of foreign nations. That sickens me. We spent nearly eighty years building bombs and equipping armies while our nation crumbled. It is time to reverse that."

Hayes knew that Baklanov was playing to the cameras. The sessions were being fed live nationwide and worldwide—CNN, CNBC, BBC, and Fox all were providing Western feeds. The answer was nearly perfect. Baklanov had dodged the real inquiry, but used the opportunity to make a global point. This man may not know how to govern, but he sure as hell knew how to pander.

Another commissioner asked, "Michael's father, Filaret, if I recall my history, actually ran the country for much of his son's reign. Michael was nothing more than a puppet. Is that a worry this nation should have from you? Will others control your decisions?"

Baklanov shook his head. "I assure you, Commissioner, I will require no one to make my decisions. But that is not to say that I will not utilize my state council for advice and wisdom. I fully recognize that an autocrat must have the support of both his government and his people to survive."

Another excellent answer, Hayes thought.

"And what of your sons? Are they prepared for the responsibility?" the same commissioner asked.

The man was pressing. He was one of the remaining three who had not been fully purchased, the price of his loyalty still being negotiated. But Hayes had been assured only a few hours ago that, by tomorrow, unanimity would be a certainty.

"My sons are ready. The oldest understands his responsibility and is prepared to become tsarevich. I have trained him for that since birth."

"You were sure of restoration?"

"My heart always told me that, one day, the Russian people would want their tsar returned. He was yanked from them in violence, his throne stolen at gunpoint. An ill deed cannot bring honor. Never has good grown from evil. This nation goes in search of yesterday, and we can only hope and pray that failure will teach us success. None of us is born to ourselves. This is particularly true of those blessed with imperial roots. The throne of this nation is a Romanov throne, and

I am the closest male Romanov to Nicholas II still alive. Great honors beget great burdens. I am prepared to shoulder those for my people."

Baklanov savored a sip of water from the glass before him. No commissioner interrupted the moment. He tabled the glass and said, "Michael Romanov was a reluctant tsar in 1613, but I make no apologies for the fact that I wish to rule this nation. Russia is my Motherland. I believe all nations have a gender, and ours is distinctly feminine. It is this strong femininity that accounts for our fertility. One of Fabergé's biographers, though an Englishman, put it best: *Give her the start, the seed, and she mothers it in her own peculiar way to quite astonishing results.* It is my destiny to see those results mature. Every seed knows its time. I know mine. The people can be forced to fear, but not to love. I understand that. I do not wish for Russia to fear me. I desire no imperial conquest or world domination. Our greatness, in the years ahead, will come from providing our people with a way of life that assures health and prosperity. It matters not that we can annihilate the world a thousand times over. What should matter is that we can feed our people, cure their sickness, provide for their comfort, and assure a prosperous nation for generations."

The words were delivered with the kind of emotion that translated easily in both audio and video. Hayes was even more impressed.

"I will not say that Nicholas II was without fault. He was a stubborn autocrat who lost sight of his purpose. We know now that his wife clouded his judgment and that the tragedy with his son made them both vulnerable. Alexandra was a blessed woman in many ways, but she was foolish, too. She allowed herself to be influenced by Rasputin, a man nearly all despised as an opportunist. History is a good teacher. I will not repeat those mistakes. This nation cannot afford weak leadership. Our streets must be safe, our legal and governmental institutions stocked with truth and confidence. Only then can this country move forward."

"It sounds, sir," one of the commissioners said, "as if you have already chosen yourself tsar."

The question came from the same aggravating commissioner.

"My birth made that choice, Commissioner. I have no say in the matter. The throne of Russia is a Romanov throne. That is an indisputable fact."

"But did not Nicholas renounce the throne for himself and his son, Alexei?" came a question from the panel.

"He did for himself. But I doubt any legal scholar would conclude that he had the right to also renounce for Alexei. At the moment Nicholas abdicated in March 1917, his son became Alexei II. He possessed no right to take that throne away from Alexei. The throne is Romanov, from the bloodline of Nicholas II, and I am the nearest living male."

Hayes was pleased with the performance. Baklanov knew exactly what to say and when. He delivered his pronouncements with enough inflection to make his point without offending.

Stefan I would make an excellent tsar.

Provided, of course, that he followed orders as well as he wanted to give them.

33

LORD GLANCED OVER AT AKILINA. THEY WERE SITTING ON THE port side of a United Airlines L1011, forty thousand feet over the Arizona desert. They'd left Atlanta at five minutes after noon and, thanks to a five-hour flight and a three-hour time difference, they would arrive in San Francisco a little after two PM. Over the past twenty-four hours Lord had traveled three-quarters of the way around the globe, but he was glad to be back on U.S. soil—or over it—even if he wasn't sure what they were going to do in California.

"Are you always so restless?" Akilina quietly asked in Russian.

"Not usually. But this isn't usual."

"I want to say something."

He heard the edge in her voice.

"I was not totally honest with you earlier . . . in the apartment."

He was perplexed.

"You asked if there had ever been anyone special in my life, and I said no. Actually, there was."

Apprehension clouded her face and he felt compelled to say, "You don't have to explain anything to me."

"I want to."

He settled back into the seat.

"His name was Tusya. I met him in the performers' school where I was sent after secondary education. It was never assumed I would attend university. My father was a performer and it was expected I would be one as well. Tusya was an acrobat. He was good, but not quite good enough. He was not elevated beyond the school. But he still wanted us to marry."

"What happened?"

"Tusya's family lived in the north, near the frozen plains. Since he was not of Moscow, we would have been forced to live with my parents until securing permission for an apartment of our own. That meant obtaining their permission for the marriage and for Tusya to live in Moscow. My mother refused."

He was surprised. "Why?"

"By then she was a bitter woman. My father was still in the labor camp. She resented him for that, and for the fact that he wished to leave the country. She saw happiness in my eyes and quelled that to satisfy her own pain."

"Why not just live somewhere else?" he asked.

"Tusya wouldn't allow it. He wanted to be a Muscovite. Everyone who wasn't wanted to be. Without consulting me, he joined the army. It was either that or be banished to factory work somewhere. He told me that once he earned the right to live where he desired, he'd be back."

"What happened to him?"

She hesitated before saying, "He died in Chechnya. For nothing, since, in the end, everything was as before. I never forgave my mother for what she did."

He heard the bitterness. "Did you love him?"

"As much as any young girl could. But what is love? For me it was a temporary respite from reality. You asked me before if I thought things would be different with a tsar. How could they get any worse?"

He did not argue with her.

"You and I are different," she said.

He didn't understand.

"In many ways my father and I are much alike. Both of us were refused love thanks to the harshness of our Motherland. You, on the other hand, hate your father, but profited from the opportunity of your homeland. Interesting how life creates such extremes."

Yes, it was, he thought.

San Francisco International Airport was crowded. They'd both packed light, toting only the shoulder bags Semyon Pashenko had provided. If nothing was learned after a couple of days, Lord intended on returning to Atlanta and contacting Taylor Hayes—Pashenko and Rasputin be damned. He'd almost called the office before they left Georgia, but decided against it. He wanted to respect Pashenko's wishes as long as possible, giving at least partial credence to a prophecy he once thought complete malarkey.

They passed baggage claim, crowded with a crush of travelers, and headed outside. Beyond a wall of glass, the West Coast afternoon loomed bright in clear sunshine.

"What now?" Akilina asked him in Russian.

He did not answer her. Instead, his attention was riveted on something across the crowded terminal.

"Come on," he said, grabbing Akilina's hand and leading her through the phalanx of people.

On the far wall beyond an American Airlines baggage claim area was a lit placard, one of hundreds that lined the terminal walls. The colorful signs advertised everything from condo developments to long-distance calling plans. He stared at the words superimposed over a templelike building:

CREDIT & MERCANTILE BANK OF SAN FRANCISCO
A LOCAL TRADITION SINCE 1884

"What does it say?" Akilina asked in Russian.

He told her, then found the key in his pocket, staring again at the initials etched into brass.

C.M.B.

"I think we have a key to a box in the Credit and Mercantile Bank. It was here during the reign of Nicholas II."

"How can you be sure that is the correct place?"

"I can't."

"How do we find out?"

"Good question. We need a convincing story to gain access. I doubt if the bank is just going to let us waltz in with a key that's decades old and open the box for us. There'll be questions." His lawyer mind started working again. "But I think I know a way around that."

The taxi ride from the airport downtown took thirty minutes. He had selected a Marriott just beyond the financial district. The gigantic mirrored building looked like a jukebox. He picked the hotel not only for location but for its well-equipped business center.

After depositing their bags in the room, he led Akilina downstairs. On one of the word processors he typed out an order headed PROBATE COURT OF FULTON COUNTY. He'd clerked in the probate division of a firm during his last year of law school and was familiar with letters testamentary—the formal order from a probate court that authorized an individual to act on behalf of a deceased. He'd written several, but to be sure he accessed the Internet. The Web was littered with legal addresses that offered everything from the latest appellate opinions to templates that could be used to draft even the most obscure documents. There was one site, hosted by Emory University in Atlanta, he routinely used. There he found the right language from which to fashion fake letters of testamentary.

When the printer spat out a hard copy, he showed it to Akilina. "You're the daughter of one Zaneta Ludmilla. Your mother has recently died and left you this key to her safe-deposit box. The probate court of Fulton County, Georgia, has appointed you her personal representative, and I'm your lawyer. Since you speak little English, I'm here to handle things for you. As the personal representative, you must inventory everything your mother possessed, including whatever is in this box."

She smiled. "Just like in Russia. Fake papers. The only way to succeed."

Unlike the perception left by its advertisement, the Credit & Mercantile Bank was not located in some granite, neoclassical building, but inside one of the newer steel structures within the city's financial district. Lord knew the names of the high-rises surrounding it. The Embarcadero Center, the Russ Building, and the distinctive Transamerica Tower. He was familiar with the district's history. Banks and insurance companies predominated, giving the area the label *Wall Street of the West*. But oil companies, communications giants, engineering firms, and clothing conglomerates were also heavily represented. California gold had originally fueled the district's creation, but Nevada silver secured its place in the American financial world.

The interior of the Credit & Mercantile Bank was a trendy combination of laminated wood, terrazzo, and glass. The safe-deposit boxes were located on the third floor, and there a woman with sun-yellow hair waited behind a desk. Lord produced his key, phony letters of administration and state bar of Georgia identification card. He smiled and was

STEVE BERRY / 262

pleasant, hoping there would be few questions. But the curious look on the woman's face was not encouraging.

"We have no box with that number," she coolly informed them.

He motioned to the key she held. "C.M.B. That's your bank, right?"

"It's our initials," was all she seemed willing to concede.

He decided to try firmness. "Ma'am, Miss Ludmilla here is anxious to settle her mother's affairs. This death has been particularly painful for her. We have reason to believe this box would be quite old. Doesn't the bank maintain boxes for long periods of time? According to your advertisements, this institution has been here since 1884."

"Mr. Lord, maybe I can speak a little slower and you'll understand." He was liking her tone less and less. "This bank has no box numbered seven sixteen. Our numbering system is different. We use a letter-and-number combination. Always have."

He turned to Akilina and spoke in Russian. "She isn't going to tell us anything. She says the bank has no box numbered seven sixteen."

"What are you saying?" the woman asked.

He turned back toward her. "I'm telling her that she'll have to control her pain a bit longer because there are no answers here."

He looked back at Akilina. "Give her a sad look. Maybe some tears if you can."

"I'm an acrobat, not an actress."

He gently clasped her hands and threw her an understanding look. He kept his face animated and said in Russian, "Try. It'll help."

Akilina glanced over at the woman and for a moment showed concern.

"Look," the woman said, handing the key back to him.

"Why don't you try the Commerce and Merchants Bank. It's down the street about three blocks."

"Did it work?" Akilina asked.

"What's she saying?" the woman wanted to know.

"She wants me to explain what you said." He turned to Akilina and said in Russian, "Maybe this bitch has a heart after all." He switched to English and asked the woman, "Do you know how long that bank has been around?"

"They're like us. Old as dirt. Eighteen nineties. I believe."

The Commerce & Merchants Bank was a broad-shouldered monolith with a rusticated granite base, marble exterior, and a Corinthian-columned front. It offered a stark contrast to the Credit & Mercantile Bank and the other sky-scrapers that flanked it on all sides, their reflective silvery glass and geometric metal grids demonstrative of a more re-cent time.

Entering, Lord was immediately impressed. The look and feel was of an old-style banking hall. Faux marble columns, inlaid stone floor, and teller cages—all remnants of an era when decorative iron bars did the job high-tech security cameras performed today.

They were directed to an office that controlled access to the safe-deposit vault located, as a uniformed guard in-formed them, one floor below in the basement.

A middle-aged black man with gray-flecked hair waited in the office. He wore a tie and vest, the gold fob of a pocket watch dangling across the beginnings of a potbelly. Their host introduced himself as Randall Maddox James, and he seemed proud of the fact that his name contained three parts.

Lord showed James his letters testamentary and the key. There were no negative remarks or questions beyond a few perfunctory inquiries, and James promptly led them through the main hall and down into an elaborate basement. The safe-deposit boxes comprised several spacious rooms, each lined with row after row of rectangular stainless-steel doors. Beyond one, they were led to a row of old boxes, the green metal exteriors tarnished, the locks black dots.

"These are the oldest the bank maintains," James said. "They were here when the 1906 earthquake struck. There are only a few of these dinosaurs left. We often wonder when the contents will all be claimed."

"You don't check after a time?" he asked.

"The law doesn't allow it. As long as the rent is paid each year."

He held up the key. "You're telling me the rental on this box has been paid since the twenties?"

"That's right. Otherwise we would have declared it dormant and drilled the lock. Surely your decedent made sure that happened."

He caught himself. "Of course. Who else?"

James pointed out the box marked 716. It was halfway up the wall, the access door about a foot across and ten inches high.

"If you need anything, Mr. Lord, I'll be in my office."

Lord waited until he heard the grille gate close, signaling that they were alone. Then he slid the key into the lock.

He opened the slot and saw another metal container. He slid the rectangle out, noticing the weight of whatever was inside, and deposited the inner box on a nearby walnut table.

Inside were three purple velvet bags, all in much better condition than the one Kolya Maks had harbored in death. There was also a newspaper, folded once, from Bern, Switzerland, dated September 25, 1920. The paper was brittle but still intact. He gently massaged the outside of the longest bag and discerned distinct outlines. He quickly opened the bag and withdrew two gold bars, both identical to the one waiting in the Kiev airport, NR and a double-headed eagle stamped on top. He then reached for another bag, this one fatter, almost round. He loosened the leather straps.

What he withdrew shocked him.

The egg was an enameled translucent rose on a guilloche field, supported by green cabriolet legs that, on close inspection, were actually overlapping leaves veined with what appeared to be rose diamonds. On top was a tiny imperial crown set with two bows, dotted with more rose diamonds and what appeared to be an exquisite ruby. The entire oval was quartered by four lines of diamonds and lilies in pearls and diamonds, more leaves enameled translucent green on gold. The whole egg was about six inches tall from leg to crown.

And he'd seen it before.

"This is Fabergé," he said. "It's an imperial Easter egg."

"I know," Akilina said. "I have seen them in the Kremlin Armory."

"This one was known as the Lilies of the Valley Egg. It was presented to the Dowager Empress Maria Feodorovna, Nicholas II's mother, in 1898. There's just one problem, though. This egg was in a private collection. Malcolm Forbes, an American millionaire, bought twelve of the fifty-four known to have existed. His collection was larger than the Kremlin Armory's. I saw this exact egg on display in New York—"

Metal clanked as the iron grille at the far end of the chamber opened. He glanced around a row of silver boxes and saw James strolling toward them. He quickly rebagged the egg and pulled the leather straps tight. The gold bars were still in their bag.

"Everything okay?" the man asked as he approached.

"Just fine," he said. "Would you perhaps have a cardboard box or paper bag we could use to transport these items?"

The man gave the table a quick perusal. "Of course, Mr. Lord. The bank is at your disposal."

Lord wanted to examine the rest of the box's contents but thought it wise to first leave the bank. Randall Maddox James was a bit too inquisitive for his current paranoid personality. But it was an understandable paranoia, he kept telling himself, considering what he'd endured the past few days.

He carried their new possessions in a Commerce & Merchants Bank paper bag with rope handles and led Akilina outside, where they took a cab to the public library. He recalled the building from a previous visit, a regal three-story structure of late-nineteenth-century design that had survived both the 1906 and 1989 earthquakes. A newer building stood next door, and they were directed there by a woman at an information desk. Before turning his attention back to the items in the bag, Lord located some books on Fabergé, including one that cataloged all known imperial Easter eggs.

Inside a study room with the door locked, he spread the contents from the safe-deposit box on a table. He then opened one of the books and learned that fifty-six eggs had been created, starting in 1885 when Tsar Alexander III commissioned Carl Fabergé to fashion for his wife, Empress Marie, a gift for Easter. That holy day was the most important feast of the Russian Orthodox Church, traditionally celebrated with an exchange of eggs and three kisses. The trinket was so well received that the tsar commissioned one every Easter thereafter. Nicholas II, Alexander's son who assumed the throne in 1894, continued the tradition, except that two were now crafted—one for his wife, Alexandra, and one for his mother.

Each of the unique creations, all of enameled gold and jewels, contained a surprise—a tiny coronation coach, a replica of the royal yacht, a train, windup animals, or some other intricate mechanical miniature. Forty-seven of the original fifty-six eggs were known to exist, their locations noted in captions beneath the photos. The remaining nine had never been located after the Bolshevik revolution.

He found a full-page photo of the Lilies of the Valley Egg. The caption beneath read:

Workmaster Michael Perchin of the Fabergé workshop created this marvel. Its surprise is three miniature portraits of the tsar and Grand Duchesses Olga and Tatiana, the first two imperial children. Presently part of a private collection, New York.

The volume showed a color photo of the egg in nearly full size. A trefoil of portrait miniatures fanned from the top, the diamond crown with ruby above. Each photographic oval was gold-backed and framed in rose diamonds. The center photo showed Nicholas II in uniform, his bearded face, shoulders, and upper chest clearly visible. To his left was Olga, the firstborn, her angelic three-year-old face surrounded by curly blond hair. To the right was the infant Tatiana, not yet a year old. The back of each photo was engraved: APRIL 5, 1898.

He held up the egg from the safe-deposit box beside the picture. "These two are identical."

"But ours has no photos," Akilina said.

He glanced back at the book and read a little of the text, learning that a geared mechanism allowed the picture fan to rise. A gold-mounted pearl button on the side, when turned, supposedly activated the crank.

He studied the egg from the safe-deposit box and saw a gold-mounted pearl button. He tabled the legs and held the egg steady as he turned the tiny knob. Slowly, the diamond-studded crown rose. Beneath, a photo of Nicholas II appeared, the image identical to the one from the other Lilies of the Valley Egg pictured in the book. Then two more tiny oval photos fanned out, the left face male, the right female.

The knob would turn no farther and he stopped.

He stared at the pictures and recognized both faces. One was Alexei—the other, Anastasia. He reached over to one of the books and thumbed through it until he located a photo taken of the imperial children in 1916, before their captivity. He was right on their identity, but the faces from the egg were definitely older, both dressed in distinctive Western clothes, the tsarevich in what appeared to be a flannel shirt, Anastasia in a light-colored blouse. Behind each gold-and-diamond oval was the engraving: APRIL 5, 1920.

"They're older," he said. "They survived."

He reached for the newspaper and unfolded the yellowed bundle. He could read Swiss-German reasonably well and noticed a story on the bottom fold, apparently the reason why it had been included in the safe-deposit box. The article was headlined: GOLDSMITH FABERGÉ SUCCUMBS. The text reiterated the death of Carl Fabergé the day before at the Hotel Bellevue in Lusanne. He'd only recently arrived from Germany, where he'd fled in exile after the Bolshevik takeover in October 1917. The story went on and noted that the House of Fabergé, which Carl Fabergé had headed for forty-seven years, ended with the demise of the Romanovs. The Soviets had seized everything and closed the business, though a vain attempt was made to keep the enterprise open for a short while under the more politically correct name of "Committee of the Employees of the Fabergé Company." The reporter noted that the lack of imperial patronage was not the only reason for the business's decline. The First World War had tapped the resources of most of the rich clientele Fabergé had served. The article concluded with an observation that privileged Russian society seemed gone forever. The photograph that accompanied the article showed Fabergé as a broken man.

"This newspaper is here to prove authenticity," he said.

He rolled the egg over and found the goldsmith mark of the man who crafted it: HW. He thumbed through one of the volumes and came to a section that dealt with the various workmasters Fabergé had employed. He knew that Fabergé himself actually designed and made nothing. He was the presiding genius of a conglomerate that, at its height, produced some of the finest jewelry ever crafted, but it was the workmasters who actually conceived and assembled everything. The book noted that Michael Perchin, the head workmaster who created the Lilies of the Valley Egg, died in 1903. The text reflected that Henrik Wigström took over the managerial reigns until the House's demise, dying himself in 1923, a year before Fabergé. The volume likewise contained a photograph of Wigström's mark—HW—and Lord compared the picture with the initials stamped into the bottom of the egg.

They were identical.

He saw that Akilina held the contents of the third velvet bag—another gold sheet with engraved writing in Cyrillic. He came close and had to strain to read it, but was able to translate:

To the Raven and the Eagle: This country has proven the haven it claims to be. The blood of the imperial body is safe, awaiting your arrival. The tsar reigns but does not govern. You must remedy that. The rightful heirs will remain forever silent until you properly awaken their spirit. What I wish for the despots who destroyed our nation Radishchev said best more than a hundred years ago: "No you shan't be forgotten. Damned for ages to come. Blood in your cradle, hymns and the battle roar. Ah, drenched in blood you tumble into the grave." See to it.

F. Y.

"That's it?" he said. "This tells us nothing. What about Hell's Bell? The last engraving from Maks's grave said only Hell's Bell can point the way to the next portal. There's nothing here about any Hell's Bell." He lifted the egg and shook it. Solid. No sound from inside. He carefully studied the exterior and noticed no lines or openings. "Obviously, we're supposed to know more at this point than we do. Pashenko said parts of the secret had been lost with time. Maybe there was another step we missed, one that would tell us what Hell's Bell is."

He brought the egg closer and examined the three small photos extending from the top. "Alexei and Anastasia survived. They were here, in this country. Both are long dead, but maybe their descendants aren't. We're so close to finding them, but all we have is some gold and an egg worth a fortune." He shook his head. "Yussoupov went to a lot of trouble. Even involving Fabergé, or at least his last workmaster, to craft this."

"What do we do now?" Akilina asked.

He sat back in the chair and considered her question. He wanted to offer some hope, an answer, but finally he spoke truthfully.

"I have no idea."

34

HAYES WALKED QUICKLY TOWARD THE PHONE RINGING BESIDE his bed. He'd just finished showering and shaving, preparing for another day at the commission proceedings, a pivotal day when a decision would be made on the three candidates to be considered in the final voting. There was certainly no doubt Baklanov would be included, his final selection now assured since the Secret Chancellory had confirmed the previous night that all seventeen commission members were purchased. Even the pesky bastard who'd grilled Baklanov during his last appearance had named his price.

He answered the phone on the fourth ring and instantly recognized Khrushchev's voice.

"A call came in about half an hour ago from the Russian consulate in San Francisco, California. Your Mr. Lord is there with Miss Petrovna."

Hayes was shocked. "What's he doing there?"

"He appeared at a local bank with a safe-deposit key. Apparently that was what he retrieved from Kolya Maks's grave. The Commerce and Merchant's Bank is one of several institutions worldwide the Soviets monitored through the years. The KGB was obsessed with finding tsarist wealth. They were convinced gold bullion was sitting in bank vaults, hidden away before the revolution. Actually, there was some truth to that, because millions were found in accounts after 1917."

"You're telling me that your people still monitor banks for money that's almost a hundred years old? No wonder your government is broke. You need to give it up and move on."

"Do we? Look what's happening. Perhaps we are not as foolish as you think. Some of what you say, though, is correct. After the communist fall, endeavors such as this were deemed unaffordable. But I had the foresight to recultivate past contacts when our secret association was formed. Our consulate in San Francisco has maintained a discreet relationship with two banks there for decades. They were both depositories used before the revolution by tsarist agents. Luckily, one of our sources reported access to a safe-deposit box we suspected of a tsarist connection."

"What happened?"

"Lord and Miss Petrovna appeared with a cover story of representing some deceased person's estate. The clerk thought nothing of it until they produced a key for one of the oldest boxes the bank still maintains. It is one of the boxes we have watched. Lord left the bank with three velvet bags, contents unknown."

"We know where they are now?"

"Mr. Lord signed in for access to the safe-deposit boxes and left a local hotel address. We have confirmed he and Miss Petrovna are there. He apparently feels safe back in America."

His mind raced. He checked his watch. A little after seven AM on a Tuesday in Moscow meant it was still eight PM. Monday in California.

Twelve hours before Lord started another day.

"I have an idea," he told Khrushchev.

"I thought you might."

LORD AND AKILINA EXITED THE ELEVATOR IN THE LOBBY OF the Marriott, the contents from the safe-deposit box stored in their room's floor safe. The San Francisco Public Library opened at nine AM and he wanted to be there first thing to do more research and try and determine what they were missing, or at least develop an avenue down which they could head for answers.

This search, which at first seemed only a way to get out of Moscow, had turned interesting. Originally, he'd planned on seeing what was in Starodug, then catching the first plane back to Georgia. But after what happened to the Makses, and what he'd found both in Starodug and the bank, he realized that there was much more here than first contemplated. He was now determined to see it through. Where that might lead he had no idea. But the quest was being made even more interesting by what was happening between him and Akilina.

He'd booked only one room in the Marriott. They'd slept separately, but their talks last night revealed an intimacy he'd not felt in a long while. They'd watched a movie, a romantic comedy, and he'd translated the dialogue. With his commentary she'd enjoyed the film, and he'd enjoyed sharing it with her.

There'd only been one major romance in his life, a fellow law student at the University of Virginia whom he'd ultimately learned was far more interested in furthering her career than developing a relationship. She'd abruptly left him right after graduation, taking an offer with a Washington, DC, firm, where he assumed she was still inching her way up the hierarchy to full partnership. He'd moved to Georgia and been hired at Pridgen & Woodworth, dating some, but nothing serious and no one as interesting as Akilina Petrovna. He'd never been a believer in fate—the concept always seemed more suitable to the faithful who'd worshipped his father—but what was happening could not be denied, both the search they'd accepted and the attraction they shared.

"Mr. Lord."

The use of his name, called out across the expansive hotel atrium, caught him by surprise. No one in San Francisco should know who he was.

He and Akilina stopped walking and turned.

A sprightly gnome of a man with black hair and matching mustache approached. He was dressed in a double-breasted suit with wide lapels cut in a European style. He walked with an even gait aided by a cane and did not hurry his step as he came close.

"I am Filip Vitenko, from the Russian consulate," the man said in English.

Lord's back stiffened. "How did you know where to find me?"

"Could we sit down somewhere? I have some things to discuss with you."

He had no intention of venturing far with this man, so he motioned to an ensemble of chairs nearby.

As they sat, Vitenko said, "I am aware of the incident in Red Square last Friday—"

"Could you speak Russian so Miss Petrovna can understand? Her English is not nearly as good as yours."

"Of course," Vitenko said in Russian, throwing a smile at Akilina.

"As I said, I am aware of what happened in Red Square last Friday. A policeman was killed. A bulletin has been issued by the Moscow police for your detention. It states that you are wanted for questioning."

Now he was concerned.

"I am also aware of your contact with an Inspector Feliks Orleg. I realize, Mr. Lord, that you have no complicity in the Red Square affair. Rather, it is Inspector Orleg who is under suspicion. I have been directed to make contact and secure your cooperation."

He was not convinced. "You still haven't said how you located us."

"Our consulate has, for a number of years, maintained a watch on two financial institutions in this city. Both existed in tsarist times and were used as depositories by imperial agents. Nicholas II was said to have secreted away gold before the revolution. When you appeared yesterday, at both institutions, and wanted access to a safe-deposit box we have long suspected as having an imperial connection, we were notified."

"That would be against the law," he said. "This isn't Russia. There is bank confidentiality in this country."

The envoy seemed unperturbed. "I am aware of your laws. Perhaps they likewise cover the use of false court papers to gain access to a safe-deposit box owned by someone else?"

He got the message. "What do you want?"

"Inspector Orleg has been under investigation for some time. He is connected to some sort of organization that is intent on influencing the outcome of the Tsarist Commission. Artemy Bely, the young lawyer who was gunned down, was killed because he was asking questions about Orleg and this association. You, unfortunately, happened to be present. The individuals who murdered Bely thought perhaps he confided in you, which explains their interest in you. I am aware of the chases in Moscow and Red Square—"

"And also on a train from St. Petersburg."

"I was unaware of that."

"What kind of organization is attempting to influence the commission?"

"That, we were hoping you might know. My government is only aware that individuals are working together and large sums of money have changed hands. Orleg is connected to them. Their purpose seems an attempt to assure that Stefan Baklanov is selected tsar."

The man's words were making sense, but he wanted to know, "Are any American businessmen suspected of being involved? My firm represents a large number of them."

"We believe so. In fact, that appears to be the cash source. We were hoping you could help us there, too."

"Have you talked with my boss, Taylor Hayes?"

Vitenko shook his head. "My government has tried to confine its inquiries to keep their knowledge secret. Arrests are about to be made, but I have been asked to question you and see if you could add more. In addition, a representative from Moscow would like to speak with you, if possible."

Lord was now extremely concerned. He didn't like the idea that anyone from Moscow knew where he was.

His apprehension must have seeped through his expression. Vitenko said, "There is nothing to fear, Mr. Lord. Your conversation will be by phone. I assure you, I represent a government that is interested in everything that has happened over the past few days. We need your assistance. The commission will take a final vote in two days' time. If there has been a corruption of the process, we must know."

He said nothing.

"We cannot begin a new Russia with vestiges of the old. If commission members are being bribed, perhaps Stefan Baklanov himself has been compromised. That cannot be allowed."

He shot a quick glance at Akilina, who signaled her concern with a lingering gaze. As long as the envoy was talking, he wanted to know some things. "Why does your government continue to be concerned with tsarist wealth? It seems ridiculous. So much time has passed."

Vitenko settled back in his chair. "Nicholas II hid millions in imperial gold prior to 1917. The Soviets thought it their duty to find every last bit of that wealth. San Francisco became the hub of all Allied support for the White Army. Much tsarist gold was deposited here for the London and New York banks, which were financing rifle and ammunition purchases. Russian émigrés followed that gold into San Francisco. Many were merely refugees, but some came for a purpose." The envoy sat straight in his chair, a ramrod back matching his stuffy personality. "The Russian consul general here at the time openly declared himself anti-Bolshevik and was actively involved with American intervention in the Russian civil war. That man personally profited from the many gold-for-arms deals that flowed through local banks. The Soviets became convinced large amounts of what they regarded as *their* gold was still here. Then there is the matter of Colonel Nicholas F. Romanov."

The pitch and tone of the man's voice signaled something important. Vitenko reached into his jacket pocket and removed a copy of a news article from the *San Francisco Examiner* dated October 16, 1919. The story told of the arrival of a Russian colonel with the same last name as the deposed imperial family. He was supposedly on his way to Washington to secure American aid for White Army efforts.

"His arrival caused quite a stir. The consulate here monitored his activities. We still have the files, in fact. Whether this man was a Romanov or not, no one knows. Most likely, he was not, the name simply a way to arouse interest. He managed to shed the surveillance placed on him, and we really have no idea what he did while here or where he disappeared to. We do know that several accounts were open at the time, one at the Commerce and Merchants Bank, along with four safe-deposit boxes, one of which was number seven sixteen, which you accessed yesterday."

He began to realize this man's interest. A few too many coincidences for events to be random.

"Care to tell me what was in the box, Mr. Lord?"

He did not trust the envoy enough to part with that information. "Not right now."

"Perhaps you could tell the representative from Moscow?"

He wasn't sure about that, either, so he said nothing. Vitenko again seemed to sense his hesitancy. "Mr. Lord, I have been straightforward with you. There is no reason to doubt my intentions. Surely you can see my government's interest in all that has happened."

"Surely you can see why I'm being cautious. I've been running for my life the past few days. And by the way, you never did say how you located us."

"You listed this hotel on the sign-in sheet at the bank."

Good answer, he thought.

Vitenko reached into his pocket and pulled out a business card. "I understand your reluctance, Mr. Lord. Here is how to contact me. Any taxi driver can deliver you to the Russian consulate. The representative from Moscow will call at two thirty this afternoon, our time. If you want to talk with him, please be at my office. If not, you will not be hearing from us again."

He accepted the card and stared hard at the envoy's face, unsure what he was going to do.

AKILINA WATCHED LORD AS HE PACED THE HOTEL ROOM. They'd spent the morning in the public library reading old newspapers, finding a couple of articles on Colonel Nicholas

F. Romanov's visit to San Francisco in the fall of 1919. There wasn't much, more gossip and social news than anything else, and she could tell that Lord was becoming frustrated. They'd also verified that the Lilies of the Valley Egg was still in a private collection, which did little to explain how they possessed a duplicate, exact in every way save for the photos.

After a light lunch in one of the street cafés, they'd returned to the room. Lord had yet to mention Filip Vitenko and his offer to appear at the Russian consulate later. She'd carefully watched the envoy while he and Lord talked, trying to gauge for herself his sincerity, but it was hard to ascertain.

She glanced over at Lord. He was a handsome man. The fact that he was "of color," as she'd been taught to think, meant nothing to her. He seemed a genuine and sincere individual thrust into something extraordinary. They'd so far spent five nights together and never once had he even intimated anything improper. That was unusual for her, since the men in the circus, and the few she associated with outside work, seemed fixated on sex.

"Akilina."

She looked at Lord.

"Where were you?" he asked.

She didn't want to tell him what she was really pondering, so she said, "Filip Vitenko seemed sincere."

"He did. But that doesn't necessarily mean anything."

Lord sat on the edge of the bed. He was holding the Fabergé egg. "We must be missing something. A part of the secret has been lost. Clearly, we're at a dead end."

She knew what he really meant. "You are going to the consulate?"

He stared at her. "I don't think I have a choice. If somebody is trying to manipulate the commission, I have to help where I can."

"But there's nothing you know."

"I'm curious to see what I can learn from the Moscow representative. The information might be helpful to the man I work for. Don't forget, my original purpose was to ensure Stefan Baklanov's selection. I have to do my job."

"We'll go together, then."

"No. I may be taking a chance, but I'm not going to be foolish. I want you to take all this stuff and check into another hotel. Leave through the parking garage. Don't use the front or the lobby. This place could be watched. You never know, you might be followed, so take a roundabout path to the new hotel. Use the subway, a bus, maybe a taxi, too. Take a couple of hours to move around. I'll go to the consulate at two thirty. You call at three thirty. Use a pay phone somewhere. If I don't answer or they say I'm unavailable or I've already gone, go to ground. Stay low."

"I don't like this."

Lord stood and walked to the wall table where the velvet bag lay. He slid the egg inside. "I don't either, Akilina. But we have no choice. If there are direct Romanov heirs still alive, the Russian government needs to know that. We can't govern our lives with what Rasputin said decades ago."

"But we have no idea where to look."

"Publicity might bring any descendants of Alexei and Anastasia out into the open. DNA testing can easily weed the real thing from frauds."

"We were told to do this alone."

"We're the eagle and the raven, right? So we can set the rules."

"I don't think we can. I believe that we must find the tsar's heirs as the *starets* predicted."

Lord leaned against the table. "The Russian people need the truth. Why is openness and honesty so foreign a concept to you folks? I think we should let your government and the

U.S. State Department handle this. I'm going to tell the guy from Moscow everything."

She was uneasy about the course Lord was about to take. She preferred anonymity, the protection that a city of hundreds of thousands could provide. But maybe he was right. Perhaps the proper authorities should be alerted and something done before the Tsarist Commission selected Stefan Baklanov, or anyone else, as the next Tsar of All Russia.

"My job was to find anything that might affect Baklanov's claim. I think this definitely qualifies. The man I work for needs to know what we know. There's a lot at stake here, Akilina."

"Perhaps your career?"

Lord went silent for a moment. "Perhaps."

She wanted to ask more, but decided not to. It was obvious he'd made up his mind and he did not look the sort to change it. She would just have to trust that he knew what he was doing.

"How will you find me after you leave the consulate?" she asked.

He lifted one of the brochures stacked with several others. It was a colorful pamphlet with pictures of a zebra and tiger on the front.

"The zoo stays open till seven PM. I'll meet you there. At the Lion House. Your English is good enough to get you there. If I'm not there by six, go to the police and tell them everything. Ask for a U.S. State Department representative to be called. The man I work for is Taylor Hayes. He's in Moscow with the commission. Have the American representatives get in touch with him. Explain it all. When you call at three thirty, unless I personally come on the phone and speak with you, don't believe a word you are being told. Assume the worst and do as I say. All right?"

She didn't like what she was hearing and told him so.

"I understand," Lord said. "Vitenko seemed okay. And we are in San Francisco, not Moscow. But we have to be realistic. If this is something more than we've been led to believe, I doubt we'll see each other again."

35

THE RUSSIAN CONSULATE WAS LOCATED ON A TRENDY STREET west of the financial district, not far from Chinatown and the opulence of Nob Hill. The consulate, a red-brown sandstone two-story with an end turret, sat on the corner of a busy intersection. Balconies lined with richly scrolled metal balustrades adorned the upper floor. The roof was trimmed in a cast-iron cresting.

Lord was deposited out front by a taxi. A cool fog ebbed inland from the nearby ocean and sent a shiver down his spine. He paid the driver, then followed a brick path to a granite stoop. Twin marble lions guarded the entrance. A bronze placard attached to the stone announced, CONSULATE OF THE RUSSIAN FEDERATION.

He entered a foyer of golden oak paneling, elaborate statuary, and mosaic flooring. A uniformed guard directed him upstairs to the second floor, where Filip Vitenko waited.

Vitenko shook his hand and offered him a seat in one of two brocaded armchairs. "I am so glad you decided to cooperate with us, Mr. Lord. My government will be pleased."

"I have to say, Mr. Vitenko, I'm uncomfortable with even being here. But I thought I'd do what I could."

"I mentioned your reluctance to my superiors in Moscow,

but they assured me nothing would be done to pressure your assistance. They understand fully what you've experienced and are sorry for your misfortunes while in Russia."

Vitenko reached for a pack of cigarettes, surely the source of the bitter odor that permeated the room. His host offered one, but Lord declined.

"I, too, wish I didn't enjoy the habit so much." Vitenko balanced the filter end in a long silver holder and lit the tip. Thick smoke curled upward.

"Who is it I'll be speaking with?" Lord asked.

"A representative of the government in the Justice Ministry. He knew Artemy Bely. Arrest warrants are being prepared for Feliks Orleg and several others. This man is spearheading that action. More facts, though, could help seal the case against these criminals."

"Has the Tsarist Commission been warned?"

"The chairman is aware of what is happening, but no public announcement is to be made, as I am sure you can understand. This would do nothing but undermine the investigative process. Our political situation is most fragile, and the commission's deliberations are at a critical juncture."

He was starting to relax. The situation appeared nonthreatening, and he noticed nothing in Vitenko's words or actions that caused alarm.

The phone on the desk sprang to life with a shrill ring. Vitenko answered in Russian and directed that the call be placed through. He replaced the receiver and pushed another button on the console. A voice came through the speakerphone.

"Mr. Lord. I am Maxim Zubarev. I work within the Justice Ministry in Moscow. I trust your day has been fine."

He wondered how the caller knew he understood the language, but he assumed Vitenko had passed the information along. "So far, Mr. Zubarev. You're up late."

A chuckle crackled through the speaker. "It is the middle of the night here in Moscow. But this is most important. When you turned up in San Francisco, we breathed a sigh of relief. We were afraid the men who were after you may have succeeded."

"I understand they were actually after Artemy."

"Artemy was working for me, making discreet inquiries. I feel somewhat responsible. But he wanted to help. I failed to realize the reach of the men involved with this treason, and my heart aches over that failure."

He decided to try to learn what he could. "Has the commission been compromised?"

"We are not sure at this point. But we suspect that is so. It is our hope the corruption has not run too deep and may be caught in time. The original belief was that unanimity would prevent this type of abuse, but I am afraid that the requirement only heightened the extent of any bribery that may have developed."

"I work for Taylor Hayes. He is an American lawyer with extensive ties to foreign business investment in Russia—"

"I am familiar with Mr. Hayes."

"Could you contact him and let him know my whereabouts."

"Of course. But could you tell me why you are in San Francisco and why you accessed the safe-deposit box at the Commerce and Merchants Bank?"

He leaned back in the chair. "I'm not sure you would believe me if I told you."

"Why not let me be the judge of your sanity?"

"I am looking for Alexei and Anastasia Romanov."

There was a long pause from the other end. Vitenko gave him a surprised look.

"Could you explain, Mr. Lord?" the voice said through the speaker.

"It appears that two Romanov children escaped Yekaterin-burg and were brought to this country by Felix Yussoupov. He was fulfilling a prophecy laid down by Rasputin in 1916. I found written confirmation of that in the Moscow archives."

"What evidence do you have to support this?"

Before he could answer, the wail of a siren seeped in from outside as an emergency vehicle passed on the street below. Not something he usually paid much attention to, except that the same siren could be heard through the speakerphone.

The implications came in an instant.

He shot to his feet and bolted from the room.

Vitenko called out his name.

He yanked open the door and was met by Droopy's smil-ing face. Standing behind him was Feliks Orleg. Droopy slammed a fist into his face. He staggered back toward Vitenko's desk. Blood gushed out his nostrils. The room blinked in and out.

Orleg rushed forward and pounded him.

He slumped to the parquet floor. Somebody said some-thing, but he could no longer register the words.

He fought the feeling, but blackness enveloped him.

36

LORD AWOKE. HE WAS STRAPPED TO THE SAME CHAIR HE'D been sitting in while talking to Vitenko, duct tape now holding his arms and legs, another piece slapped over his mouth. His nose ached, and blood stained his sweater and jeans. He could still see, but his right eye was swollen, and the images of the three men standing before him were blurred.

"Wake up, Mr. Lord."

He focused hard on the man who was speaking. Orleg. Talking Russian.

"You certainly understand me. I would suggest you acknowledge whether you hear me or not."

He lightly shook his head.

"Good. So nice to see you again here, in America, land of opportunity. Such a wonderful place, no?"

Droopy stepped forward and rammed a fist between Lord's legs. The pain electrified his spine and brought tears to his eyes. The tape over his mouth deadened his scream. Each breath wheezed from a desperate attempt to suck air through his aching nostrils.

"Fucking *chornye,*" Droopy said.

He reared back to strike again, but Orleg grabbed his fist. "Enough. He'll be no good to any of us." Orleg pushed Droopy back toward the desk, then stepped closer. "Mr. Lord, this gentleman does not like you. On the train you sprayed his eyes with an aerosol, then in the woods you pounded his head. He would very much like to kill you and I really don't care, except that the people I work for desire some information. They have authorized me to say that your life will be spared if you cooperate."

Lord did not believe that for a second. His eyes apparently betrayed his mistrust.

"You don't believe me? Excellent. It is a lie. You are going to die. Of that we are sure. What I will say is that you can affect the manner of that death." Orleg was close and he caught the scent of cheap alcohol through the aroma of his own blood. "There are two options. A bullet to the head, which is quick and painless, or this." Orleg displayed a piece of duct tape dangling from his outstretched index finger, which he yanked free and then crumpled over Lord's broken nose.

The pain brought renewed tearing to his eyes, but it was the sudden loss of air that got his attention. With his nose and mouth sealed, his lungs quickly exhausted the remaining bits of oxygen. But not only couldn't he inhale, he couldn't exhale, either, and the skyrocketing carbon dioxide levels made consciousness strobe in and out. His eyes felt like they were about to explode. In the instant before darkness overcame him, Orleg yanked the tape from his nose.

He sucked in lungfuls of air.

Blood leaked down his throat with each breath. He couldn't spit it out, so he swallowed. He continued to breathe through his nose, savoring what until now he'd taken for granted.

"Option two is not pleasant, is it?" Orleg said.

If it was possible, he would have killed Feliks Orleg with his bare hands. There would be no hesitation, no guilt. Again, his eyes betrayed his thoughts.

"Such hate. You would much like to kill me, would you not? Too bad you will never have the chance. As I said, you are going to die. The only question is whether it will be quick or slow. And whether Akilina Petrovna will join you."

At the mention of her name, his gaze locked tight on Orleg.

"I thought that might get your attention."

Filip Vitenko stepped up behind Orleg. "Is this not going a bit too far? There was no mention of murder when I relayed this information to Moscow."

Orleg turned to face the envoy. "Sit down and shut up."

"Who do you think you are talking to?" Vitenko barked. "I am the consul general of this station. No Moscow *militsya* gives me orders."

"This one does." Orleg motioned to Droopy. "Get this idiot out of my way."

Vitenko was jerked back. The envoy quickly shrugged off Droopy's grasp and retreated across the room, saying, "I am calling Moscow. I do not believe any of this is necessary. Something is not right here."

The door leading out of the office opened and an older man with a long smashed face and crinkly eyes the color of burnished pennies stepped into the room. He wore a dark business suit.

"Consular Vitenko, there will be no calls to Moscow. Do I make myself clear?"

Vitenko hesitated a moment, considering the words. He also recognized the voice. It was the man from the speakerphone. Vitenko shrank to the corner of the office.

The new man stepped forward. "I am Maxim Zubarev. We spoke earlier. Apparently, our little ruse did not work."

Orleg backed away. This older man was obviously in charge.

"The inspector was correct when he said you are going to die. That is unfortunate, but I have no choice. What I can promise is that Miss Petrovna will be spared. We have no reason to involve her, provided that she does not know anything of relevance or possess any information. Of course, we never learned what it is you know. I am going to have Inspector Orleg remove the tape from your mouth." The older man motioned to Droopy, who promptly closed the door leading out of the office. "But there is no need to waste your voice screaming. This room is soundproof. Perhaps you and I can have an intelligent conversation. If I am convinced you are being truthful, Miss Petrovna will be left alone."

Zubarev stepped back and Orleg yanked the tape from Lord's mouth. He worked his jaw and loosened the stiffness.

"Better, Mr. Lord?" Zubarev asked.

He said nothing.

Zubarev pulled a chair over and sat down, facing him. "Now tell me what you failed to tell me on the phone. What evidence do you have to support a conclusion that Alexei and Anastasia Romanov survived the Bolsheviks?"

"You own Baklanov, don't you?"

The older man heaved a long breath. "I see no reason why that is relevant, but in the hope that you will cooperate I will indulge you. Yes. The only thing that could stand in the way of his ascension is the reemergence of a direct bloodline to Nicholas II."

"What's the point to all this?"

The older man laughed. "The point, Mr. Lord, is stability. The reinstitution of a tsar could greatly affect not only my interests, but a great deal of other individuals' interests as well. Was that not your purpose for being in Moscow?"

"I had no idea Baklanov was a puppet."

"He is a willing puppet. And we are clever puppeteers. Russia will thrive under his rule, and so will we." ˙

Zubarev casually examined the fingernails of his right hand, then looked at Lord. "We know that Miss Petrovna is here in San Francisco. She is no longer at your hotel, though. I have men looking for her now. If I find her before you tell me what I want to know, there will be no mercy. I will let them enjoy her and do as they please."

"This is not Russia," he said.

"True. But that is where she will be when all that occurs. A planc is waiting at the airport to return her. She is wanted for questioning and we have already cleared that with your customs authorities. Your FBI has even offered to assist in locating both you and her. International cooperation is such a wonderful thing, is it not?"

He knew what he had to do. He could only hope that after he failed to show at the zoo, Akilina would leave town. He was sad he would never see her again. "I'm not going to tell you a damn thing."

Zubarev stood. "Have it your way."

As the older man left the room, Orleg slapped another strip of tape over his mouth.

Droopy stepped close and smiled.

He hoped the end would be quick, but knew that it wouldn't.

HAYES LOOKED UP FROM THE SPEAKER AS MAXIM ZUBAREV entered the room. He'd listened to the entire exchange with Lord from down the hall, courtesy of a room microphone.

He, Khrushchev, Droopy, and Orleg had left Moscow the previous night within hours after the call verifying Lord's location. An eleven-hour time difference had allowed them to travel nine thousand miles and arrive by the time Lord was having lunch in San Francisco. Thanks to Zubarev's government connections, police visas had been arranged for Orleg and Droopy. What Khrushchev had just told Lord was true. A call had secured the help of the FBI and customs in locating Lord and Akilina Petrovna if needed, but Hayes had declined American intervention, hoping to keep the situation confined.

An easy exit from California and back to Russia for Lord and Petrovna was arranged through the State Department, few questions to be asked by Immigration at the San Francisco airport, a Russian warrant for murder the means of securing unquestioned American assistance. The idea was to contain exposure and stop whatever it was Lord was intent on finding. The problem was they still did not really know what *that* was, beyond some incredible assertion that perhaps somewhere in the United States was a direct descendant of Nicholas II.

"Your Mr. Lord is a defiant man," Khrushshev said, as he closed the door.

"But why?"

Khrushchev sat. "That is the question of the day. When I left, Orleg was stripping two wires from one of the lamps. Some electricity surging through his body might loosen his tongue before we kill him."

Through the speaker Hayes heard Droopy's voice as he told Orleg to cram the plug back in the wall socket. An amplified scream that lasted fifteen seconds pierced the room.

"Maybe you might reconsider telling us what we want to know," Orleg's voice said.

There was no reply.

Another scream. This one longer.

Khrushchev reached across the desk to a candy dish and fingered a chocolate ball. He unwrapped the gold foil and popped the morsel into his mouth. "They will continue lengthening the amount of electricity until his heart gives out. It will be a painful death."

The tone was cold, but Hayes had little sympathy for Lord. The fool had placed him in a difficult situation, his irrational actions jeopardizing a lot of planning and millions of dollars. He now wanted to know everything as badly as these Russians.

Another scream rattled the speaker.

The phone on the desk buzzed and he lifted the receiver. A voice on the other end informed him that a call had come in through the switchboard downstairs for Miles Lord. The receptionist thought it important and decided to see if Mr. Lord was available to take the call.

"No," Hayes said. "Mr. Lord is in a conference right now. Put the call through to here." He cupped his hand over the mouthpiece. "Shut that speaker off."

A click in his ear and a female voice asked through the phone, "Miles. Are you all right?" She spoke Russian.

"Mr. Lord is not available at the moment. He asked me to speak with you," he said.

"Where is Miles? Who are you?"

"You must be Akilina Petrovna."

"How do you know that?"

"Miss Petrovna. It is important we speak."

"I've got nothing to say."

He motioned to switch the speaker back on. A crackled scream instantly blared.

"Did you hear that, Miss Petrovna? That is Miles Lord. He's being questioned at the moment by a determined Moscow *militsya*. You could end his pain by simply telling us where you are and waiting there."

Silence on the other end.

Another scream.

"Electricity is being passed through his body. I doubt his heart can take much more."

The phone clicked dead.

He stared at the receiver.

The screaming stopped.

"The bitch hung up." He looked at Khrushchev. "Determined people, aren't they?"

"Very. We must learn what they know. Your idea of tricking Lord was a good one, but it failed."

"I'm betting these two are more coordinated than we think. Lord was smart to hide her. But they had to have a way to reconnect, if this wasn't a trap."

Zubarev sighed. "I'm afraid there's no way to find her now."

He smiled. "I wouldn't say that."

37

4:30 PM

AKILINA WAS FORCING BACK TEARS. SHE STOOD AT A PAY phone, the surrounding sidewalk busy with shoppers and pedestrians. She could still hear Lord's scream. What was she going to do? Lord had expressly forbidden her to call the police. He'd also made it clear that she was not to go to the Russian consulate. Instead, she was to find a new hotel, check in, and go to the zoo at six PM. Only when he failed to show was she to go to the American authorities, preferably somebody with the U.S. State Department.

Her heart ached. What had the man on the phone said? *Electricity is being passed through his body. I doubt his heart can take much more.* The words were delivered as if killing meant nothing to him. His Russian was good but she detected an American twist, which was curious. Were American authorities likewise compromised? Were they working with the same Russians who seemed intent on discovering what she and Lord were doing?

Her hand continued to grasp the phone, her gaze down to the sidewalk, and she failed to notice anyone until a hand touched her right shoulder. She turned and an elderly woman said something. The only words she caught were *you* and *over*. Tears were now dripping from her eyes. The woman noticed the crying and her face softened. She caught herself and quickly swiped the moisture from her eyes and mouthed a *spasibo,* hoping the woman understood Russian for "thank you."

She stepped from the phone and merged into the sidewalk rush. She'd already checked into another hotel using the money Lord had provided. She'd not stashed the egg, gold bars, and newspaper in the hotel's safe-deposit box, though, as he recommended. Instead, she carried them in one of the bags that had originally held Lord's toiletries and change of clothes. She did not want to trust their safety to anyone or anything.

She'd wandered the sidewalks the past two hours, darting in and out of cafés and shops, making sure no one was following. She was fairly sure she was alone. But where was she? Definitely west of the Commerce & Merchants Bank, beyond the city's main financial district. Antiques stores, art galleries, jewelers, gift shops, bookstores, and restaurants abounded. Her drifting had led her in no particular direction. The only thing important was to know the way back to her new hotel, but she'd brought one of the brochures and could always show it to a taxi driver.

What had drawn her to this spot was the bell tower she'd noticed a few blocks back. The architecture was Russian with gilded crosses and a distinctive dome. The design was a breath of home, but there were clearly foreign influences in the pedimented main door, rusticated surfaces, and a balustrade she'd never seen on any Orthodox church. She could read the sign out front, thanks to a Cyrillic translation beneath the English—HOLY TRINITY CATHEDRAL—and concluded this was a local Russian Orthodox church. The structure harked of safety, and she quickly crossed the street and entered.

The interior was traditional, built in the form of a cross, the altar facing east. Her eyes were drawn upward to the dome and a massive brass chandelier that dangled from its center. The distinctive smell of beeswax drifted from brass stands holding thick candles that flickered in the muted light, the mild scent softening a lingering presence of incense. Icons stared back from all around—on the walls, in the stained glass, and from the iconostasis that separated the altar from the congregation. In the church of her youth the barrier had been more open, offering a clear view of the priests beyond. But this was a solid wall filled with crimson and gold images of Christ and the Virgin Mary, only the open doorways offering glimpses beyond. There were no pews or benches anywhere. Apparently people here, as in Russia, worshipped standing.

She moved to a side altar, hoping perhaps God could help with her dilemma. She started to cry. She'd never been one for tears, but the thought of Miles Lord being tortured, perhaps to death, was overwhelming. She needed to go to the police, but something cautioned her that this might not be the right course. Government was not necessarily a salvation. That was a lesson her grandmother had hammered into her.

She crossed herself and started to pray, muttering lines taught to her as a child.

"Are you all right, my child?" a male voice asked in Russian.

She turned to face a middle-aged priest dressed in black Orthodox robes. He did not wear the headdress common to Russian clergy, but a silver cross dangled from his neck, an accessory she vividly recalled from childhood. She quickly dried her eyes and tried to regain control.

"You speak Russian," she said.

"I was born there. I heard your prayer. It is odd to hear someone speak the language so well. Are you here for a visit?"

She nodded.

STEVE BERRY / 298

"What is the trouble that makes you so sad?" The man's calm voice was soothing.

"It is a friend. He is in danger."

"Can you help him?"

"I don't know how."

"You have come to the right place to seek guidance." The priest motioned to the wall of icons. "There is no better adviser than our Lord."

Her grandmother had been devoutly Orthodox and tried to teach her to trust in heaven. Not until this moment, though, had she ever really *needed* God. She realized the priest would never understand what was happening, and she did not want to say much more, so she asked, "Have you followed what is occurring in Russia, Father?"

"With great interest. I would have voted yes for restoration. It is the best thing for Russia."

"Why do you say that?"

"A great destruction of souls occurred in our homeland for many decades. The church was nearly destroyed. Maybe now Russians can return to the fold. The Soviets were terrified of God."

That was a strange observation, but she agreed. Anything that might have gelled the opposition was viewed as a threat. The Mother Church. Some poetry. An old woman.

The priest said, "I have lived here many years. This country is not the awful place we were taught it was. The Americans elect their president every four years with great fanfare. But at the same time, they remind him he is human and may be wrong in his decisions. I have learned that the less a government deifies itself, the more it should be respected. Our new tsar should take a lesson from that."

She nodded. Was this a message?

"Do you care for this friend who is in trouble?" the priest asked.

The question brought her attention into focus, and she answered truthfully. "He is a good person."

"You love him?"

"We have only recently met."

The priest motioned to the bag draped from her shoulder. "Are you going somewhere? Running away?"

She realized this holy man did not understand, nor would he ever. Lord said to talk to no one until after he failed to show at six PM. And she was determined to respect his wishes. "There is nowhere to run, Father. My troubles are here."

"I am afraid that I do not understand your situation. And the Gospel says that if the blind lead the blind, both shall fall into the ditch."

She smiled. "I don't really comprehend it myself. But I have an obligation to fulfill. One that is tormenting me at the moment."

"And it involves this man, whom you may or may not love?"

She nodded.

"Would you like for us to pray for him?"

What could it hurt? "That might help, Father. Then, after, could you tell me the way to the zoo?"

38

LORD OPENED HIS EYES, EXPECTING EITHER ANOTHER JOLT OF electricity or another piece of duct tape to be pressed over his nose. He didn't know which was worse. But he realized that he was no longer strapped to the chair. He was sprawled on a hardwood floor, his bindings cut loose and dangling from the chair's legs and arms. None of his torturers were around, the office lit only by three lamps and pale sunlight filtering past opaque sheers that covered floor-to-ceiling windows.

The pain of raw electricity surging through his body had been excruciating. Orleg had delighted in varying the contact points, starting with his forehead, then his chest, and finally his crotch, his groin now aching both from Droopy's blow and the bare wires that had sent voltage surging through his genitals. It was like cold water doused on a raw toothache, intense enough to black him out. But he'd tried to hang on, stay tough, keep alert. He couldn't slip and let anything out about Akilina. Some mythical heir of the Romanovs was one thing. She was another.

He struggled to lift himself from the floor, but his right calf was numb and he was barely able to stand. The numerals on his watch blurred in and out. He was finally able to make out five fifteen PM. Only forty-five minutes left to meet Akilina.

He hoped they'd not found her. His still being alive was perhaps confirmation of their failure. Surely when she'd called at three thirty and he hadn't spoken with her, she'd followed his instructions.

He'd been a fool to trust Filip Vitenko, thinking thousands of miles between here and Moscow enough insulation. Apparently, whoever was interested in what he was doing had sufficient connections to transcend international borders, which meant high-level government involvement, and Lord resolved not to make that mistake again. From now on he would trust no one, except Akilina and Taylor Hayes. His boss had connections. Maybe enough to counteract what was happening.

But first things first. He needed to get out of the consulate.

Orleg and Droopy were surely nearby, probably just outside. He tried to remember what happened before he passed out. All he could recall was more electricity surging through his body, enough that his heart had fluttered. He'd stared hard into Orleg's bleak eyes and seen joy. The last thing he recalled before succumbing to unconsciousness was Droopy shoving the inspector aside, saying it was his turn.

He tried once more to push himself from the floor. A wave of vertigo swirled through his head.

The office door flew open. Droopy and Orleg strolled in.

"Good, Mr. Lord. You're awake," Orleg said in Russian.

The two Russians yanked him from the floor. Instantly the room spun and nausea invaded his stomach. His eyes rolled toward the ceiling and he thought he was about to black out when a sudden rush of cold water soaked his face. The initial feeling was like the electricity, but where voltage burned, the water soothed and his dizziness began to abate.

He focused on the two men.

Droopy was holding him upright from behind. Orleg stood before him, an empty pitcher in hand.

"Still thirsty?" the inspector asked with sarcasm.

"Fuck you," he managed to say.

The back of Orleg's hand slapped his wet jaw hard. The pain from the blow roused his senses. He tasted blood on the corner of his mouth and wanted to pull free and kill the sonovabitch.

"Unfortunately," Orleg said, "the consul general is concerned about a murder taking place here. So we have arranged a little journey for you. They tell me a desert lies not far away. A perfect place to bury a body. I live in the cold. Some warm, dry air would be nice." Orleg stepped close. "There is a car waiting in the rear of this building. You will go quietly. There is no one present to hear any cry for help, and if you make one sound outside, I will slit your throat. I personally would kill you here. Right now. But orders do need to be followed, would you not agree?"

A long, curved knife appeared in Orleg's hand, its edge boasting a recent sharpening. The policeman handed it to Droopy, who pressed the flat of the blade to Lord's throat.

"I suggest you walk slow and straight," Orleg said.

The warning mattered little to Lord. He was still woozy from the torture and barely possessed the strength to stand. But he was trying to muster enough stamina to be ready if an opportunity presented itself.

Droopy shoved him out of the office and into a secretarial area devoid of people. Down a staircase they made their way toward the rear of the ground floor, past a cadre of offices, all of which were dark and empty. The glimpses he caught through windows showed that day was surrendering to night.

Orleg stepped ahead, now leading the way, stopping at a

paneled wooden door outlined in elaborate molding. He unlocked the latch and opened it. Beyond, the growl of a car
motor could be heard, and he saw the open rear door of a
black sedan, exhaust smoke whipping mist up and over the
roof. The inspector motioned for Droopy to bring their charge
forward.

"Stoi," a voice called out from behind. Stop.

Filip Vitenko brushed past and moved straight toward Orleg. "I told you, Inspector, there would be no more violence
where this man is concerned."

"I told you, diplomat, this does not concern you."

"Your Mr. Zubarev is gone. I am in authority here. I have
spoken to Moscow and have been told to do as I see fit."

Orleg grabbed two handfuls of the envoy's jacket and
slammed him to the wall.

"Xaver," Vitenko screamed.

Lord heard the gait of someone rushing down the hall,
then a stump of a man rushed at Orleg. The second of commotion allowed Lord to jam his elbow into Droopy's stomach. The muscles were hard and flat, but he managed to
wedge the point between ribs, then wrench upward.

Droopy's breath left him in a *swoosh.*

Lord shoved the hand holding the knife away. The big
man atop Orleg noticed the attack and turned his attention to
Droopy, leaping onto the Russian.

Lord lunged toward the outer door. Vitenko momentarily
interfered with Orleg, which allowed Lord to leap out under
the porte cochère harboring the idling vehicle. He saw no
one in the car and jumped into the front seat. He rammed the
gearshift into drive and plunged the accelerator to the floor-
board. Tires grabbed pavement and the car rocked forward,
the rear door slamming shut.

Ahead loomed an open iron gate.

He raced through.

Out in the street, he wheeled right and roared off.

"ENOUGH," HAYES SAID.

Droopy, Orleg, Vitenko, and the aide stopped their tussle.

Maxim Zubarev stood beside Hayes in the corridor. "Good show, gentlemen."

"Now," Hayes said. "Let's go track that motherfucker and find out what this is all about."

39

LORD SWUNG THE CAR AROUND ANOTHER CORNER, THEN slowed. In the rearview mirror he noticed no cars following, and the last thing he needed was to attract the attention of the police. The dashboard clock glowed five thirty. He still had half an hour to make the rendezvous. He was trying to remember the local geography. The zoo was south of town center, adjacent to the ocean, near San Francisco State University. Lake Merced was nearby. On an earlier trip, he'd fished there for trout.

That seemed like an eternity ago. Back when he was just an associate in a huge law firm, nobody beyond his secretary and supervising attorney caring what he did. Hard to believe all this had started just a week ago after a simple lunch in a Moscow restaurant. Artemy Bely had insisted on paying the tab, saying the next day's meal would be on Lord. He'd allowed the courtesy, knowing the Russian lawyer made less in a year than he did in three months. He'd liked Bely, a seemingly knowledgeable, easygoing young man. Yet all he now remembered was the image of Bely's bullet-ridden corpse, lying on the sidewalk, Orleg telling him there were too many dead to bother covering them.

The bastard.

He turned at the next intersection and headed south, away from the Golden Gate Bridge, toward the ocean side of the peninsula. It helped when signs started appearing for the zoo, and he followed them through evening traffic. Soon he left the congestion of commercialism behind for the quiet hills and trees of St. Francis Wood, the villas set back from the road, most with iron gates and fountains.

He was amazed that he was even able to drive, but a rush of adrenaline surging through him had charged his senses. His muscles still ached from the electricity and he was winded from repeated strangulations, but he was starting to feel alive again.

"Just let Akilina be there, waiting," he whispered.

He found the zoo and motored into a lighted parking lot. He left the keys in the sedan and trotted to the admission gate where he paid for a ticket, the attendant warning him that the park would be closing in little more than an hour.

The front of his sweater was wet from Orleg's dousing, the bloodied green wool carrying the feel of a damp towel in the chilly evening air. His face ached from the blows, and surely some swelling had contorted his features. He was probably quite a sight.

He trotted down the concrete walkway, amber lights illuminating the way. A few visitors milled about, several more strolling in the opposite direction back toward the exit. He passed a primate center and elephant exhibit and followed direction signs to the Lion House.

His watch read six PM.

Darkness was starting to conquer the sky. Only the sounds of animals muted by thick walls disturbed an otherwise peaceful scene. The air smelled of fur and food. He entered the Lion House through a set of double glass doors.

Akilina stood before a pacing tiger. He sympathized with the animal trapped in a cage—exactly where he'd been the entire afternoon.

Her face reflected relief and joy. She rushed toward him

and they hugged, her grip desperately tight. He held her as she trembled.

"I was just about to leave," she said. Her hand gently traced his swollen jaw and bruised eye. "What happened?"

"Orleg and one of the men who's been after me are here."

"I heard you scream through the phone." She told him about her call and the man she'd talked with.

"The Russian in charge called himself Zubarev. There must be others at the consulate helping them besides Vitenko. But I don't think Vitenko is one of them. If it wasn't for him, I wouldn't be here." He told her what had happened just a few minutes before. "I checked all the way here, but nobody was behind me." He noticed the bag slung over her shoulder. "What's that?"

"I didn't want to trust these things to the hotel. Better to keep everything with me."

He decided not to argue about her foolishness. "We're getting out of here. As soon as we're safe, I'm calling Taylor Hayes and getting some help. This is way out of control."

"I'm glad you are okay."

He suddenly realized they were still in each other's arms and drew back to look at her.

"It's okay," she said softly.

"What do you mean?"

"You can kiss me."

"How do you know I want to?"

"I just do."

He touched his lips to hers, then pulled away. "This is really strange."

One of the cats across the viewing chamber suddenly roared.

"Think they approve?" he said, a smile creeping onto his face.

"Do you?" she asked.

"Very much. But we need to get out of here. I used one of their cars to get across town. Probably not a good idea to use it again. They might report it stolen and involve the local police. We'll get a cab. I noticed a few parked out front when I came in. We'll go back to the hotel you found and in the morning find a rental car. I don't think we need to be using the local airport or bus stations."

He slipped the bag off her shoulder and draped it onto his, feeling the weight of the two gold bars. He took her by the arm and they headed out of the Lion House, past a group of teenagers ambling in for a last look.

A hundred yards away, under one of the lights illuminating the walkways, he caught a glimpse of Orleg and Droopy racing his way.

Mother of God. How had they found him?

He grabbed Akilina and they bolted in the opposite direction, past the Lion House, toward a lit building labeled PRIMATE DISCOVERY CENTER. Monkeys screeched from their outdoor habitats. They followed the paved path deeper into the complex, then made a sharp left. Before them was a lighted naturalistic setting of trees and rocks, a deep moat separating a concrete retaining wall from an open enclosure beyond. Gorillas lumbered about in a forestlike setting, a couple of adults and three babies.

Still running, it took Lord only an instant to register the fork in the path ahead and the fact that the concrete walk apparently encircled the exhibit, making a teardrop-shaped loop that both began and ended before him. A high fence ran the length of the property to his left, and beyond to the right was an open area designated MUSK OXEN EXHIBIT. About ten people were intently watching the gorillas feeding on a huge pile of fruit in the middle of the habitat.

"There's nowhere to go," he said, desperation in his voice.

He needed to do something.

Then, in the far rock wall of the gorilla exhibit he spotted an open iron gate. He studied the animals and the portal. Perhaps it was where the beasts ventured at night. Maybe they could get there and close the gate before the gorillas became interested.

Anything was preferable to the alternative. Orleg and Droopy were racing toward them. He knew what that sadistic pair were capable of and decided to take his chances with the apes. Through the open portal in the rock wall he spied a door with lights. There was movement inside. Perhaps an attendant.

And maybe a way out.

He hurled the travel bag through the air into the ape exhibit. The bundle landed hard near a pile of fruit. The gorillas reacted to the intruder with a vocal start, then moved forward to investigate.

"Come on."

He hopped onto the retaining wall. The other visitors gave him a strange look. Akilina followed. The distance across the moat was about ten feet. The wall itself was about a foot wide. With a running start he leaped forward, propelling his stocky frame through the air and praying he hit solid earth on the other side.

He did, pounding the ground, pain searing up through his sore legs and thighs. He rolled once and looked back just as Akilina landed on her feet.

Droopy and Orleg appeared at the retaining wall.

He was counting on the fact they wouldn't follow or use weapons with people around. Several of the spectators cried out and he heard one of them scream for the police.

Droopy leaped onto the wall. He was about to jump when one of the adult gorillas raced forward to the edge of the moat. The animal raised up on its hind legs and bellowed. Droopy retreated.

Lord scrambled to his feet and motioned for Akilina to head for the gate. The other adult gorilla lumbered his way. The massive animal waddled on all fours, soles and knuckles skipping off the hard ground. From the size and manner, Lord reasoned this was a male. The fur was a satiny brown-gray highlighted by jet-black skin on the chest, palms, and face, a silver saddle decorating his back. The animal stood upright, his nostrils flaring, broad chest extended, bulky arms waving. The ape let out a roar and Lord stood perfectly still.

The smaller gorilla, more reddish brown, apparently a female, moved toward Akilina and was now challenging her. Lord wanted to help but had problems of his own. He hoped everything he'd ever seen on the Discovery Channel about gorillas was true. They were supposedly more bark than bite, the physical display an attempt to generate some reaction in their opponent, perhaps enough to scare him away, or at least to distract.

Out of the corner of his eye he noticed Orleg and Droopy watching, then saw as they headed back from where they came. Perhaps the attention was becoming a bit much.

Not only did Lord not want another meeting with his Russian pursuers, but he didn't want to have to explain any of this to the local police—at least not yet—and surely they'd been called.

He needed to get to the portal. But the big male standing before him started pounding his chest.

The female concerned with Akilina started to back away, and Akilina used the moment to inch toward him. Suddenly the female surged forward and Akilina reacted, vaulting toward the outstretched limb of one of the poplars that dotted the habitat. She quickly rolled up onto the limb, her acrobatic grace obvious as she leaped to a higher branch. The female ape seemed almost astonished by the move and started her own climb. Lord noticed that the female's face had softened. It was almost as if the ape thought the whole thing play. The trees dotting the enclosure were heavily intertwined, surely an effort to provide the animals with a more natural habitat, but what it did now was provide Akilina a way to avoid her pursuer.

The male before him stopped pounding his chest and hinged down on all fours.

From behind, a female voice whispered, "Whoever you are, I'm the tender of this exhibit. I would strongly suggest you stand perfectly still."

"I can assure you, I'm not moving," he said in his own low voice.

The ape's gaze stayed tight, the head cocked at a curious angle.

"I'm inside the rock wall. Beyond the open gate," the disembodied voice said. "They come in here for the night. But they won't bother until all the food's gone. You've got King Arthur there. He's not overly friendly. I'll try to distract him while you make your way inside."

"My friend out here has her own problems," he said.

"I see that. But we'll take it one at a time."

King Arthur slowly backed away, toward the travel bag. Lord could not leave without the bag. He eased toward it. The ape rushed forward and screeched, as if commanding him to stay still.

He obeyed.

"Don't challenge him," the voice said.

The gorilla bared his canines. Lord harbored no desire to feel their effects. He watched as Akilina and the female ape vied with each other through the branches. Akilina did not appear to be in any danger, staying outside the reach of the animal, winding herself up, then down over a thick branch, landing square on the ground. The female tried to mimic the action, but her great bulk drew her downward in a swinging arc and she slammed to the earth. Akilina used the moment to rush into the portal.

Now it was his turn.

King Arthur jerked up the travel bag and fumbled with it in an attempt to see what was inside. Lord moved to grab it, hoping he might be quick enough to snatch the satchel and make it into the opening. But King Arthur was quick, too. The ape's arm swept up and a hand grabbed a bundle of his sweater. The gorilla now had him in his grasp and he tried to fall back. The ape, though, did not relinquish his grip and the sweater slowly tore from his chest. King Arthur stood with the travel bag in one hand, sweater in the other.

Lord did not move.

The gorilla tossed the sweater aside and returned to rummaging the bag.

"You need to come on," the woman said.

"Not without that bag."

The ape tugged and pulled at the stitching, several times sinking long teeth into the exterior. The stiff green cloth held firm and, in obvious frustration, the gorilla slung the bag hard against the rock wall. Rushing over, King Arthur again flung the bundle into the stone.

Lord winced.

The Fabergé egg could not withstand such abuse. Without thinking, he lunged forward as the bag fell to the ground from a third throw. King Arthur came with him, but Lord reached the bag first and snatched up the bundle. The female dashed over and moved between him and the male, reaching for the bag herself, but King Arthur wrenched her neck hair, eliciting a belch and grunt from the smaller gorilla. The male pulled her away, and Lord used the moment to dart for the open gateway.

But King Arthur cut him off only a few steps from safety.

The big ape stood not five feet away, his body odor nause-ating. An intense stare accompanied a low growl. The ani-mal's upper lip flared, displaying incisors as long as Lord's fingers. The gorilla slowly reached out and fingered the travel bag, caressing the cloth exterior.

Lord stood still.

The ape poked his right index finger into Lord's chest. Not enough to hurt, just enough to test the skin beneath his shirt. It was an almost human gesture, and for a moment Lord's fear abated. He stared deep into the animal's glowing eyes and sensed an acknowledgment that he was in no danger.

King Arthur withdrew his finger and stepped back.

The female had likewise withdrawn after her rebuke.

The big male continued to inch away until the path into the portal was clear. Lord crept inside and the iron gate closed after him.

"I've never seen King Arthur react like that before," said the woman, who locked the gate shut. "He's an aggressive ape."

Lord stared through the bars at the gorilla, who continued to watch him, the sweater now back in hand. Finally, the an-imal lost interest and headed for the pile of food.

"Now you want to tell me what you were doing in there?" the woman asked.

"Is there a way out?"

"Not so fast. We're going to wait for the police."

He could not do that. No telling how far the reach of those after him extended. He spied a closed exit door with a hall-way beyond visible through wire-reinforced glass. He grabbed Akilina and headed that way.

The uniformed woman intercepted him. "I said we're go-ing to wait for the police."

"Look, I've had a rough day. There are men trying to kill

us and I just stared down a three-hundred-pound gorilla. I'm not in the mood to argue, if you get my meaning."

The attendant hesitated, then stepped out of the way.

"Good choice. Now, where's the key for that door?"

The woman reached into her pocket and tossed him a ring with a single key. He and Akilina left the chamber, and he closed and locked the door behind them.

They quickly found an exit that led beyond the public viewing areas, toward two large sheds filled with equipment. Farther on was an empty parking lot. A sign noted that the space was for employees only. He knew they could not return to the main entrance, so he headed toward the ocean and a road that paralleled the shore. He wanted to get out of the area immediately and was relieved when a cab appeared. He flagged the vehicle down and they climbed inside, the driver depositing them at Golden Gate Park ten minutes later.

He and Akilina walked inside the park.

A darkened soccer field spread before them, a small pond to the right. The grounds extended for miles in all directions, trees and meadows nothing but featureless shadows. They stopped at a bench and sat down. His nerves were shot, and he wondered how much more he could take. Akilina put her arm around him, then laid her head on his shoulder.

"That was amazing what you did with the ape," he said. "You're a hell of a climber."

"I don't think the animal would have hurt me."

"I know what you mean. The male could have attacked, but he didn't. He even prevented the female from charging."

He thought about the travel bag slamming into the rock wall. He lifted the bag from the damp grass. An overhead streetlight gave off an orange radiance. No one else was in sight. The air was chilly and he wished he still wore his sweater.

He unzipped the bag.

"When King Arthur slammed this thing, all I could think about was the egg."

He withdrew the velvet sack and slipped the egg out. Three of the legs were broken and many of the diamonds were loose. Akilina quickly cradled her hands underneath and caught the precious debris. The egg was cracked down the center of its oval, laid open like a grapefruit.

"It's ruined," he said. "That thing was priceless. Not to mention it may spell the end of our search."

He studied the gaping slit in the masterpiece, a sick feeling grew in his stomach. He dropped the velvet bag and, with his finger, gently probed what was inside the egg. White and fibrous. Like some sort of packing material. He squeezed a pinch and discovered it was cotton, stuffed so dense it was difficult to loosen even a sample. He continued to probe, expecting at some point to find the mechanism that controlled the rising of the three tiny portraits, but instead he struck something else.

The tip of his finger explored farther.

Definitely something hard.

And smooth.

He moved close to the ambient glow from the overhead light and continued to bore with his finger.

He caught a glint of gold with something etched on it.

Writing.

He grasped the sides of the egg with both hands and parted the divide, opening up the thin gold exterior as if it were a ripe pomegranate.

PART
THREE

PART
THREE

40

HAYES WATCHED AS ORLEG AND DROOPY EXITED THE ZOO'S main gate and hustled for the car. He and Khrushchev had been waiting patiently in the parking lot for the past ten minutes. The tracking device Hayes had placed on Lord had worked, a tiny dot no larger than a button. The consulate possessed a quantity of such equipment, holdovers from the Cold War when San Francisco was central to Soviet intelligence gathering in the important computer- and defense-oriented California region.

They'd allowed Lord to escape as a means of finding Akilina Petrovna, whom Hayes believed possessed whatever it was Lord found in Kolya Maks's grave and in the safe-deposit box. The ability to covertly track their prey had allowed them to stay back a discreet distance as Lord wove his way through evening traffic. He thought the meeting place odd, but reasoned that Lord had wanted a public locale. Public attention was one thing Hayes did not need.

"I don't like the looks on their faces," Khrushchev said.

Hayes didn't, either, but said nothing. He was still comforted by the fact the LCD screen before them beeped, signifying a lock on Lord. He pushed a button and the rear window of the Lincoln whined down. Orleg and Droopy stopped outside.

"He jumped into the gorilla pit," Orleg said. "We tried to follow, but one of the fucking beasts stopped us. I didn't think you wanted a lot of show, so we came out. We'll just track him again."

"That was wise," he said. "We still have a strong signal." He turned to Zubarev. "Shall we?" He opened the door and they climbed out into the night. Orleg grabbed the handheld LCD display and they all moved forward. In the distance, sirens could be heard approaching.

"Someone has called the police. We need to end this fast," he said. "This is not Moscow. The police here ask lots of questions."

The zoo's front gate was unattended and they quickly darted inside. A crowd had gathered at the gorilla expo. The tracking device Orleg carried continued to signify Lord's presence nearby. "Put that thing under your jacket," he said to Orleg, not wanting any questions from the curious.

They approached the primate exhibit and Hayes asked what was going on. A woman told him that a black man and a white woman had jumped over the moat and the gorillas had gone after them. They eventually slipped into an open gate in the rock wall and disappeared. He moved back to Orleg and learned the signal was still active. But when he focused out into the lit habitat he immediately saw what a large silver-back gorilla held in his clenched hand.

A dark green sweater.

The same sweater into which the tracking device had been sewn. He shook his head and suddenly recalled what Rasputin had predicted to Alexandra. *The innocence of beasts will guard and lead the way, being the final arbiter of success.*

"The ape has the sweater," he told Zubarev, who moved close to the retaining wall and saw for himself.

The look on the wiry Russian's face conveyed that he, too, remembered the *starets*'s prediction. "The beast certainly guarded the way. I wonder if he led it, as well."

"Good question," Hayes said.

LORD PEELED BACK THE GOLDEN EDGES OF THE EGG. DIA-
monds popped off like drops of juice from a split orange. A
small golden lump fell to the damp grass. Akilina reached
down and lifted the object.

A bell.

The exterior shone bright in the glow from the lamp
above, surely the first time that this gold had touched fresh
air in decades. She stepped closer to the light and he spied
tiny words etched on the bell's exterior.

"It's written in Cyrillic," she said, the bell close to her
eyes.

"Can you read it?"

" 'To where the Princess tree grows and Genesis, a Thorn
awaits. Use the words that brought you here. Success comes
if your names are spoken and the bell is formed.' "

He was tiring of riddles. "What does that mean?"

He grabbed the bell and studied it in detail. It was no more
than three inches high and a couple of inches wide. No clapper hung inside. Its weight suggested that it was solid gold.
Other than the etched letters encircling the outside, there
were no words or symbols. Apparently, this was Yussoupov's
last message.

He retreated to the bench and sat down.

Akilina followed.

He looked at the destroyed Fabergé egg. For the better part
of the twentieth century and into the twenty-first, descendants of Nicholas II had apparently survived. While communist premiers dominated the Russian people, heirs to the
Romanov throne lived on, in obscurity, *where the Princess
tree grows*—wherever that was. He wanted to find those descendants. Actually, he needed to find them. Stefan Baklanov was not the rightful heir to the Russian throne, and

perhaps the reemergence of a direct Romanov might galvanize the Russian people in a way nothing else could. But at
the moment he was too tired to do any more. He'd originally
planned to leave town tonight, but now he decided against
that. "Let's go back to the hotel you found and get some
sleep. Maybe this will be clearer in the morning."

"Could we get something to eat along the way? I have not
eaten since breakfast."

He looked at her, then reached up and lightly caressed her
cheek. "You did good today," he said in Russian.

"I was wondering if I'd ever see you again."

"You weren't the only one."

Her hand came up to his. "I did not like the thought of
that."

Nor did he.

He gently kissed her lips, then took her in his arms. They
sat for a few minutes in the darkness, savoring the solitude.
Finally he stuffed what was left of the egg back into its velvet sack, along with the bell. He shouldered the travel bag
and they walked from the park to the boulevard beyond.

Ten minutes later a cab appeared and he told the driver the
name of the hotel Akilina had selected. They sat together in
the backseat as the cab made its way into the city. He was
thinking about what was inscribed on Hell's Bell.

*To where the Princess tree grows and Genesis, a Thorn
awaits. Use the words that brought you here. Success comes
if your names are spoken and the bell is formed.*

Apparently another cryptic direction—enough to lead the
way if you knew what to look for, but not enough to be a di-
vining rod for intruders. Trouble was, he didn't know what
they were looking for. Those words had been scripted sometime after 1918, when the imperial family was murdered, and
before 1924, when Fabergé himself had died. Perhaps
their meaning was clearer then, time clouding what was once

an unambiguous message. Through the cab's dingy windows he studied the parade of cafés and restaurants that rolled by. He recalled Akilina's request for food and, though he did not want to be exposed for long, he, too, was hungry.

A thought occurred to him.

He told the driver what he wanted and the man nodded in recognition, finding the appropriate establishment a few minutes later.

He led Akilina inside a building marked CYBERHOUSE, one of many places that combined Internet access with food and drink. Right now he needed both food and information.

The interior was half full and lined with shiny stainless-steel walls and lots of smoky glass panels with local scenes etched into them. A large-screen TV with a small crowd gathered around dominated one corner. Hefty draft beers seemed the specialty, along with thick deli sandwiches.

He darted into the bathroom, doused his face with cold water, and tried to make the bruises appear less threatening.

He and Akilina then grabbed a booth with a terminal and ordered, the waitress explaining how to use the keyboard and providing them a password. While they waited for the food, he found a search engine and typed: PRINCESS TREE. Some three thousand findings appeared. Many dealt with a jewelry line being peddled and known as the Princess Tree Collection. Others dealt with the rain forest, forestry, horticulture, and medicinal herbs. One, though, instantly drew his attention with the summary:

```
Paulownia Tomentosa—Princess Tree, Karri
Tree—fragrant violet flowers. Aug./Sept.
```

He clicked on the site and the screen exploded with a narrative explaining that the princess tree originated in the Far East, but was imported to America in the 1830s. The species had spread all along the eastern United States thanks to seed-pods used for packing material in crates shipped from China. Its wood was light and water-resistant, used by the Japanese for rice bowls, utensils, and coffins. The growth rate was fast—five to seven years to maturity—and its blooms were quite striking, with an elongated lavender flower that was mildly fragrant. A mention was made of utilizing the species in the timber and pulp industries due to its fast growth and low production cost. It was particularly prominent in the mountains of western North Carolina, where attempts at cultivation had occurred repeatedly through the years. But it was the explanation of the name that caught his attention. The text noted that the tree was named for Princess Anna Paulownia, daughter of Tsar Paul I, who ruled Russia from 1797 to 1801. Paul I was Nicholas II's great-great-grandfather.

He told Akilina what he read.

She was amazed. "To learn so much. So fast."

He realized Internet access was something only just beginning in Russia. Some of Pridgen & Woodworth's clients were working feverishly to better connect the country to the World Wide Web. Problem was, a single computer cost more than most Russians made in two years.

He scrolled down and checked a couple more sites. None provided any useful information. The waitress arrived with their food and two Pepsis. They ate and, for a few minutes, he forgot about their dire situation. He was finishing up the last of his baked chips when another thought hit him. He backtracked to the search engine. There he typed NORTH CAROLINA and found a site that contained a detailed state map. He focused on the mountainous western region and called up an enlarged portion.

"What is that?" Akilina asked.

"A hunch I'm playing," he said, eyes not leaving the screen.

In the center of the screen was Asheville, a cross of dark red lines emanating in four directions, signifying Interstates 40 and 26. To the north were towns like Boone, Green Mountain, and Bald Creek. To the south were Hendersonville and the South Carolina–Georgia border. Maggie Valley and Tennessee lay to the west, and Charlotte loomed off to the east. He studied the Blue Ridge Parkway snaking a path to the northeast from Asheville to the Virginia line. The towns carried interesting names. Sioux, Bay Book, Chimney Rock, Cedar Mountain. Then, just north of Asheville, south of Boone, near Grandfather Mountain, he saw it.

Genesis. On State Route 81.

To where the Princess tree grows and Genesis, a Thorn awaits.

He turned to Akilina and smiled.

41

WEDNESDAY, OCTOBER 20

LORD AND AKILINA ROSE EARLY AND CHECKED OUT OF THE hotel. The past week had been the first time in many years he'd slept with a woman. There'd been no sex, as they were both too exhausted and scared, but they'd lain in each other's arms, he dozing in and out, half expecting Droopy and Orleg to burst into the room any minute.

They'd awakened just after dawn and headed to an Avis rental agency in the financial district. Then, they'd driven ninety miles northeast to Sacramento, reasoning that the airport there might be safe from watchful eyes. After dropping off the car, they boarded an American Airlines nonstop to Dallas. On the plane, he took the time to read a *USA Today*. A front-page story recounted how the Tsarist Commission was nearly finished with its work. Defying all odds, the commission had completed its interviews and narrowed the field to three finalists, one of whom was Stefan Baklanov. A final vote, originally scheduled for the next day, had been changed to Friday because of a death in one commission member's family. Since unanimity was required on any final vote, there was no choice but to institute a one-day delay. Analysts were already predicting Baklanov's selection and heralding the choice as the best course for Russia. One historian was quoted as saying, "He is the closest we have to Nicholas II. The most Romanov of the Romanovs."

Lord stared at the phone recessed into the headrest of the seat ahead. Should he contact somebody at the State Department, or Taylor Hayes, and tell them what he knew? The information he and Akilina were privy to would almost certainly change the outcome of the commission's vote. At least it would delay any final resolution until the validity of his information could be checked. But the prophecy said he and Akilina must complete the task alone. Three days ago he would have dismissed all of this as the drunken ravings of a power-hungry peasant who managed to worm his way into the graces of Russia's imperial family. But the ape. *The beast.* He'd smashed the egg. He'd also stopped Droopy from leaping over the moat.

The innocence of beasts will guard and lead the way, being the final arbiter of success.

How could Rasputin have known something like that would happen? Was it coincidence? If so, it stretched the bounds of probability to the breaking point. Was the heir to the Russian throne living peacefully in America? Genesis, North Carolina, population 6,356, according to the atlas he'd bought in the airport. The seat of Dillsboro County. A tiny town in a tiny county nestled in the mountains of Appalachia. If he or she was there, that fact alone could change the course of history. He wondered what the Russian people would think when they learned two heirs had survived Yekaterinburg and hid in America, a place the entire nation had been taught for decades to mistrust. He also wondered what the heir would be like—a child or grandchild of Alexei or Anastasia, or perhaps both, raised American. What type of connection would he or she have to a Motherland that now beckoned them home to rule a country in utter turmoil?

This was incredible. And he was a part of it. An integral

part. The raven to Akilina's eagle. Their job was clear. Finish this quest and locate a Thorn. But somebody else was also looking. People who were trying to influence the commission's outcome. Men who'd used money and power to dominate what was supposedly a neutral process. Was it all a lie concocted by the people who controlled Filip Vitenko, simply to lure him to the Russian consulate? He didn't believe so. Maxim Zubarev had shown a callousness that gave credence to his words. Stefan Baklanov was owned. Nothing more than a *willing puppet*. And, as Zubarev had said, they were *clever puppeteers*. What else had Zubarev said? *The only thing that could stand in the way is the reemergence of a direct bloodline to Nicholas II*. But who were *they*? And had they really managed to stack the commission? If so, what did it matter since Stefan Baklanov was the man he'd traveled to Moscow to champion? His clients wanted that result. Taylor Hayes wanted that to happen. It would be good for everybody.

Or would it?

Apparently the very factions, both political and criminal, that had brought Russia to its knees now controlled its absolute-monarch-to-be. And this wasn't some eighteenth-century ruler with cannons and guns. This autocrat would have access to nuclear weapons, some small enough to fit into a suitcase. No single person should ever have that kind of authority, but Russians would never consider anything less. To them, the tsar was sacred, a link to God and a glorious past they'd been denied for a century. They wanted a return to that time, and a return was what they were about to get. But would they be better off? Or simply trading one set of problems for another? Something else Rasputin had said occurred to him.

Twelve must die before the resurrection can be complete.

He mentally tallied the dead. Four the first day, including

Artemy Bely. The guard in Red Square. Pashenko's associate. Iosif and Vassily Maks. So far everything else the *starets* said had come to pass.

Would four more die?

HAYES WATCHED KHRUSHCHEV SQUIRM IN THE CHAIR. THIS former communist and long-standing government minister, highly placed and highly connected, was nervous. He realized that Russians tended to wear their emotions on their sleeves. When happy, there was an exuberance that could sometimes be frightening. When sad, their despair ran deep. They naturally gravitated to either extreme, rarely set in a middle ground, and he'd come to learn from nearly two decades of dealing with them that trust and loyalty were indeed important attributes. Problem was, it could take years before one Russian actually trusted another, even longer before a foreigner was accepted.

Khrushchev was, at the moment, acting particularly Russian. Twenty-four hours ago he'd been confident and assured, knowing Lord would soon be in his hands. Now he was quiet and detached, saying little since the previous night at the zoo when they realized there was no way to track their quarry, and he would have to explain to the other members of the Secret Chancellory that he'd approved the idea of deliberately letting Lord escape.

They were on the second floor of the consulate, alone in Vitenko's office with the door locked. On the other end of the speakerphone were the Chancellory members, all gathered in the study of the Moscow house. No one was happy with the present predicament, but no one openly criticized the course of action.

"It is not a problem," Lenin said through the phone. "Who could have predicted the intervention of a gorilla?"

"Rasputin," Hayes said.

"Ah, Mr. Lincoln, you are beginning to understand our concern," Brezhnev said.

"I'm beginning to think Lord is definitely after a survivor to Alexei and Anastasia. *The* heir to the Romanov throne."

"Apparently," Stalin said, "our worst fear has become a reality."

"Any thoughts on where he might go?" Lenin asked.

Hayes had been thinking about just that for the past few hours. "I have his apartment in Atlanta being watched by a private investigative firm. If he returns there we'll have him, and this time we won't let him go."

"That's all well and good," Brezhnev said. "But what if he ventures straight to wherever this supposed heir is waiting?"

That was the other possibility he'd been pondering. He knew people in law enforcement. FBI. Customs. DEA. Those contacts could be utilized to covertly track Lord, especially if he was using credit or bank cards to finance his journey. They would have access to information trails he could never duplicate. But bringing them into the loop would entangle him with folks he preferred to keep at arm's length. His millions were safely tucked away under a mountain of Swiss protection, and he intended to enjoy those dollars—and several more million he planned to acquire— over the coming years. Then he would retire from the firm, taking the seven-figure buyout the partnership agreement guaranteed him. The remaining senior partners would surely want him to stay on in some capacity, enough that his name would continue to appear on the letterhead and assure the loyalty of clients he'd cultivated. He would, of course, agree. Provided a reasonable annual stipend was paid— enough to cover modest living expenses for a man residing in a European château. It was all going to be perfect. He sure as hell was not going to give anyone the opportunity to screw the whole thing up. So, in answer to Brezhnev's query, he lied.

"I have some avenues available that I can pursue. There are men here, as you provided to me there." He'd really never had any need for such men before, and did not know where to secure them, but his Russian pals didn't need to know that. "I really don't think it's going to be a problem."

Khrushchev's eyes met his. The speakerphone was silent, his Moscow listeners apparently waiting for more.

"I believe Lord will contact me," he declared.

"Why would you say that?" Khrushchev asked.

"He has no reason not to trust me. I'm his employer, and I have contacts in the Russian government. He's got to call me, especially if he actually finds somebody. I'd be the first person he'd want to tell. He knows what our clients have at stake and what that would mean to them and him. He'll contact me."

"So far he has not," Lenin said.

"But he's been under fire and on the move. And as of now, he doesn't have anything to show for his efforts. He's still looking. Let him. Then he'll contact me. I'm positive."

"We have only two days left to contain this," Stalin said. "Luckily, after Baklanov is selected it will be hard to undo his ascension, especially if public relations are handled carefully. If any of this comes to light, we could simply paint the matter as another conspiracy hoax. No one will seriously believe any of it."

"Not necessarily," Hayes said. "DNA testing could demonstrate a conclusive connection to Nicholas and Alexandra since the Romanov genetic code is now cataloged. I agree, the situation can be contained, but we need corpses for heirs, not living human beings, and those corpses should never be found. They must be cremated into oblivion."

"Can that be handled?" Khrushchev wanted to know.

He wasn't sure how he'd do it, but knew what was at stake, both for him and for the other men. So he gave them the correct answer.

"Of course."

42

LORD STARED OUT THE WINDSHIELD AND ADMIRED WITH RE-newed interest the thick stands of tall trees rising on both sides of the steeply graded highway. Their bark was a patchy dark gray, the long leaves a verdant green. He'd visited the area several times on weekend getaways and recognized the more common sycamore, beech, and oak. But he'd always thought the bushy trees just another form of poplar. Now he knew them for what they were.

"Those are princess trees," he said, pointing. "I read last night that this time of the year is when the big ones release their seeds. One tree sends out twenty million seeds. Easy to see why the things are everywhere."

"Have you visited here before?" Akilina asked.

"I've been to Asheville, which we passed a while back, and Boone, which is farther north. This is a big ski area in winter and wonderful during summer."

"It reminds me of Siberia. Near where my grandmother lived. There were low mountains and forests just like this. The air there was cool and fresh, too. I loved it."

All around autumn had grabbed hold, the peaks and valleys ablaze with red, gold, and orange, a smoky mist curling out of the deepest valleys. Only the pines and princess trees retained a lively summer facade.

They'd changed planes in Dallas and caught a flight to Nashville. From there, a half-full commuter shuttle had brought them to Asheville about an hour ago. He'd run out of cash in Nashville and had been forced to use his credit card, a move he hoped they would not regret, knowing full well how credit card receipts could be traced. But airline ticket purchases could likewise be monitored. He could only hope that Maxim Zubarev's boast that the FBI and customs were helping was only talk. Why, he could not say for sure, but he believed the Russians were working independent of the U.S. government—maybe there was some peripheral co-operation, minor and covert, but nothing reaching a full-scale effort to locate one American lawyer and a Russian acrobat. That, he reasoned, would require some in-depth explanation. And there was simply too much risk that he would tell the Americans everything before the Russians could contain the situation. No. The Russians were working alone—at least for the moment.

The drive north from Asheville had been pleasant, across the Blue Ridge Parkway, then onto State Route 81 for the final trek through rolling hills and stunted mountains. Genesis itself was a picture-book town of brick, wood, and fieldstone buildings filled with quaint art galleries, gift shops, and antiques stores. Benches lined Main Street, roofed by bushy sycamore trees. An ice-cream parlor dominated one corner at the central intersection, two banks and a drugstore the others. Franchise operations, condominiums, and vacation homes were zoned to the outskirts. As they cruised into town, the sun was already low, transforming the sky from a bright blue to a pale salmon as the trees and peaks faded to a deep violet. Evening apparently came early here.

"This is it," he told Akilina. "Now we have to find out who or what Thorn is."

He was just about to pull into a convenience store and check the local telephone directory when a sign caught his eye. The wrought-iron display hung from the side of a two-story redbrick building. The county courthouse was a block beyond on a tree-filled square. The words announced in black lettering: OFFICE OF MICHAEL THORN, LAWYER. He pointed and translated for Akilina.

"Just like Starodug," she said.

He'd already thought the same thing.

He parked close to the curb a block down. They quickly made their way into the law office where a secretary informed them that Mr. Thorn was at the courthouse, finishing up some deed work, and should be back shortly. He expressed a desire to talk with Thorn immediately and the woman told them where to find him.

They walked to the Dillsboro County Courthouse, a neoclassical brick-and-stone building with the pedimented portico and tall cupola customary for legal buildings in the South. A bronze plaque near the front door noted that the structure had been completed in 1898. Lord had rarely visited courthouses, his practice confined to the boardrooms and financial institutions of America's largest cities or Eastern European capitals. He'd never actually appeared in court for anything. Pridgen & Woodworth employed hundreds of litigators who handled that chore. He was a deal maker. The behind-the-scenes man. Until one week ago, when he'd been catapulted to the forefront.

They found Michael Thorn in the deed vault, hunched above an oversized volume. In the harsh fluorescent light Lord saw that Thorn was a balding, middle-aged man. Short and stocky, but not overweight, the thin bridge of his nose was prominent, his cheekbones high, the face certainly more youthful than his age.

"Michael Thorn?" he asked.

The man looked up and smiled. "That's right."

He introduced himself and Akilina. There was no one else in the windowless room.

"We've just arrived from Atlanta." Lord showed him his state bar of Georgia card and used the same line that had worked at the San Francisco bank. "I'm here working on an estate that involves a relative of Miss Petrovna."

"Looks like you do a bit more than practice law," Thorn said, motioning to his bruised face.

He thought quickly. "I do a little amateur boxing on the weekends. Got a bit more than I gave the other day."

Thorn smiled. "How can I help you, Mr. Lord?"

"Have you practiced here long?"

"All my life," Thorn said, a touch of pride in his voice.

"This town is beautiful. My first time up here. You're a local-bred guy, then?"

A curious look came onto Thorn's face. "Why all the questions, Mr. Lord? I thought you were here working on an estate. Who is your deceased? I'm sure I know them."

Lord reached into his pocket and removed Hell's Bell. He handed it to Thorn and carefully watched the lawyer for some reaction.

Thorn casually inspected the bell, inside and out. "Impressive. Solid gold?"

"I think so. Can you read what's on it?"

Thorn reached for a pair of eyeglasses on the chest-high table and carefully studied the exterior. "Small letters, aren't they?"

Lord said nothing, but glanced at Akilina, who was watching Thorn intently.

"I'm sorry, this is some sort of foreign language. I'm not sure what. But I can't read it. I'm afraid English is my only means of communication, and some say I'm not real good at that."

"He that endureth to the end shall be saved," Akilina said in Russian.

Thorn stared at her for a moment. Lord could not decide if the reaction was surprise, or the fact that he did not understand her. He caught Thorn's gaze with his own.

"What did she say?" Thorn asked.

"He that endureth to the end shall be saved."

"From the Gospel of Matthew," Thorn said. "But what docs that have to do with anything?"

"Do those words have any meaning to you?" he asked.

Thorn handed the bell back. "Mr. Lord, what is it you want?"

"I know this must seem strange, but I need to ask a few more questions. Would you indulge me?"

Thorn removed his glasses. "Go ahead."

"Are there many Thorns living here in Genesis?"

"I have two sisters, but they don't live here. There are a few other families with that name, one quite large, but we're not related."

"Would they be easy to find?"

"Just look in the phone book. Does your estate involve a Thorn?"

"In a manner of speaking."

He was trying hard not to stare, but was equally intent on discerning any sort of family resemblance to Nicholas II. Which was nuts, he realized. He'd only seen Romanovs in grainy black-and-white movies and photographs. What did he know of any family resemblance? The only thing he could say for certain was Thorn was short, like Nicholas, but beyond that he was merely imagining anything else. What had he expected? The supposed heir to read the words and suddenly be transformed into the Tsar of All Russia? This wasn't a fairy tale. It was life and death. And if any supposed heir knew what he did, the fool would keep his or her mouth shut and blend back into the woodwork that had served as sanctuary for all these years.

He pocketed the bell. "I'm sorry to have bothered you, Mr. Thorn. You must think us a little odd, and I don't blame you."

Thorn's expression softened and a smile crept onto his face. "Not at all, Mr. Lord. Obviously you are on some sort of mission that involves client confidences. I understand that. It's quite okay. So, if that's all, I'd like to finish this title search before the clerk shoos me out of here."

They shook hands.

"It was nice to meet you," Lord said.

"If you require any assistance finding those other Thorns, my office is just down the street. I'll be there all day tomorrow."

He smiled. "Thanks. I'll keep it in mind. You could, though, recommend somewhere to stay for the night."

"That may be tough. This is prime tourist season and most places are booked. But with it being a Wednesday, there's probably a room for a night or two. The weekends are the real problem. Let me make a quick call."

From his suit jacket Thorn withdrew a cellular phone and dialed a number. He spoke a moment, then beeped off. "I know the owner of a bed-and-breakfast who was telling me this morning that he was a little slow right now. It's called the Azalea Inn. Let me draw you a map. It's not far."

The Azalea Inn was a lovely Queen Anne–style building on the outskirts of town. Beech trees dominated the landscaping and a white picket fence encircled the property. The front porch accommodated a row of green rockers. The interior was an old-fashioned decor of quilts, cracked-beam ceilings, and wood-burning fireplaces.

Lord rented a single room, the request meeting with a strange stare from the elderly woman who operated the front desk. He recalled the reaction of the clerk in Starodug when he refused a room to what he thought was a foreigner. But then he realized this lady's attitude was different. A black man and white woman. Hard to believe color still mattered, but he certainly wasn't naïve enough to think that it didn't.

"What was the concern downstairs?" Akilina asked, after they were in the room.

The second-floor space was airy and light, with fresh flowers and a fluffy comforter on a sleigh bed. The bath contained a claw-foot tub and white eyelet window lace.

"Some here still think the races shouldn't mix."

He tossed their travel bags on the bed, the same two that Semyon Pashenko had provided what seemed an eternity ago. He'd stashed the gold bars in a locker at the Sacramento airport. That made three pieces of imperial bullion awaiting his return.

"Laws can make people change," he said, "but more than that is needed to adjust attitudes. Don't take it wrong, though."

She shrugged. "We have prejudice in Russia. Foreigners, anyone dark-skinned, Mongols. They are all treated badly."

"They're also going to have to adjust to a tsar who was born and raised in America. I don't think anyone ever figured on that contingency." He sat on the edge of the bed.

"The lawyer seemed genuine. He did not know what we were talking about."

He agreed. "I looked at him carefully when he was studying the bell and when you said the words."

"He said there were others?"

He stood and walked to the phone and the directory that

lay beneath. He opened to the Ts and found six Thorns and two Thornes. "Tomorrow, we'll see about these people. We'll visit each one if we have to. Maybe we can take Thorn up on his offer and enlist his help. Some local talent might make the difference." He looked over at Akilina. "In the meantime, let's get some dinner, then a little rest."

They ate at a quiet restaurant two blocks from the Azalea Inn that came with the unique characteristic of being adjacent to a pumpkin patch. Lord introduced Akilina to fried chicken, mashed potatoes, corn on the cob, and iced tea. At first he found her unfamiliarity amazing, but then he'd never eaten leavened buckwheat pancakes, beetroot soup, or Siberian meat dumplings until visiting Russia.

The evening weather was perfect. There was not a cloud in the sky and the Milky Way streaked overhead.

Genesis was definitely a day place—none of the businesses, beyond a few restaurants, lingered open after dark. After a brief walk they made it back to the inn and entered the downstairs foyer.

Michael Thorn was perched on a settee next to the staircase.

The lawyer was dressed casually in a tan sweater and blue slacks. He rose as Lord closed the front door and calmly said, "Do you still have that bell?"

He reached into his pocket and handed it to Thorn. He watched as Thorn fitted a gold clapper inside and, with a slight waggle of his wrist, tried to ring it. Only a dull *tap* came where a ding would be expected.

"Gold is too soft," Thorn said. "But I imagine you need something else to confirm who I am."

He said nothing.

Thorn faced him. *"To where the Princess tree grows and Genesis, a Thorn awaits. Use the words that brought you here. Success comes if your names are spoken and the bell is formed."* He paused. "You are the raven and the eagle. And I'm who you seek."

Thorn's words came in a whisper, but were delivered in flawless Russian.

43

LORD STARED IN DISBELIEF.

"Could we go to your room?" Thorn said.

They walked upstairs in silence. Once inside with the door locked, Thorn said in Russian, "I never thought I would ever see that bell or hear those words. I kept the clapper safe for decades, knowing what I had to do if ever presented with the opportunity. My father warned me the day would come. He waited sixty years and never got his chance. Before he died he told me that it would happen in my lifetime. I didn't believe him."

Lord was still stunned, but he motioned to the bell and asked, "Why is it called Hell's Bell?"

Thorn stepped to the window and gazed out. "It's from Radishchev."

Lord recognized the name. "He was also quoted on a gold sheet left in the San Francisco bank."

"Yussoupov was a fan. A great lover of Russian poetry. One of Radishchev's verses read: *God's angels shall proclaim heaven's triumph with three peals of Hell's Bell. Once for the Father, once for the Son, a final for the Holy Virgin.* Quite apt, I'd say."

Lord was regaining his composure and, after a moment of silence, asked, "Have you been following what's happening in Russia? Why haven't you come forward?"

Thorn turned back. "My father and I many times argued the point. He was an ardent imperialist, truly of the old school. He knew Felix Yussoupov personally. Talked with him many times. I always believed the time for monarchy had long passed. No room in modern society for such antiquated concepts. But he was convinced Romanov blood would be resurrected. Now that is happening. Still, I was always told not to reveal myself unless the raven and eagle appeared and the words were uttered. Anything less was a trap laid down by our enemies."

"The Russian people want your return," Akilina said.

"Stefan Baklanov will be disappointed," Thorn said.

Lord thought he sensed a twinge of humor in the observation. He told Thorn about his interest in the Tsarist Commission and all that had happened over the past week.

"That was precisely why Yussoupov kept us hidden. Lenin wanted every remnant of Romanov blood extinguished. He wanted no possibility of a restoration. Only later, when he realized Stalin was going to be worse than any tsar ever could have been, did he realize the mistake he made in killing the imperial family."

"Mr. Thorn," Lord began.

"Michael, please."

"Perhaps Your Imperial Majesty is more in order?"

Thorn frowned. "That's a title I will definitely have trouble adjusting to."

"Your life is in real danger. I assume you have a family?"

"A wife and two sons who are both in college. I have yet to discuss this with any of them. That was one condition Yussoupov insisted upon. Total anonymity."

"They need to be told, along with the two sisters you mentioned earlier."

"I plan to tell them. But I'm not sure how my wife's going

to react at being elevated to tsarina. My oldest son is going to have some adjusting to do. He's the tsarevich now, his brother a grand duke."

Lord had so many questions, but there was one thing he really wanted to know. "Can you tell us how Alexei and Anastasia made it to North Carolina?"

For the next few minutes, Thorn spoke, telling a tale that made Lord's spine tingle.

It started on the evening of December 16, 1916, when Felix Yussoupov fed cyanide-laced cakes and wine to Gregorii Rasputin. After the poison failed to kill his victim, Yussoupov shot the starets *once in the back. When that bullet did not finish the task, others chased the fleeing holy man into a snow-covered courtyard and shot him repeatedly. Then they tossed the body into the frozen Neva River, pleased with their night's work.*

After the murder, Yussoupov openly basked in his glory. He saw a political future that might even include a change in the ruling house of Russia from Romanov to Yussoupov. Talk of revolution was spreading throughout the nation. It seemed only a matter of time before the fall of Nicholas II. Yussoupov was already the wealthiest man in Russia. His holdings were vast and wielded considerable political influence. But a man named Lenin was riding a wave of resentment toward ultimate power, and no nobles, regardless of their name, would survive.

The effect of Rasputin's murder on the imperial family was profound. Nicholas and Alexandra retreated more into themselves, and Alexandra began to exercise even greater influence over her husband. The tsar presided over a huge clan who were simply indifferent to their public reputation. They spoke French better than Russian. They stayed abroad more than at home. They were jealous of name and rank, but casual about public obligations. Divorce and bad marriages sent a wrong message to the masses.

All the Romanov relatives hated Rasputin. None lamented his death and some were so bold as to tell the tsar how they felt. The murder drove a wedge into the imperial house. Some of the grand dukes and duchesses even began to openly talk of change. Ultimately, the Bolsheviks exploited that imperial rift by deposing the provisional government that succeeded Nicholas II and forcibly seizing power, murdering as many Romanovs along the way as possible.

Yussoupov, though, continued to publicly state that killing Rasputin was right. Banished by the tsar to one of his estates in central Russia as punishment for the murder, he was conveniently out of reach during the February and October Revolutions of 1917. He'd at first been somewhat supportive of change, even offering his assistance, but once the Soviets seized all his family assets and threatened to arrest him, he realized the mistake he'd made. Rasputin's death had come far too late to alter the course of events. By his misguided attempt to save the realm, Yussoupov actually dealt the Russian monarchy a fatal blow.

It was shortly after the October 1917 revolution and Lenin's rise to power that Yussoupov decided what needed to be done. Being one of the few nobles left with monetary resources, he managed to assemble a group of ex–imperial guardsmen. Their task would be to secure the freedom of the imprisoned royal family and restore the monarchy. He hoped that his change of heart, although late, would be recognized by Nicholas, and the murder of Rasputin forgiven. Yussoupov saw in this quest a way to cleanse his guilt—not for ridding the world of Rasputin, but for the subsequent imprisonment of the tsar.

When the imperial family was removed from Tsarskoe Selo and transported to Siberia in early 1918, Yussoupov knew it was time to act. Three attempts were made at a rescue, but none developed beyond the initial planning. The Bolsheviks maintained a close watch on their imperial captives. George V, king of England and cousin to Nicholas II, was approached about offering the Romanovs safe haven. He initially agreed, but eventually bowed to pressure and refused permission to immigrate.

It was then Yussoupov realized what fate had decided.

He recalled Rasputin's prediction that if a noble was his murderer, Nicholas II and his family would not survive two years. He was the highest ranking of all the non-Romanov nobles, and his wife was an imperial niece. It seemed the starets had been right.

But he was determined to undermine fate.

He dispatched Kolya Maks and others to Yekaterinburg with orders to perfect a rescue at all costs. He was thrilled when Maks was able to work his way close to the men guarding the imperial family. But it was nothing short of a miracle that Maks was present at the actual execution and managed to save both Alexei and Anastasia, secreting them off the transport truck and ultimately returning to find both alive in the forest. Amazingly, Alexei had been untouched by bullet or bayonet. A blow to Anastasia's head, delivered by Maks himself during the executions, cracked her skull, but the girl was otherwise little harmed, her corset of diamonds and jewels shielding her from the guns. She did sustain bullet wounds to one of her legs, but they were treated and she ultimately recovered, the only lasting effect a limp that stayed with her the rest of her life.

Maks took both children to a cabin west of Yekaterinburg. Three of the other men sent by Yussoupov were there waiting. Yussoupov's orders were clear. Take the family east. But there was no family. Just two teenagers, scared to death.

In the days after the murder, Alexei did not utter a word.

The boy sat in a corner of the cabin. He would eat and drink some, but otherwise had withdrawn into himself. He would later say that the sight of his parents being gunned down, his precious mother choking on her own blood, bayonets being jabbed into the bodies of his sisters, stole his mind, and the only thought that kept him going was something Rasputin had once told him.

You are the future of Russia and must survive.

He'd instantly recognized Maks from the man's time at the Imperial Court. The burly Russian had acted as carrier for the tsarevich, one of several whose job it was to haul the heir in their arms when his hemophilia would not allow his legs to work. He recalled Maks's gentleness and obeyed without question when told to lie still.

It took nearly two months for the survivors to be trekked east to Vladivostok. The seeds of revolution preceded their arrival, but few there had any idea what the Romanov children actually looked like. Luckily, the tsarevich experienced a period without any attacks of hemophilia, though he did suffer a minor bout once there.

Yussoupov already had men waiting on Russia's Pacific coast. Originally, he planned to keep the royal family in Vladivostok until the time was right, but the rapidly deteriorating civil war was waning toward the Reds. Soon the communists would be in complete charge. He knew what had to be done.

Russians were emigrating by the boatload to America's West Coast, San Francisco the main port of entry. Alexei and Anastasia, along with a Russian man and his wife recruited for the task, boarded one of the departing ships in December 1918.

Yussoupov himself fled Russia in April 1919 with his wife and four-year-old daughter. For the next forty-eight years he traveled Europe and America. He wrote a book and periodically protected his reputation with slander and libel lawsuits when he felt films and manuscripts did not accurately portray him. Publicly he remained a proud and defiant rebel, his murder of Rasputin the right course under the circumstances. He took no blame for any of the subsequent actions and accepted no responsibility for what happened to Russia. Privately was another matter. He seethed at Lenin and later Stalin. He had wanted Rasputin dead and Nicholas freed from the German yoke of Alexandra, but he had also wanted imperial Russia to survive. Instead, just as Rasputin had predicted, the Neva River ran red with the blood of nobles. Romanovs died indiscriminately.

Russia ended.

The Union of Soviet Socialist Republics was born.

"What happened after Alexei and Anastasia traveled to the United States?" Lord asked.

Thorn was sitting on the sofa in front of the windows. Akilina was perched on the bed. She'd listened in open amazement as Thorn filled in the gaps of what they already knew. Lord, too, was amazed.

"There were two others already here. Yussoupov had sent them ahead to find a safe place. One of them had been to the eastern part of the United States and traveled through Appalachia. He knew of the princess trees and thought the connection meaningful. So the two children were brought to Asheville first, then farther north, to Genesis. They settled with the Russian couple who came on the boat with them. The name *Thorn* was chosen because of its local popularity. They became Paul and Anna Thorn, the only two children of Karel and Ilka Thorn, a Slavic couple from Lithuania. At the time, millions were immigrating into this country. Nobody paid these four any attention. There's a large Slavic community in Boone. And back then, no one in this country knew anything about the Russian imperial family."

"Were they happy here?" Akilina asked.

"Oh, yes. Yussoupov was a big investor in American stocks and the dividends were used to finance relocation. But every effort was made to conceal wealth. The Thorns lived simply, their contact with Yussoupov solely through intermediaries. It was only decades later that Yussoupov himself talked with my father."

"How long did the two of them live?"

"Anastasia died in 1922. Pneumonia. Sadly, it happened only weeks before she was to marry. Yussoupov finally found a suitable man, one who met royal criteria, except that his noble lineage was a strain. Alexei had married the year before. He was eighteen, and there was concern his illness would eventually become too much for him to bear. There was little that could be done for hemophiliacs in those days. A marriage was arranged with one of the daughters of the men working with Yussoupov. The young girl, my grandmother, was only sixteen, but she met the statutory requirements for a tsarina. Her emigration was arranged and the two were wed by an Orthodox priest in a cabin not far from here. I still own the place."

"How long did he survive?" Lord asked.

"Only another three years. But it was enough for him to sire my father. The child was healthy. Hemophilia passes from female to male, not the other way around. Later, Yussoupov would say fate had even intervened there as well. If Anastasia had been the one to survive and ultimately mother a son, the curse may have continued. But it ended with her death, and my grandmother birthed a son."

A strange pang of sadness swept through Lord. One reminiscent of when he'd learned that his own father was dead. A curious mixture of regret and relief, combined with longing. He flushed the feeling away and asked, "Where are they buried?"

"A beautiful place decked with princess trees. I can show you tomorrow."

"Why did you lie to us earlier?" Akilina asked.

Thorn was quiet for a moment. "I'm scared to death. I go to Rotary Club on Tuesdays and fish on Saturdays. People trust me with their adoptions, house purchases, divorces, and I help them. But now I'm being asked to run a nation."

Lord felt for the man sitting across the room. He did not envy his task. "But you may be the catalyst that solidifies that nation. The people remember the tsar now with affection."

"But I worry about that. My great-grandfather was a difficult man. I've studied him in detail, and historians have not been kind to him. They've been particularly harsh on my great-grandmother. I worry about the lessons to be learned from their failure. Is Russia really ready for autocratic rule again?"

"I'm not sure they ever lost it," Akilina said.

Thorn's look was far away. "I think you're right."

Lord listened to the solemn tone the lawyer used. Thorn seemed to consider each word, each syllable, careful with his choices.

"I was thinking of the men who are after you," Thorn said. "My wife. I need to make sure she's going to be all right. She didn't ask for any of this."

Lord asked, "Was the marriage arranged?"

Thorn nodded. "My father and Yussoupov found her. She comes from a devout Orthodox family with a vestige of royal blood. Enough, under the circumstances, to satisfy any objectors. Her family came here in the nineteen fifties from Germany. They fled Russia after the revolution. I love her dearly. Our life has been good."

There was something else Lord wanted to know. "Did Yussoupov ever relate what happened with the bodies? Iosif Maks told us what happened up until the point where his father found Alexei and Anastasia in the woods the morning after the murders. But Kolya left that day—"

"That's not true."

"That's what his son said."

"He left, but not after finding Alexei and Anastasia. He returned to the House of Special Purpose. It was three days later that he left with the two children."

"Was he involved with the ultimate disposal of the bodies?"

Thorn nodded.

"I've read a lot of speculation and the spurious firsthand accounts. Did Yussoupov say what actually happened?"

Thorn nodded. "Oh, yes. He related it all."

44

KOLYA MAKS RETURNED TO YEKATERINBURG AROUND NOON. He'd taken Alexei and Anastasia to the safe house outside town and managed to hike back without anyone knowing where he'd gone. He learned that Yurovsky had returned to Yekaterinburg also and dutifully reported to the Ural Regional Soviet that the executions had been accomplished. The committee was pleased, and a dispatch had been sent to Moscow detailing their success.

But the men Yurovsky chased from the Four Brothers mine the night before, the men led by Peter Ermakov, were telling anyone who would listen where the tsar and his family lay. There was talk of jewel-encased bodies and men who wanted to venture back into the woods. None of which was surprising. Too many had been involved in the disposal to even hope secrecy could be maintained.

It was midafternoon when Maks met up with Yurovsky. He, along with three others, had been ordered to appear in town and assist the commandant.

"They're going back out there," Yurovsky told them. "Ermakov is determined to win this fight."

Artillery could be heard booming in the distance.

"The Whites are within days of here. Maybe even hours. We have to get those bodies out of that mine." Yurovsky's black eyes narrowed. "Particularly given our numerical problem."

Maks and the others knew what he meant. Nine corpses, instead of the required eleven.

Yurovsky directed two men to requisition kerosene and sulfuric acid from whatever merchant had a stock available. Maks was told to get into the car and he and Yurovsky left town on the Moscow highway. The afternoon had turned cool and dingy, the morning sun gone behind a thick bank of gunmetal-gray clouds.

"I've been told there are deep mines filled with water west of here," Yurovsky said along the way. "We will drop them in there with stones tied around them. But first they will be burned and disfigured with acid. Even if found, no one will recognize who they are. Every hole in the ground around here has a body or two."

Maks did not relish the thought of retrieving nine bloodied corpses from the bottom of the Four Brothers mine. He recalled Yurovsky tossing hand grenades down the shaft, and his spine shivered at the prospects that lay ahead.

Fifteen miles west of Yekaterinburg, the car broke down. Yurovsky cursed the engine, then led the way on foot. They discovered three deep mines about five miles away filled with water. It was eight PM when they finally returned to town, the journey made partly by foot, the rest on a horse commandeered from a peasant. Not until shortly after midnight on July 18, twenty-four hours after the debacle of the night before, did they finally return to the Four Brothers mine.

It took several hours to light the deep shaft and prepare. Maks listened as each of the three who came with Yurovsky hoped not to be the one chosen for the descent. When all the preparations were in order Yurovsky said, "Kolya, climb down and find them."

Maks thought of objecting but it would show weakness, and that was the last thing he wanted to demonstrate before these men. He had their confidence. Most important, he had Yurovsky's confidence, and that was something he would need in the days ahead. Without saying a word, he tied a rope around his waist and two men slowly lowered him into the shaft. The black clay was oily to the touch. A bituminous stench mixed with mildew and lichens permeated the cold air. But there was also another odor, one more pungent and sickly sweet. One he'd smelled before. The scent of decaying flesh.

Fifty feet down, his torch illuminated a pool. In the flickering light he saw an arm, a leg, the back of a head. He called up for the lowering to stop. He hovered just above the surface.

"Down. Slow," he yelled.

His right boot touched, then submerged. The water was icy. A chill swept through him as his legs were soaked. Luckily, the water was only waist-deep. He stood shivering and called out that they should stop lowering.

Another rope suddenly fell from above. He knew what it was for. He reached over and grabbed its end. Yurovsky's grenades had apparently done little damage. He reached out for the closest body part and pulled naked flesh toward him. It was Nicholas. Maks stared down at the mutilated tsar, the face barely recognizable. He remembered the man as he was. Slender body, square face, impressive beard, expressive eyes.

He tied the rope around the corpse and signaled that it should be raised. But the earth seemed not to want to yield its charge. Water gushed from the lifeless shell. Limp muscles and flesh gave way, and Nicholas II crashed back into the pool.

Frigid water drenched Maks's face and hair.

The rope dropped back down. He waded to the corpse and this time tied the noose tighter, pinching the torso and tearing flesh.

It took three more attempts to lift the tsar from the shaft.

Fighting back nausea, he repeated the task eight more times. It took hours to finish, the cold, darkness, and decay complicating everything. He'd gone back up three times to warm himself by a fire, the water chilling him to the bone. When he was lifted out the final time, the sun was high in the sky and nine mutilated corpses lay on the wet grass.

One of the men produced a blanket for Maks. The dry wool smelled of ox, but felt good.

"Let's just bury them here," one of the men said.

Yurovsky shook his head. "Not in this mud. The grave would be easily discovered. We need to transport them to a new site. These demons need to be covered forever. I'm tired of seeing their cursed faces. Bring the carts forward. We'll take them to a new place."

Three flimsy wooden carts were rolled from where the cars were parked. The wheels bucked on the rough, muddy ground. Maks stood with the blanket wrapped around him, near Yurovsky, waiting for men and carts to draw near.

Yurovsky stood rigid, staring down at the bloated bodies. "Where could the other two be?"

"Not here," Maks answered.

The burly Jew's glare came with the speed and accuracy of a bullet. "I wonder if that might one day be a problem."

Maks considered whether the short-necked man in the black leather jacket standing before him knew more than he should. Then he dismissed the thought. Those two missing corpses could mean Yurovsky's life. No way he'd let that pass.

"How could it be?" Maks asked. "They are dead. Is that not all that matters? A body is just confirmation."

The commandant stepped close to one of the females. "I fear we have not heard the last of these Romanovs."

Maks said nothing. The comment had not called for a response.

The nine bodies were tossed onto the carts, three each, a blanket draped over the piles and pinned tight beneath. Then they rested for a few hours and ate black bread and garlic ham. It was midafternoon when they finally started off toward the new site. The road was a decayed mass of rutted mud. The word had been passed the day before that White Army forces were lurking in the woods. Red search parties would be on the move. Any of the villagers found in the restricted area would be shot. The hope was that the warning would provide some measure of privacy so they could finish their task.

Less than two miles passed before one of the carts' axles broke. Yurovsky, following in a car, ordered the procession stopped.

The other two carts were not in any better shape.

"Stay here and guard," Yurovsky ordered. "I'll drive into town and find a truck."

Darkness had enveloped them by the time the commandant returned. The bodies were transferred to the truck bed and the trip resumed. One of the vehicle's headlights did not work, and the other barely pierced the coal-black night. The wheels seemed to find every pothole in the muddy road. The going was further slowed by planking that had to be spread periodically to negotiate the slippery ground. Four times the tires bogged and had to be forced forward with backbreaking efforts.

They stopped to rest again for an hour.

July 17 became July 18.

It was nearly five AM when the mud caught wheels again, this time permanently, and no amount of effort could vanquish the earth's grip. It did not help that they were all exhausted from the past two days.

"This truck is going nowhere," one of the men finally said.

Yurovsky looked skyward. Dawn was not far away. "I've lived with the corpses of these stinking royals for three days. Enough. We'll bury them right here."

"In the roadway?" one of the men asked.

"Precisely. This is the perfect spot. This whole thing stays a mud bog. No one would notice our digging."

Shovels were fetched and a common grave about eight feet square and six feet deep was dug. The bodies were tossed in, faces doused with sulfuric acid to prevent any subsequent identification. The hole was filled and covered with branches, lime, and planks. The truck was finally freed and the site driven over several times. When they finished, no evidence remained of their digging.

"We are twelve miles to the northwest of Yekaterinburg," Yurovsky said. "From where the railroad tracks cross the road, it is about seven hundred feet in the direction of the Isetsk factory. Remember this spot. It is where our glorious tsar will rest. Forever."

LORD SAW THE EMOTION ON THORN'S FACE.

"They left them there. In the mud. And there they stayed until 1979. One of the searchers, at the time, was quoted as saying when they dug into the ground and found planking, 'Let me find nothing underneath.' But they did. Nine skeletons. My family." Thorn stared at the carpeted floor. A car passed on the street below. Finally, the lawyer said, "I've seen pictures of the bones resting on lab tables. It shames me to see them displayed like museum curiosities."

"They couldn't even agree on where to finally bury them," Akilina said.

Lord recalled how the battle had raged for years. Yekaterinburg claimed the family should be interred there, where they had died. St. Petersburg urged that they be laid to rest in the Cathedral of Peter and Paul, where all the previous tsars were interred. But the debate was not over respect or protocol. Yekaterinburg officials saw a revenue potential in having the last tsar buried nearby. So did St. Petersburg. And just as Thorn had said, while the argument continued for nearly eight years, the remains of the imperial family rested on metal shelving in a Siberian laboratory. St. Petersburg eventually won after a government commission decided all nine skeletons should be buried with the remaining Romanovs. The whole affair was another Yeltsin fiasco in which he tried to offend no one and irritated everyone.

Thorn's face screwed tight. "So many of my grandfather's things were sold by Stalin to raise money. Years ago, my father and I went to the Virginia Museum of Fine Arts to see an icon of St. Pantalemion that monks gave to Alexei when he was once very sick. It used to be in his room at the Alexander Palace. I read recently where a pair of his skis were sold at auction in New York." He shook his head. "The damn Soviets hated anything imperial, but had no problem using that heritage to finance their evil."

Lord asked, "Was it because of what Kolya Maks did that Yussoupov entrusted him with the first piece of the puzzle?"

"He was the ideal choice, and apparently kept the secret even in his grave. His son and nephew did well, too. God rest their souls."

"The world has to know this," Lord said.

Thorn heaved a deep sigh. "Do you think Russia will accept an American-born tsar?"

"What does that matter?" Akilina quickly asked. "You are a Romanov. Pure to the bone."

"Russia is a complicated place," Thorn said.

"The people want only you," she made clear.

Thorn smiled weakly. "Let's hope your confidence is infectious."

"You will see," she said. "The people will accept you. The world will accept you."

Lord stepped to the phone beside the bed. "I'm calling the man I work for. He's got to know this. The commission vote must be stopped."

No one said a word as he dialed long distance for Pridgen & Woodworth's Atlanta office. It was nearly seven PM, but the firm operated around the clock. Secretaries, paralegals, and lawyers worked throughout the night to accommodate satellite offices and clients scattered in every time zone.

The switchboard directed his call to Hayes's night secretary, whom he knew well from many long evenings at his own desk.

"Melinda, I have to talk with Taylor. When he calls in from Russia—"

"He's on the other line, Miles. He told me to put him on hold when they buzzed your call through."

"Make it a conference."

"I'm already pushing the buttons."

A few seconds later Hayes came on the line. "Miles, where are you?"

He took a few minutes and explained everything. Hayes listened in silence, then said, "You're telling me that the heir to the Romanov throne is sitting there with you?"

"That's exactly what I'm saying."

"No doubt?"

"None to me. But DNA will put any questions to rest."

"Miles. Listen and listen good. I want you to stay right there. Don't leave that town. Give me the name of the place you're staying."

He did.

"Don't leave that inn. I'll be there by tomorrow afternoon. I'll get the first plane out of Moscow for New York. This has to be handled carefully. When I get there, we'll involve the

State Department and whoever else we need. I'll be in touch with the right people while en route. I'll take care of this from now on. You got that?"

"I understand."

"I hope so. I'm pissed as hell you've waited until now to call."

"The phones are not safe. I'm not even sure about now."

"This phone is clean. I guarantee it."

"I'm sorry about not involving you, Taylor. But I had no choice. I'll explain all of it when you get here."

"I can hardly wait. Now get some sleep and I'll see you tomorrow."

45

LORD FOLLOWED THE DIRECTIONS MICHAEL THORN PROVIDED. The lawyer sat in the backseat of the Jeep Cherokee he'd rented yesterday at the Asheville airport. Akilina filled in the front passenger's seat.

Lord and Akilina had spent a restless night at the Azalea Inn, both deeply affected by what they'd found. There was no doubt in Lord's mind the balding, middle-aged man with soft gray eyes sitting behind him was heir to the Romanov throne. Who else would have known exactly how to respond? Not to mention possessing the gold clapper that formed the bell. He'd satisfied all the criteria Yussoupov had established to confirm his identity. Science could now provide undisputed verification in the form of DNA testing, which surely the Tsarist Commission would order.

"Turn up there, Miles," Thorn said.

They'd gone to first names last night after two hours of conversation and the call to Taylor Hayes. At breakfast Thorn had asked if they would like to see the graves. Lord recalled Hayes's instruction to stay close but didn't think a short trip would be a problem, so they'd driven a few miles south of Genesis into a lovely hollow of copper and gold trees. The day was bright and sunny. Like an omen from heaven, Lord thought, that everything was going to be all right.

But was it?

Here, in this tiny corner of America, known for homespun Appalachian common sense and misty blue ridges, lived the Tsar of All Russia. A country lawyer college-educated at the University of North Carolina, then at nearby Duke for law school. All paid for by a student loan and part-time jobs that helped feed a wife and two kids.

Thorn had told them all about himself. They were entitled to know. He'd come back to Genesis after graduating and had practiced law the past twenty-four years, opening an office and making sure a shingle hung outside for all to see. That had been one of Yussoupov's instructions. A way to mark the trail. Of course the odd little Russian had never conceived of computers, satellite communications, and the Internet, or the ability to locate someone with the push of a button, a world so small that there were few, if any, places left to hide. Yet Kolya Maks and Thorn's father, along with Thorn himself, had adhered to Yussoupov's instructions, and that single-minded determination had paid off.

"You can park over there," Thorn said.

Lord nestled the front bumper close to the trunk of an oversized oak. A light breeze rustled the surrounding boughs and whisked leaves into a twirling dance.

Unlike the frozen plot in Starodug, the cemetery in the grove beyond was immaculate. The grass around every grave was cut and trimmed, and many were adorned with fresh flowers and wreaths. No moss or mold stained the markers, though many showed the effects of time. A gravel path bisected the center and branched off in shoots leading to the far corners of the rolling site.

"Our local historical society maintains the plots. They do

an excellent job. This site has been used for burials since the Civil War."

Thorn led them to the outer perimeter of the grassy meadow. A line of princess trees rose not fifty feet away, their limbs dotted with colorful pods.

Lord stared at the stone markers, a cross chiseled into the top of each:

ANNA THORN
BORN JUNE 18, 1901—DIED OCTOBER 7, 1922

PAUL THORN
BORN AUGUST 12, 1904—DIED MAY 26, 1925

"Interesting that they used the correct dates of birth," he said. "Wasn't that a little foolish?"

"Not really. Nobody knew who they were."

On both of the monoliths the same epitaph appeared below the names. HE THAT ENDURETH TO THE END SHALL BE SAVED.

Lord motioned to the words. "A last message from Yussoupov?"

"I always thought it fitting. From what I was told, they were each quite special. Perhaps if they'd continued as the tsarevich and grand duchess, their personalities would have been corrupted. But here they were merely Paul and Anna."

"What was she like?" Akilina asked.

A smile crept onto Thorn's mouth. "She matured wonderfully. As a teenager, Anastasia was plump and arrogant. But here she thinned and I'm told was quite beautiful, like her mother at that age. She walked with a limp and her body was scarred, but her face was untouched. My father made a point of telling me everything that Yussoupov said about her."

Thorn stepped over to a stone bench and sat. The hoarse croaking of crows echoed in the distance.

"She was to be the hope, though there was fear of hemophilia passing from her to a male child. No one seriously believed Alexei would survive long enough for a wife to be found and children produced. It was a miracle he made it out of Yekaterinburg without an attack. He had many attacks here. There was a local doctor, though, who had some success with him. Alexei learned to trust him, as with Rasputin, and in the end it was simple flu that killed him, not his defective blood. Rasputin was right on that, too. He predicted hemophilia would not be the cause of the heir's death." Thorn gazed off at the mountains in the distance. "My father was a year old when Alexei died. My grandmother lived until the nineteen seventies. She was a wonderful person."

"Did she know about Alexei?" Lord asked.

Thorn nodded. "She was Russian-born to noble blood. Her family fled when Lenin took over. She knew it all. Alexei's physical afflictions were impossible to hide. They spent only three years together, but you would have never known from listening to her. She loved Alexei Nicholaevich."

Akilina stepped toward the markers and knelt down on the grass. He watched as she crossed herself and said a prayer. She'd told him about her experience in the San Francisco church, and he now realized this Russian woman was more religious than she wanted to admit. He, too, was moved by the tranquil scene, disturbed by nothing other than the rustle of squirrels through princess trees.

"I come here often," Thorn said. He motioned toward three more markers, their backs facing them. "My father and mother and grandmother are all buried there."

"Why wasn't your grandmother placed here, with her husband?" Akilina asked.

"She refused. The sister and brother should be buried together, she said. They are divine, of royal lineage, and should rest alone. She was insistent on that."

They drove back to Genesis in silence and Lord headed straight for Thorn's office. Inside, he noticed photographs of a woman and two young men displayed on a dusty credenza. The woman was attractive, with dark hair and a smile that transmitted warmth. Thorn's sons were both handsome with dusky-hued complexions, strong features, and wide Slavic cheekbones. They were Romanovs. One-quarter each. In direct line with Nicholas II. He wondered how Thorn's siblings would react when told they were now nobles.

He'd brought the travel bag from San Francisco and laid it on a wooden table. Last night, in the excitement of the moment, he'd not shown Thorn the Fabergé egg. Now he gently removed the shattered treasure and found the two tiny portraits of Alexei and Anastasia. Thorn studied them closely.

"I've never seen what they looked like after they came here. No other photographs were ever taken. My grandmother told me about these pictures. They were made at the cabin, not far from here."

Lord's gaze returned to the photos of Thorn's family on the credenza. "What about your wife?"

"I didn't say anything to her last night. Once your employer arrives and we determine what's to be done, then I'll speak to her. She's gone for the day. Down to Asheville to visit her sister. It'll give me time to think."

"What's her background?"

"What you really mean is, does she qualify as tsarina?"

"It's something that has to be considered. The Succession

Act is still in place, and the commission intended on following it as closely as possible."

"Margaret is Orthodox by birth, with some Russian blood, as much as could be found twenty-five years ago here in the United States. My father personally searched for candidates."

"You make it sound so impersonal," Akilina said.

"I didn't mean to. But he realized the depth of our responsibility. Every effort was made to maintain a continuity with the past."

"She's American?" Lord asked.

"From Virginia. Which makes two Americans Russia will have to accept."

There was something else he wanted to know. "The man who sent us here told us about tsarist wealth that might still be in banks. Were you privy to that information?"

Thorn set the photos of his ancestors beside the clump of debris that was once a Fabergé egg. "I was given a safe-deposit key and told where to go when the time arrived. I guess that's now. I assume the information will be in the deposit box. I was told never to attempt access unless you arrived. New York will have to be our first stop."

"Are you sure the box still exists?"

"I pay the rental every year."

"Did you pay the rental in San Francisco?"

Thorn nodded. "Both are paid from automatic withdrawals on accounts that were opened decades ago under fictitious names. I don't mind telling you we had a problem when the law changed and Social Security numbers had to be attached to every account. But I managed to use a couple of deceased clients' names and numbers. I was concerned about a trail, but I never considered my position dangerous. That is, until last night."

"I can assure you, Michael, the threat is real. But Taylor

Hayes will provide protection. You'll be okay. Only he knows where we are. That much I can assure you."

HAYES CLIMBED FROM THE CAR AND THANKED THE PRIDGEN & Woodworth associate who'd been waiting at the Atlanta airport. He'd called ahead and told his secretary to have somebody there, and with three dozen lawyers in his division, and that many and more in paralegals to choose from, the task should not have been difficult.

Droopy and Orleg had traveled with him from California and they, too, stepped out into a foggy morning. Neither of the Russians had uttered a word since the airport.

Hayes's house was a stone-and-brick Tudor monstrosity that sat on three wooded acres in north Atlanta. He had no wife. The divorce had come a decade ago. Luckily, there'd been no children. And there would be no more wives. He harbored no desire to share anything he possessed with anyone, much less a greedy woman who'd want a respectable percentage of his assets as compensation for the privilege of having lived with her.

He'd called from the car and told his housekeeper to have food prepared. He wanted to clean up, eat, and get on the road. There was business waiting a few hours north in the North Carolina mountains. The kind of business that would shape his future. Serious men were depending on him. Men he did not want to disappoint. Khrushchev had wanted to come with him, but he'd vetoed the idea. Bad enough he was strapped with two burly Russians who could use personality lessons.

He led Droopy and Orleg through a wrought-iron gate. Leaves slid across the brick pavers, riding a wet morning breeze. Inside the house, he saw that his housekeeper had followed directions and prepared an early lunch of cold cuts, cheese, and bread.

While his two Russian associates gorged themselves in the kitchen, he stepped into his trophy room and unlocked one of several gun cases that lined the paneled walls. He selected two high-powered rifles and three handguns. Both rifles were equipped with sound suppressors—usually used for hunting in heavy snow to avoid avalanches. He unbolted the clips and peered down the barrels. He checked the scopes and sites. All seemed in order. The handguns were loaded with ten shots each. All three were Glock 17L Competition pistols. He'd bought them on a hunting trip in Austria a few years back. Droopy and Orleg had certainly never been privileged enough to handle weapons like these.

He gathered spare ammunition from the locked closet on the other side of the room, then walked back to the kitchen. The two Russians were still eating. He noticed open beer cans. "We'll leave here in an hour. Easy on the alcohol. Drinking has limits here."

"How far away is this place?" Orleg asked through a mouthful of sandwich.

"About a four-hour drive. That will put us there by mid-afternoon. Let me make myself clear. This isn't Moscow. We do this my way. Understand?"

Neither Russian said a word.

"Is it necessary I call Moscow? Perhaps more instructions could be given to you by phone."

Orleg swallowed his food. "We understand, lawyer. Just get us there and tell us what you want us to do."

46

LORD WAS IMPRESSED WITH WHERE MICHAEL THORN LIVED. IT was a lovely neighborhood of older homes with forested lots and deep lawns. *Ranch style* was the description he recalled appended to the design, most of the houses single-story brick structures with gabled roofs and chimneys.

They'd driven over so Thorn could tend to his dogs. The lawyer's wooded backyard was dotted with pens and Lord immediately recognized the breed. The males were notice-ably larger and all of the animals, about a dozen, varied in color from sable red to tan and black. The heads were long and narrow and slightly domed. The shoulders sloped, the chests narrowed. They stood about three feet tall, each ani-mal a hundred pounds or so, and muscular, the fur long and silky.

They were in the sight hound family and their name, *bor-zoi,* meant "swift." Lord smiled at Thorn's choice of breed. These were Russian wolfhounds, bred by nobility for the de-mands of coursing wild game through open terrain. Tsars since the 1650s had raised them.

This one apparently no exception.

"I've loved these dogs for years," Thorn said as he walked about the pens, filling water bowls with a hose. "I read about them years ago and finally bought one. They're like chocolate-chip cookies, though. Can't have just one. I ended up breeding them."

"They're beautiful," Akilina said. She stood close to the cages. The borzois stared back at her through oblique brown eyes encased by black rims. "My grandmother cared for one. She found him in the woods. He was a fine animal."

Thorn opened one of the cages and dumped scoops of dry food into a bowl. The dogs did not move and had yet to bark. The animals' gazes followed Thorn's movements, but they did not otherwise advance toward the meal. The lawyer then motioned with his forefinger to where the food bowls lay.

The dogs pounced.

"Well trained," Lord said.

"No sense having beasts like these unless they obey. This breed trains well."

Lord noticed that the scene was repeated in the other cages. Not one of the dogs challenged Thorn or disobeyed a command. He knelt in front of one of the cages. "Do you sell them?"

"By next spring this litter will be gone, and I'll have puppies again. Each time I breed the best of the lot. Only those two, there, stay continually."

Lord stared at two dogs in the pen closest to the back porch. A male and female, both sable red, coats like silk. Their pen was larger than the others and included a wooden enclosure.

"The best of a litter from six years ago," Thorn said, pride in his voice. "Alexei and Anastasia."

Lord grinned. "Interesting choice of names."

"They're my purebred show dogs. And my friends."

Thorn moved toward the cage, unlocked the gate, and

gestured. The two animals immediately smothered him with affection.

Lord watched his host. Thorn appeared levelheaded and genuinely in awe of his ancestral responsibilities. Nothing like Stefan Baklanov. He'd heard Hayes speak of Baklanov's arrogance and the fear that Baklanov was far more interested in the title than actually ruling. Michael Thorn seemed quite different.

They returned to the house and Lord examined Thorn's library. The shelves were filled with treatises on Russian history. There were biographies of various Romanovs, many from nineteenth-century historians. Most of the titles he recognized from his own reading.

"You have quite a collection," he said.

"You'd be surprised what you can find at secondhand bookstores and library sales."

"Nobody ever questioned the interest?"

Thorn shook his head. "I'm a long-standing member of our historical society, and everyone knows my love of Russian history."

On one shelf he spied a book he was quite familiar with. Felix Yussoupov's *Rasputin: His Malignant Influence and Assassination.* Yussoupov had published the account in 1927, a scathing attack on Rasputin that repeatedly tried to justify the murder. Beside the volume rested the two memoirs Yussoupov published in the 1950s, *Lost Splendor* and *En Exil.* Vain attempts at raising money, if Lord recalled what later biographers had concluded. He motioned to the shelf. "Yussoupov's writings were anything but flattering to the imperial family and Rasputin. If I remember, he particularly attacked Alexandra."

"All part of the deception. He knew Stalin was interested in what he was doing and didn't want to do anything that might raise suspicion. So he kept up the facade till his death."

He noticed a few volumes on Anna Anderson, the woman who maintained to her death that she was actually Anastasia. He pointed to the books. "I bet those were amusing."

Thorn smiled. "Her real name was Franziska Schanzkowska. Born in Prussia. She wandered in and out of sanatoriums until Yussoupov learned of her resemblance to Anastasia. He taught her everything she needed to know, and she was an eager student. By the time she died, I actually think she believed herself Anastasia."

"I read about her," Lord said. "All spoke of her in loving terms. She seemed an exceptional lady."

"A fitting stand-in," Thorn said. "One I never really minded."

The faint sound of car doors slamming could be heard through the front windows. Thorn stepped over and peeked out plantation shutters. "A sheriff's deputy is here," he said in English. "I know him."

Lord stiffened and Thorn seemed to understand. The lawyer moved to the double doors leading to the entrance foyer. "Stay here. I'll see what this is about."

"What is it?" Akilina asked in Russian.

"Trouble."

"When is your employer due?" Thorn asked at the doorway.

He checked his watch. "Anytime now. We really need to get back to the inn."

Thorn closed the double doors, but Lord crossed the room and cracked them open just as a doorbell chimed.

"Evening, Mr. Thorn," a deputy said. "The sheriff wanted me to come over and talk with you. I tried your office, your secretary said you were home."

"What's the trouble, Roscoe?"

"Has a man named Miles Lord and a Russian woman come to see you yesterday or today?"

"Who is this Miles Lord?"

"How about you answer my question first."

"No. I haven't had any visitors. Much less Russian ones."

"Kind of strange to hear you say that. Your secretary said a black lawyer named Lord and a Russian woman were at your office last evening and with you all today."

"If you already knew the answer, Roscoe, why'd you ask?"

"Just doin' my job. Care to tell me why you lied to me?"

"What's the big deal about these two?"

"A Moscow warrant for murder. They're both wanted for the death of a city cop there. Shot in Red Square."

"How do you know that?"

"Those two there in my car told me. Brought the warrant with 'em."

Lord raced from the door to the study's front window. He glanced out just as Droopy and Feliks Orleg climbed out of the police cruiser.

"Oh, shit," he whispered.

Akilina was instantly by his side and saw what he did.

The two Russians started their march from the curb. Both reached under their coats and guns appeared. Shots popped like firecrackers in the distance. Lord bolted for the double doors and yanked them open just as the deputy's body crumpled forward into the front doorway. Apparently the first salvo had been meant for him.

He leaped forward and grabbed Thorn, jerking him back and slamming the wooden door shut. He clicked the lock just as bullets pounded the outside.

"Down," he screamed.

They lunged to the tile floor, rolling toward a far hall.

Lord glanced at the deputy. Three large holes were spewing blood. No sense wasting time with him. "Come on," he said, springing to his feet. "That door won't stop 'em long."

He sprinted down the hall toward sunlight at the far end. Thorn and Akilina followed. He listened as the front door was rattled, then more shots. He entered the kitchen and yanked open the back door, motioning Thorn and Akilina out onto the terrace. More shots echoed and, in the instant before he followed, he heard the front door splinter.

He watched as Thorn raced for the nearest dog pen, the one harboring Alexei and Anastasia. He heard Thorn tell Akilina to move toward the others and open the gates. Thorn pointed to the back door leading into the kitchen and screamed to the dogs, "Move. Strike."

Akilina had managed to open only a couple of pens, but the two dogs in each, along with Alexei and Anastasia, responded to the command and galloped toward the back door. In the second that Orleg appeared in the doorway, one of the borzois pounced and the Russian screamed.

Three more snarling dogs followed the first inside.

Shots came in rapid succession.

"I don't think we can hang around to find out who wins," Lord said.

They sprinted toward the gate that led to the front drive, back to where the rental Jeep was parked, and climbed inside.

Lord held the ignition key.

More shots came from the back of the house.

"My poor dogs," Thorn said.

Lord gunned the engine and jammed the gearshift into reverse. He wheeled out of the drive and spun around, ending up beside the police cruiser parked at the curb. He caught a glimpse of one of the dogs loping down the drive.

"Wait," Thorn yelled.

Lord hesitated before slamming his foot onto the accelerator. Thorn popped open the back door. The dog leaped inside, panting hard.

"Go," Thorn screamed.

Tires peeled off the asphalt as the Jeep lurched forward.

47

"WHY WAS IT NECESSARY TO KILL THAT DEPUTY?" HAYES tried to keep his low voice calm. "Are you two complete idiots?"

He'd waited for them at the sheriff's department after convincing local officials of Orleg's credentials and using a fabricated warrant faxed from Moscow. Khrushchev had arranged the document in San Francisco, similar to the one used there to enlist FBI and customs assistance, and few questions were asked when Hayes explained that his firm often represented the Russian government in its American affairs.

They were standing outside in the cool evening, away from a door where deputies streamed in and out. The place was abuzz after what had happened an hour earlier. Hayes was trying to keep his composure and not draw any attention, but it was damn difficult.

"Where are the guns?" he whispered.

"Under our jackets," Orleg said.

"What did you tell them happened?"

"That the deputy went inside and we heard shots. We rushed in and the man was on the floor. We chased after Lord and the woman, but the dogs attacked. Last we saw, Lord was driving off with Thorn at gunpoint."

"They accepted it?"

Droopy smiled. "Completely."

But he wondered for how long. "You told them about the dogs?"

Orleg nodded. "That we shot them? There was no choice."

"Which one of you geniuses shot the deputy?"

"I did," Orleg said. The fool sounded proud.

"And who shot the dogs?"

Droopy admitted he had, since Orleg had been attacked. "They were aggressive."

He realized he needed to replace Orleg's pistol before somebody decided to confiscate both as evidence. He couldn't just dispose of it, thanks to Orleg's admission, and he certainly couldn't leave the damn thing around since the slugs in the deputy would be a conclusive match. He reached under his jacket and found the Glock.

"Give me yours."

He switched guns with Orleg. "Hopefully, no one will notice the full magazine. If they do, say you changed out and lost the other one in all the excitement."

The sheriff exited the building and walked over to where they stood. He watched the little man's approach. "We have an alert out on the car. It's a Jeep Cherokee and the description y'all provided was helpful."

Orleg and Droopy acknowledged the compliment.

The sheriff looked at Hayes. "Why didn't you tell us Lord was dangerous?"

"We told you he was wanted for murder."

"That deputy had a wife and four kids. If I'd thought for one moment this lawyer was capable of gunnin' a man down in cold blood, I'd have sent the whole fuckin' department over there."

"I realize emotions are running high here—"

"First time we've ever had a deputy killed in this county."

He ignored the information. "Are state officials being involved?"

"You're goddamn right."

He realized that if he played the situation right, these folks might permanently rid him of the problem. "Sheriff, I don't think Inspector Orleg cares if Lord leaves here in a body bag."

Another deputy rushed up.

"Sheriff, Mrs. Thorn's here."

Hayes and his two associates followed the sheriff inside. A middle-aged woman sat in one of the offices crying. She was being consoled by another woman, younger, who was also upset. Hayes listened to the conversation and quickly learned the older of the two was Thorn's wife, the other his secretary. Mrs. Thorn had been away most of the day in Asheville and had arrived back home to find a swarm of patrol cars in front of the house and a dead body being carted off by the coroner. Some of her husband's prized borzois littered the family kitchen. One dog was missing completely. Only four had escaped the carnage. Their cages had not been opened. The dead dogs were causing the deputies some concern. *Why had they been released in the first place?* was the question they kept repeating.

"Obviously to stop Inspector Orleg," Hayes said. "Lord is smart. He knows how to handle himself. After all, they've been chasing him across the globe with little success."

The explanation seemed to make sense and no one questioned any further. The sheriff turned his attention back to Mrs. Thorn and assured her everything would be done to find her husband.

"I have to call our sons," she said.

Hayes did not like that. If this woman was indeed the Tsarina of All Russia, he certainly did not want a further containment problem by involving the tsarevich and a grand duke. Lord could not be allowed to pass on what he knew beyond Michael Thorn, so he stepped forward and introduced himself. "Mrs. Thorn, I think it might be better to see if this matter plays itself out over the next few hours. It might be resolved and there'd be no need to worry your children."

"Why are you here?" she asked in a blunt tone.

"I'm assisting the Russian government in trying to find a fugitive."

"How did a Russian fugitive manage to get into my home?"

"I have no idea. It was only through luck we were able to trace him to this point."

"Actually," the sheriff said, interrupting, "you never explained how you did trace Lord here."

The man's tone had now shifted to suspicion but, before Hayes could respond, a female deputy burst into the room.

"Sheriff, we got a spot on that Jeep. Damn thing drove right past Larry on Highway 46, about thirty miles north of town."

LORD PASSED A ROADSIDE STAND WHERE LOCALS PEDDLED AP-ples and saw the patrol car. The brown-and-white sedan was parked on the shoulder, an officer out talking to a man in overalls beside a flatbed truck. He watched in his rearview mirror as the policeman hustled into his car and roared onto the highway.

"We have company," he said.

Akilina turned back. Thorn's head also turned, and the dog in the rear compartment shifted back and forth. Thorn gave a command and the dog disappeared down.

Lord worked the accelerator, but the engine was only a six-cylinder and the rolling terrain was taxing their horsepower. Even so, he was doing nearly seventy-five on a narrow highway with forested embankments on either side. Ahead, the trunk of another car rapidly approached. He cut

STEVE BERRY / 380

the steering wheel left and darted past just as a car in the opposite lane appeared around a curve. He hoped the turn in the
road would prevent the deputy from duplicating his feat, but
in the rearview mirror he saw a blue glow appear in the opposite lane, then cut back in hot pursuit.

"That cruiser's got more power than us," he said. "Only
a matter of time before he catches up. Not to mention his
radio."

"Why are we running?" Akilina asked.

She was right. There was no need to flee the deputy. Orleg
and Droopy were forty miles to the south, back in Genesis.
He should stop and explain the situation. The search was
over. Secrecy was no longer required. The sheriff's department could probably help.

He slowed the Jeep, then braked and veered onto the
shoulder. In seconds the patrol car had likewise halted. Lord
opened the door. The deputy was already out using the
driver's-side door as a shield, gun drawn.

"To the ground. Now," the policeman screamed.

Cars whizzed by in a whirlwind.

"I said on the ground."

"Look, I need to speak with you."

"If your ass ain't pointin' to the sky in three seconds, I'm
goin' shoot you."

Akilina was now out of the car.

"Down, lady," the deputy screamed.

"She doesn't understand you," he said. "We need your
help, Officer."

"Where's Thorn?"

The rear door opened and the lawyer climbed out.

"Come toward me, Mr. Thorn," the deputy yelled over the
traffic, gun still leveled.

"What's happening?" Thorn whispered.

"I don't know," said Lord. "You know him?"

"Face isn't familiar."

"Mr. Thorn, please come here," the officer said again.

Lord took a step. The gun jutted forward. Thorn stepped in front of him.

"Down, Mr. Thorn. Get down. That bastard killed a deputy. Get down."

Had Lord heard right? *Killed a deputy?*

Thorn did not move. The gun continued to waggle, the officer trying to find a clear shot.

"Down," the deputy said again.

"Alexei. Out," Thorn softly said.

The borzoi snapped to attention and leaped from the car. The deputy had moved from behind the door and was approaching with his gun leveled.

"There," Thorn said to the animal. "Move. Jump."

The animal braced his hind legs, then charged and pawed the air as his muscular body slammed into the deputy. They both crumpled to the graveled shoulder, the deputy screaming. The gun went off twice. Lord rushed over and managed to kick the pistol away.

The dog growled and writhed.

In the distance, more sirens could be heard.

"I suggest we get out of here," Thorn said. "Something is wrong. He said you killed a deputy."

Lord didn't need to be told twice. "I agree. Let's go."

Thorn commanded the dog to the car. They all three climbed in as the deputy tried to scramble to his feet.

"He'll be okay," Thorn said. "There were no bites. I didn't give that command."

Lord slammed the transmission into drive.

HAYES WAITED AT THE SHERIFF'S DEPARTMENT WITH ORLEG and Droopy. He'd almost gone with the sheriff and his men as they raced northward. The radio call had come twenty minutes earlier. A gray Jeep Cherokee was spotted on Highway 46, heading north toward the next county and Tennessee. A cruiser was in pursuit and the last report was that the Jeep was slowing to a stop. The officer had requested backup, but was ready to handle the situation alone.

He could only hope emotions were running high enough that one of the pursuers would get trigger-happy. He'd made it clear the Russians cared nothing about a warm body, only a body, so perhaps someone would end this nightmare with a well-placed shot. Yet even if Lord and the woman were killed, or just Lord, there was still the problem of Michael Thorn. The police would do what they could to save him, and God knows Lord wasn't going to hurt him. If indeed he was a direct descendant of Nicholas II, as Lord insisted, DNA testing would lay to rest any lingering doubts.

And that would be a problem.

He was standing in a dispatch room, an array of communications equipment banked before him. A female deputy was working the console. Static gristled from an overhead speaker.

"Central. Dillsboro One. We're at the scene."

The voice was the sheriff's and Hayes waited for the report. While he did, he stepped close to Orleg, who stood in the corner near the exit door. Droopy was outside, smoking. He whispered in Russian, "I'm going to have to call Moscow. Our friends will not be happy."

Orleg seemed unfazed. "We had our own orders."

"What's that supposed to mean?"

"I was told to make sure the woman, Lord, and anyone Lord thought important does not return to Russia."

He wondered if that included him. "You'd like to kill me. Wouldn't you, Orleg?"

"It would be a pleasure."

"Then why haven't you?"

The inspector said nothing.

"It's because *they* still need me."

More silence.

"You don't scare me," he said, his mouth close to Orleg's face. "Just remember. I know it all, too. Let them know that. There are two sons who possess Romanov genes. They will have to be dealt with. Whoever sent Lord and the woman will send others. Assure our friends that my death will result in the world learning the truth faster than that problem can be solved. Sorry to deny you the pleasure, Orleg."

"Don't overestimate your importance, lawyer."

"Don't underestimate my resilience."

He stepped away before there could be any response. As he did, the speaker crackled to life.

"Central. Dillsboro One. Suspect fled with captive. Deputy down, but okay. Attacked by a dog the suspect has in his possession. Cars in pursuit. But suspect has a lead, probably still heading north on Highway 46. Alert who you can up ahead."

The dispatcher acknowledged the report and Hayes heaved a silent sigh of relief. Where a few minutes before he'd hoped Lord would be found, now he realized that would further complicate matters. He needed to be the one to find him and apparently Lord was not trusting the locals. These fools thought Lord had a hostage and was fleeing. Only he knew Lord, Thorn, and the woman were all on the run.

And they'd have to get off the road fast.

Lord would most likely assume Orleg and Droopy were working in conjunction with the sheriff, so he wouldn't contact local law enforcement again. He would probably find a place to hide, with the others, at least until he could think the situation through.

But where?

He assumed Lord knew nothing of the area. Michael

Thorn would know the surroundings intimately. Perhaps there was a way to learn something.

He left the dispatch room and walked to where Mrs. Thorn and the secretary sat. The wife was occupied out in the hall with another female deputy, so he said to the secretary, "Excuse me, ma'am."

The woman looked up.

"I heard you tell the sheriff that Lord and his companion were at Mr. Thorn's office today."

"That's right. They came in yesterday. Then, back today. They actually spent the day with Mr. Thorn."

"Do you know what they were discussing?"

She shook her head. "They stayed in his office with the door closed."

"This is terrible. Inspector Orleg is so upset. One of his men was killed in Moscow. Now a deputy here."

"Lord said he was a lawyer. He didn't look like a killer."

"Who does? Lord was in Moscow on business. No one knows why he shot the policeman. Something was happening. Same is probably true here." He let out a breath, ran a hand through his hair, then pinched the bridge of his nose. "This area is so beautiful. Particularly this time of year. A shame something like this has to spoil it."

He moved toward a coffeepot and poured a cup into a stained mug, offering some to the secretary, who waved the offer off.

"I come up here from Atlanta occasionally to hunt. Rent a house in the woods. Always wanted one myself, but couldn't afford the luxury. Did Mr. Thorn have one? Seems like everybody has a cabin around here." He came back to where she sat.

"His cabin is lovely," she said. "It's been in his family for generations."

"Near here?" he asked, trying to sound disinterested.

"An hour north. He owns about two hundred acres including a mountain. I used to tease him about what he'd do with that mountain."

"What did he say?"

"Just sit and look at it. Watch the trees grow."

Her eyes dampened. This woman had obviously been close to her boss. He sipped his coffee. "That mountain have a name?"

"Windsong Ridge. I always liked it."

He slowly stood. "I'll leave you be. You're upset."

She thanked him and he walked outside. Orleg and Droopy stood puffing cigarettes.

"Come on," he said.

"Where are we going?" Orleg asked.

"To solve this problem."

48

AFTER LEAVING THE DOWNED DEPUTY, LORD QUICKLY ABANdoned the main highway and steered east on a county road. A few miles later he turned north, following directions to the land Thorn's family had owned for close to a hundred years.

The mile-long dirt road wound through foothills and across two rock-strewn streams. The cabin was a one-story rectangle, built of pine logs bound together with thick mortar in colonial style. The front porch held three rockers with a rope hammock suspended from one end. Cedar shingles on the gabled roof looked new. A flagstone chimney rose from one end.

Thorn explained this was where Alexei and Anastasia first lived after arriving in North Carolina in late 1919. Yussoupov had the cabin built on two hundred acres of old-growth forest, with a mountain, that a century before had been christened Windsong Ridge. The idea was to provide a place of solitude for the heirs, far away from anyone who might associate them with the Russian royal family. The hills of Appalachia offered the perfect setting, while providing a climate and scenery not unlike home.

Now, sitting inside the cabin, Lord could almost feel their presence. The sun had set and the air had turned cold. Thorn had started a fire using some of the split logs abutting one of the exterior walls. The interior was about fifteen hundred square feet filled with thick quilts, varnished wood, and a lingering scent of hickory and pine. The kitchen was stocked with canned food and they'd suppered on chili with beans washed down with Cokes from the refrigerator.

Thorn had suggested the cabin. If the police thought he was being held against his will, they would never look on his own property. Most likely, the roads all the way into Tennessee were being watched and a bulletin had been issued on the Jeep Cherokee, which was all the more reason to get off the highway.

"Nobody lives within miles," Thorn said. "Back in the twenties it was a great hiding place."

Lord noticed that nothing in the decor pointed to the cabin's unique heritage. But it was certainly the dwelling of a nature lover—framed prints of skyward birds and grazing deer decorated the walls. No mounted trophies, though.

"I don't hunt," Thorn said. "Except with a camera."

Lord pointed to the framed oil of a black bear that dominated one wall.

"My grandmother painted that," Thorn said. "And the rest, too. She loved to paint. She lived here until the end of her life. Alexei died in the bedroom over there. My father was born in the same bed."

They were gathered before a fire, two lamps illuminating the great room. Akilina sat on the plank floor, a wool quilt around her. Lord and Thorn filled two leather chairs. The dog was curled up in the corner, beyond the heat of the open hearth.

"I have a close friend in the North Carolina Attorney General's office," Thorn said. "We'll call him tomorrow. He can help. I trust him." Thorn sat silent a moment. "My wife must be a wreck. I wish I could call her."

"I wouldn't advise it," Lord said.

"Couldn't if I wanted to. I never put a phone here. I have a mobile that I bring when we stay the night. Electricity was only added in the past decade. The company charged me a bunch to run the line out here. I decided phones could wait."

"You and your wife come here often?" Akilina asked.

"Many times. I really feel a connection with my past here. Margaret never fully understood, only that this place seemed to calm me. My spot of solitude, she called it. If she only knew."

"She will soon," he said.

The borzoi suddenly alerted and a soft growl rumbled from his throat.

Lord's eyes locked on the dog.

A knock came at the front door. He sprang to his feet. None of them said a word.

Another knock.

"Miles. It's Taylor. Open the door."

He hustled across the room and glanced out one of the windows. In the dark he could see nothing except the form of a man standing before the door. He moved toward the locked entrance.

"Taylor?"

"It isn't the tooth fairy. Open the damn door."

"You alone?"

"Who else would be with me?"

He reached for the hasp and released the lock. Taylor Hayes stood in the doorway, dressed in a pair of khaki pants and a thick jacket.

"Man, am I glad to see you," Lord said.

"Not half as glad as I am to see you." Hayes stepped into the cabin. They shook hands.

"How did you find me?" Lord asked, after closing and re-locking the front door.

"When I got to town, I learned about the shooting. Seems two Russians are here—"

"Two of the men who have been chasing me."

"That much I gathered."

Lord noticed the quizzical look on Akilina's face. "Her English isn't the best, Taylor. Speak Russian."

Hayes faced Akilina. "And who are you?" he asked in Russian.

Akilina introduced herself.

"It's a pleasure to meet you. I understand my associate has been dragging you across the globe."

"We have had quite a journey," she said.

Hayes looked at Thorn. "And you must be the object of that journey."

"Apparently so."

Lord introduced the two, then said, "Maybe now we can get something done. Taylor, the local police think I killed a deputy."

"They're quite intent on that."

"Did you speak with the sheriff?"

"I decided to find you first."

For the next forty-five minutes, they talked. Lord related everything that had happened in detail. He even showed Hayes the shattered egg and gold-leaf messages brought inside from the Jeep. He explained about the gold bars and where they were stored, and all about Semyon Pashenko and the Holy Band that had kept Felix Yussoupov's secret safe.

"Then you are Romanov?" Hayes asked Thorn.

"You never explained how you found us," Thorn said.

Lord noticed the suspicion in the lawyer's voice. Hayes seemed unfazed by the abruptness.

"Your secretary gave me the idea. She and your wife were at the sheriff's department. I knew that Miles hadn't kidnapped you, so I figured a hiding place would have to be found. Who would ever look here? No kidnapper would use the victim's own house. So I took a chance and drove up."

"How is my wife?"

"Upset."

"Why didn't you tell the sheriff the truth?" Thorn asked.

"This is a delicate situation. International relations are involved. Literally, the future of Russia. If indeed you are a direct descendant of Nicholas II, the throne of Russia would belong to you. Needless to say, your reemergence will create a shock. I don't want to trust all that to the sheriff of Dillsboro County, North Carolina. No offense to the area."

"None taken," Thorn said, his voice still carrying an edge. "What do you suggest we do?"

Hayes stood and moved toward windows that fronted the house. "That's a good question." He peered out past the curtains.

The borzoi came alert again.

Hayes opened the front door.

Feliks Orleg and Droopy walked inside. Both men cradled rifles. The dog came to his feet and started to growl.

Akilina let out a gasp.

Hayes said, "Mr. Thorn, your animal is quite beautiful. I've always been partial to borzois. I would hate to order one of these gentlemen to shoot it. So would you direct the dog to leave through the front door, please?"

"I sensed something about you," Thorn said.

"I could tell." Hayes motioned at the still-growling dog. "Do I shoot it?"

"Alexei. Gone." Thorn pointed to the door and the dog bolted out into the night.

Hayes closed the door. "Alexei. Interesting name."

Lord was in shock. "It was you all along?"

Hayes motioned to his two associates who fanned across the room. Orleg took up a position at the door leading to the kitchen, Droopy at the bedroom door.

"Miles, I have some associates in Moscow who became quite upset with you. Hell, I sent you into the archives to find out if Baklanov had any problems, and you come out with the heir to the Russian throne. What did you expect?"

"You sonovabitch. I trusted you." He rushed toward Hayes. Orleg stopped his advance with a leveling of his rifle.

"*Trust* is such a relative term, Miles. Especially in Russia. I'll give you credit, though. You're a tough man to kill. Lucky as hell, too." Hayes reached under his jacket and withdrew a pistol. "Sit down, Miles."

"Fuck you, Taylor."

Hayes fired the gun. The bullet ripped across Lord's right shoulder. Akilina screamed and lunged toward him as he fell back in the chair.

"I told you to sit," Hayes said. "I don't like to repeat myself."

"Are you okay?" she asked.

Lord saw the concern in her face. But he was okay. The bullet had only grazed him, enough to draw blood and hurt like hell. "I'm all right."

"Miss Petrovna, sit down," Hayes said.

"Do it," Lord urged.

She retreated to a chair.

Hayes moved close to the hearth. "If I wanted to kill you, Miles, I would have. Lucky for you I'm a good shot."

Lord's hand clamped onto the wound and he used his shirt to stem the bleeding. His gaze drifted to Michael Thorn. The lawyer sat perfectly still. He'd said nothing and had not reacted when Hayes fired the gun.

"I think you are Russian," Hayes said to Thorn. "The look in your eye. I've seen it many times over there. Heartless, every damn one of you."

"I am no Stefan Baklanov." The words came in a near whisper.

Hayes chuckled. "I should say not. I think you might actually be able to govern those idiots. It'll take somebody with nerve. The best tsars all had it. So I'm sure you understand why you cannot leave here alive."

"My father said there would be men like you. He warned me. And I thought him paranoid."

"Who would have thought the Soviet empire so fragile?" Hayes asked. "And who would have ever guessed the Russians would want their tsar back?"

"Felix Yussoupov," Thorn said.

"Point taken. But all that is meaningless now. Orleg." Hayes motioned to the inspector, then to the front door. "Take our dear heir and this woman out and do what you do best."

Orleg smiled and stepped forward, grabbing Akilina. Lord started to rise, but Hayes rammed the pistol into his throat.

"Sit down," Hayes said.

Droopy yanked Thorn up from the chair and placed the tip of his rifle to the lawyer's head. Akilina started to resist. Orleg wrapped his right forearm around her neck and clamped hard, yanking her off the ground. She struggled for a second, then her eyes rolled skyward as her breath was blocked.

"Stop," Lord screamed. Hayes jammed the pistol deeper into his neck. "Tell him to stop, Taylor."

"Tell her to be a good girl," Hayes said.

He wondered how he was supposed to tell her to calmly walk outside and be killed. "Stop," he said to her.

She ceased struggling.

"Not here, Orleg," Hayes said.

The Russian relaxed his grip and Akilina went weak-kneed to the floor, gasping for breath. Lord wanted to rush to her, but couldn't. Orleg grabbed her by the hair and brought her to her feet. The pain seemed to wrench her back to life.

"Get up," Orleg said in Russian.

She staggered to her feet and Orleg shoved her toward the front door. Thorn was already there and exited first, followed by Droopy.

The door closed behind them.

"I do believe you like that woman," Hayes said, switching to English.

The gun was still pressed to his throat. "What do you care?"

"I don't."

The gun moved away and Hayes stepped back. Lord slumped into a chair. The pain in his shoulder amplified, yet the rage surging through him was keeping his reflexes ready. "Did you have the Makses killed in Starodug?"

"You left us no choice. Loose ends and all that."

"And Baklanov really is a pawn?"

"Russia is like a virgin, Miles. So many sweet pleasures that none have tasted. But to survive you have to play by their rules, and they are some of the toughest anywhere. I adapted. Murder, for them, is an accepted means of achieving an end. In fact, it seems the preferable means."

"What happened to you, Taylor?"

Hayes sat, gun leveled. "Don't give me any of that crap. I did what had to be done. Nobody at the firm ever complained about the fees rolling in. Sometimes risks have to be taken to achieve great things. Controlling the tsar of Russia seemed worth it. Actually, the whole thing was nearly perfect. Who would have ever guessed a direct heir was still alive?"

Lord wanted to lunge at him and Hayes seemed to sense the hatred. "Not going to happen, Miles. I'll shoot you dead before you leave that chair."

"I hope it's worth it."

"Beats the shit out of practicing law."

He thought he'd try to stall. "How do you plan to contain this? Thorn's got a family. More heirs. They all know, too."

Hayes smiled. "Nice try. Thorn's wife and children know zero. My containment problem is right here." Hayes motioned with the gun. "Look, you've got nobody to blame but yourself. If you'd left this alone, done just what I told you, there'd be no problem. Instead you had to traipse off to St. Petersburg and California and involve yourself in a whole lot of things that simply don't concern you."

He asked what he really wanted to know. "You going to kill me, Taylor?" Not a hint of fear entered his voice. He was surprised at himself.

"Nope. But those two out there are. Made me promise not to harm a hair on your head. They don't like you. And I certainly can't disappoint the hired help."

"You're not the man I knew."

"How the shit would you know me? You're a damn associate. We're not blood brothers. Hell, we're barely friends. But, if you have to know, I've got clients depending on me and I aim to deliver. Along with providing a retirement fund for myself."

He glanced beyond Hayes, toward outside.

"You worried about your little Russian darling?"

He said nothing. What was there to say?

"I'm sure Orleg's enjoying her . . . right about now."

49

AKILINA FOLLOWED THE MAN LORD CALLED DROOPY AS THEY plunged through the woods. A bed of leaves cushioned their steps and moonlight flickered through the branches, strobing the forest in a milky glow. Freezing air slapped her skin, her sweater and jeans offering little warmth. Thorn was in the lead, a rifle to his back. Orleg followed her, gun in hand.

They plowed ahead for ten minutes before entering a clearing. Two shovels stood spiked in the earth. Apparently, some planning had occurred prior to Hayes's appearance.

"Dig," Orleg said to Thorn. "Like your ancestors, you'll die in the woods and be buried in the cold ground. Perhaps in another hundred years somebody will find your bones."

"And if I refuse?" Thorn calmly asked.

"I'll shoot you, then enjoy her."

Thorn's gaze moved toward Akilina. The lawyer's breathing was rhythmic and she saw no concern in his eyes.

"Look at it this way," Orleg said. "A few more precious minutes of life. Every second counts. Anyway, it's more time than your great-grandfather got. Lucky for you, I'm no Bolshevik."

Thorn stood rigid and made no attempt to grasp the shovel. Orleg tossed his rifle aside and grabbed Akilina's sweater. He pulled her close and she started to scream, but his other hand cupped her mouth.

"Enough," Thorn yelled.

Orleg stopped his assault, but raised his right hand to her neck, not tight enough to strangle, but enough to let her know he was there. Thorn grasped the shovel and started to dig.

Orleg fondled her breast with his free hand. "Nice and firm." His breath stank.

She reached up and dug her fingers into his left eye. He jerked back, recoiled, and slapped her hard across the face. Then he shoved her to the moist ground.

The inspector retrieved his rifle. He chambered a round and slammed his right foot across her neck, pinning her head to the ground. He wiggled the end of the barrel into the corner of her mouth.

Her gaze darted to where Thorn stood.

She tasted rust and grit. Orleg pressed the end of the barrel deeper and she fought to avoid gagging. Terror built inside her.

"You like that, bitch?"

A black form surged from the woods and slammed into Orleg. The policeman tumbled back and lost his grip on the rifle. In the instant it took Akilina to shove the barrel away, she realized what happened.

The borzoi had returned.

She whirled as the rifle butt found the ground.

"Attack. Kill," Thorn screamed.

The dog's head whipped as fangs found flesh.

Orleg shrieked in agony.

Thorn swung the shovel and slammed the blade into Droopy, who seemed momentarily stunned by the animal's arrival. The Russian moaned as Thorn thrust the shovel again, the point digging into Droopy's stomach. A third blow across the skull and Droopy pounded the ground. The body twitched for a few seconds, then all movement stopped.

Orleg was still screaming as the dog attacked with a relentless furor.

Akilina grabbed for the rifle.

Thorn rushed over. "Halt."

The dog withdrew and heeled, panting a cloudy mist. Orleg rolled over, gripping his throat. He started to rise, but Akilina fired one shot into his face.

Orleg's body lay still.

"Feel better?" Thorn calmly asked her.

She spit the taste of metal from her mouth. "Much."

Thorn moved toward Droopy and checked for a pulse. "This one's dead, too."

She stared at the dog. The animal had saved her life. Words Lord and Semyon Pashenko told her flashed through her mind. Something a supposed holy man had proclaimed a hundred years ago. *The innocence of beasts will guard and lead the way, being the final arbitor of success.*

Thorn moved to the dog and caressed the silky mane. "Good boy, Alexei. Good boy."

The borzoi accepted his master's affection, pawing gently with sharp claws. Blood framed his mouth.

She said, "We need to see about Miles."

A DISTANT SHOT ECHOED, AND LORD USED THE MOMENT Hayes glanced away to grab a lamp with his uninjured arm and sling the heavy wooden base. He rolled out of the chair as Hayes recovered and fired a shot.

The room was now lit by a single lamp and a glow from the dying fire. He quickly belly-crawled across the floor and sent the other lamp in Hayes's direction, diving up and over a sofa that faced the fireplace. His right shoulder ached from the effort. Two more bullets tried to find him through the sofa. He scrambled across the floor toward the kitchen and rolled inside just as another bullet shattered the doorjamb. The wound to his shoulder reopened and started to bleed. He was trying to stem the blood flow with his hand and hoping the transition from light to dark would affect Hayes's aim—he couldn't take any more bullets—but he knew it would only be a few moments before the man's eyes adjusted.

In the kitchen he pushed to his feet, then momentarily lost his balance from the pain. The room spun and he grabbed hold of his emotions. Before bolting outside, he yanked a checkered towel from the counter and slapped it over the shoulder gash. Exiting, he slammed the door shut with his bloodied left hand and tipped a trash can over.

Then he rushed into the woods.

HAYES COULDN'T DECIDE IF HE'D HIT LORD OR NOT. HE TRIED to count the number of shots. Four, he could recall, maybe five. That meant five or six bullets left. His eyes were quickly adjusting to the darkness, the faint glow of embers in the hearth providing only minimal light. He heard a door slam and assumed Lord had left. He leveled the Glock and moved forward, entering the kitchen cautiously. His right toe slipped on something wet. He bent down and dabbed the fluid. A coppery stench confirmed blood. He stood and moved toward the door leading out. A trash can blocked the way. He kicked the plastic container aside and stepped out into the cold night.

"Okay, Miles," he called out. "Looks like it's time for a little 'coon hunting. Hope your luck's not as good as your grandfather's."

He popped the magazine from the Glock and replaced it with a fresh one. Ten shells were now ready to finish what he'd started.

AKILINA HEARD THE SHOTS AS SHE AND THORN RACED BACK toward the cabin. She carried Orleg's rifle. Just outside the cabin, Thorn stopped their advance.

"Let's not be foolish," he said.

She was impressed by the lawyer's reserve. He was handling the situation with a calm she found comforting.

Thorn stepped onto the porch and approached the closed front door. From behind the cabin, he heard a man say, "Okay, Miles. Looks like it's time for a little 'coon hunting. Hope your luck's not as good as your grandfather's."

She crept up behind Thorn, the dog beside her.

Thorn turned the knob and swung open the door. The interior was black, except for the smoldering hearth. Thorn moved inside and went directly to a cabinet. A drawer opened and he returned with a handgun.

"Come on," he said.

She followed him into the kitchen. The exterior door was swung open. She noticed Alexei sniffing the plank floor. She bent down and spied dark splotches leading from the great room outside.

The dog was intent on them.

Thorn bent down. "Somebody's been hit," he quietly mouthed. "Alexei. Scent. Take."

The dog sucked another noseful of one of the stains. Then the animal's head raised, as if to say he was ready.

"Find," Thorn said.

The dog charged out the door.

50

LORD HEARD HAYES'S WORDS AND THOUGHT ABOUT THE CON-
versation they'd had in the Volkhov nine days before.

Damn, it seemed longer.

His grandfather had told him all about the times when
southern rednecks vented their anger on blacks. One of his
friend's granduncles had even been snatched from his home
and hanged because somebody suspected him of thievery.
No arrest, no charges, no trial. He'd often wondered what it
took to hate that much. One thing his father had always done
was make sure both blacks and whites never forgot that past.
Some called it populism. Others pandering. Grover Lord
said it was a *friendly reminder from the Man-Up-Top's representative.* Now he was the one racing through the Carolina
mountains with a man following, determined that he never
see dawn.

The dish towel he'd jammed onto the shoulder wound
helped, but the steady brush of limbs and shrubs was doing damage. He had no idea where he was going. He remembered Thorn saying the nearest neighbors were miles
away. With Hayes, Droopy, and Orleg behind him, he figured his chances weren't all that good. In his mind he
could still hear the shot just before he'd made his move on
Hayes. He wanted to double back and find Akilina and
Thorn, but realized the futility of that effort. In all likeli-

hood they were both dead. He was better off losing himself in the night—making it out to tell the world what he knew. He owed that to Semyon Pashenko and the Holy Band, especially to all who'd died. Like Iosif and Vassily Maks.

He stopped his advance. Each breath came in short gulps and evaporated before his eyes. His throat was parched and he was having trouble orienting himself. His face and chest were covered in perspiration. He wanted to peel off his sweater, but there was no way his shoulder could take the effort. He was light-headed. The blood loss was affecting him, and the altitude wasn't helping, either.

He heard thrashing behind him.

He brushed back a low-hanging limb and slipped into thick brush. The ground began to harden. Rocky outcrops appeared. The elevation was likewise rising and he started up a short incline. Gravel crunched, the sound amplified in the stillness.

A wide panorama opened ahead.

He stopped at the end of a cliff overlooking a blackened gorge. A fast-moving stream rambled below. But he wasn't trapped. He could go left or right, back into the woods, but decided to use the spot to his advantage. If they found him, perhaps the element of surprise might give him an edge. He couldn't keep running. Not with three armed men after him. Besides, he didn't want to be gunned down like some animal. He'd take a stand and fight. So he pulled himself up the rocks, onto a ledge that overlooked the precipice. Open sky stretched for what seemed an eternity. He now possessed a vantage point from which he could see anyone who approached.

He groped in the dark and found three rocks the size of softballs. He extended the muscles in his right arm and determined he could throw, but not far. He tested the weight of each rock and readied himself for anybody who might approach.

HAYES HAD TRACKED ENOUGH ANIMALS TO KNOW HOW TO follow a trail and Lord had thrashed the woods with no regard for the broken branches he was leaving behind. There were even footprints in places where the thatched floor gave way to moist earth. In the bright moonlight the path was easy to decipher. Not to mention the bloodstains, which came with predictable regularity.

Then the trail stopped.

He stopped, too.

His eyes darted left and right. Nothing. No more branches pointing the way. He tested the foliage all around and found no blood, either. Strange. He readied a shot, just in case this was the place Lord had chosen for a showdown. He was certain the fool would fight at some point.

Maybe here was the place.

He inched forward. No instinct told him he was being watched. He was about to change directions when he noticed a dark smear on a fern ahead. He crept ahead, one step at a time, gun out front. The ground turned to stone and forest was replaced with granite outcroppings that rose all around him in myriad misshapen shadows. He didn't like the look or feel of the situation, but continued forward.

His eyes searched for clues—perhaps a bloodstain on the rocks—but it was hard to distinguish splotches from shadows. He slowed his pace to one step every few seconds, trying to minimize the crackle of rock beneath his soles.

He stopped at the edge of a cliff, water below, trees left and right. Beyond was a vast velvet sky dotted with a billion stars. No time for aesthetics. He turned and was just about to reenter the woods when he heard something *whoosh* through the air.

AKILINA FOLLOWED THORN AS HE HEADED OUT THE KITCHEN door. She noticed a bloodstained handprint and thought of Lord. The borzoi had already disappeared, but a low whistle from Thorn caused the animal to bolt from the trees.

"He won't venture far. Just enough to find the trail," Thorn whispered.

The dog heeled at his feet and Thorn stroked his forehead.

"Find, Alexei. Move."

The animal disappeared into the trees.

Thorn moved in the same direction.

She was worried about Lord. He'd most likely been shot. The voice she'd heard earlier was Taylor Hayes's. Lord probably thought both she and Thorn were dead, the chances of them escaping two professional killers slim. But they had an edge with the borzoi. The animal was remarkable, showing a loyalty that was to be admired. Michael Thorn had a way about him, too. This man had royal blood coursing through his veins. Maybe that was what gave him such presence. She'd heard her grandmother speak of imperial times. The people had worshipped the tsar for his strength and will. They looked to him as the embodiment of God on Earth and sought his protection in times of need.

He *was* Russia.

Perhaps Michael Thorn understood that responsibility. Perhaps he also felt enough of a connection with the past to be unafraid of what lay ahead.

Yet she was afraid. And not only for herself, but for Miles Lord as well.

Thorn stopped and whistled softly. Alexei appeared a few moments later, panting hard. He knelt down and stared the dog in the eyes.

"You have the trail, don't you?"

She almost expected the animal to answer back, but he simply rested on his hindquarters and caught his breath.

"Find. Move."

The dog ran off.

They headed in pursuit.

A shot exploded in the distance.

LORD ARCHED THE ROCK INTO THE AIR JUST AS HAYES TURNED. He felt something tear in his shoulder, then a blinding pain reverberated down his spine. He'd torn open the flesh wound again.

He saw the rock slam into Hayes's chest and heard the gun fire. He leapt from his position, crashing into his employer. The two men collapsed to the ground, electrified pain surging through his right shoulder.

He ignored the pain and slammed his fist into Hayes's face, but Hayes used his legs and thighs to send Lord up and over, onto his back. Sharp stones wedged into Lord's spine and added more agony.

In the next instant, Hayes was on him.

AKILINA STARTED TO RUN. THORN DID, TOO. BOTH IN THE DI-rection of the gunshot. The ground began to harden and she noticed rocks all around. Ahead, she could hear heavy breathing and bodies rolling.

The forest ended.

Before them Taylor Hayes and Miles Lord were fighting.

She halted beside Thorn. The borzoi stopped, too, watching the battle thirty feet away.

"End it," she said to Thorn.

But the lawyer did not use his weapon.

LORD WATCHED HAYES SPRING TO HIS FEET AND POUNCE. Amazingly, he still possessed some strength and managed to swing with his left fist, catching Hayes square on the jaw. The blow momentarily stunned his attacker. He needed to find the gun he'd seen. It had fallen from Hayes's grip when the rock had made contact.

He kicked with his right knee and forced Hayes up. He rolled once before regaining his balance and crouching to his knees. He was tired of rocks grinding his already sore body. His shoulder was definitely bleeding. But he was not about to be cowed at this point. The sonovabitch had to be stopped here and now.

He searched the blackened earth for the gun, but could not distinguish its outline. He thought he sensed two forms beyond the outcroppings, toward the trees, but it was hard to focus. Probably Orleg and Droopy, watching the fight with amusement, able to decide the winner with a single shot.

He tackled Hayes around the waist. They slammed into a pile of granite and he felt something in the other man give way, perhaps a rib. Hayes cried out, but managed to wedge two thumbs deep into Lord's neck and twist, the pressure affecting his windpipe. He struggled for breath and, in the instant his grip relaxed, Hayes brought a knee into his midsection, then punched hard, sending Lord reeling toward the cliff's edge.

He readied himself for the next volley as Hayes leapt forward, pivoting himself off the ground and kicking hard. But

Hayes had somehow sensed the move and stopped his advance.

So his feet found only air.

AKILINA WATCHED AS LORD ROLLED ONCE AFTER A MISSED kick, coming to his knees and turning toward Hayes.

Thorn knelt down in front of the borzoi. She knelt, too. The animal growled low in his throat, his eyes never leaving the shadowy scene before them. The jaws snapped a couple of times and she spied sharp fangs.

"He's deciding," Thorn said. "He can see much better than we can."

"Use the gun," she said.

Thorn's gaze leveled on her. "We must see the prophecy through."

"Don't be foolish. Stop it now."

The borzoi took a step forward.

"Use the gun, or I'll use the rifle," she said.

The lawyer gently placed a hand on her arm. "Have faith." His voice and manner exuded something that was not easily explained.

She said nothing.

Thorn turned back to the dog.

"Easy, Alexei. Easy."

LORD MANAGED TO SCRAMBLE TO HIS FEET AND MOVE AWAY from the cliff's edge. Hayes had stopped his attack, seemingly trying to regain his breath.

He stared at his boss.

"Come on, Miles," Hayes said. "We've got to finish this. Just you and me. No way out of here, except through me."

They circled around each other like cats, Lord moving right toward the trees, Hayes coming left toward the edge.

Then Lord saw it. The gun. Lying on the rocks not six feet away. But Hayes seemed to spot it, too, pouncing and grasping the stock before he could muster the strength.

In an instant the barrel was palmed, Hayes's finger on the trigger, the barrel aimed directly at him.

AKILINA WATCHED AS THE BORZOI RUSHED FORWARD. No command was given by Thorn. The animal simply moved on his own, somehow knowing this was the moment and likewise knowing exactly where to strike. Perhaps the dog was able to distinguish the scents and was familiar with Lord's from the blood. Perhaps he was being influenced by the spirit of Rasputin. Who knew? Hayes never saw the animal until the moment before they made contact, the rushing weight of the borzoi enough to stagger him backward.

LORD SEIZED THE MOMENT AND LUNGED FORWARD, PUSHING Hayes and the dog over the edge. A scream pierced the night, slowly fading as the two bodies dissolved into blackness. A second later he heard a distant thud as flesh met stone, accompanied by a yelp that made his heart ache. He could not see the chasm's bottom.

But there was no need to.

Footsteps came from behind.

He whirled, expecting to see Droopy and Orleg, but instead Akilina appeared, followed by Thorn.

She hugged him hard.

"Easy," he said, reacting to the pain in his shoulder.

She relaxed her grip.

Thorn stood at the edge and stared down.

"A shame about the dog," Lord said.

"I loved that animal." Thorn turned toward him. "But it's over now. The choice has been made."

And in that moment, illuminated in the glow of a quarter moon, within a hardened face and unblinking eyes, Miles Lord saw the future of Russia.

51

MOSCOW
SUNDAY, APRIL 10
11:00 AM

THE INTERIOR OF THE CATHEDRAL OF THE DORMITION GLOWED with radiance from hundreds of lights and candles. The vast interior had been specially illuminated to accommodate the television cameras that were transmitting the ceremony live to the world. Lord stood near the altar, in a place of prominence, Akilina beside him. Above them four tiers of icons dotted with jewels twinkled in the glow, signaling that all was well.

Two coronation chairs sat at the front of the cathedral. One was the throne of the second Romanov tsar, Alexei. Nearly nine thousand diamonds were embedded in it, along with rubies and pearls. It was 350 years old, a museum curiosity for the last 100. Yesterday the chair had been transported from the Kremlin Armory, and Michael Thorn now sat upright in it.

Beside him, in the Ivory Throne, sat his wife, Margaret. Her chair had been brought to Russia by Ivan the Great's Byzantine bride, Sophia, in 1472. It had been Ivan who had proclaimed, *Two Romes have fallen, but the third now stands, and a fourth there will not be.* Yet today, on a glorious April morning, a fourth Rome was about to be born. A merger of the secular and sacred in one entity—the tsar.

Russia once again ruled by Romanovs.

Thoughts of Taylor Hayes flashed through Lord's mind. Even now, six months after Hayes's death, the full extent of the conspiracy was still unknown. There was talk that the patriarch of the Russian Orthodox Church, Adrian, had himself been a party. But he'd steadfastly denied any involvement, and nothing had yet materialized to the contrary. The only for-certain accomplice was Maxim Zubarev, the man who'd tortured Lord in San Francisco. But before authorities could question him, his body had been found in a shallow grave outside Moscow, two bullet holes in the skull. The government suspected a widespread conspiracy, one even involving the *mafiya,* but as yet no witnesses had been found to substantiate anything.

The threat these unknowns posed to the emerging monarchy was real, and Lord was worried about Michael Thorn. But the lawyer from North Carolina had shown remarkable courage. He'd charmed the Russian people with a sincerity they found compelling, even his American ancestry was seen as a positive factor, world leaders expressing relief that a nuclear superpower would be ruled by somebody with an international outlook. Yet Thorn had made clear he was a Romanov—Russian blood coursed through his veins—and he intended to reassert Romanov control over a nation his family had once ruled for three hundred years.

Thorn had early on announced that a cabinet ministry would be appointed to help rule. He'd enlisted Semyon Pashenko as an advisor and charged the leader of the Holy Band with structuring a government. There would also be an elected Duma, one with enough of a voice to ensure that no monarch would have absolute power. The rule of law would be honored. Russia must force itself into the new century. Isolationism was no longer possible.

Now this simple man was sitting on the Diamond Throne,

his wife beside him, both looking cognizant of their responsibilities.

The church was filled with dignitaries from around the world. The English monarch had come, along with the president of the United States and prime ministers and heads of state from every major nation.

There'd been a great debate over whether the new tsar would be II or III. Nicholas II's brother had been named Michael and supposedly ruled for a day, before himself abdicating. But the Tsarist Commission had silenced any argument when it decided that Nicholas had been able to renounce the throne only for himself, not for his son, Alexei. At his abdication, therefore, his son and not his brother had become tsar. Which meant that Nicholas's direct descendants retained the sole claim to the throne. Michael Thorn, as the nearest male in line, would be known as Mikhail II.

It had been Thorn's friend in the North Carolina Attorney General's office who'd summoned a representative of the State Department to Genesis the day after Taylor Hayes died. The U.S. ambassador to Russia was called, and he immediately appeared before the Tsarist Commission to reveal what had transpired seven thousand miles away. A final vote was delayed pending the heir's arrival before the commission, which occurred three days later to much fanfare and worldwide attention.

DNA testing positively confirmed Michael Thorn as a direct descendant of Nicholas and Alexandra. His genetic structure matched Nicholas's exactly, even containing the same mutation scientists had found when Nicholas's bones were identified in 1994. The probability of error was less than a thousandth of 1 percent.

Again, Rasputin had been right. *God will provide a way to be sure of righteousness.*

Rasputin had also been right about another prediction.

Twelve must die before the resurrection can be complete. First four in Moscow, including Artemy Bely, then the guard in Red Square, Pashenko's associate in the Holy Band, then Iosif and Vassily Maks, the deputy in Genesis, and finally Feliks Orleg, Droopy, and Taylor Hayes. A procession of twelve corpses from Russia to the United States.

But one more should be added to the casualty list.

Alexei, a six-year-old borzoi.

They'd buried the dog in the cemetery only paces away from his namesake, Thorn believing the animal had earned the right to dwell eternally with Romanov ancestors.

Lord's attention was drawn to the altar as Michael Thorn rose from the throne. Everyone else in the church was already standing. Thorn was wearing a silk robe that had been draped across his shoulders two hours before in the first act of the coronation ceremony. He adjusted the folds and gently knelt, while everyone else remained standing.

Patriarch Adrian approached.

In the silence that followed, Thorn prayed.

Adrian then anointed the forehead with holy oil and administered an oath. In a building built by Romanovs, protected by Romanovs, and ultimately lost by Romanovs, a new Romanov assumed the mantle of power, one that had been stolen through murder and ambition.

The patriarch slowly placed a gold crown on Thorn's head. After a moment of prayer, the new tsar rose and approached his wife, who also wore a beautiful silk robe. She stood from her throne and knelt before him. Thorn placed the same crown on her head, then replaced it on his. Thorn then led his wife back to her throne, seated her, and sat beside her.

A steady procession of Russian dignitaries approached to swear allegiance to the new tsar—generals, government ministers, Thorn's two sons, and many of the surviving Romanov family, Stefan Baklanov included.

The would-be tsar had escaped the scandal by denying any involvement and challenging anyone to prove the contrary. He professed no knowledge of any conspiracy and proclaimed that he would have been a good ruler, if chosen. Lord thought the move smart. Who could have come forward implicating Baklanov in treason? Only fellow conspirators, and no one seriously believed they would ever say anything. The Russian people appreciated his candor and he remained popular. Lord knew without a doubt that Baklanov had been deeply involved. Maxim Zubarev had told him so. *A willing puppet.* He'd questioned whether to challenge Baklanov, but Thorn had vetoed the idea. There'd been enough dissension. Let it die. And Lord finally agreed. But he couldn't help wondering if they'd made the right decision.

He glanced at Akilina. She was watching the ceremony through damp eyes. He reached over and gently grasped her hand. She was radiant in a pearl-blue dress trimmed in gold. Thorn had arranged for the garment and she'd been grateful for his thoughtfulness.

He caught her gaze with his own. She returned his touch with a light squeeze of her hand. He saw affection and admiration reflecting from the eyes of a woman he'd come to perhaps love. Neither of them was sure what was going to happen. He'd stayed in Russia because Thorn wanted him and Akilina nearby. Lord had even been asked to remain on as a personal adviser. Though an American, he came with a stamp from the past. He was the raven. The one who had helped resurrect the blood of the Romanovs. In that capacity, his presence in what would otherwise be a devotedly Russian scene seemed fitting.

But Lord was undecided about staying in Russia. Pridgen & Woodworth had offered him a promotion. Head of the International Division. Taylor Hayes's replacement. He would vault ahead of others, but he'd earned the privilege, his name now known worldwide. He was considering that offer, but what stopped him was Akilina. He didn't particularly want to leave her, and she'd expressed a strong desire to stay and work with Thorn.

The ceremony ended and the newly crowned monarchs walked from the church, wearing, just as Nicholas and Alexandra had in 1896, brocaded mantles embroidered with the Romanov double-headed eagle.

Lord and Akilina followed them out into a brisk midday.

The gold onion domes of the four surrounding churches glistened in a bright sun. Cars awaited the tsar and tsarina, but Thorn declined. Instead he shed his mantle and robe and led his wife across the cobbles toward the Kremlin's northeast wall. Lord and Akilina accompanied them and he noticed the vibrant look sweeping Thorn's face. Lord, too, sucked in the brisk air and felt rejuvenation for both himself and a nation. The Kremlin was once again the fortress of the tsar—a *people's citadel,* as Thorn had come to call it.

At the base of the northeast wall a wooden staircase rose sixty feet to the ramparts. The tsar and tsarina slowly wound their way up, and Lord and Akilina climbed next. Beyond the wall was Red Square. Open cobblestones now spanned the spot where Lenin's tomb and the Tribunes of Honor had once stood. Thorn had ordered the mausoleum leveled. The towering silver firs had been allowed to remain, but the Soviet graves were no more. Sverdlov, Brezhnev, Kalinin, and all the others were dug up and reburied elsewhere. Only Yuri Gagarin was allowed to remain. The first man in space deserved a place of prominence. Others would follow. Good, decent people whose lives would be worth honoring.

Lord watched as Thorn and his wife approached another platform just below the merlons, high enough to elevate them above the wall. Thorn smoothed his suit and turned.

"My father told me about this moment. How I would feel. I hope I'm up for this."

"You are," Lord said.

Akilina reached up and hugged Thorn. He returned the gesture.

"Thank you, my dear. In ancient times, you would now be killed. Touching the tsar like that in public." A smile crept onto his face.

Thorn turned to his wife. "Ready?"

She nodded, but Lord saw the apprehension in the woman's eyes. And who could blame her? A decades-old wrong was about to be righted. Peace made with history. Lord, too, had decided to make peace with his own conscience. When he returned home, he would visit his father's grave. It was time to say good-bye to Grover Lord. Akilina had been right when she told him that his father's legacy was more than he realized. Grover Lord had molded him into the man he'd become. Not by example, but by mistakes. Still, his mother loved the man dearly, and always would. Maybe it was time he stopped hating.

Thorn and his wife climbed three short steps onto the plywood platform.

He and Akilina stepped to one of the merlons.

Beyond the Kremlin wall, as far as the eye could see, people spread. Press reports had earlier put their number at two million. They'd flocked into Moscow over the past few days. In Nicholas's time there would have been pageantry and balls to celebrate a coronation. Thorn wanted none of that. His bankrupt nation could ill afford such luxury. So he'd ordered that the platform be built and it be known that at precisely noon he would appear. Lord noted the new tsar's punctuality as the tower clock banged its chimes.

Out of loudspeakers mounted all around Red Square, a voice proclaimed words that were surely reverberating throughout the nation. Lord, too, was caught in the enthusiasm. Moved by an announcement that for centuries had been a rallying cry for Russians searching for leadership. Four simple words that kept pouring from the speakers. Even he started to mouth them, his eyes misting at their meaning.

Long live the tsar.

WRITER'S NOTE

The idea for this novel came to me during a tour of the Kremlin. As with my first novel, *The Amber Room,* I wanted the information to be accurate. The subject of Nicholas II and his family is fascinating. In many ways, the truth of their ultimate fate is far more scintillating than fiction. Ever since 1991, when the royal remains were exhumed from their anonymous grave, there has existed a great debate as to which two children's bodies are actually missing. First a Russian expert examined the bones and concluded, from photographic superimposition, that Maria and Alexei were not there. Then an American expert analyzed dental and bone specimens and determined the missing to be Alexei and Anastasia. I chose Anastasia simply because of the fascination that has developed around her.

A few more items:

There is indeed a royalist movement in Russia, as described in chapter 21, but no contemporary Holy Band. That was my invention. Russians are likewise fascinated with the concept of a "national idea" (chapter 9), an ideology that the populace can rally behind. The one used in the story is mine, and simple—God, Tsar, and Country. Also, Russians clearly have a fondness for commissions and routinely assign important decisions to a collective resolution. It seemed only natural that a new tsar would be chosen that way.

The flashback sequences (chapters 5, 26, 27, 43, and 44),

which describe what happened during the Romanov execution and thereafter, including the bizarre way in which the bodies were disposed of, are based on fact. I tried to recreate those events precisely as related by the participants. The task was complicated, though, by contradictory testimony. Of course, how Alexei and Anastasia escaped is purely my concoction.

The letter from Alexandra (chapter 6) is fictional, except that much of the prose was taken verbatim from other correspondence Alexandra sent to Nicholas. Their relationship was truly one of love and passion.

The affidavit from a fictional guard at Yekaterinburg quoted in chapter 13 is from an actual account.

Rasputin's predictions are correctly reported, save for the one addition about a "Romanov resurrection," which I fashioned. Whether the predictions were actually Rasputin's, voiced during his life, or manufactured by his daughter after his death, remains a matter of debate. Clearly, though, Rasputin could affect Alexei's hemophilia and his efforts, as depicted in the prologue, are based on actual accounts.

The information on Felix Yussoupov is all true, except for his involvement with any plan to save Alexei and Anastasia. Sadly, unlike my Yussoupov, who ultimately is honorable, the real man never realized the folly of Rasputin's murder and the damage he inflicted on the royal family.

Yakov Yurovsky, the dark Bolshevik who murdered Nicholas II, is accurately portrayed, his own words used in most instances.

The accomplishments of Carl Fabergé are all true, save for the duplicate Lilies of the Valley Egg. It was hard to resist including it. That masterpiece seemed the perfect repository in which to secrete photos of the surviving heirs.

The princess tree detailed in chapters 40 and 42 flourishes in western North Carolina. Its connection with the Russian royal family is likewise accurate. The lovely Blue Ridge Mountains would have, indeed, offered a perfect sanctuary for Russian refugees since (as mentioned by Akilina in chapter 42) the area is similar, in many ways, to parts of Siberia.

The borzoi (Russian wolfhound), which plays such an important part in the story (chapters 46, 47, 49, and 50), is a dynamic breed, and its link to the Russian nobility is all true.

Let it be clear that Nicholas II was in no way a benevolent and benign ruler. The negative observations Miles Lord makes about him in chapter 23 are accurate. But what happened to the Romanov family was nonetheless tragic. All the assorted Romanov family murders detailed throughout actually happened. There was, indeed, a systematic effort to eradicate that entire genetic line. Also, Stalin's paranoia with the Romanovs, and his sealing of all records relating to them (chapters 22, 23, and 30), occurred. To imagine a resurrection brings some meaning to their awful ending. Sadly, though, the actual fate of Nicholas II, his wife, and three of his daughters was not as romantic. As detailed in chapter 44, after the graves were exhumed in 1991, the Romanovs' bones remained on a shelf in a laboratory for more than seven years while two cities—Yekaterinburg and St. Petersburg— fought over possession. Finally, another infamous Russian commission chose St. Petersburg and the family members were entombed, with royal pomp and circumstance, alongside their ancestors.

They were buried togther. Which is perhaps fitting, since all observers agree that in life they were a close, loving family.

And in death, so shall they remain.

An Interview with the Author

Question: Why write about the Romanovs?
Steve Berry: The idea for the novel came during a tour of the Kremlin. The guide kept mentioning the phrase "the fourth Rome." Being unfamiliar with that term I inquired, and she told me that Ivan the Great, who was the first man to be called tsar and ruled Russia in the fifteenth century, made a comment one day. He said, "Two Romes have fallen [Rome and Constantinople], a third now stands [Moscow], and a fourth there will never be." That was an intriguing thought, and over the next few days, the novel was born. The whole scenario dealing with Nicholas II and his family, their arrest, imprisonment, murder, burial, and exhumation is fascinating. As is Russia itself.

Q: Is there really a tsarist restoration movement in Russia?
SB: The All-Russian Monarchist Assembly referred to in the book is an actual Russian organization dedicated to not only tsarist remembrance but a Romanov restoration to the throne.

Q: Why include Felix Yussoupov?
SB: What a fascinating character. His family was the richest in Russia, he was married to Nicholas II's favorite niece, yet he murdered Rasputin thinking he was saving the country from ruin. Unfortunately, that act saved nothing and only hastened the tsar's downfall. He's described in the book as a man of sudden ideas, which is apt. He was never meant to be head of the Yussoupov family, and inherited the reins only when his older brother was killed in a duel. He was a disappointment from birth. His mother wanted a girl, so to console herself she kept him in long hair and dresses, a habit

Felix maintained into adulthood. He was a man of glaring contradictions and extreme beliefs, one I thought readers would enjoy meeting.

Q: Is that why Fabergé is part of the story, too?
SB: No question. Interestingly, as is noted in the book, Fabergé himself actually designed and made nothing. He was simply the presiding genius of a conglomerate that, at its height, produced some of the finest jewelry ever crafted. His workmasters actually conceived and assembled everything, and the two men mentioned in the story are real. The Lilies of the Valley Egg is, without question, a spectacular object. Once I saw a photo of the egg, with its tri-fold photos of the tsar and two of his children, I knew it had to be part of the story.

Q: Was Rasputin always a part of the plot?
SB: His prophecies are what spur the plot forward. It's not really known whether he uttered those predictions during his life, or whether they were added after his death by his daughter, who became his biographer, but there is no denying this Siberian peasant was a skillful manipulator. I fictionalized some to give his words even more credence, but they still remain mysterious and intriguing. There's a whole other novel there to do on his life.

Q: Was the research difficult?
SB: Finding primary and secondary sources that deal with the Romanovs and Nicholas II is easy. There are hundreds of books available. The trouble comes with the lack of consistency between the various primary accounts. I read many so-called eyewitness reports from a variety of participants in the imperial murders. There is a Russian saying quoted in the book:—"He lies like an eyewitness"—which is right on

target. The accounts conflict far more than they agree—to the point that you have to wonder if the various witnesses were all present at the same event. It took time to cull the consistent information, then I filled in the blanks. The Writer's Note at the end of the novel makes clear what's fact and what's fiction.

Q: When was the book written?
SB: I first wrote the novel in 1996. It was submitted for publication in 1998 and rejected by seventeen major publishers. It then sat in a drawer until 2002, when *The Amber Room* was bought by Ballantine Books. I then submitted the manuscript as the second of the two books Ballantine wanted, and it was accepted. Just goes to show, don't toss out those old manuscripts.

Q: Will we ever see Miles Lord again?
SB: It's entirely possible. I'd love to revisit the new Russia created in *The Romanov Prophecy* and take Miles, and the surviving cast of charcters, on a new adventure. In fact, I have several in mind.

Read on for an excerpt from

THE
COLUMBUS
AFFAIR

by

STEVE BERRY

Published by Ballantine Books

TOM SAGAN GRIPPED THE GUN. HE'D THOUGHT ABOUT
this moment for the past year, debating the pros and
cons, finally deciding that one pro outweighed all
cons.

He simply did not want to live any longer.

He'd once been an investigative reporter for the
Los Angeles Times, knocking down a high six-figure
salary, his byline generating one front-page, above-
the-fold story after another. He'd worked all over
the world—Sarajevo, Beirut, Jerusalem, Beijing, Bel-
grade, Moscow. His confidential files had been filled
with sources who'd willingly fed him leads, knowing
that he'd protect them at all costs. He'd once proved
that when he spent eleven days in a D.C. jail for refusing to reveal his source on a story about a corrupt
Pennsylvania congressman.

The congressman went to prison.

Sagan received his third Pulitzer nomination.

There were twenty-one awarded categories. One
was for distinguished investigative reporting by an individual or team, reported as a single newspaper article or a series. Winners received a certificate, $10,000,
and the ability to add three precious words—Pulitzer
Prize winner—to their name.

He won his.

But they took it back.

Which seemed the story of his life.

Everything had been taken back.

His career, his reputation, his credibility, even his self-respect. In the end he came to see himself as a failure in each of his roles—reporter, husband, father, son. A few weeks ago he'd charted that spiral on a pad, identifying that it all started when he was twenty-five, fresh out of the University of Florida, top third in his class, with a journalism degree.

And his father disowned him.

Abiram Sagan had been unrelenting. *"We all make choices. Good. Bad. Indifferent. You're a grown man and made yours. Now I have to make mine."*

And that he had.

On that same pad he'd jotted down the highs and lows that came after. His rise from a news assistant to staff reporter to senior international correspondent. The awards. Accolades. The respect from his peers. How had one observer described his style? *Wide-ranging and prescient reporting conducted at great personal risk.*

Then, his divorce.

The estrangement from his only child. Poor investment decisions. Even poorer life decisions.

Finally, his firing.

Eight years ago.

And since then—nothing.

Most of his friends had abandoned him, but that was as much his fault as theirs. As his depression deepened, he'd withdrawn into himself. Amazingly, he hadn't turned to alcohol or drugs, but neither had ever appealed to him. Self-pity was his intoxicant.

He stared around at the house's interior. He'd decided to die here, in his parents' home. Fitting, in some morbid way. Thick layers of dust and a musty smell evidenced the three years the rooms had sat empty. He'd kept the utilities on, paid the meager taxes, and had the lawn tended just enough so the neighbors wouldn't complain. Earlier, he'd noticed that the sprawling mulberry tree out front needed trimming and the picket fence painting. But he'd long ignored both chores, as he had the entire interior of the house, keeping it exactly as he'd found it, visiting only a few times.

He hated it here.

Too many ghosts.

He walked the rooms, conjuring a few childhood memories. In the kitchen he could still see jars of his mother's fruit and jam that once lined the windowsill. He should write a note, explain himself, blame somebody or something. But to whom? And for what? Nobody would believe him if he told them the truth.

And would anyone care when he was gone?

Certainly not his daughter. He'd not spoken to her in two years. His literary agent? Maybe. She'd made a lot of money off him. Ghostwriting novels paid bigtime. What had one critic said at the time of his downfall? *Sagan seems to have a promising career ahead of him writing fiction.*

Asshole.

But he'd actually taken the advice.

He wondered—how does one explain taking his own life? It's, by definition, an irrational act, which, by definition, defies rational explanation. Hopefully, somebody would bury him. He had plenty of money in the bank, more than enough for a respectable funeral.

What would it be like to be dead?

Are you aware? Can you hear? See? Smell? Or is it simply an eternal blackness? No thoughts. No feeling. Nothing at all.

He walked back toward the front of the house.

Outside was a glorious March day, the noontime sun bright. He stopped in the open archway and stared at the parlor. That was what his mother had always called the room. Here was where his parents had gathered on Shabbat. Where Abiram read from the Torah. The place where Yom Kippur and Holy Days had been celebrated. He stared at the pewter menorah on the far table and recalled it burning many times. His parents had been devout Jews. After his bar mitzvah he, too, had first read from the Torah, standing before the room's twelve-paned windows, framed by damask curtains his mother had taken months to sew. She'd been talented with her hands. What a lovely woman. He missed her. She died six years before Abiram, who'd now been gone for three.

Time to end the Sagan clan.

There were no more.

He'd been an only child.

He studied the gun, a pistol bought a few months before at an Orlando gun show. He sat on the sofa. Clouds of dust rose then settled. He recalled Abiram's lecture about the birds and the bees as he'd sat in the same spot. He'd been what—twelve? Thirty-three years ago, though somehow it seemed like last week. As usual, the explanations about sex had been short, brutish, and efficient.

"Do you understand?" Abiram asked him. "It's important that you do."

"I don't like girls."

"You will. So don't forget what I said."

Women. Another failure. He'd had precious few relationships as a young man, marrying the first girl who'd shown serious interest in him. There'd been a few since the divorce, and none past the downfall. Michele had taken a toll on him, in more ways than just financially.

"Maybe I'll get to see her soon, too," he muttered.

His ex-wife had died two years ago in a car crash.

Her funeral marked the last time he and his daughter had spoken, her rebuke still loud and clear.

Get out. She would not want you here.

And he'd left.

He stared again at the gun, his finger on the trigger. He steeled himself, grabbed a breath, and then nestled the barrel to his temple. He was left-handed, like nearly every Sagan. His uncle, a former professional baseball player, told him as a child that if he could learn to hurl a curveball he'd make a fortune in the major leagues. Left-handers were rare. But he'd failed at sports, too.

He felt the metal on his skin. Hard. Unbending.

Like Abiram.

And life.

He closed his eyes and tightened his finger on the trigger, imagining how his obituary would start. *Tuesday, March 5th, former investigative journalist Tom Sagan took his own life at his parents' home in Mount Dora, Florida.*

A little more pressure on the trigger and—

Rap. Rap. Rap.

He opened his eyes.

A man stood outside the front window, close enough to the panes for Tom to see the face—older than himself, clean-cut, distinguished—and the right hand.

Which held a photograph pressed to the glass.

He focused on the image of a young woman, bound and gagged, lying down, arms and feet extended as if tied.

He knew the face.

His daughter.

Alle.